JUN 18 2012

W9-BFY-844

DATE DUE

BRODART, CO.

Cat. No. 23-221

THE TINTERN TREASURE

THE TINTERN TREASURE

Kate Sedley

This first world edition published 2012
in Great Britain and in the USA by
SEVERN HOUSE PUBLISHERS LTD of
9–15 High Street, Sutton, Surrey, England, SM1 1DF.
Trade paperback edition first published
in Great Britain and the USA 2012 by
SEVERN HOUSE PUBLISHERS LTD

Copyright © 2012 by Kate Sedley.

All rights reserved.
The moral right of the author has been asserted.

British Library Cataloguing in Publication Data

Sedley, Kate.
  The Tintern treasure.
  1. Roger the Chapman (Fictitious character)–Fiction.
  2. Great Britain–History–Richard III, 1483-1485–
  Fiction. 3. Detective and mystery stories.
  I. Title
  823.9'14-dc23

ISBN-13: 978-0-7278-8164-9 (cased)
ISBN-13: 978-1-84751-420-2 (trade paper)

Except where actual historical events and characters are being
described for the storyline of this novel, all situations in this
publication are fictitious and any resemblance to living persons
is purely coincidental.

All Severn House titles are printed on acid-free paper.

Severn House Publishers support The Forest Stewardship Council [FSC],
the leading international forest certification organisation. All our titles that
are printed on Greenpeace-approved FSC-certified paper carry the FSC logo.

Typeset by Palimpsest Book Production Ltd.,
Falkirk, Stirlingshire, Scotland.
Printed and bound in Great Britain by
MPG Books Ltd., Bodmin, Cornwall.

ONE

I would never have been involved in the affair if the handle of Adela's best iron cooking pot hadn't come loose. Or if the travelling tinker hadn't knocked so opportunely at our door the following morning. Or if the said tinker hadn't passed through Hereford some months earlier and performed a similar repair for a certain Goody Harker. On such trivial chances does the course of my life depend. As I frequently observe to myself, it may not be other people's fault, but it's all too often my misfortune.

To begin with, the conversation was all between the tinker and myself. As he settled at our kitchen table to begin mending the damaged pot, he enquired what we both thought of the summer's dramatic events. There was, of course, no need to ask what he was referring to: the bastardizing of the late King Edward IV's children and Parliament's subsequent offer of the crown to his brother, Richard, Duke of Gloucester, thus deposing the boy king, Edward V, had been the talk of every ale-house, of every home, in the country and beyond.

'Folk don't care for it, you know,' the man said as he opened his satchel and took out the tools of his trade, laying them in a neat row in front of him. 'They don't like seeing a child done out of his rights.'

'He hasn't been done out of his rights,' I retorted irritably. 'The late King Edward was already betrothed to Lady Eleanor Butler when he married Elizabeth Woodville. The Bishop of Bath and Wells has testified to the fact and he should know. He officiated at the handfasting. And in the eyes of the Church, a promise to wed is the same as a marriage, so the children are illegitimate.'

'All right! All right!' the tinker said with a grin. 'No offence, I'm sure. Our new king seems to have found a partisan in you, at any rate. And I must admit I liked the look of him, myself.'

'You've seen King Richard?' Adela asked eagerly. Anything to do with royalty always commanded her attention.

'Saw him at Oxford back in July, when he started on his progress up north. Outside Magdalen College, it were. He was being given a right enthusiastic welcome by an old fellow someone told me was the college chancellor, whatever that is. Said he'd founded the place and all. I was close enough to overhear what they were saying.'

'And what were they saying?'

'Dunno. They were talking in Latin. It was all Greek to me.' The tinker guffawed loudly. (I hate people who laugh at their own jokes.) When he found we weren't inclined to share his mirth, he continued hastily, 'Saw him again a few days later, at Gloucester. The king, that is. There was no getting near him that time, though. That other one was there.'

'What other one?' I asked, although I had a good idea.

The tinker raised his head from his task and thought for a moment. 'Some duke or other. They say he was the one what helped King Richard to his throne. But if you'd seen him and the way he was carrying on, the airs and graces he was giving himself, you could've been forgiven for thinking he was the one what was wearing the crown. Such importance! You've never seen the like!'

'The Duke of Buckingham,' I said, recalling uneasily my sight of the duke in King Richard's coronation procession and the same impression I had received of a man growing rapidly too big for his breeches; a man who was perhaps wondering why, as another Plantagenet prince, he hadn't seized power for himself. If I read the situation right, it had been no part of Buckingham's plan to put his cousin on the throne, merely to bolster the duke's position as lord protector and thwart his own wife's family, the Woodvilles, from wielding too much influence. 'Has he accompanied the king on progress?'

The tinker cursed as he dropped a rivet, then shook his head. 'Don't think so. Talk was that His High and Mightiness was going home to his estates in Wales. Brecon way. Taking some prelate who'd been plotting against the king with him, under house arrest. Anyway, that were the story I heard.'

'The Bishop of Ely. The prelate who'd been plotting against King Richard,' I elucidated. 'He was a party to Lord Hastings' plot.'

The tinker eyed me curiously. 'You seem to know a lot about it.'

'Like yourself, only what I hear as I go about my business.' I excused myself hurriedly, and made the mistake of adding, 'I'm a chapman by trade.'

Our guest paused yet again, this time glancing significantly around him. 'Big house for a pedlar and his wife.'

I didn't enlighten him as to how we came by it. It was none of his business. Besides, he'd only have to ask his next customer about us and he would learn more of our affairs than we knew ourselves. Bristol was a hotbed of gossip.

'We have three children,' Adela told him cheerfully, as if this explained everything. My wife then proceeded to add some totally unnecessary detail (if only she hadn't!). 'My son, Nicholas, from my first marriage, when I lived in Hereford, Roger's daughter from his first marriage and our son, Adam.'

'You say you lived in Hereford?' The tinker looked up from boring a fresh hole in the pot to take the new rivet for the handle. 'I was there back in the spring. Or early summer. It's not important. I did a similar job to this for a Goody Harker. Did it for nothing, too,' he added virtuously. 'Poor old soul, she's fallen on hard times.'

'Whereabouts did she live in Hereford?' my wife asked sharply. 'Was it in the Butchery, towards the market end?'

The tinker chewed a thumbnail.

'I rather think it was.' He nodded. 'Yes, now you mention it, I'm certain of it. D'you know her?'

'She and Goodman Harker were very kind to me after Owen, my first husband, died. I lived next to them.'

'Well, if it's the same goody, she's a widow woman now. Husband died a good few years back, she told me, and she's not found things easy since then, I reckon. Fair poverty-stricken, she is – which is why I wouldn't take no payment for mending her pot. There! That's done.' He straightened his back and regarded the mazer of ale I was offering him with a glistening eye.

Adela had her purse at the ready. 'And you must let me pay you for Goody Harker's pot, as well,' she offered before I could stop her. 'You mustn't be out of pocket for an act of kindness. No, no! I insist!' This after the tinker had made a half-hearted – very half-hearted – attempt at refusal.

'You're a fool,' I told her roundly when he had finally departed with two lots of money in his pouch. 'Who is this woman, anyway?'

'I've told you! Well, I told the tinker and I'm sure you were listening. Anne and Goodman Harker were our neighbours in the Butchery. Gerald was indeed a butcher and owned the cottage that Owen and I rented. Things must have gone terribly wrong since he died for Anne to be in such poverty now.'

Adela said no more at the time, but she was very quiet for the rest of the day – when I was at home, that is – and throughout the evening. She was also short-tempered with the children, which was unlike her, but even so, idiot that I was, I failed to see the request coming, and was completely taken aback when it did.

We had finished making love – something Adela had permitted rather than actively encouraged – and I was lying on my back, staring at the ceiling and feeling, as always, quite unjustifiably pleased with myself, when a quiet voice beside me asked, 'Would you do something for me, Roger?'

I turned my head on the pillow to smile at her. 'Of course, sweetheart. Anything.'

Rash fool that I was!

Adela snuggled closer and wound me in her embrace. (The serpent in Eden must have been a female.) 'Would you go to Hereford and visit Goody Harker for me? If she's in desperate want, give her some money. We can afford it just at present and I owe her such a lot. You could make it a working trip.'

I was staggered and far from pleased at the suggestion. I had been away in London for most of the summer and had only finally returned home in the early weeks of July. A few days' time would see the end of September, which meant that after a mere two and a half months and with the worst of the year's weather ahead of me, I should be on my travels again.

'You could be home easily before October's out,' Adela wheedled, cuddling even closer. Then, when I remained silent, she withdrew a little and said in a sharper tone, 'You'd do it fast enough if the duke asked it of you.'

'The king,' I corrected her. 'And that's unfair. You can't refuse royalty; at least, not without making things very uncomfortable for yourself.'

'Well . . .' Her sense of justice came into play. 'I suppose that's true. All the same' – a shapely leg slid sinuously across one of mine and she nibbled my left earlobe suggestively – 'I don't often ask you for a favour.'

She might, with perfect truth, have said that she had never asked me for a favour in all the six years of our marriage and that I was an ungrateful oaf even to think of refusing her now. But after my near death by drowning and subsequent debilitating illness of the summer, I had been looking forward to a long autumn and winter of comfort and coddling in the bosom of my loved ones.

Now, this!

I was just plucking up my courage to say flatly that I couldn't – and wouldn't – go, when Adela heaved a forlorn sigh and said no, she supposed it was too much to demand of me in the circumstances and that she was deeply ashamed of herself for having even suggested it. It was just that Goody Harker and her husband had been so very kind to her and Nicholas after Owen died that . . . And there she let the sentence hang on the breath of another sigh.

Women! They have more tricks up their sleeves than a conjuror! They are the wiliest creatures on God's earth. (But if I'm honest, I suppose I must admit that they have to be. It's their only armour in a world ordered always to the advantage of men.)

Of course, the moment I was offered a way out, a refusal with honour, I was unable to take it. The old, familiar urge for freedom stirred my blood. It was true that I should have to spend the second of October, my thirty-first birthday – a date and age I shared with our new king – away from my family, but other congenial company was certain to be found on the road; plenty of wayfarers like myself who would be more than willing to drink my health in the convivial atmosphere of tavern or ale-house. It might not be what I had planned, and it might be that I was reaching an age when independence was not quite as important as it had once been, but the thought of the open road and being my own man still held its attractions.

'I'll do it,' I said, adding nobly, 'for your sake, sweetheart.'

I had my reward, and this time it was Adela who was the more enthusiastic of the two of us. If the truth be told, I found it a bit of an effort, a fact which worried me considerably and led to something of a sleepless night. Thirty-one might be creeping on towards middle age but it wasn't that old, surely?

In the morning, we decided that I should set out as soon as possible in order to avoid the worst of the autumnal storms, so I fixed my departure for the following day, the last but one day of September. The children were as indifferent as always to my going. Or were they? In recent months they had all three demonstrated resentment and, in one instance, downright hostility, to my absences from home. On this occasion, however, realizing that their mother was actively encouraging my journey and that it was a favour to her, they only repeated their usual demand that I bring them something back.

'Promise!' my daughter Elizabeth demanded.

'Promise!' echoed her half-brother, five-year-old Adam.

My stepson, Nicholas, contented himself with giving me a steely look, but one, nevertheless, that spoke of serious consequences should I forget.

I gave my solemn promise.

It was little more than a fortnight later that I reached Hereford, on Monday, October the thirteenth. I might have covered the distance in less time had I not taken Adela's advice and stopped to sell my wares along the way. For the first week I had done good business and my pack was considerably lighter than when I started. But for the past seven days, the weather had deteriorated with frightening speed, bringing lashing rain and high winds to flood the countryside and uproot trees. By the time my destination came in view late on the Monday morning, I was, in spite of my good weatherproof cloak and hat, soaked to the skin, in a foul temper and cursing myself roundly for being such a fool as to set out on such a lengthy journey at that time of year. Discomfort might not have worried me once, but my recent illness and advancing age made me less and less inclined to endure adverse conditions with any sort of stoicism. As for actively enjoying pitting my strength against the elements, that kind of nonsense had vanished long ago.

Nor was my state of mind in any way improved by the discovery that the object of my journey was in no sort of distress. Goody

Harker was living comfortably in her old home, well looked after by kindly neighbours and, far from having been unable to pay the tinker for his services, she had given him more money than he demanded, having been pleased by the speed and dexterity with which he had mended her broken pot.

'He was having you and Adela on, the rogue,' she chortled, after inviting me in to partake of a bowl of her winter pottage and a mug of her home-brewed ale. 'He saw a way of getting double the money out of you,' she added, setting my cloak and hat to dry before the fire burning merrily on the hearth. 'Now, tell me, how is Adela and that dear little son of hers?'

I'm afraid she found me a poor conversationalist, my mind being preoccupied with devising all the worst forms of torture I could think of to inflict upon the tinker should he ever be unfortunate enough to cross my path again. I was furious with the conniving little toad's duplicity, with my own and Adela's gullibility and most of all with having allowed my wife to persuade me into undertaking this journey against my better judgement. But in time, my sense of well-being slowly began to return. The warmth of the little parlour and a bellyful of excellent food gradually did their work and I was able to answer Goody Harker's enquiries with tolerable politeness. However, the arrival, just as I was finishing my meal, of an elderly woman who, it soon became clear to me, was the goody's lodger, made it plain that I should be unable to beg a bed for the night before setting out on my homeward voyage, it having been obvious from the exterior that the cottage boasted no more than two bedchambers. Instead, I asked for the name of a decent inn where I might rest my weary bones.

Both dames having heartily recommended one in Behindthewall Lane, I thanked Goody Harker for her hospitality, donned my still-not-dry hat and cloak and emerged once more to brave the elements. The rain had eased a little, but the clouds piling up in the western sky suggested that there was more to come, so I wasted no time in making my way to the inn – whose name, after all these years, escapes me – and paying for a bed for the night.

The landlord at first eyed my pedlar's pack askance, but the colour of my money put paid to any qualms he might have had about offering me a room. I suspected, too, that the sudden burst of bad weather was making him short of customers because, just before suppertime, another pedlar with his pack, urgently seeking shelter from a further violent storm, was ushered into the room next to mine. I had been standing on the covered courtyard gallery as he arrived and we gave one another a nod of mutual under-standing. Then a sudden flurry of hailstones made me descend to the ale-room and the comfort of a sizzling bacon collop served with pease pudding and a mazer of rough red wine.

'That was good.'

The stranger pushed his stool away from the table and rubbed his belly in satisfaction.

It was dark by now and candles had been lit in the ale-room. By the sound of things, the weather had worsened yet again. No locals had ventured out of doors and no other traveller had arrived to disturb the peace of my fellow pedlar and myself.

'You were hungry.' I nodded at the empty plate.

He nodded. 'Aye, I was that.'

'You're from up north,' I said. 'I recognize the accent.'

He grinned assent. 'God's own country. You know those parts?'

'I passed through York on my way up to Scotland with the army last year.' I naturally didn't enlarge upon the circumstances of my journey. 'Your speech is not so thick as some of your countrymen. I couldn't understand a lot of 'em.'

My companion laughed as we drew our stools closer to the old-fashioned central hearth and settled down to a steady drinking session, the considerate landlord having left a full jug of ale on the table behind us.

'Your own accent is none so easy to follow,' he complained, then held out his free hand. 'Name of Oliver Tockney,' he said. 'What's yours?'

I returned his clasp warmly. 'As a child I was known as Roger Stonecarver or Carverson. It was my father's trade. But nowadays everyone calls me Roger Chapman and it's the name I answer to in general.'

The other nodded. 'It's the way you get labelled in life. My guess is that you're from somewhere in the west. Your speech has got that burr to it. Now us, up north, our Viking ancestors gave us our distinctive way of talking.'

I took a swig of ale as another, even more violent gust of wind rattled the shutters. 'More than likely,' I agreed. 'They never got a foothold in my part of the world, thanks to King Alfred and the great battle at Ethandune.' The candles guttered in a sudden draught. 'You're a fair distance from home.'

'Aye. And going further.' He gave me a leery look and added succinctly, 'Wife and five children.' He offered no other explanation, and perhaps none was necessary. 'You?' he enquired with equal brevity.

'Wife and three children. But I'm starting for home tomorrow.' And I gave him a short history of how I came to be in Hereford in the first place.

He grinned appreciatively. 'You've to watch yon tinkers. They've a reputation for being rogues and rascals. Don' know why it should be so, but there it is.' A squall of rain hit the shutters with the force of a handful of thrown pebbles. 'By the Virgin, it's a rotten evening. Saint Christopher will have his work cut out tonight, guiding any travellers foolish enough to be out in this. Let's hope it'll have eased off by morning.' He hesitated for a second or two, then asked, 'Would you be willing to have some company on your journey? I'm minded to go all the way with you to Bristol. Never seen the place and I doubt I'll ever be this far south again. Nor will I be in the mood to give my dame the slip for so long a while.' His pleasant face darkened. 'But this time she deserves it.'

Once again, he didn't enlarge on the subject, and it was obvious that he was labouring under a strong sense of grievance. But it was also obvious that he regretted having said so much. He wriggled uncomfortably on his stool and was plainly casting about in his mind for some other topic of conversation.

I supplied it for him. 'Were you still in York back in late summer, early autumn?' I asked.

'I was just on the point of leaving. Why?'

'Before I left Bristol there was talk of King Richard having staged a second coronation in the Minster. Talk that someone – Sir Walter Tyrrell was the name bandied about – had been sent back to London to collect extra robes and jewels from the Wardrobe at the Tower. The rumour wasn't too well received down south, I can tell you. There's always the feeling there that our new king favours the north over the southern counties.'

Oliver Tockney threw back his head and laughed out loud. 'Oh, aye! He's a Yorkshireman to his fingertips all right is our Richard, God bless him! That would make the southrons spit, I daresay. But no one'll ever alter him. Yorkshire's bred in his bones. And in our new queen's. But it wasn't a second crowning that was held in the Minster, and so you can tell all your friends when you get back.'

'What was it then?'

'It was the ceremony to make his son, young Edward, Prince of Wales.'

'Ah! No one down south seems to have thought of that.'

Yet again, wind and rain together lashed the inn. My companion and I huddled yet closer to the fire, and I threw on another log to keep it blazing. It was the sort of night when all the demons of hell seemed to be abroad.

'I've heard the French king's dead,' Oliver remarked after several minutes' silence.

I nodded. 'I've heard the rumour, too. Whether it's true or not, I couldn't say. But if it is, it'll be no loss to King Richard. King Louis never liked him, not after his refusal to take French bribes eight years back when the English invasion of France came to nought. Or was bought off, which is nearer the mark.'

My new friend regarded me curiously. 'You speak with some authority.'

I cursed inwardly. I was always making mistakes like that. It's not that I am, or ever have been, a particularly modest man, but the recounting of my various exploits and the answering of all the old, familiar questions has become a chore, a penance to be endured rather than relished.

'Oh, one hears things in our line of business,' I prevaricated. 'You know how it is.'

To my relief, my companion seemed to accept this and lapsed once more into silence, staring gloomily into the fire, lost in his own thoughts.

There was a loud banging on the inn door, and I heard the landlord yelling for one of the potboys to go and open it. The sound of voices penetrated our cosy retreat, followed by the sound of someone trying to shake the rain from his cloak. The landlord was speaking – I could hear his questioning tone, then the tramp of feet as he and the newcomer mounted the stairs to the upper chambers. After some minutes, someone clattered down again and the landlord entered the ale-room.

'A guest,' he said sharply. 'A gentleman. I'll have to ask you two to move and continue your gossip elsewhere.' He ignored our glares of resentment. Indeed, I doubt he even noticed them, preoccupied as he was by news that the stranger had brought. 'He says a rebellion's broken out in the south against the new king.'

TWO

'Rebellion?'

Oliver Tockney and I framed the word together, incredulity in both our voices.

'Whose rebellion?' I added, dismay adding an edge of challenge and disbelief.

'It's no use asking me,' the landlord retorted, understandably annoyed by my belligerent attitude. 'I'm only repeating what the gentleman's told me. And now, if you two will remove yourselves while I and my goodwife prepare his supper . . .'

But I was going nowhere until I had seen and questioned this visitor for myself. My companion obviously felt the same way, because he settled himself more firmly on his stool and glared defiantly.

'We've paid our shot like honest citizens,' he announced, his north country speech becoming thicker with every word as his indignation grew.

'Besides,' I chorused, 'we'd like to discover just what foundation there is for these rumours. Indeed, if they have any foundation.'

The landlord began to bluster, but before he could threaten us with eviction, the door into the ale-room opened and the new arrival appeared.

I knew him at once, although it took him a minute or two to recognize me. He was a Bristol lawyer by the name of Heathersett, an elderly bachelor who lived with his mother and had chambers in an alleyway that ran between two of the Broad Street houses, curving to the right and emerging into Wine Street, near the castle. Whatever its original name – probably Crooked or, perhaps, Elbow Lane – it was known generally as Runnymede Court on account of the fact that there were at least three men of law practicing there.

'Lawyer Heathersett,' I said, rising respectfully to my feet and nudging the Yorkshireman to do the same. 'What's this story, sir, of rebellion in the south?'

He peered at me short-sightedly with his protuberant, pale blue eyes, then fiddled in his pouch, finally producing a pair of spectacles which he perched precariously on the bridge of his nose.

'Do you know me, my man?' He stared harder, then suddenly added, 'Ah! Yes! It's Roger the chapman, isn't it? Forgive me for not knowing you at once, Master Chapman. My eyes are not what they were.'

Oliver Tockney and the landlord turned to stare at me. The latter looked thoroughly taken aback. 'You're acquainted with this man, Your Honour?' he asked dubiously.

The lawyer nodded vigorously. 'Oh, yes. Most certainly. He's very well known in Bristol, where we come from. Quite one of our more famous citizens.' His tone was dry and, I thought, a little mocking, but to my relief, he didn't elaborate.

Curiosity was written in every line of the landlord's face, but all he said was, 'I'm just about to get Your Honour's supper. Indeed, my goodwife's already preparing it. But . . . But if you'd be obliging enough to tell us what you know . . . how these rumours of rebellion came about . . . where you heard them . . . if they're true or not . . .'

'Yes, yes.' Lawyer Heathersett drew nearer the fire, spreading his delicate, almost transparent hands to the flames, his thinning grey hair still damp from the storm and plastered to his skull. A thought struck him. 'Is my horse being properly cared for?' he enquired anxiously.

'As if he were my own,' the landlord reassured him. A jerk of his head indicated that Oliver Tockney should vacate his stool, and promptly. Our host had patently become nervous of me, unsure of my status. A pedlar who was hailed almost as an equal by a lawyer was outside of his experience.

Master Heathersett – his Christian name was Geoffrey, I suddenly recalled – took the proffered seat and shivered as yet another squall of wind and rain hit the shutters and the candles once more guttered in the draught.

'The first rumours reached Bristol before I left home, last Thursday. Who brought them I've no idea, but the town is always full of strangers, as you know, Master Chapman. I think the first I heard was on the Monday and, to begin with, I discounted it all as malicious gossip. Up until then, everyone had spoken well – more than well, if the truth be told – of King Richard, and it seemed universally acknowledged that Parliament's offer of the crown to him had been a very good thing. But as the week wore on, other and more convincing details reached us. Many of the late king's friends and loyal supporters in the south and west had risen on behalf of his son and were determined to restore the boy to his throne. There was a story that an attempt had been made to rescue him and his brother, the little Duke of York, from the Tower. By the time I left Bristol for Hereford early Thursday morning, the rumours were gaining credence everywhere, and when I reached Gloucester, proclamations against the rebels confirmed their truth.'

The lawyer paused as his supper was borne triumphantly into the ale-room by the goodwife, who had produced a fricassee of chicken and mushrooms in very short order and was expecting to be congratulated on her efforts.

Nothing but silence greeted her, however, and she unloaded her tray, setting a place for one on the table with an offended sniff. There was also a certain amount of thumping and spilled ale as she placed another full jug and a fresh beaker alongside the dish of fricassee. Then the door banged behind her and we heard her muttering angrily to herself as she retreated to the kitchen. The landlord raised his eyebrows at my fellow pedlar and myself – a look which plainly said, *Women!* – but which went unnoticed by the lawyer as he drew his stool to the table and set about his supper with a will.

I gave up my stool to the landlord, dragged forward a bench from beside the opposite wall and shared it with Oliver Tockney.

We allowed Master Heathersett to take the edge off his hunger before continuing to question him.

I got in first. 'You were saying, sir, that proclamations against the rebels were being issued at Gloucester, in which case there can be no doubt that these rumours are true and that there has been a rising in the south and west in favour of the lord Edward. Do you have any idea of what is happening elsewhere?'

The lawyer made no answer, his mouth being full, rendering it impossible for him to reply immediately. But Oliver Tockney said, 'If the news has reached York, King Richard will be on his way south to confront the rebels. He may in any case have already started on his return journey to London.'

And not before time, I thought to myself. The king had, in my estimation, lingered far too long in his beloved Yorkshire. It would not endear him to his subjects in the south, whose suspicions of anyone living north of The Wash were ineradicably inbred.

With a determined effort, Lawyer Heathersett cleared his mouth, waving his spoon about in an agitated manner as he did so. When he was at last able to speak, he said excitedly, 'But that's not all! I haven't told you everything yet.' He took a gulp of ale and continued, 'I'm here on business with a fellow lawyer. Here, in Hereford. He, himself, has only just returned from Wales and he says that the Welsh are also up in arms on behalf of Henry Tudor . . .'

'Henry Tudor!' I broke in scornfully. 'No one's going to rebel in favour of Henry Tudor! He hasn't a shred of entitlement to the throne!'

Geoffrey Heathersett's judicial instincts asserted themselves. 'Indeed, he has,' he argued with asperity, 'on both the spear and distaff side.'

'Both bastard lines,' I contested hotly. 'Neither the Beauforts nor the Tudors have a legal claim to the throne.'

The lawyer shrugged. 'That won't stop the disaffected backing them. Henry Tudor is the last scion of the House of Lancaster, and the Lancastrians, as you know, have never accepted the Yorkist claim to be the legitimate heirs of Richard II. Besides' – he gestured once more with his spoon, flicking bits of fricassee in all directions and his voice rising almost to a squeak – 'according to my friend, there's another, much more serious rumour gaining ground in Wales.' He drew a deep breath and lowered his voice to its normal level. 'And that is that the two boys, the two princes, have been murdered in the Tower on the orders of the king.'

There was an aghast silence. The landlord sat as though turned to stone while Oliver Tockney and I looked at one another in total and utter disbelief.

'What a fucking great lie!' Oliver roared, so loudly that the lawyer jumped and spilled gravy down his tunic.

At the same moment, I pounded the table and demanded, 'Surely you don't believe such vicious nonsense, do you?'

I was remembering some words of King Richard's, spoken to me back in the summer. 'You have saved the life of a young boy, a very precious thing.' Moreover, I knew the man – had known him, on and off, for the past twelve years – and I would swear to his probity and honour. He was deeply religious, but even if he weren't, he would never order the death of any child, let alone his own nephews. And in any case, why would he need to? Parliament had accepted his right and title to the crown. He had been consecrated king in Westminster Abbey.

I felt confident that the rebellion would come to nothing. King Richard had been a seasoned soldier since the age of eleven. He was perfectly capable of putting down any revolt against him. The story of the murders would then be disproved. The lie had been concocted by someone or other for his or her own ends. But who that person was and what those ends were was not yet clear.

And they were still not clear when I finally climbed the inn stairs to bed. The intervening two hours had been spent in fruitless discussion of the news with Master Heathersett and Oliver Tockney – the landlord had been called away by his irate wife to deal with some emergency, either real or imagined – but I was perfectly satisfied in my own mind that the rumour was false and would soon be quashed by the king's public denial.

In spite of this conviction, however, I found it hard to fall asleep, and for this, my unruly thoughts were as much, if not more, to blame than the storm still raging outside. (There would be some loose tiles and missing thatch come daybreak.) The news of the uprisings had disturbed me and, for a while, I stubbornly refused to acknowledge the cause. Instead, I feigned astonishment that a king so universally acclaimed – from all I could gather – wherever he had been received on his royal progress, whose coronation had been among the best attended for a hundred years or more, whose acceptance of the throne, in place of his twelve-year-old nephew, had been hailed with apparent relief by everyone of note, could so soon be facing rebellion. But in the end, I forced myself to face the truth.

The fact was that by no means had everybody been happy with the change of sovereign. There were many people who remained dubious about the legitimacy of King Richard's claim. Even I, with the knowledge gleaned from my journey to Paris the previous year, was uneasy. Robert Stillington, Bishop of Bath and Wells, had sworn that he had betrothed the late King Edward to the Lady Eleanor Butler well before the former's wedding to Elizabeth Woodville, and there seemed no reason to doubt his word. In the eyes of the Church, the bishop had maintained, a betrothal was as good as a marriage. Maybe it was, but it should have had the endorsement of a papal court before declaring King Edward V and his siblings bastards. Besides, I had heard it argued, if the children of everyone who broke off a betrothal to marry elsewhere were declared illegitimate, half the population would be bastardized.

Then there was the uncomfortable fact of the young Earl of Warwick, who came before King Richard in the line of succession, but who was barred from the throne by the fact of his father's attainder. But an Act of Attainder was easily reversed, and considering King Richard had always stoutly declared that George of Clarence's execution had been entirely due to the machinations of the Woodvilles, why did he not choose to right this apparent wrong? The answer to that, unfortunately, was all too obvious . . .

Here, I abruptly got out of bed to use the chamber pot. As I relieved myself, I could see clearly where my thoughts were leading me. After all these months, I was forcing myself to accept what, deep down, I had felt all along: that I was not entirely convinced by the validity of Richard's right to be king. And what was more, as I climbed back into bed, I perceived with a sudden, startling clarity that he might not be entirely convinced, himself.

And with this thought in mind, I fell asleep and slept uneasily until morning.

With the coming of daylight, I suppressed the whole idea as nonsense. Of course, King Richard was rightfully king and I was one of his most loyal subjects. Moreover, as I cautiously opened the shutters and looked out on a wet and bedraggled world, the reason for the rumour about the deaths of the princes struck me with the force of a sledgehammer. If the Welsh were rising on behalf of Henry Tudor, what better way to get the dissident Yorkist supporters on their side than to persuade people that Richard had villainously had his nephews murdered? I trusted that the king would be swift to deny it.

Here, a knock on the door heralded a chambermaid with a jug of hot water for me to wash and shave. I also cleaned my teeth with my customary piece of willow bark, fished out of my pack my one spare shirt which I had resisted putting on until now, having noticed at supper last night that I was beginning to smell, and descended to the ale-room where Oliver Tockney was awaiting me.

'Has Lawyer Heathersett gone?'

It was the landlord who answered as he bustled in with a tray of hot oatcakes and small beer. 'He's a busy man. He has several days' business yet to complete in the town. He'll be back tonight, but you two will be gone by then, I daresay. You'll be wanting to be on your way. And now the weather's improving a little, trade's bound to pick up again.'

The Yorkshireman grinned at me and winked. 'I might stay around for a day or so and try selling some o' my wares in this town. What about you, Master Chapman?'

'A good idea, Master Tockney,' I concurred.

'Then you must both find other accommodation,' the landlord declared, finally showing his hand.

We didn't hurry our breakfast and by the time we finally left the inn, the weather had improved yet again. What clouds there were, shuttling busily across the face of a watery sun, were thin and transparent, like gossamer. It seemed at last as though the gods were smiling and that the terrible storm had blown itself out.

So Oliver Tockney and I spent a couple of days touting our packs around the town, making sure that we didn't tread – literally – on one another's toes, and doing a surprising amount of business among the goodwives of Hereford who had been housebound for too long by the inclement weather and were in urgent need of spending a little money. And for the hours of darkness, which were growing longer with each passing day, we found an ale-house tucked away in Bye Street, where we were offered a couple of verminous blankets and the use of the ale-room floor when the locals had departed. Both Oliver and I suspected that it was something of a thieves' den, but we didn't let that worry us. We were strangers and it was none of our business.

On the third day, we decided it was time to move on. We had covered most of the streets pretty well between us and in any case, I was anxious to start for home as the weather again seemed to be deteriorating. We were a little later setting forth than we had intended, and I noticed anxiously that the whole of the eastern sky appeared to be on fire, banks of grey cloud against the red which burned and smouldered as the sun rose. 'Red sky in the morning, shepherd's warning,' my mother had often quoted to me when I was young, and frequently it had proved to be true. My companion appeared undeterred by these signs and portents, declaring himself firm in his resolve to get as far south as Bristol if he could.

As we approached the marketplace, wrapped warmly in our cloaks and hoods, we could hear the town crier's stentorian voice demanding our attention. We paused on the edge of the crowd that had gathered about him and so heard the first official confirmation of the rebellions that had broken out in the south-west and in Wales. But the news that sent me rocking back on my heels, that set my senses reeling, was the information that the Welsh uprising was being led by no less a person than the Duke . of Buckingham himself.

Buckingham!

Henry Stafford, the one man who had done more than any other person to set the crown on his cousin Richard's head had turned against him, was even now raising his tenantry in rebellion against their lawfully crowned king.

As we left the town behind us and began to walk southwards, Oliver Tockney could barely contain his anger and bewilderment. What could possibly have provoked this act of betrayal and treachery from one on whom King Richard had heaped reward after reward for his loyalty and friendship? And when, on the second day, an itinerant ladies' tailor, whom we encountered sheltering in a barn during a heavy rainstorm, suggested that the duke's defection was because he had learned of the young princes' murder and was horrified by it, it took all my strength to prevent my travelling companion from attacking him with his knife.

'Never,' Oliver panted, picking himself up from the pile of hay where I had flung him and addressing the cowering tailor, 'say that to a Yorkshireman again! You may not be so fortunate next time to have someone to defend you. You'll be cut down like the lying bastard you are.'

'Well, it stands to reason –' the tailor was beginning hotly, but I signalled to him not to push his luck, so he subsided, muttering defiantly to himself, and took himself off as soon as the rain had eased.

'And good riddance to bad rubbish,' Oliver growled as we, too, made preparations to resume our journey. He eyed me severely as I humped my pack on to my back and took hold of my cudgel. 'You haven't passed an opinion, chapman. So what do you make of that idiot's slanderous theory?'

I grinned at him. 'If I said I thought there might be some truth in it, would you try to murder me, as well?'

He returned grin for grin. 'No, because I shouldn't believe you.' He followed me out into the rain and sleet, carefully closing the barn door behind him. 'Would I be right?'

I staggered a little as a heavy gust of wind buffeted me and almost swept me off my feet.

'I think I've always distrusted Buckingham,' I said, raising my voice slightly to make myself heard above the storm. 'I saw him back in the summer, riding along the Strand in King Richard's coronation procession, and he looked . . .' How had he looked? I struggled to recall the expression that had worried me. 'He looked,' I continued after a moment, 'sullen. Resentful. Not like a man triumphing in the elevation of his kinsman and friend, knowing that he will be his right-hand man. I don't believe he

ever envisaged Richard taking the crown. I think . . . I think
he thought of the two of them, equal in importance, governing
the young king. You see, he, too, is an uncle of young Edward,
although only by marriage. Buckingham's wife is a Woodville,
sister of . . .' I hesitated. How did one refer now to the former
queen? '. . . the Lady Elizabeth.' I finished, before continuing.
'I think, too, that the ease with which parliament and the nobility,
both laymen and churchmen, accepted Duke Richard as king
might have made him wonder if he couldn't have made a
successful bid for the throne himself. As a direct descendant of
one of Edward III's sons, he has a claim of sorts. Perhaps someone
persuaded him . . .' I broke off as some words of the tinker's
surfaced. 'Of course!'

My companion grimaced as another gust of wind hit us in the
face and tightened the strings of his hood. 'Of course what?'

'The king had placed the Bishop of Ely in Buckingham's
charge, under house arrest. The tinker I told you about saw them
at Gloucester and said that the duke was riding off to his Brecon
estates, taking John Morton with him.'

'And this bishop? He's no friend of the king's?'

'A sworn enemy. Hates him. Richard is too straightforward
for a man with such a tortuous mind.'

Oliver Tockney shrugged as well as he could with a pack on
his back and a wet cloak clinging to his shoulders. 'That would
seem to explain matters, then.'

'It's possible,' I admitted cautiously. 'It's possible.'

After that, we let the subject drop, battling against the elements
and each occupied with his own thoughts. I was growing increas-
ingly worried at my failure to recognize any markers along the
track we were following. No familiar wayside shrines, dwellings,
churches, or ale-houses emerged from the veil of rain and mist
to reassure me that we were on the road to Gloucester. And when
Oliver and I finally stopped at a slate-roofed cottage – the first
habitation we had encountered for some miles – to beg food and
shelter for the night, and when the cottager addressed us in a
strange language which I guessed to be Welsh, my heart sank. I
knew without doubt that I had missed my way and instead of
approaching Gloucester, we were travelling south on the Welsh
side of the River Severn.

This fact was confirmed by the wife of our host who, providentially, turned out to be an Englishwoman.

'Then where, in the name of the Blessed Virgin, are we?' I demanded, struggling to rid myself of my sodden cloak and boots.

'About four miles north of Monmouth,' the goodwife answered, throwing more wood on the fire in an effort to heat up the pot of stew that hung above it. 'On foot, you should reach there by midday tomorrow. Perhaps sooner if you make an early start. Mind you,' she added, as the whole cottage was shaken by the wind, 'that depends on the weather. Never known anything like it in all the years we've lived here, have we, Huw?'

Her husband looked at her vaguely and she repeated the question in Welsh. Immediately, he broke into a spate of words, none of which Oliver and I could understand, accompanied by a wealth of gesticulation. The goodwife continued to stir the pot, not paying him a great deal of attention except to nod occasionally and grunt. When he eventually fell silent, she said, 'He blames it all on the English. Says we're a godless lot and that all the sins of the world are on our heads.' She laughed, a deep-throated, guttural sound. 'Daresay he's right. What d'you think, gentlemen?'

We both joined in her laughter and agreed. As a race, we've never much cared what other people think of us: we imbibe the consciousness of our superiority with our mothers' milk. Foreigners down the centuries have upbraided us for our laziness, lack of personal cleanliness, inedible food and the unattractiveness of our habits in general, but we just raise two fingers and carry on our merry way. If anything, we rather relish the opprobrium.

A short time later, Oliver and I were warm, if not completely dry, and fed. In exchange for her hospitality, we regaled the goodwife with information about the outside world, although news of rebellion breaking out in other parts of Wales disturbed her. She said she wouldn't tell her husband as it was more than likely he'd want to go off and fight for Henry Tudor, something of which, as a loyal supporter of the House of York, she couldn't approve.

She herself was a Gloucester girl and I asked her if she knew a Juliette Gerrish.

A shake of the head preceded the fact that she hadn't lived in the city for many years. 'And yet . . .' The goodwife paused, frowning. 'Now you mention it, someone did pass this way a while back – a long while back – who mentioned her name. At least, I think that's what it was. I seem to have heard it before. Whoever it was said she'd had a child, but the talk was that it wasn't her husband's.'

'She's no longer a widow, then?' I asked sharply.

Our hostess shook her head. 'I wouldn't know. If she was once, she must have married again.' She regarded me curiously. 'What's the lady to you?'

'Nothing. Nothing at all,' I said, with just a little too much emphasis. 'I met her a year or so back when I was working the Gloucester streets.' No need to say more than that. 'A chance encounter, that's all. I just happened to remember her when you said you came from the city, but I didn't realize you'd been away from it so long.' I changed the subject abruptly and nodded at Oliver Tockney. 'We'll be off at first light, mistress. We'll retrace our steps to Gloucester and cross the Severn there. I hope we don't keep you and your goodman awake with our snoring.'

'It won't bother us,' she answered, beginning to douse the fire. 'We sleep like logs. You'll find some old blankets and sacks and things in that chest over by the wall. You can see where our bed is. You're welcome to the other half of the room. And if you'll both look away while I take off my gown and shift, we shall get on tolerably well. We've no chamber pot, I'm afraid, so you'll just have to piss in the corner where the pile of straw is, or out of the door.'

The weather being what it was, we chose the straw, and half an hour later, in spite of the hardness of the cottage's beaten-earth floor, Oliver Tockney and I were both fast asleep.

THREE

We set out betimes the following morning – after a breakfast of oatmeal and warm ale provided by our hostess and watched in glum silence by our reluctant host – to retrace our path to Gloucester. We had not gone more than a mile or two, however, before we encountered a sour-faced cottager, driving his pig ahead of him.

He said something to us in Welsh.

Oliver and I both mimed our inability to understand him, whereupon he dropped into English with the ease that many borderers have. Most of them, of necessity, speak both languages. 'I asked where you're bound for. Gloucester, is it?'

I nodded and he came to a halt, letting his pig wander off to rootle among the wayside bushes, their leaves still dripping from the previous night's storm. 'You won't make it then,' he announced lugubriously. 'There's a great tree uprooted not three or four furlongs up the track from here. It'll take a day or so before it's moved, I reckon. I was hoping to get my pig to Gloucester market and sell him. I need to buy provisions before the winter sets in. Just my luck! Now I've to leg it to Marstow to get help.' He glanced upwards, regarding the lowering sky, the full-bellied clouds pregnant with rain. 'If you've any sense, you'll turn around and head for Monmouth. Get under shelter before the next storm comes. Try again for Gloucester in a day or so. Maybe me and a few other boyos will have got the path cleared by then.'

'What about the sidetracks?' I asked, loath to abandon our journey and start in the opposite direction. The further south we went, the wider became the Severn and the more difficult its crossing.

'The sidetracks!' The man was scathing. 'They're nothing but quagmires after all this rain. A lot of hamlets and settlements must be entirely cut off. I've been a countryman all my life and I tell you I've never experienced weather as bad as this. Rivers and streams are bursting their banks. It's like the Great Flood.

If we'd any sense, we'd all be building arks.' With which, he hooked his pig out of the bushes with his long, curved stick and, cursing to himself, went on his way.

Oliver Tockney and I stood looking at one another.

'What do you reckon, then?' he said. 'Do we take yon fellow's advice?'

'It seems we don't have much choice,' I answered reluctantly. Heavy raindrops suddenly splattered the earth around our feet, sending up little fountains of mud. 'It seems as if it's starting up again.'

The Yorkshireman nodded and turned about. 'We'd better go back to the cottage and get directions and let the goodwife know about the tree.' He gave a sudden shout of laughter. 'The goodman will probably die of an apoplexy on seeing us again, just as he's heaving a sigh of relief at having rid himself of us.' We trudged in silence for a while, then Oliver asked curiously, 'Who was this woman in Gloucester you were asking about? A friend of yours?'

'A woman I knew for a short period once. A woman I'd almost forgotten – certainly never expected to hear from again – but who suddenly resurfaced in my life earlier this year to make trouble for me.'

I sensed my companion's hesitation, but his curiosity got the better of his manners and the unwritten rule of the road that you don't enquire too closely into other travellers' affairs. 'What sort of trouble?'

'She claimed I was the father of her child.' The unspoken question fairly shouted at me. 'No, I was not,' I snapped. 'What's more, at the time the child must have been conceived I was out of the country. First Scotland and then Paris.'

Fortunately for my patience and good manners, and for the sake of peace between us, this last piece of information drove all other questions from Oliver's mind. 'You've been to Paris?' he breathed. 'Paris? What's it like? Is it true that even the children speak French over there?'

'Perfectly true.'

Oliver furrowed his brow, and not just because a squall of wind and rain had buffeted him.

'But how do they communicate with God and the saints, then?

Everyone knows that God and the heavenly host all speak English.'

It took us all day and well into the evening to cover the four miles to Monmouth. The goodwife's instructions how to get there had been lucid and concise when we reappeared at her door, and I think even she had been relieved that we hadn't been seeking further shelter. She had thanked us for the information concerning the tree blocking the northern track and been moved to provide us with slices of bread and cheese to sustain us during the hours ahead.

'Not too many dwellings hereabouts to beg food from,' she had said.

She was right. Nor did we meet many people as foolish as ourselves, out of doors in such terrible weather. We passed a woodcutter once, going in the opposite direction, but he merely grunted in response to our greeting, too wet and sorry for himself to linger. A young girl carrying a basket of eggs, her skirts bunched up around her knees, scurried down a stony path leading heaven alone knew where. There was no house in sight that we could see. A discalced friar, not even allowing himself the permitted luxury of sandals, joined us for half a mile or so, his bare feet swollen and blue with cold. But he discoursed cheerfully enough of this and that, speculating with Oliver and myself on whether or not we believed the rumours that placed Buckingham at the head of a Welsh uprising to be true. Or whether, indeed, there was an uprising at all.

'For I've seen nobody but you two gentlemen on the roads all day. Hardly surprising in this sort of weather.'

He didn't mention the other rumour concerning the death of the young princes in the Tower, so I assumed they hadn't yet come his way. And before I could ask him, he left us with a blessing and a hastily sketched sign of the cross as he disappeared abruptly into the woods which stretched, gloomy and dark, on either side of the track. After that, we trudged doggedly along, all our energies concentrated on putting one foot in front of the other and avoiding the worst of the puddles. Sometimes there was no help for it but to wade straight through the larger ones which stretched the width of the path, from one tangle of bushes and undergrowth to the other.

We ate our bread and cheese beneath the shelter of a tree, our silent thanks going out to the cottager's wife who had so thoughtfully provided it. By mid-afternoon – or what we judged to be mid-afternoon – a thin sun emerged from between the clouds, striking down between the tree trunks in patterns of fretted gold. But there was no warmth in it. A wind had sprung up, whispering among the black and silver shadows of the leaves and making us shiver under our rain-soaked cloaks.

The sound of hoof-beats made us draw into the side of the track, and only just in time as a horse and rider went past us at a decent pace and with little regard for our safety. To be fair, the rider was so hunched up against the elements, I doubt if he was even aware of us.

I stared after his receding back.

'I feel certain that that was Lawyer Heathersett,' I said at last.

'Did you see his face?' Oliver asked.

'No.'

'Then how do you know?' My companion was sceptical.

'There was just something about his appearance.'

A snort was my only answer and I decided to say no more. Nevertheless, I was quite sure in my own mind that it had been Geoffrey Heathersett who passed us, and I was therefore not in the least astonished, two hours later, as Oliver and I entered an inn close to Monmouth's St Mary's Church, that the first person I clapped eyes on was the lawyer.

He was seated at a table near the door, deep in conversation with two other men who I also recognized. They, too, were Bristol citizens, the slightly younger one being Gilbert Foliot, a man of about forty, fair-haired and blue-eyed in a typically English fashion, a wealthy goldsmith with a shop in St Mary le Port Street and an expensive new house close to St Peter's Church. He had been a widower for the past eight years and was the father of an only child, a daughter, whose name I seemed to remember was Ursula. (Although how I knew that, I wasn't quite sure.)

The second man, Henry Callowhill, was a wine importer with at least three ships plying between Bristol and Bordeaux and southern Spain. Not quite as wealthy perhaps as Gilbert Foliot, but certainly rich enough to be venerated in a city that regarded the making and accumulation of money as one of, if not the most, desirable goals in life. He was a large, jolly man who might well have run to fat in old age had it not been for his height of almost six feet. He was married and had named his three ships after his three children, Martin, Edmund and Matilda.

'You were right, Roger,' Oliver Tockney breathed in my ear. 'I owe you an apology.'

At that moment, the landlord came bustling towards us, none too pleased to have his inn invaded by a couple of pedlars, their homespun cloaks dripping water all over his nicely sanded floor. (Gentlemen, of course, were different. They were allowed to drip anywhere they chose.)

'We're full,' he said before either of us could speak, 'and very busy. You two will have to look for some other kitchen to sleep in. There's an ale-house in the street next to this.'

'We can pay,' Oliver snapped and produced a handful of coins from his pouch, rattling them under the innkeeper's nose.

The man hesitated, then, glancing over his shoulder at the trio seated behind him, shook his head.

'This is a hostelry for gentlemen,' he hissed. 'You can see that for yourselves.'

'It's for anyone who can pay,' Oliver answered aggressively. 'You wouldn't get away with this sort of attitude where I come from. One man's as good as another up north.'

I doubted that and so, by the look on the landlord's face, did he. But before he had time to argue the point, there was a scraping of stool legs and Gilbert Foliot was advancing on us, one hand extended in greeting.

'Master Chapman!' he exclaimed. 'What are you doing in this part of the world? Or shouldn't I ask? Is it perhaps' – he gave an awkward laugh – 'another secret mission for the duke? I mean,' he added hurriedly, 'the king. One tends to forget.'

I was conscious that Oliver Tockney and the innkeeper were regarding me open-mouthed, and it was my turn to be embarrassed.

'No, no, sir! I'm merely earning my living which, I assure you, is what I do most of the time. Had I known what shocking storms and winds I would encounter, I should never have left Bristol.'

It was plain that the goldsmith didn't believe me, but he was willing to leave the matter there. Indeed, his discretion was so obvious that it must have raised doubts in everyone's mind concerning the true reason for my presence.

'It's all right, landlord,' he said. 'These two gentlemen' – he choked slightly over the word, but continued gallantly – 'will eat with us. And I feel sure you can find somewhere for them to sleep tonight.'

The innkeeper muttered something in reply, but he was still too busy goggling at me to argue, and merely ordered the potboy to place two more stools at Master Foliot's table before hurrying off to the kitchen.

'Well, Master Chapman,' the goldsmith resumed when Oliver and I were settled, 'this meeting is not altogether a surprise. Lawyer Heathersett here told us he'd run into you in Hereford.'

'Yes.' I helped Oliver to shed his pack. For all his brave talk earlier, I could see that he was a little overawed at being in the company of men so far above him in the social hierarchy.

Henry Callowhill gave me a hearty slap on the back, causing me to spill some of the ale which the potboy had just placed in front of me.

'No necessity for you to say anything further,' he said. 'No need at all. We quite understand.'

Geoffrey Heathersett made no comment, simply giving me a hard stare and a sour smile, both of which might have meant anything or nothing according to how I liked to interpret them.

I made one last effort to convince the three that they were wrong. 'Gentlemen, you are labouring under a misapprehension. I was in Hereford on some business for my wife and doing a little trade on my own account. Master Tockney – who comes from Yorkshire, by the way – and I met quite by chance, and we are here because I missed the road to Gloucester and landed us on the Welsh side of the Severn by mistake. We intended to retrace our steps to Gloucester, but when we started out this morning, we were told that the track was impassable because a large tree had been blown down overnight. According to our informant, it will probably be several days before the path is clear again, and the sidetracks are also impassable because of the mud.'

There was a moment's silence, then Master Callowhill administered a second resounding slap on my shoulder. 'Quite so! Quite so! We'll say no more about it, eh?'

I gave up. And in any case, at that moment the food arrived; roast fowl with buttered parsnips and a beef pudding on the side. We all picked up spoons and knives, setting to with a will, and for quite some while there was nothing to be heard but the champing of jaws. Gradually, however, conversation became possible again.

Gilbert Foliot smiled at me across the table. 'Gossip has it, Master Chapman, that you attended King Richard's coronation at his personal command.'

There was no point in denying it. My former mother-in-law, Margaret Walker, and her cronies had made sure that all Bristol knew this unimportant fact.

'In a very, very lowly position, sir, I assure you.'

'And also the coronation banquet afterwards.'

I squirmed. 'Again, on the very lowliest benches. If you've heard otherwise, it's a blatant lie.'

The goldsmith laughed. 'I'll accept your word for it. I understand it was the best attended coronation for many years. Is that so?'

I grimaced. 'As to that, I'm in no position to say. I've never been to a coronation before. But certainly, no one who is anyone appeared to be missing. Even Henry Tudor's mother and stepfather were present. Lady Stanley carried Queen Anne's train, or so I was informed by one who knew.'

'Is that so?' my interlocutor questioned smoothly. 'Well, I suppose there can be very little possibility of her son ever obtaining the crown. She might as well throw in her lot with the Yorkists. Although I must admit I'm surprised. Wasn't Thomas Stanley implicated in that plot to kill King Richard, back in the summer? The one which ended with Hastings summarily losing his head?'

'Not summarily,' I protested indignantly. 'I know there were malicious rumours that he was beheaded out of hand, but I can assure you they were false. Lord Hastings was not executed until a week later, after due trial and sentence.'

'You know that for a fact, do you?' Lawyer Heathersett asked, staring hard at me and raising his brows.

'Yes.'

The three older men exchanged significant glances, as much as to say that I had confirmed all they had ever heard about me was true, and I realized that I must have been steadily gaining a reputation for being the Duke of Gloucester's – now the king's – man without being aware of it. I opened my mouth to lodge another protest, but Gilbert Foliot suddenly decided that enough was enough, and abruptly changed the subject. 'How's your daughter, Henry?' he asked, looking across the table at the wine merchant. 'How old is she now?'

'Nine,' Master Callowhill answered thickly through a mouthful of beef pudding.

The goldsmith continued, 'And I believe you also have a daughter about the same age, Master Chapman? I've seen her with your wife. A pretty little thing.'

I wasn't sure that I'd describe Elizabeth as pretty and certainly not little. Her physique was too much like mine. She would be a big woman. But I nodded agreement just the same.

Gilbert Foliot heaved a sentimental sigh. 'A lovely age, gentlemen, when girls think their fathers are gods.' I very much doubted this in Elizabeth's case, but I held my tongue and tried to show a Greek profile to the others. 'But things change,' the goldsmith went on sadly. 'Girls grow up and become openly defiant and sulky when their wills are crossed.'

Geoffrey Heathersett, a childless bachelor, gave a superior smile. 'Is Ursula still giving you trouble, Gilbert? Still wanting to marry young Peter Noakes?'

There was another sigh. 'I'm afraid so.'

'You don't intend to allow it?'

The younger man snorted. 'No, I do not. Oh, Anthony Roper is quite a good sort of man and pretty plump in the pocket, I grant you. But that nephew of his is a ne'er-do-well if ever I saw one. And who exactly was his father, can anyone tell me that?' His friends glumly shook their heads. 'That sister of Roper's was always a wild piece. Ran away when she was fifteen, a year younger than Ursula is now, had a child by some fellow who deserted her as soon as he'd made her pregnant, came home destitute to her brother, gave birth and incontinently died. And her son has grown up just as feckless as far as I can see. Shows

no interest at all in the rope-making business. Just likes spending
his uncle's money and loafing around the town. And hanging
around my daughter. Well, I don't need to tell you, gentlemen,
that's not the sort of husband I want for my only child.'

We all shook our heads and pursed our lips in solemn agreement. But I couldn't help reflecting that Master Foliot would
have his work cut out keeping that motherless chit in leading
reins. I knew by sight the woman he had installed as Ursula's
companion: one Margery Dawes, a younger cousin of Geoffrey
Heathersett, a buxom woman with the lawyer's protuberant blue
eyes and a roguish smile entirely her own. According to my
former mother-in-law and her best friend, Bess Simnel – and
believe me, those two knew everything that went on in Bristol:
nothing escaped their eagle gaze – Margery was more inclined
to encourage her charge and young Noakes than not, and arranged
lovers' trysts for the pair of them. But of course I said nothing.

At this point another jug of ale and a syllabub of pears arrived
at the table to replace the fowl and beef pudding, now shadows
of their former selves. We fell to with a will and the conversation
flagged again until once more our plates were empty. But even
then, the talk was desultory. We were all by now feeling the effects
of the second jug of ale and a long, hard day and beginning to
think longingly of our beds. Outside, the rain still beat down
and the wind had risen, causing the locals to hurry home and
leave the five of us in sole command of the ale-room. The landlord, evidently impressed by our apparent friendship with three
men of substance, offered Oliver and myself the use of an attic
where, he assured us, we should find a comfortable bed provided
with clean sheets and good wool blankets. We accepted with
alacrity and, having bidden the others goodnight, followed him
up three flights of rickety stairs to a room so small and low-pitched
that I was unable to stand upright in it. Stripping to our shirts,
we fell into bed without more ado, my eyes closing almost as
soon as my head touched the pillow.

My companion, however, was not so sleepy, his natural curiosity
keeping him awake until he had received some answers to his
questions. I could tell by the way he wriggled around in the bed,
snorted and started forming sentences which he then abandoned,
that he was intent on finding out exactly what sort of a pedlar I

was and why my superiors deferred to my opinion. But I was far too weary for such a catechism – although I realized that I should have to take Oliver into my confidence at some time, particularly if he insisted on travelling with me to Bristol – so I pretended to sleep, emitting some really lifelike snores and keeping them going until they became genuine.

I slept dreamlessly and soundly. And the next thing I knew, it was morning.

I was the first of the guests to awaken and made my way downstairs, where one of the servants directed me to a pump in the yard. I removed my shirt under the interested scrutiny of two chambermaids leaning over the balcony rail above me and, working the handle with my right hand, cupped my left to help pour the icy water all over my shivering body, although I might just as well have stood in the middle of the yard and let the sluicing rain do the work for me, for the weather had not improved. Indeed, it seemed to have worsened during the night; even if the wind had dropped a little, the downpour continued.

I was fully dressed by the time that Oliver finally roused himself and managed, temporarily at least, to postpone any explanations he felt were his due by urging him downstairs to breakfast. The meal was once more laid out in the ale-room, and the mouth-watering smell of hot oatcakes and fried bacon collops greeted us as we entered. One of the potboys, obviously bursting with news, started to tell us something, but was thwarted by the arrival of the landlord, closely followed by Master Foliot and his two companions.

The landlord was speaking to them over his shoulder as he deposited a dish of honey and another of dried figs on the table alongside the oatcakes and bacon.

'There are terrible rumours in the town this morning, sirs. Rivers are bursting their banks, bridges have been swept away during the night, animals are being drowned in the fields where they stand. Some say the Severn itself has flooded. I'm afraid you might find it difficult to continue your journey.'

Lawyer Heathersett chewed his bottom lip. 'I shall at least have to try,' he said uncertainly. 'I have an important case coming up next week at the Bristol Assize.'

'And I have a consignment of wine due from Spain in three days' time,' added Henry Callowhill.

Gilbert Foliot made no comment but he, too, looked dubious, as though there were affairs of the moment calling him home. I wasn't any too happy myself, wanting to get back to Adela and the children before the weather suddenly became colder and all the rain turned to snow and ice. Nevertheless, it would be more than foolish to set out and find ourselves stranded somewhere without hope of reaching food and shelter.

'Your Honours are welcome to remain here as long as is necessary,' the landlord offered hopefully and already, no doubt, feeling the coins from this extra custom jingling in his pocket.

'We'll discuss it over breakfast,' the goldsmith said, moving towards the laden table.

The rest of us nodded agreement and seated ourselves around the board, Henry Callowhill taking charge of the jug of ale and pouring us all generous measures.

We talked over the situation while we ate, but came to no definite conclusion. Geoffrey Heathersett gave it as his opinion that these rumours were often gross exaggerations of the truth and, while the rest of us desperately wanted to agree with him, the question, *What if they're not?* was uppermost in everyone's mind.

We were still debating the subject – no man willing to decide for himself because it was instinctively felt that, in the circumstances, it would be much better to travel as a company rather than individually – when the ale-room door burst open and the landlord reappeared, looking white and shaken.

'Gentlemen!' he gasped. 'Word has just come that the Welsh rebels, under the Duke of Buckingham's command, are closing in on Monmouth. If the town elders decide to withstand the rebels and close the Monnow Bridge Gate, there might well be a siege of lengthy proportions.'

Henry Callowhill and the lawyer both got hastily to their feet.

'That decides it, then,' Geoffrey Heathersett said. 'I must leave at once and take my chance on the road.'

'Me, too,' the wine merchant agreed.

Gilbert Foliot looked up, asking in his calm way, 'And if the rebels capture you? Do we know how far off they are, landlord?'

'Report reckons about three miles, sir. They're seemingly
moving at a walking pace because most of 'em aren't mounted.'

The other two paused in their headlong dash for the door.

'But I don't want to be caught up in any siege,' Henry
Callowhill objected. 'It might go on for months.'

'True,' grunted the lawyer. 'But neither do I want to be captured
by Buckingham and his rabble. They might hold us to ransom.'

The goldsmith gave a sarcastic smile and rose to his feet.
'Highly unlikely, I should think. However, let us err on the safe
side. Landlord, how far is it to Tintern Abbey from here, would
you reckon?'

The man pursed his lips. 'About ten miles or so, Your Honour.
Maybe a bit more, maybe a bit less.'

'A day's walk, a morning's ride on horseback,' Gilbert mused.
He thought for a moment while we all waited for his decision.
At last, he nodded. 'Then I suggest that's what we do. We make
for Tintern and ask for sanctuary. The rebels won't dare besiege
us there.'

FOUR

Of course, with hindsight I know that the rebels never
had any intention of besieging Monmouth, never came
within miles of it; that even then, the rebellion was
beginning to lose momentum. But at the time, with rumours
flying about like leaves in autumn, the emergency seemed very
real.

'Will the abbot be willing to give us all shelter?' the lawyer
queried, and was met with a haughty stare from Gilbert Foliot.

'Apart from the fact that it is his religious duty to offer shelter
to wayfarers in need, he will certainly not refuse me,' was the
crisp retort. Then, as there was a baffled silence from his listeners,
the goldsmith added with asperity, 'My late wife was a Herbert.'

If he expected this fact to explain matters, he was due for a
disappointment. The silence was as profound as before. He
continued impatiently, 'Sir William Herbert, late Earl of Pembroke,

was buried in Tintern Abbey after his execution fourteen years ago. My wife, as a member of a cadet branch of the family, attended his funeral. I accompanied her.'

Memories came flooding back. Fourteen years previously, I had just begun my novitiate at Glastonbury, but I still maintained a lively interest in what was happening in the outside world. And in that year of Our Lord, 1469, the country was again in a state of insurrection, with the mighty Earl of Warwick and his son-in-law, the Duke of Clarence, in revolt against the late King Edward, who had briefly become their prisoner. Yorkists and Lancastrians were once more at war and, after the battle at Edgecote, which the former lost, the loyal William Herbert had been executed out of hand. His body had, it seemed, later been interred at Tintern Abbey.

'Ah!' I said, indicating by a nod that I had grasped the goldsmith's meaning. As a relation, if only by marriage, of one of the martyrs of the Yorkist cause, he would be welcomed by the abbot.

Gilbert Foliot smiled gratefully at me. 'I suggest, Master Chapman, that you and your, er, companion' – he eyed Oliver Tockney somewhat askance – 'set forth immediately. You should reach the abbey easily by nightfall. We' – he indicated the other two men – 'will no doubt pass you on the road and, if no misfortune befalls us, should be at Tintern by noon. I shall ensure that the brothers are ready to receive you; that beds and food are prepared for you. You will only have to present yourselves at the main gate to be allowed immediate access.'

I noticed he didn't suggest that Oliver and I hire horses and ride with him and the others. I didn't press the point because, for one thing, I wasn't sure that Oliver could ride and had no wish to embarrass him. Another reason, and perhaps the more cogent of the two, was that I had no desire to spend more time than necessary in our new-found acquaintances' company. They were all three perfectly pleasant, but I knew very well that their friendliness stemmed from a wariness of me and uncertainty as to my exact relationship with King Richard, who was himself something of an unknown quantity to all southerners. Underneath their polite words and manners, I could detect a certain resentment at the need for courtesy towards someone whom they regarded as little better than a peasant, but were frightened to offend. And who could blame them? Finally, it occurred to me that if we should encounter armed rebels, it would be easier to seek shelter among the trees and undergrowth bordering the track than attempt to outstrip them along paths that were ankle-deep in mud and pitted with potholes from the recent storms: veritable stumbling blocks for fast-moving horses.

Oliver Tockney duly expressed his gratitude as we left Monmouth and headed south, following the rough map which the landlord had drawn for us.

'For it's not that I couldn't have afforded to hire a nag,' he said when he had voiced the same misgivings as my own. 'And I feared it was what they might suggest. But I'm no good astride any beast, unless it were my old grandfather's cow, and would only have fallen off and made a right fool of myself. Besides, they don't like me, I can tell. And they're afraid of you. So,' he added as the rain once more began to fall, 'why don't you enliven what looks like being another miserable journey by telling me what it's all about. For you're no ordinary pedlar, that's clear.'

The hills rose all around us in the encroaching dark, the trees foaming in dusky waterfalls between the primeval humps, loose scree and shale ribbing their slopes. Below us, we could just make out the shape of the abbey and its sprawl of attendant buildings, candle- and lamplight starring the gathering dusk.

Our journey had been uneventful except for the need to take frequent shelter from the rain, which had increased in volume as the day progressed towards late afternoon. Several times it had turned to hail, and once, on the higher ground, to snow, but we had ploughed on doggedly and now had our reward. Food – hot food – and shelter were both at last within sight.

I had told Oliver Tockney my life story, or as much of it as I had thought fit to impart, with the unfortunate result that he, too, had now lost his ease of manner with me. I could feel the distance between us growing – not physically, of course – and a certain deference had crept into his manner when addressing me.

'Look, man!' I said as we descended the path to the main gate. 'I'm just a pedlar, like yourself. I'm not a spy or an agent for King Richard. I just happen to have done one or two good

turns for him over the years. That's all. I daresay that you and
your fellow Yorkshiremen have seen a great deal more of him
than I have, for most of the time I've been in Bristol and he's
been up north. So, for the Virgin's sake, don't start treating me
as though I'm something that I'm not. We shall need each other's
support once we're inside the abbey. Now, let's hope that Master
Foliot has been as good as his promise and that we're expected.
I don't know about you, but I could eat an ox. And I'm too cold
and wet to start bandying words with the gate-porter.'

All was well, however. Not only were we expected, but the
porter was on the lookout for us and had the gate open before
we had even rung the bell. As we entered, I noted that the River
Wye, which bounded two sides of the abbey, was swollen and,
here and there, overflowing its banks.

'I'm to take you first, sirs,' the porter said, 'to the infirmary
hall where you and the other gentlemen are to sleep and which,
at the moment, is happily free of patients. You may stow your
baggage there. Afterwards, I am to conduct you to Father Abbot's
lodging where you will eat.'

Oliver and I had no fault to find with this programme and
followed our guide, his white Cistercian robe glimmering palely
in the darkness, between various buildings and across a cloister
and garden to a single-storey building on the eastern perimeter
of the enclave. The brother opened the door and ushered us inside.
Oliver and I paused on the threshold, both equally surprised.

I have been in a few infirmaries in my time, including
Glastonbury's, but this was the most imposing I had seen. A
broad central aisle was flanked on both sides by separate bays,
each with its own fireplace and lit by a pair of lancet windows,
between which stood a bed and a bedside cupboard. Perfect
privacy could be obtained by pulling a curtain across the front
of the bay. There was a large, traceried window in the eastern
wall which must, in the daytime, give more than ample light,
while we later discovered that in the north-west corner, hidden
from view, was a private latrine.

'Luxury, indeed,' Oliver murmured in my ear. 'The monks do
themselves well here.'

'More than well,' I answered softly, first making sure that our
guide wasn't listening.

There were six bays in all, and in three of them, I could see
the saddle-bags of the goldsmith and his companions already
stowed. The porter indicated that we should take two of the three
on the opposite side of the aisle where the third one, judging by
the drawn curtain, was occupied.

I raised my eyebrows. 'I thought you said the infirmary was
empty.'

The brother nodded.

'That's not a patient,' he said. 'It's another traveller, like yourselves and the gentlemen, seeking sanctuary from the weather. A
young man who arrived early this morning and who has kept to
his bed ever since. He's feeling unwell and has particularly asked
not to be disturbed. He suffers, it seems, from severe headaches
which attack him from time to time and for which the only real
cure is rest. Complete rest. So Brother Infirmarian has given
instructions that he is to be left alone to sleep.' He smiled. 'Now,
sirs, if you will follow me again, I'll take you to Father Abbot's
private lodging, and then I must return to my gate. I've left it for
far too long as it is.'

We were buffeted by another squall of wind and rain as we
stepped outside and once more drew our cloaks about us. We
recrossed the cloister – 'the infirmary cloister,' our guide informed
us, skirted a small chapel, 'Father Abbot's private chapel' – and
were finally shown into the abbot's private parlour, a haven of warmth
and light.

Good wax candles shed their glow across shining, polished
surfaces, and a fire of scented pine logs burned on the generous
hearth, around which Gilbert Foliot, Henry Callowhill and Lawyer
Heathersett were standing. Each held a brimming glass of wine,
the liquid jewel-red in the flickering light, and were, at the moment
of our entry, pledging the health of their host.

Gilbert Foliot turned and saw Oliver and myself hesitating
just inside the doorway. 'Ah!' he exclaimed, setting down his
glass – fine Venetian glass if I were not mistaken. 'Here are
the two men I was telling you about, Lord Abbot. Our two
companions from Monmouth.' He patted my shoulder. 'Truth
to tell, Roger, you're not that far behind us. Our journey must
have been worse than yours, I think. The roads were almost
impassable in places. And as I don't recall overtaking you, I

guess you must have found some sidetracks that saved you a mile or so.'

I smiled noncommittally. I thought it best not to mention the fact that the three men had indeed passed us, but failed to notice two such insignificant travellers. A lay brother, who was evidently in attendance on the abbot that evening, handed a glass of wine to both Oliver and myself – although I could see that he thought it a case of casting pearls before swine – and then ushered everyone to the long oak table and bade us be seated. My fellow pedlar and I found ourselves sitting opposite one another at the bottom of the board.

A bowl of rich, hot oyster soup was placed in front of each of us and a large basket of white bread graced the middle of the table. For a while, talk was suspended as we all set to with a will, letting the hot liquid course through our frozen bodies and thaw out numbed extremities. After a time, however, conversation was gradually resumed with, inevitably, discussion of the rebellion taking precedence.

'What in heaven's name could have possessed My Lord of Buckingham to raise his standard against King Richard?' the abbot wanted to know. 'If all the stories which have reached us here are true, he practically put the crown on Richard's head himself, with the result, or so we hear, that the king's gratitude has been boundless. The duke was the mightiest subject in the land. Or does his defection have anything to do, I wonder, with this rumour of the princes' murder?'

I saw Oliver Tockney's hand clench around the handle of his spoon and, without being asked for my opinion, hurried into speech. 'I am convinced, My Lord, that that is a malicious rumour put about by the supporters of Henry Tudor in order to get the Yorkist insurgents on their side. I am persuaded that the king will refute all such stories once the rebellion has been put down and the ringleaders punished.'

The abbot raised his eyebrows in haughty surprise, then glanced questioningly at Gilbert Foliot. The latter, seated at his right hand, gave an almost imperceptible nod before muttering something that I was unable to catch.

'Ah!' The abbot gave me a piercing stare. 'So this is the man you were telling me about. A chapman who is also a confidant of our new royal master. Remarkable. Quite remarkable. But then, I'd always heard that Gloucester, as he then was, made friends of some oddly assorted people.' What he meant, of course, but did not like to say, was low-born scum like me. He need not have worried. I got the message. His tone of voice said it for him.

The goldsmith sent him a warning glance, then smoothly changed the subject. Looking around him, he said, 'Allow me to congratulate you, Lord Abbot, on your new accommodation. This lodging of yours is a great improvement on the old.'

The abbot frowned slightly. 'It must be many years since you were last here, sir. It is some time since the old house was in use.'

The by now empty soup bowls were removed and replaced by clean plates and a large haunch of venison, which was set in front of the abbot. Dishes of leeks and parsnips and water chestnuts were also arranged on the table by servants who were both deft and quick. A couple of them gave Oliver and me resentful looks, just to let us know that they were unused to waiting on anyone below the rank of gentleman; but, with Oliver following my lead, we returned high-nosed stares, indicating that being waited on was something to which we were entirely accustomed.

Master Foliot was replying to the abbot. 'It is many years, Father, as you surmise. Fourteen, to be precise. It was at the interment of my late wife's kinsman, William Herbert, Earl of Pembroke. He was executed on the orders of Warwick and Clarence after the unfortunate defeat at Edgecote. He was not the only one, of course. Earl Rivers and one of his sons, the, er, the Queen Dowager's father and brother, also lost their lives during that rebellion.'

'Should one call her Queen Dowager now?' mused Lawyer Heathersett.

'It's difficult to know exactly what to call anyone since . . . since the summer,' Henry Callowhill complained.

There was a reflective silence. I had the odd feeling that much more might have been said, but for my presence. I wasn't sure why. As far as I knew, everyone present was a supporter of the Yorkist cause and a loyal subject of our new king. But then, I thought, as recent events had shown, one did not necessarily march hand-in-hand with the other.

Gilbert Foliot once again took charge of what could have proved an awkward hiatus in the conversation. 'On the last occasion when I was here, My Lord,' he said, addressing the abbot, 'that secret hiding place in your old lodgings had just been discovered. Was anything more found afterwards?'

'More than those old documents?' The prelate shook his head. 'No, nothing.' He laughed. 'A most disappointing treasure trove.'

Master Foliot, noting the curious, enquiring looks of the rest of us, condescended to explain. 'Fourteen years ago, when, as you will have gathered, I was here with my late wife for her kinsman's funeral, some alterations had recently been made to the hearthstones of the abbot's previous lodging, during the course of which, a cavity had been revealed beneath one of the tiles. It had, it seemed, caused great excitement when it was first discovered, but sadly proved to contain nothing more than a couple of ancient account books and a few pages of a diary kept by one of the monks over a century and a half ago.'

There was a general murmur of interest.

'What were the diary pages about?' I asked.

The goldsmith laughed. 'Ah! You scent a mystery, Roger. Unfortunately, if my memory serves me right, there was little of interest in them.'

The abbot nodded in confirmation, adding, 'Nothing more than a description of the daily round, the reporting of one or two of the inevitable squabbles among the brothers – such disagreements are bound to happen from time to time in enclosed communities – and, I think, the mention of some strangers received by the then abbot who stayed at Tintern for a night or two. I remember that because there appeared to have been an argument between the brothers and their superiors about the advisability of granting these men sanctuary. But I may be wrong. It is many years now since I read the diary.'

'Is it still here, in the abbey?'

The abbot made a dismissive gesture. 'In the library somewhere, I believe. Brother Librarian could show it to you if you're really interested. But I assure you it would be a waste of your time and his. It's the merest fragment.'

'Dating from when exactly?' Geoffrey Heathersett queried. His lawyer's mind liked to have things neatly labelled.

The abbot speared a slice of venison on the end of his knife and waved it with an airy gesture. 'My dear sir, I've told you! It's no more than a page or so. There is nothing to date it with any accuracy. It's only because of the books of accounts that were found with it that Brother Librarian considers we might date it to the year 1326. But of course there is no reason why we should make that assumption.'

'I wonder,' I observed, helping myself liberally from the dish of parsnips, 'why it was considered necessary to conceal such an innocuous collection of documents in a secret hiding place.'

Gilbert Foliot signalled his agreement. 'I've often thought the same thing, Master Chapman.' He again turned to the abbot. 'I suppose the secret compartment is now sealed?'

Our host looked surprised. 'It was sealed almost immediately after its discovery. Its contents were removed and then it was closed. Did you ever see it?'

The goldsmith nodded. 'I was shown it at the time of the funeral, and the documents as well. As you so rightly say, Lord Abbot, an unremarkable collection. A couple of abbey account books and the diary pages. One can see no reason at all why they should have been hidden. That was why I asked if anything more had ever been discovered.'

'Not to my knowledge,' the abbot answered thickly, his mouth full of venison. He was plainly tired of the subject. 'Well, gentlemen, tell me what brings you to this part of the country, and in such terrible weather.'

He so obviously did not include Oliver and myself in this invitation that we were able to apply ourselves wholeheartedly to our food and listen with only half an ear to what the others were saying. The lawyer had had business both in Hereford and on this side of the Severn – something to do with bequests from a will, I think – and the same was true of the other two. Business had brought them from home in weather that, they declared, had not been so very bad at the outset of their journeys. It had, it seemed, been pure chance that had seen all three fetch up at the same inn at Monmouth.

'Nevertheless,' Gilbert said, 'it was a happy circumstance as things fell out. It's better to have company in the sort of storms we have experienced these past few days than to be on one's own.'

The other two murmured their hearty agreement, but for my own part, while not doubting their sincerity, I had reservations about the goldsmith's. It seemed to me that there had been a certain constraint in his tone that suggested he was not entirely pleased at this reunion with old friends and acquaintances; that he would be happier on his own. I fancied I was not alone in this opinion: I saw the lawyer give him a shrewd, sidelong glance beneath half-closed lids, but he made no comment.

'News has reached us from overseas,' said the abbot, 'that the king of France is dead.'

I raised my head sharply from the contemplation of my empty plate. The rumour I had heard was true, then. The others seemed unsurprised.

'Yes, so I believe,' Gilbert Foliot answered. 'At the end of August.'

'The penultimate day,' Geoffrey Heathersett agreed pedantically.

The abbot murmured, 'The feast day of Saint Felix.'

At this juncture, our dirty plates were removed and clean ones set before us. A truly majestic apple pie was placed in the centre of the table, together with a pitcher of cream, and we were all invited by our host to help ourselves and not to stint our portions. This being done, silence reigned once more as we again filled our mouths and bellies. A different wine was produced and poured into our glasses by the head server – a slightly more acidic-tasting drink, this, to counterbalance the luscious sweetness of the pie – and I could not help reflecting that this style of living had surely never been envisaged by Robert of Molesme when he established his new Order at Citeaux. In fact, I was absolutely certain it hadn't, Robert having been the original aesthete. However, I wasn't grumbling.

It concerned me somewhat that I had not previously heard definite confirmation of King Louis's death, and that almost two months had elapsed since King Edward's old enemy and bene-factor had followed him to the grave. It proved – had I needed proof – that I had been away from Bristol far too long (and for no good reason as it had turned out). Bristol's trade with very nearly every country in Europe, with foreign ships tying up daily along the Backs, ensured that the town's citizens were early recipients of news from abroad.

Someone nudged me in the ribs and I realized that the abbot was condescending to address me. 'Master Foliot, here, tells me that you were at the king's coronation, Master, er, Chapman. And also afterwards, at the coronation feast.' He smiled incredulously.

'In a very humble capacity, My Lord. Extremely humble.'

'Don't overdo it,' Oliver Tockney muttered.

'It was well attended, I believe?'

I inclined my head. 'I have it on good authority that it was the best attended coronation within living memory.'

'Mmm.' This noncommittal noise might have meant something or nothing. I waited. The prelate continued after some moments, 'I understand a bill is to be passed at the next meeting of Parliament confirming Richard's right and title to the crown.' He regarded me thoughtfully for a moment or two before glancing at the others around the table. 'Which makes these rumours of the young princes' death absurd, wouldn't you agree, gentlemen? Why order the commissioning of such a crime, when the prize is his already?'

'There has been a rising in the south-west on behalf of the princes and, as far as I know, it has not yet been put down,' Gilbert Foliot pointed out. 'Maybe the king feels his crown is unsafe while his nephews are alive.' He saw me look at him and smiled. 'Oh, it's all right, Roger. You needn't doubt my loyalty. I don't think for one moment that King Richard is capable of such a heinous sin. I'm no supporter of either young Edward or of Henry Tudor.'

'Talking of the latter,' the abbot broke in, 'didn't he at one time live in the household of your wife's kinsman? The Earl of Pembroke who is buried here?'

The goldsmith nodded. 'He did indeed, My Lord, for several years after his uncle, Jasper Tudor, fled abroad. William Herbert was eventually given Jasper's old title and there was some thought at one time of marrying Henry to William's daughter, Maud. I understood from my wife – whom God assoil! – that William was very fond of the boy, although he never wavered in his loyalty to the House of York.'

'No, indeed,' agreed the abbot. 'A loyalty for which he paid with his life.' He gave another glance around the table. 'Well, my masters, if everyone has finished, no doubt you would like to retire for the night. You have all had long and tiring journeys. I am sure you are ready for your beds. Compline will be in an hour's time, if any of you care to join us.'

There was a general murmur which might have signified assent or then again, might not. I think we all hoped that we could well be asleep by then and not to be roused without difficulty. I was good at feigning sleep when necessary, but felt that in the present case I wouldn't have to pretend. I was bone weary and could hardly keep my eyes from closing. I was sure the others must feel the same.

A general scarping back of stools ensued as we rose at last from the table. Half the pie remained uneaten, but I think I spoke for everyone when I pressed a hand to my belly and said I was unable to eat another crumb.

As we moved towards the dining-parlour door, it was suddenly flung open and one of the brothers appeared, out of breath and slightly dishevelled. He was plainly agitated and forgot to close the door behind him. Outside, the storm still raged.

'Father Abbot, come quickly,' he urged. 'There's someone in the old abbot's lodgings. I can see the glow of a lamp.'

FIVE

The abbot frowned and lowered the glass he had been raising to his lips.

'Are you sure, Brother Mark?' he asked. 'No one uses those rooms now unless we have an important guest.' (Presumably none of those present rated this distinction.)

The brother nodded vigorously. 'I saw the light between the slats of the shutters as I passed, Father. And I could hear someone moving about inside.'

'You didn't go to investigate?' Gilbert Foliot queried, raising his eyebrows.

The brother gave a shamefaced gulp. 'No, sir.' He added in extenuation, 'There were other noises.'

'Such as?'

'Oh . . . I don't know how to describe them, sir.' Brother Mark turned back to his superior. 'Please come, Father!'

The abbot heaved a sigh and got to his feet, glancing round the table as he did so.

'Master Chapman,' he said, 'you look a sturdy, broad-shouldered fellow. Perhaps you would accompany me. Meanwhile, Brother Mark, rouse some of the other brothers and come after us, although I feel certain you're starting at shadows. If there is anyone there, there will be a perfectly sound explanation for it.'

'I'll come as well,' the goldsmith offered, rising briskly from his seat. He looked enquiringly at the others. 'Anyone else?'

No one volunteered. I couldn't blame them. We could all hear the rain hammering down outside.

Gilbert Foliot shrugged. 'Lead the way, then, Lord Abbot. Master Chapman and I will be right behind you.'

We followed the abbot out of doors, leaving the warmth of candle- and firelight to be soaked in the first two minutes by sharp spears of rain falling from a storm-riven sky. Fortunately it was only a short walk across a patch of muddy ground, past a couple of outhouses, before the abbot paused in front of a two-storey building, listened for a moment, then motioned us to accompany him round to the front. Here, there were two rows of three windows apiece, all being closed and silent except for one on the ground floor, which did indeed show chinks of light between the slats of the shutters. We moved closer.

'Brother Mark is right,' the abbot said. 'There is someone in there. One of the novices, no doubt, up to some mischief.'

He squared his shoulders, marching back around the corner to a side door which he pushed open with a resounding crack, before leading the way along a short passage to another door on the left. But just as he was about to fling this wide, words of reprimand on his lips, it was jerked open from inside and a figure stood framed in the doorway.

The abbot gasped and we all fell back a pace, startled by this sudden apparition, but that momentary hesitation was our undoing. The young man – for, despite the hood pulled well forward to obscure his face, there was no doubting either his youth or sex – simply charged between us and out into the night. I was the first to recover and, pushing Master Foliot unceremoniously aside, rushed after him. By this time, however, reinforcements had arrived in the shape of Brother Mark and an intrepid band of his fellow monks who, on sighting their quarry, gave an excited whoop and set off in pursuit. Confident that the intruder would soon be caught, I returned to the abbot's old lodging to discover what had been going on there.

This was immediately apparent. Several tiles had been prised loose from around the hearthstone, revealing a gaping hole beneath. The abbot and Gilbert Foliot were standing over it, regarding the empty space, but the latter turned his head sharply at my entrance. 'Did you catch him?'

'No. But don't worry. Brother Mark and his posse are hard on his heels.' I, too, stared into the hole. 'Is this the . . . er . . .?'

The goldsmith nodded. 'Yes, this is the secret hiding place that was accidentally found fourteen years ago.'

The abbot chewed a thumbnail. 'But why would anybody want to open it up again? Everything that was in there was removed when it was discovered. Everyone knows that.'

'I wonder,' I mused. 'Is what we can see of the hole all that there is, Father?'

'What do you mean?'

'I'm wondering if the hiding place is perhaps bigger than was thought at the time. If it was properly explored back then.'

The abbot looked bewildered, but Gilbert Foliot nodded excitedly. 'I see what you're getting at, Chapman. You mean that when the account books and scraps of old diary were found, nothing else was searched for. It was assumed that that was all there was.'

'Yes.' I dropped to my knees and, leaning forward, thrust my arm into the aperture, bending lower so that I could probe sideways. Sure enough, there was a far larger space than was obvious at first sight. My arm disappeared almost up to the shoulder. I could also feel loose crumbs of cement as though some kind of barrier had been broken down.

I stood up and reported my findings. Once again, the goldsmith was the first to grasp the implications. 'You're thinking,' he said, 'that a century and a half ago, something was concealed in that hole and then sealed up with a wall of cement? The old accounts books and the pages of diary were put in to fill the remaining space and act as a decoy if anyone – for some unknown reason – should go searching for the secret hiding place?'

I nodded. 'And the other noises which Brother Mark heard, and was unable to identify, was our young friend either chiselling up the hearth tiles or else breaking through the cement wall into the inner compartment.' I added, 'I don't fancy the wall was very strong, and in any case, it may well have begun to crumble after a hundred and fifty odd years.'

'But who would know about this inner compartment?' the abbot demanded fretfully. 'I didn't know about it, and as far as I know, no one has talked or even thought about that secret hiding place for years. Well, certainly not within my hearing.'

'We shall only have the answer to that,' I pointed out, 'when we interrogate our prisoner.'

'Do you think he found anything?' Gilbert Foliot asked me.

'Yes.' I closed my eyes and tried to visualize the man as he had charged between us. 'Yes,' I repeated. 'I feel almost certain that he was holding something. Oh, not his bag of tools. That was in his right hand. But I would stake my life he was also clutching something in his left. Something small because his fist was clenched around it.'

The goldsmith nodded slowly.

'I don't understand any of this,' the abbot complained even more fretfully than before. 'So let's go and demand an explanation of this young man. Brother Mark and the others should surely have him in custody by now.'

But he was to be disappointed. Barely were the words out of his mouth than Brother Mark appeared in the doorway very much out of breath and wearing a distinctly hangdog expression. It didn't need his stumbling apology to know that our quarry had eluded us.

'We . . . We thought we had him cornered, Father. We did indeed! He was about half a furlong ahead of us – maybe a little more – when he ran into the infirmary . . .'

'Ah!' I exclaimed. 'Of course! The unknown traveller who, according to the gatekeeper arrived here earlier today, but had kept to his bed with the curtains drawn, pleading a sick headache. He had to go back to the infirmary to collect the rest of his gear.'

'Yes! You've got it, Master Chapman!' Gilbert Foliot clapped me on the shoulder.

'Never mind that,' the abbot said impatiently. He turned back to Brother Mark. 'Well? What happened then?'

The young monk shuffled his feet. 'We . . . we all rushed into the infirmary, Father, thinking he couldn't possibly get away, but . . . but he'd gone.' The boy swallowed, his prominent Adam's apple bobbing up and down like a fisherman's float. 'We . . . we forgot about the latrine drain. He must have followed it down to the cesspit, then climbed over the wall.'

The abbot closed his eyes and took a deep breath, the picture of frustration. But he was a fair-minded man and at last forced himself to say, 'I suppose that wasn't your fault.'

'He can't have got far,' the goldsmith said. 'I'm going out after him. See if I can track him down.'

I laid a restraining hand on his arm. 'Don't be a fool, man!' For the moment, I had forgotten the difference in our stations. 'Listen to that rain! You'll be soaked to the skin in less than a minute. It's worse than it was quarter of an hour ago. You've only to look at Brother Mark, here. He's like a drowned rat.'

The boy nodded, shivering miserably, and the abbot added his voice to mine.

'I beg you not to think of it, my son. We're not even sure the abbey's been robbed of anything yet. It's all speculation. It's certainly not something worth the risk of catching your death of cold.'

But Gilbert Foliot was not in the mood to listen to either of us. He shook off my hand and plunged out into the darkness.

It was at least half an hour before he returned, wet, furious and more than a little dishevelled. His hair was plastered flat to his head and his hands were covered in scratches where he had searched the scrubland on the slopes above the abbey. He was also limping, having, he said, badly twisted his ankle. There was a rent about three inches long in his fur-trimmed tunic.

The abbot and I had by this time rejoined the others in the dining parlour of the former's lodgings and given them a graphic account of the happenings so far.

'We thought there was a lot of noise,' Henry Callowhill remarked comfortably.

'We did look out,' Geoffrey Heathersett added, 'but it was too dark and too wet to see anything clearly.'

They both roundly condemned the goldsmith's folly in continuing the pursuit and gave it as their considered opinion that he would be laid up tomorrow and unable to resume his journey. In the event, none of us could do so, the storm of the previous evening having worsened and there being rumours, brought by one of the lay brothers, of there being rebel forces in the surrounding hills. It was therefore reluctantly agreed by all of us that, for another twenty-four hours at least, we must stay where we were.

In the presence of the abbot and the infirmarian, I made a close search of the infirmary, particularly the bay occupied by the stranger, but to no avail. He had left no trace of himself. The porter confirmed that he had arrived on foot so there was no horse left behind in the stables which might have yielded up a clue to his identity.

'A mystery,' the abbot said with dissatisfaction, but concluded in a resigned tone, 'and a mystery I'm afraid it will have to remain. If he got what he came for – and if our friend the chapman is correct in what he thinks he saw, he probably did so – then he won't be visiting us again.'

And that was his last word on the subject, the daily running of a great abbey making too many demands on his time for him to waste any on a problem he was unable and unlikely to solve. But that didn't prevent the rest of us discussing the subject ad nauseum and propagating the wildest theories as to what the unknown might have found and how he knew of its existence in the first place. Only Gilbert Foliot seemed a little reluctant to take part, but that was because he was very tired and somewhat feverish. His stupidity of the evening before was taking its inevitable toll and he was eventually forced to admit that was feeling unwell. At his friends' insistence, he finally agreed to pay a visit to Brother Infirmarian and swallow one of his potions.

By dinnertime, the rest of us, cooped up together in the infirmary, unable to ease our cramped limbs with exercise and finding nothing new to say concerning the subject uppermost in all our minds, were beginning to get on one another's nerves. Oliver Tockney's north country speech, which I had at first found so fascinating, was now starting to irritate me beyond measure. And I could tell that my flat West Country vowels and Saxon diphthongs were annoying him equally. So, after dinner, between the services of Nones and Vespers, I took myself off to the abbey library and introduced myself to Brother Librarian. 'Father Abbot told me that if I asked, you would be pleased to show me what was originally found in the secret hiding place,' I said, investing a somewhat loose remark of the abbot's with an authority it did not really warrant. 'And I should very much like to see the diary, if nothing else.'

Brother Librarian was a sour-faced little man who, like so many others of his calling whom I have encountered from time to time, regarded the books and documents in his charge as his personal property, to be handed over to outsiders only with the greatest reluctance.

He began by claiming that he didn't know where the papers were: no one had asked to look at them for as long as he could remember and he had no idea where they were filed. I stared him down and repeated, mendaciously, that the lord abbot had promised me a sight of them, managing to convey that his superior would be extremely displeased if my desire were thwarted. So finally, after much grumbling under his breath and a token search, Brother Librarian produced the necessary papers with comparative ease from one of the lower shelves. They were enclosed in a cover bound with purple silk which he dropped on to one of the reading stalls, standing in a line along one wall.

'There you are, then,' he snapped ungraciously. 'Just be careful how you handle them, that's all I can say. They're over a century and a half old, and fragile.' He advanced his tight, weasel-like little face to within an inch of mine. 'I don't suppose you've ever heard of Richard de Bury?' he sneered.

Not for the first time in my life, I blessed the teaching and knowledge of Brother Hilarion, our Novice Master at Glastonbury, and the endless trouble he had taken to hammer that knowledge into our unreceptive heads. 'Bishop of Durham, sometime Chancellor and close friend of King Edward III in the last century,' I answered with a smirk.

'Oh.' For a moment my interlocutor was nonplussed, but he soon made a recovery. 'He was also,' he went on, 'one of the greatest bibliophiles this country has ever known, and he wrote a treatise on the disgusting way in which people handle books. Ever read it?'

'No,' I said foolishly – but consoled myself with the reflection that even had I answered, 'Yes,' he would still have told me what it said. He was one of those who, once he was riding his hobby-horse, there was no way of stopping.

'Richard de Bury complains' – and the little man spoke as one who had learned the passage by heart – 'about the abuser of books who underlines favourite passages with his dirty nails, who marks his place with straws because his memory is poor, who stains the parchment with fruit and wine, who drops into the open pages crumbs of bread and cheese and other such vict-uals, who falls asleep over his book and in so doing creases the leaves, who turns back the corners of pages and presses wild flowers between them with his sweaty hands, who marks the vellum with soiled gloves and who, finally, flings aside the sacred object so that its leaves are splayed and will no more shut.' Brother Librarian finished, breathless, on a triumphant shout, an admonitory finger waggling beneath my nose. 'I trust,' he added, a gleam of hatred for the despised reader in his eye, 'that you are not one of those!'

'No, no!' I assured him hastily and sat down in the reading stall, spreading out the pages of the account books and diary in front of me.

At last he seemed to take the hint that I wished to be left alone and, still muttering under his breath, moved away to busy himself elsewhere.

The pages I had before me were written on neither vellum nor parchment, but on a cheap paper made of rags. Those belonging to the two account books were the most numerous and, as Father Abbot had warned me, of very little interest except, perhaps, to the abbey's present manciple as an indication of what was being ordered a hundred and fifty years ago, and for the date. This latter was repeated twice, in Roman numerals, as 1326, which suggested that the pages of the diary were possibly written about the same time. Not necessarily, I reminded myself, but probably.

I turned to them eagerly and was disappointed to see that there really was little more than a page and a half of black, spidery, very upright writing, very difficult to read. This was not the fault of the ink which had retained its colour after all those years and was still beautifully vivid. I wondered if it had been made from blackthorn bark or oak galls, or to one of the abbey's secret recipes. (Most religious establishments had their own, which they zealously guarded.) It certainly wasn't thickened blackberry juice mixed with blood, which faded early.

I applied my mind to deciphering the narrative. This wasn't easy, the writing being extremely uneven and the style discursive. Almost all the first page was devoted, as the abbot had said, to squabbles amongst the brothers, with particular attention being paid to the disagreement between a certain Brother Barnabas and another named Philip. What it was about, I couldn't have told you even ten minutes later, so rapidly did I skip the lines, searching eagerly for the incident of the strangers' arrival.

I came to it at last at the top of the second page. "'They came last night as we had feared they might, having had warning that they were close by. Two others were with them; Reading, I think, and Baldock were the names, but I cannot be sure. We had begged Father Abbot not to give them sanctuary; their crime is too great, but he ignored our wishes. Perhaps he was afraid to do otherwise. It seems they will stay here again tonight, but after that Father Abbot has assured us they will be gone. God have mercy on their souls. They will need it.'"

This, disappointingly, was all on that head, and for the next twenty or so lines, the writer returned to the feud between Brothers Philip and Barnabas until breaking off mid-sentence and leaving the rest of the page blank. What had happened to make him stop writing so abruptly it was impossible to say with any certainty after a century and a half; but if I was forced to hazard a guess it would be that someone had snatched the paper from him to stuff into the abbot's secret hiding place, along with pages torn from the account books. He had probably protested violently, but if his fellow monks suspected that he wrote about them in his diary, someone must have borne him a grudge and taken malicious pleasure in frustrating him.

But that was just idle speculation and not the riddle that was teasing me. I stared down at the black lettering thoughtfully. The longer I considered the problem, the more I felt convinced that whatever our thief had stolen tonight, whatever it was that had lain concealed in the hiding place for so long, had been brought by the strangers that night a hundred and fifty-odd years ago. It had been hidden for them by the abbot and walled in, the papers then being placed in the remaining space and the tiles of the hearth replaced. Had the strangers intended to return for what they had left? I thought it more than likely, but something had prevented them. Imprisonment? Death? The diarist had spoken of them and their crimes with revulsion, so either was probable if the law had eventually caught up with them and exacted reparation. Their treasure, whatever it was, had lain buried and forgotten as the long progression of years went by and those who had placed it there had died. Indeed, knowledge of the hiding place itself had been lost until its accidental discovery fourteen years earlier.

So far, so good. Exactly why the abbot of the time had agreed, not only to give sanctuary to four criminals for two nights but also to keep their treasure for them was beyond my comprehension, but indisputable. And it was impossible that I should discover the reason now, so there was little point in agonizing over it. What did exercise my mind was the fact that this treasure had suddenly been rediscovered and stolen at the very time that Gilbert Foliot had been talking to the abbot on the subject of its hiding place. Coincidence, one might say. But I have never liked coincidences. All right, so they do happen or, as I have remarked somewhere else in these chronicles, there wouldn't be a word for them. I still don't like them.

But if there was a connection between the two events, I had to admit that I had no inkling what it was.

My travelling companions must have found me rather taciturn for the rest of the day, but as I refused to say what was bothering me, they soon shrugged and left me alone with my thoughts. And I can't say that those did me much good. In fact by evening, with an incipient pain nagging behind my eyes, I was thoroughly sick of the whole subject. So when, next morning, the weather was found to be greatly improved, with a watery sun struggling to show its face between the clouds, and when news was brought that rumours of rebels in the vicinity had yet again proved to be a false alarm, I was as happy as the others to set out for home.

It was my intention to walk back to Gloucester in order to cross the Severn there, and Oliver Tockney said he would accompany me. We both needed to refill our packs, which we could do either from the ships anchored in the town's docks or from its market. I didn't say so, but I had another, more cogent, reason for wishing to visit the place, having arrived quite suddenly at the decision to seek out Juliette Gerrish and demand an explanation for her unpardonable conduct earlier in the year.

Gilbert Foliot, Lawyer Heathersett and Master Callowhill would follow the same route, but on horseback and would no doubt be home in Bristol some days ahead of us.

'The horse ferry won't be running after all this rain,' Gilbert Foliot wisely remarked, 'so, my friends, we have no choice but to retrace our steps and cross the Severn higher up.' He smiled graciously at me across the table in the lay brothers' refectory, where we were having breakfast. 'I'm sorry I can't offer to take you up behind me, Master Chapman, but you and your pack together are too weighty, I'm afraid.'

I inclined my head with a graciousness equal to his own. 'I thank you for the thought, Master Foliot, but I should prefer to walk. I'm used to it and, like Master Tockney, I'm not easy on horseback. He and I have kept one another company from Hereford. We shall do so still.'

He had the decency to look uncomfortable, knowing full well that he preferred to overlook Oliver's presence as much as possible. (As, indeed, he would have overlooked mine had he not had this erroneous idea that I was some sort of spy for the king.)

We were just finishing our meal and preparing to return to the infirmary in order to gather our belongings together, when the abbot entered to wish us all a safe journey and give us his blessing.

'You may travel safely,' he announced. 'I have it on good authority' – people always have it on good authority but never tell you exactly how good that authority really is – 'that the roads this side of Severn are clear of rebels. Presumably they have gone to join up with their fellow insurgents in the south and west. The last rumour concerning the royal forces is that the king is moving south and is probably at Coventry by now. So—'

He was interrupted by one of the lay brothers rushing in, obviously in a state of suppressed excitement. 'Father!' he gasped. 'Come quickly!'

The abbot frowned, annoyed. 'What is it?' he snapped.

The man flapped an ineffective hand. 'A – a body! Washed up on the river bank! A young man!'

The goldsmith and I exchanged startled glances, sharing the same thought. The same certainty. Then, in the wake of the lay brother and with the others following, we both made a dash for the refectory door.

'This way!' the layman panted, urging us on across the soggy, rain-soaked ground.

A few rays of sun were filtering through the clouds to glimmer palely on wet grass and gleam corpse-like on the surface of the river. A flock of birds rose suddenly in a ragged line, screaming and cawing against the darker shapes of the surrounding hills. Crouched around something lying at the water's edge were several of the brothers, their white habits looking a dirty grey in the early morning light.

Gilbert Foliot and I reached them first, unceremoniously pushing our way between them to stare down at the ashen-faced body at their feet. The lad had been young, not more than about eighteen, I reckoned, with a snub nose in a roundish, freckled face and hair, now plastered tightly to his scalp, that was probably sandy-coloured when dry. Caught among the reeds, standing sentinel along the bank, was his travelling satchel and cloak. In his headlong flight to escape last night, he had fallen into the river and drowned.

I stared at the smooth, beardless young face, the eyes now closed in death. The features were vaguely familiar, and I realized that I had seen them at some time or another around the Bristol streets.

I turned to Gilbert Foliot, who was looking as pale as the corpse. 'Do you know him?' I asked.

'I should do,' he answered in a shaking voice. 'It's Peter Noakes, the young ne'er-do-well who's been courting my daughter.'

SIX

The abbot arrived, breathless from unaccustomed exertion. 'Has anyone searched the body?' he gasped, then recollected himself and made the sign of the Cross. He turned to Gilbert Foliot. 'Did I hear you say, sir, that you recognized this unfortunate young man?'

The goldsmith nodded. He now had himself well in hand. 'He is a Bristol youth who, much against my wishes, has recently been courting my daughter. There can be no doubt that it is from her that he learned of the secret hiding place here at Tintern, just as Ursula learned of it from me.'

This explanation gave the answer to one question that had been troubling me, but begged others. Why, for instance, after almost a decade and a half, would the hiding place have been resurrected as a subject of discussion in the Foliot household? And what had caused speculation that it might, in fact, be larger than had been previously thought? Or that it could contain something other than the papers originally found? But there was no time at the moment to look for solutions.

Two of the more elderly monks were by now hurriedly searching the body, while a third had rescued the satchel from among the reeds. The latter, however, contained only some spare clothing and a hammer and chisel, tools obviously deemed necessary by young Noakes to accomplish the job he had in mind. Of stolen treasure, there was no sign. Nor was there anything to be found on the body, although it was stripped nearly naked before the abbot, or indeed the rest of us, could be satisfied that a few coins for the lad's travelling expenses were all that was concealed about his skinny person.

'Nothing!' exclaimed the abbot disgustedly.

'Probably because there was nothing to find in the first place,' said the lawyer's dry voice. He and Henry Callowhill had just arrived, having proceeded to the scene of the accident at a more dignified pace than the goldsmith and myself. Master Heathersett went on, 'Our friend, the chapman here, must have been mistaken last night when he thought he saw something in young Peter's left hand.'

There was a general, if reluctant, nodding of heads in which I joined. It was the only explanation. A suggestion by one of the Brothers that the thief might have accidentally dropped his booty whilst in flight was considered, but eventually dismissed. It was felt by everyone that had he discovered anything of value, Peter Noakes's first priority would have been to secure it safely, either about his person or in his satchel. All the same, a half-hearted search was organized to scour the river bank and the ground between the abbey and the spot where his body had been found, but nothing came to light. I think, by this time, no one expected it to. Everyone seemed to be fast coming to the conclusion that the whole idea of undiscovered treasure was nothing more than a mare's nest; a bit of wishful thinking.

And yet, as the sad little procession made its way back to the abbey, two of the monks bearing Peter Noakes's body on an improvised stretcher, I couldn't avoid the thought that the young man must have come to Tintern under the impression that there was something – and something worthwhile – to be found. And where could he have formed that impression except in the Foliot household? Moreover, taken in conjunction with that fact, was Gilbert Foliot's raising of the matter with the abbot: did his lord-ship remember the discovery of the hiding place fourteen years before, and was it possible that it might not have been thoroughly explored at that time? It could, it was true, be my old enemy, coincidence. And then again, perhaps not.

For the time being, however, there were other things to think about, the most pressing of which was the need to get to Gloucester before there was again any worsening of the weather. Oliver Tockney and I had planned to be well on the way by this hour. The town was all of twenty-five miles distant, if not more, and we had no idea of what conditions were still to be met with on the roads. It could take us three or even four days travelling if we were unlucky, and I knew that my companion was itching to get away. Fortunately, there was nothing to delay us further. Master Foliot had undertaken to acquaint Anthony Roper of the death of his nephew as soon as he reached Bristol, and made arrangements with the monks that they would house the body decently until such time as Master Roper sent to collect it. So there was nothing further that either Oliver or I could do.

We therefore tendered thanks for the abbot's hospitality and set out.

The old English meaning of the name Gloucester is the Shining Place, but there was nothing remotely shining about the town as we crossed the bridge over the Severn that miserable late October morning and made our way into the heart of the town. Cobbles, slippery with dead leaves and mud made for uncomfortable walking, while the relentlessly grey skies shrouded the houses and shops in a pall of drizzle.

Oliver wanted to go immediately to the docks and market to replenish the goods in his pack, but I said I had other business to attend to and would meet him later at the New Inn, close to the abbey.

'We may get a bed there for the night, if we're lucky,' I said. 'Although it's usually full of pilgrims coming to pay homage at King Edward's tomb.'

'Is that the king who was murdered by having his bowels burnt out with a red hot spit?' Oliver enquired with a ghoulish leer.

'In Berkeley Castle, yes.' I turned away, repeating over my shoulder, 'The New Inn,' and adding, 'about the hour of Vespers.'

I didn't wait for his reply, striding away through the narrow streets, glad of the chance to be on my own for a while. The truth was that, after nearly two weeks, Oliver and I were growing tired of one another's company. Our companionable exchanges of the past three days had grown fewer and fewer and, on two occasions, had turned into downright squabbles. I use the word 'squabbles' deliberately for there had been nothing dignified about our disagreements, and the second time we very nearly came to blows. Only a mutual sense of the ridiculous, the picture of two grown men fighting like schoolboys, prevented it. I wondered how we were to cover the remaining distance between Gloucester and Bristol and stay friends. That, however, was tomorrow's problem. Meanwhile, as I had said, I had business of my own.

Consequently, I directed my footsteps towards the north side of the abbey, where there was a small enclave of houses known as Cloister Yard, and knocked on the first door I came to. This was the entrance to a pleasant two-storey building with a walled enclosure behind it, but showing, at that season of the year, nothing more than a network of bare hawthorn branches rising above the grey stones.

My knock went unanswered. I waited a minute or so, then knocked again. And once again, there was no reply. I stepped back and looked up at the windows, but they were all shuttered, and there was a silence about the place that convinced me no one was at home. The cloister itself was so quiet that it might have been uninhabited, and I was just preparing to leave, swearing under my breath in frustration, when an elderly woman turned into the close. She stood staring at me, saying nothing but raising her strongly marked eyebrows.

'I'm looking for Mistress Gerrish,' I said. 'Mistress Juliette Gerrish. Do you know her?'

'I should do,' she answered tartly 'I'm her companion. Who are you?'

'An – an old friend.' I cursed that slight hesitation which immediately made the woman suspicious. I went on quickly, 'I knew Juliette some years ago and, as I happened to find myself in Gloucester' – I indicated my pedlar's pack – 'I decided to pay her a visit, for old times' sake.'

The woman regarded me straitly for some moments, but evidently finding nothing in either my appearance or manner to give her any particular unease, said at last, 'As I told you, I'm her companion, Jane Spicer. Mistress Gerrish and the boy are out at this present and won't be home yet awhile. Come again tomorrow. Who shall I say called?'

'I could wait,' I offered. 'Or come again this evening.'

But this Mistress Spicer would not allow. 'I'm not prepared to be alone in the house with a stranger,' she announced flatly. 'And we don't open the door once it gets dark. So, come tomorrow. Or not at all. You still haven't told me your name.'

'What happened to her uncle, Master Moresby?' I asked.

'He died two years ago last Michaelmas.' The woman eyed me up and down, but I could see that her somewhat severe features had softened a little. The fact that I knew of Robert Moresby had reassured her. Nevertheless, she was not prepared to relax her rules in my favour. 'Come again tomorrow. But first, tell me your name.'

I could see no help for it. To withhold it would only reawaken her suspicions. On the other hand, once Juliette knew who had called, she might take steps to avoid me.

'Roger Chapman,' I said. 'Tell Mistress Gerrish that I shan't leave Gloucester without seeing her.'

This brought the frown back to Mistress Spicer's face, so before she could question me further, I turned and walked away.

It was too early yet to meet Oliver Tockney at the New Inn. I had stipulated the hour of Vespers and, by my reckoning, that would not be for another half-hour or more. So I joined a party of pilgrims making their way into the abbey but, once inside, detached myself from them and walked around on my own.

The inside of the great building was busy as always, with some of the monks making ready for the service while others stood guard over Edward II's tomb in the North Ambulatory, making sure that none of the younger pilgrims secured their own immortality by carving names or initials into the marble. For my own part, I wandered as far as the Choir to stare down at the battered image of Duke Robert II of Normandy, eldest son of the Conqueror, whose father had bequeathed him a dukedom but not a kingdom, and who had spent his life trying to wrest what he regarded as his birthright from his brothers, William and Henry.

After a little while, I, too, made my way back to King Edward's tomb, looking through the marble columns at his effigy, at the luxuriously curling beard and hair, and reflecting, somewhat cynically, that if the monks of Gloucester had not taken in and given burial to his mutilated body, the abbey would never have grown as rich as it was today. For once our forebears had finished reviling him as a weak ruler, a coward who had allowed himself to be ignominiously beaten by the Scots and, worst of all, a sodomite, they had suffered a typically English revulsion of feeling, turned on his conquering French wife and her lover and elevated Edward almost to the status of a saint. So many people began flocking to his tomb that an inn – still called the New Inn although it was now more than a hundred years old – had been built especially to accommodate them.

Which reminded me . . . I left the abbey just as the pilgrims were being herded into the nave for Vespers and made my way back to the inn.

Oliver was already there, anxious to show me some of the bargains he had obtained, but even more eager to inform me that not only had he secured us a decent room for the night, but that there was a carter staying at the inn with whom he had struck a deal to take us nearly all the way to Bristol, starting early the very next morning. His expression invited congratulation, and his face fell ludicrously when I refused the offer.

'I'm sorry, Oliver, but I've unfinished business to attend to in Gloucester tomorrow. Don't worry, we'll find another carter going our way.'

His jaw jutted ominously. 'You don't know that.'

'Not for certain, no. But it's more than possible.'

The jaw jutted even further. 'I'm not interested in "possible". This is a certainty. This man says he can take us as far as a place called Westbury, and that Bristol is only a matter of a mile or two from there.'

'That's so,' I admitted. 'All the same, I'll have to refuse.'

My companion took a deep breath. 'Well, I'm going,' he announced defiantly.

A great sense of relief – of release – flooded through me, but I tried not to sound too eager. 'You must, of course, do as you wish. Indeed, in your place I should do the same.'

'You don't mind?'

'Not in the least. Haven't I just said?'

He drew a deep breath and clapped me on the back, smiling.

Our last evening together was as convivial as those in Hereford had been two weeks earlier. We drank a great deal too much ale, laughed uproariously at the slightest thing, discussed the happenings at Tintern, propounding more and more preposterous theories as to the meaning of it all, and finally helped each other upstairs to the tiny cupboard-like chamber put at our disposal by the landlord, falling into bed fully clothed, without even bothering to remove our boots.

When I awoke next morning, Oliver had already gone.

The room smelled foul, a cross between a brewery and a

shithouse, and my mouth tasted pretty much the same. My head was thumping fit to burst, so I staggered down to the courtyard and took my turn at the pump, stripping off with the best of them and persuading a fellow sufferer to scrub my back. Then I tottered up to my room again where I stripped for a second time, shaking the fleas out of my clothes and lamenting the fact that I had no fresh shirt left to put on. However, I cleaned my teeth and combed my hair before breakfasting in the ale-room on a fried herring, oatcakes and small beer.

Thus fortified, I set out to visit Cloister Yard for the second time, hoping that I was early enough to catch Juliette Gerrish at home before she decided to avoid me by going out for the day. But as it happened, this was not her intention. She opened the door herself, neatly dressed, and invited me in.

'Hallo, Roger,' she said quietly. 'I suppose I always knew there would be a day of reckoning.'

I didn't answer for a moment. I couldn't. She was obviously extremely ill.

She was still a short woman, of course, and she still, judging by her eyebrows, hid copper-coloured curls beneath her coif. But the plump face, once so full of animation, was thin to the point of emaciation, the bones clearly delineated under the grey-toned skin. The roguish brown eyes, which had once invited with a twinkling glance, were now devoid of any expression except pain. They stared wearily up at me, but seemed to look through, rather than at me.

'Juliette?' I said cautiously.

She smiled faintly, but did not trouble herself to answer, merely holding the door a little wider.

'Come in.'

I stepped past her into the stone-flagged passageway, then stood aside for her to precede me into the dining parlour, where wine and a plate of little sweet cakes had been laid out ready on the table.

Again, that travesty of a smile. 'I remembered that you were always hungry. Put your pack and cudgel in the corner, then please' – she indicated a chair with carved arms – 'sit down.'

I did as she bade me.

From somewhere in the house a child wailed. Juliette, in the act of pouring wine into one of the mazers, glanced up sharply, then paused, listening. But there were no further cries and she nodded to herself as though satisfied.

'That was my son, Luke,' she said. 'Jane must have settled him.'

'You once told me that you couldn't have children,' I accused her.

She handed me the mazer and offered me the plate of douc-ettes, which I refused, then sat down opposite me in another carved armchair, taking a great gulp of her own wine as if it were a restorative, as perhaps it was.

'It wasn't a lie,' she pleaded. 'Not a deliberate one. I truly believed I couldn't. My husband and I tried often enough, but I never conceived. And' – a faint tinge of colour crept into her emaciated cheeks – 'there were other men before you. Never was there any sign of a child. Nor did you, with all your virility, father one on me.'

It was my turn to feel uncomfortable. I could feel the hot blood creeping up my neck. I took refuge in anger. 'But that didn't prevent you trying to foist your bastard on me, though, did it?' When she didn't answer immediately, I went on loudly, 'My wife left me because of your lies.' I slammed the by now half-full mazer down on the table, making her jump. 'Oh, yes, she left me and took two of our children with her.' No need to explain that Nicholas wasn't mine. 'I had to go after her, to London. Fortunately, for the greater part of last year, I was out of England, first in Scotland, then in France. And it was the spring of the year before that that you and I . . .' I broke off, floundering, resuming lamely, '. . . that I was in Gloucester. Fortunately, although no thanks to you, Adela believed me.'

'I'm glad,' Juliette said simply.

I stared at her. 'Is that all you've got to say? You're glad! No explanation as to why you tried to wreck my marriage? Nothing?'

I could barely speak, I was so choked with rage. I pushed the mazer away from me, slopping the wine. I felt I couldn't take another drop to drink beneath her roof and, without realizing it, I was on my feet, towering over her. It was only when I saw the flicker of fear in her eyes that I took a grip on myself and my emotions. I sat down again abruptly.

'So?' I said coldly, viciously. 'Who is the father of your little bastard? Or don't you know? Was he someone you pleasured in that casual way of yours? Did you even know his name?'

The words were barely out before I was feeling ashamed of myself. I saw the tears well up in her eyes, and she looked for a moment as though she might faint. I had to remind myself that this woman had done me a great wrong in order to prevent myself going to her assistance.

Juliette took a deep, steadying breath, then nodded. 'You are quite right, Roger. You are owed an explanation.'

'Well?' My tone was softer, more reasonable. Nevertheless, I felt that the explanation had better be good, but I was unable to imagine what it could be.

Juliette took another sip of wine. She was breathing calmly now, but her pallor was more alarming than ever. I half rose from my chair, wondering if I should summon Jane Spicer but, guessing my intention, she waved me back into my seat.

'I shall be all right,' she said. 'Just sit still and listen.'

In the spring – 'probably March' – of the preceding year, the year of the invasion of Scotland, she had met a young Irishman who told her he was seeking temporary lodgings. Juliette smiled wryly. 'He didn't tell me what he was doing in Gloucester, and I didn't ask.'

That, I thought, was typical of the woman: large-hearted, generous and fond of younger men. 'Go on,' I said resignedly. My anger had evaporated.

She gave something like a grin, but it was a feeble attempt and slid without difficulty into a grimace of pain. 'Jane had come to live with me after my uncle died. She was a cousin of his on his mother's side of the family, and I'd always known her, if only at a distance. She didn't like the thought of me being here on my own, so she shut up her own house and moved into Uncle Robert's chamber. But there was still a small attic room standing empty.'

'So you offered it to the young Irishman,' I said, not even bothering to make it a question.

'Yes. It was only for a week or so, and I persuaded Jane that we could do with the extra money.'

'But you didn't really charge him. You intended him to pay in kind.'

Again, hot colour touched the almost transparent skin. But she made no effort to refute my accusation.

'Of course,' she retorted defiantly. 'And he was only too eager to oblige. I was still strong and healthy then. Not as you see me now.'

'He couldn't believe his luck, I daresay. Free lodgings and an attractive woman anxious for his company in bed. What was he doing in Gloucester?'

'I've already told you, he didn't tell me and I didn't ask.' She passed a hand across her brow and when it came away, I could see that it was damp with sweat. She didn't seem to notice and went on, 'But I don't think it was anything legal. There was a furtiveness about his comings and goings. If I had to make a guess, it would be smuggling . . . He came to my bed three times in all during the week or so that he was with us. It was quite easy: Jane sleeps like a log and snores as well. We always knew as soon as she was asleep.'

She started to cough, a harsh, hacking sound, and I rose and poured her more wine. She thanked me and seemed better for it.

'Go on,' I said inexorably, ignoring the look of exhaustion in her face.

Juliette nodded and made a visible effort to concentrate. 'When he left, he was genuinely concerned what might happen to me should I find that I was pregnant. I assured him his fears were groundless. I was unable to conceive, I told him. I was barren. He said, quite rightly as it turned out, that nothing in this world was certain, but I just laughed at his fears. All the same, I said, if he felt so strongly, he must tell me where to find him in Ireland, but for all his solicitude, that was the one thing he refused to do – which convinced me even more that he was engaged in some criminal activity. However, he did say that if I were to find myself in serious difficulties . . .'

Here she paused, giving me a long, hard look of such significance that I wondered uneasily what was coming. And if I'd thought for a week, I don't think I could have guessed the answer.

Juliette continued: 'He said that if I were to find myself in serious difficulties, I could do no better than to go to his brother – his half-brother – in Small Street in Bristol, whose name was Roger Chapman, and beg his aid.' She ignored my gasp of incredulity and went on, 'I asked him to describe you and when he had done so, I told him you and I were already acquainted. I said you had called here on some business with my uncle the year before and that our acquaintance had . . had blossomed into something more.'

I was hardly listening to her. 'John,' I said. 'John Wedmore, that's his name. He's my father's bastard son, but I never knew of his existence until three years ago, when I cleared him of a charge of murder that was brought against him. He went back to Ireland afterwards – although he's no more Irish by birth than I am – and I've neither heard from nor seen him since. And he had the . . . the audacity to suggest that you should pass his bastard child off as mine?'

'No, no!' Juliette exclaimed, distressed. 'He only suggested that if I were in difficulties or any sort of trouble I should seek your help. Naturally, I dismissed the idea as absurd – even after I discovered that I was indeed carrying his child.'

'So what changed your mind?' I demanded savagely.

'My sickness,' she answered simply. 'Luke was born in January, on St Agnes's Day and by that time, I knew that I hadn't long to live. I first began to feel ill last summer, but thought it just the natural malaise of women in my condition. By Christmas, I feared I was wrong and by the time Luke was two months old, I knew my days were numbered. It's no good hoping that Jane will care for him when I'm gone. She doesn't really like children, and he's of no kin to her. But he is your nephew.'

'Half-nephew,' I corrected her.

She went on as though I hadn't spoken. 'I have no family of my own, and the neighbours have shunned me since Luke was born. As far as they're concerned, I'm no better than a whore. So I decided I must take John's advice and seek you out and ask for your help. But when I got to Bristol, you weren't at home and your wife didn't know when to expect you.' Juliette put up a trembling hand to her mouth. 'I didn't know what to do. The story was too difficult and too complex to explain to a stranger and I felt so ill. Oh, I know that's no excuse, but I just said the first thing that came into my head, that the child was yours and asked her – your wife – to take him in. Of course, I knew I'd done wrong as soon as I'd said it. My only comfort was that she didn't seem to believe me.'

'Maybe not at once,' I answered grimly. 'But Adela had time to think things over before I got home and decided there might be some truth in your story. As I told you, she left me for a while and I had to follow her to London.' There was a strained silence between us which I eventually broke by getting to my feet and saying, 'Well, at least now I know the truth, I shan't think quite so badly of you.'

'Would . . . Would you like to see Luke?' she asked tentatively.

I shook my head. 'No.'

I think she knew by my tone of voice that it was useless to persist.

I shouldered my pack, took a grasp on my cudgel and left.

SEVEN

Then I went back.

Some sixth sense must have told her that I would, because Juliette opened the door before I had time to knock. I followed her into the parlour only to find Jane Spicer also there with the child, a boy about ten months old, rather small for his age – but then, both parents were on the small side – with his mother's colouring of copper-red curls and large brown eyes. Held upright in the older woman's arms, he surveyed me critically before giving vent to an enormous yawn and lowering his head to Jane Spicer's shoulder. Plainly, I was dismissed as being of no interest, but not someone to be afraid of, either.

'Mistress Gerrish,' I said, 'I want you to understand that I really can't help you. I accept that I'm your son's uncle. There's no possible way you could know about my half-brother by hearsay alone. You must have met him –'

'John Wedmore is Luke's father,' she cut in earnestly. 'I swear it.'

'I believe you,' I assured her. She didn't have to convince me, either, that she was dying. 'But there's nothing I can do about it, you must see that. Between us, my wife and I already have three children and we are not rich people. To ask Adela to take in and rear my half-brother's bastard is more than I can find the courage to do. If Luke were a girl it might make a difference. A very slight difference. Our daughter, Elizabeth, is mine, not hers, and she lost a daughter of her own. But another boy . . . No! You must see that it's impossible.'

Juliette sat down rather suddenly, her face ashen, obviously in the grip of pain. The jug of wine was still on the table and she poured some into her mazer with a shaking hand, swallowing it almost at a gulp. Then she looked pleadingly at Jane.

I saw something like a spasm of pity crease the other woman's face, but the next moment her features had hardened again.

'It's no good, Juliette,' she said. 'I won't be persuaded to change my mind. At my age I'm not prepared to look after a young child single-handed. The Virgin knows I'm fond of him, but not enough to take on that responsibility. If Walter had married me as he promised, it might have been a different matter.' Her lip curled. 'But when I was fool enough to mention the possibility to him, you know very well what happened. He ran away.'

Juliette looked distressed. 'I thought he went only to take up this new position in Somerset because of the money. I thought . . . I thought he might send for you, or come back and fetch you when he was settled. Maybe,' she added, brightening a little, 'this Sir Lionel you mentioned might not have employed him after all. Perhaps he'll come home any day now.'

'He's been gone more than four months,' Jane Spicer said drily. 'Walter's not coming home again, ever. I didn't expect that he would. Any man who wants the best for his horses would be a fool to ignore Walter's way with the animals. He only has to whisper to the most savage brute to have it eating out of his hand. His name was a byword in these parts. His former master begged him on bended knees not to leave. And I don't believe he would have done – there have been Gurneys hereabouts for hundreds of years – if, as I say, I hadn't mentioned to him about keeping Luke when . . . when . . .'

'When I'm dead,' Juliette finished for her. 'But you don't know for certain that that was what made him go away.'

Jane Spicer snorted and shifted the now sleeping child to her other arm. 'I know Walter Gurney,' she said emphatically. 'And I tell you, Juliette, that as soon as that travelling barber mentioned this Sir Lionel Despenser to him, and that he'd just lost his head groom –'

'Sir Lionel Despenser?' I questioned sharply. 'Not of Keynsham, in Somerset?'

Both women turned to look at me. 'You know him?' Juliette asked.

'I know of him. He has an estate near Keynsham Abbey, and the village itself is about five miles or so south-east of Bristol, on the road to Bath. He comes into the city on occasions. He's the friend of our chief goldsmith, Gilbert Foliot.'

As I uttered the last few words, it seemed as if a giant hand had squeezed my entrails. Here was coincidence with a vengeance. Or was it? Until now, I hadn't been aware of God taking a hand in this affair. Indeed, why should He? So far, I couldn't think of anything that might interest Him. I still couldn't. But as I keep saying, I don't like coincidences; and so often in they past, they have meant that God was poking His nose into my business once again.

Juliette was addressing me eagerly, clutching at straws. 'Roger, when you get back to Bristol, could you – would you – go to this place and talk to Walter Gurney? Try to persuade him to . . . to . . .'

'Come back and marry me?' Jane Spicer finished bluntly. 'He won't, of course.'

'Why not?' Juliette cried.

Jane Spicer shrugged as well as she could with the sleeping child's arms entwined about her neck. She made no reply, but I guessed her thoughts. If her mistress couldn't see the reason for herself, it wasn't worthwhile trying to explain.

'You will, Roger, won't you?' the younger woman insisted. 'Promise me.'

What could I say? When a dying woman asks for help, it would take a harder man than I am to refuse, however useless my intervention was plainly destined to be. 'Very well,' I said.

'Promise!'

'I promise. And now I must go. God be with you.'

And this time, I really did take my leave.

I finally arrived back in Small Street on Monday, the third day of November and, although I would not learn this until the beginning of the following week, the day after Henry, Duke of Buckingham was publicly beheaded in Salisbury marketplace. The Welsh rebellion had been crushed and the king was on his way to Exeter to deal with the western uprising in an equally ruthless and efficient manner (but always, as was his way, tempering justice with mercy).

It had taken me somewhat longer than I expected to travel from Gloucester to Bristol, largely due to the state of the roads, never good but even worse than usual after the recent two months of appalling weather. This, at last, seemed to be on the mend, but the almost incessant wind and rain had left devastation in their wake. Fields were flooded, tracks ankle-deep in mud, bridges washed away, rivers in spate and fords impassable. I got a lift with a carter only once, and even then he had been unable to reach his intended destination at Fairford and been forced to turn back halfway.

Before I left Gloucester, I had followed Oliver Tockney's example and replenished my pack with a number of items including two pairs of Spanish gloves, a set of very pretty carved bone buttons and a knife with an ivory inlaid handle, all of which I knew I could sell at a substantial profit. Unfortunately, I had been so carried away with my Gloucester bargains that I had added considerably to the weight of my pack, a fact which, as well as the conditions underfoot, had impeded my progress more than a little.

Nevertheless, my family was delighted to see me. For a while, at least.

Adela had been genuinely worried once news of Buckingham's rebellion had come to her ears, and the children had sensed enough of her unease to begin to be anxious about me. My sudden appearance in the kitchen, therefore, just as they were about to sit down to ten o'clock dinner, caused a minor stampede as Adela rushed to embrace my upper half and Elizabeth, Nicholas and

Adam grabbed whatever other bits of me were available. I was installed in my seat at the head of the table, my wet boots removed by the simple expedient of the two boys seizing a leg apiece and pulling hard, while Adela served me a lavish portion of rabbit stew and my daughter poured me a beaker of ale. It was a welcome that almost convinced me that I had truly been missed.

I was able to reassure Adela straight away about her erstwhile friend, Goody Harker, with a strong animadversion on the foolishness of believing everything told one by a thieving tinker. I was just about to embark on the tale of my various adventures, when Elizabeth suddenly clapped her hands and demanded, 'Well, what have you brought me, Father?' My guilty expression must have alerted her to the truth, and she gasped, 'You can't have forgotten that today's my birthday!'

I stared aghast at Adela.

She hurried, as always, to my defence. 'Your father's been very busy and in a lot of danger, Bess. You can't blame him for forgetting your and Nicholas's birthdays.' She added for my benefit, 'Nick was nine years old last month, while you were away, Roger. Bess is nine today.'

It was no good pretending. 'Sweetheart,' I said to Elizabeth, 'I am so very sorry, but I have forgotten. And you, Nick! My deepest, most heartfelt apologies. But your mother is right. I have had quite a lot on my mind. But you shall both go with me to the market tomorrow and choose anything you like.'

'Within reason,' my wife amended, frowning at me. She was quite aware of my tendency to let my tongue run away with me.

'Oh, well!' Elizabeth granted magnanimously, 'I suppose that will have to do.' Her face brightened. 'And there are always the other presents you've bought us.'

Five-year-old Adam clapped his hands in excitement and bounced up and down on his chair. 'Presents!' he announced. 'What have you brought me, Father?'

Once again my eyes sought Adela's with a look of dismay. But this time she was at a loss for words and only had the same excuse to offer on my behalf. And this time, it wasn't good enough.

'You . . . You mean you haven't brought us anything?' my daughter quavered.

I shook my head.

There was a silence while all three children waited to see if I were joking or not. Then, having decided that I was in earnest, Elizabeth's eyes began to fill with tears, my stepson regarded me with horror, while Adam's lower lip and jaw started to tremble preparatory to his giving an almighty roar of protest. (And as I think I've mentioned in former histories, he had the best pair of lungs I've ever met with in a child.) To add to my discomfiture, Hercules chose this particular moment to return home from whatever secret foray he had been on and, having regarded me with some surprise for several seconds, began to bark aggressively. This was his way of letting me know that he deeply resented the fact that I had been away and failed to take him with me.

The crescendo of noise increased. Elizabeth was now wailing and Nicholas sobbing, adding to the bedlam of Adam's yells and the dog's barking. In general, I can bear it, my nerves having become inured over the years to the din of outraged children and animals. But the past few weeks had not been without their trials and perils and I had been looking forward to a little peace and quiet within the walls of my own home. I suddenly sprang to my feet, fairly kicked the dog aside, seized my pack from where I had dropped it in a corner, unbuckled it and emptied the contents all over the table.

'There you are!' I shouted. 'Take your pick from that! Go on! Take whatever you want. I don't care! You mercenary, ungrateful little beggars!'

And I stormed from the kitchen. But at least the noise had stopped. They were all, including Adela, staring after me with their mouths hanging open.

In the cool of the parlour, I slumped down on the window-seat, feeling extremely sorry for myself. A month ago, on the second of October, it had been my birthday, but I had been forced to celebrate it in the company of strangers. Moreover, on that day, King Richard and I had both turned thirty-one, very nearly middle-aged. And where had I been? Not among my loved ones, receiving their congratulations and presents, that was for certain. No, thanks to my wife's misplaced confidence in the words of a mendacious tinker, I had been on a wild goose chase to Hereford in the mistaken belief that some old biddy, whom I had never met, was in need of my help. I was the one who should be feeling hard done by.

But gradually, as my anger cooled, my lips begin to curl into a reluctant grin and I started to feel extremely foolish. I was behaving like a child. There was nothing to choose between me and Elizabeth, Nicholas and Adam. Indeed, I was the worse culprit because at my age I really should know better. At the same moment, I felt a cold wet nose nudge one of my hands, and then, with a leap and a scramble, Hercules was on the window-seat having come to find me and make his peace.

'Hello, old fellow,' I said and fondled his ears. He licked my face and gave a little whine of pleasure. Then he got hold of the edge of my tunic with his teeth and gave it a gentle tug. I nodded and rose to my feet. 'All right,' I told him. 'I'm coming.'

In the kitchen, it was now very quiet. My satchel had been repacked and re-buckled, tears had been dried, dirty dishes cleared from the table and a fresh beaker of ale stood waiting for me. In silence, I took my seat and glanced at Adela, who winked.

'Did each of you find something you wanted?' I asked mildly.

The relief was palpable. Their lord and master was over his tantrum and prepared to let bygones be bygones.

'Yes, thank you, Father,' my daughter said demurely. 'I took those lovely buttons.' And she patted the reticule attached to her girdle with a proprietary hand.

I cursed silently. I had meant to make a decent profit on those buttons.

'And I took the metal tags for the end of my new belt,' Nicholas added, opening his clenched fist to show me.

Another loss! They were silver. But then, I had told them to take what they liked. I couldn't go back on my word. The blame was mine and served me right for losing my temper.

I turned to Adam. 'And what did you take?'

He smiled seraphically, delved into the little pouch at his waist and produced the knife with the ivory inlaid handle. I might have guessed!

'I think he's too young to have a knife, Roger,' Adela protested, immediately provoking the usual storm signals.

I sighed and, not without a good many misgivings, took my

son's side. 'He's a boy, sweetheart. Boys need knives. You'll be careful with it, won't you, Adam?'

'Yes,' he said, scowling ferociously at his mother and echoing my words. 'Boys need knives. And I'm five.'

Adela shrugged and gave in. She knew she was beaten when the males of her household began to side with each other. Nicholas gave Adam a nod of approval, and he and I grinned at one another. I was on easy terms with my stepson and very often forgot that he was not my own. Adela's relationship with Bess was a more difficult one. My daughter had never known her mother, who had died when she was born, and I had married again when she was a mere two and a half years old. All the same, she had never wholly accepted Adela, and even after six years I still noticed in her a reluctance to use the word 'mother'. For this state of affairs I blamed Margaret Walker, Adela's cousin and my former mother-in-law, who talked far too much about Lillis to her granddaughter; not, I am sure, with any intention of alienating Elizabeth from her stepmother, but simply because it kept the memory of her child alive in her mind. (Indeed, Margaret was very fond of Adela and had been the moving spirit behind our marriage.) Nevertheless, her reminiscences were a constant reminder to Bess that Adela was not her mother, a fact which had been underlined earlier this year when my wife had fled to London taking the two boys with her, but leaving my daughter in her grandmother's charge.

Adela's voice broke in on my thoughts. 'I hope you don't think, Roger, that I encouraged them to pick those things.' She knew their value as well as I did. 'In fact, I washed up the dirty dishes so that I didn't even see what they chose.'

'Sweetheart, such a thought never so much as crossed my mind,' I lied. I wouldn't have put it past her as a punishment for behaviour of which she strongly disapproved. But if she said she didn't, then she didn't. Adela was the most truthful person I had ever known.

'And now,' she went on, 'it's time for lessons. Your knowledge of the alphabet, Adam, leaves much to be desired, while as for you two, your inability to do the simplest sums is very worrying. A little more concentration and a little less whispering and giggling would do neither of you any harm.' (For the affection between Elizabeth and her stepbrother had been instant and lasting, making them almost inseparable.)

But as my wife rose to fetch their slates from the cupboard, I stopped her. 'Couldn't you let them off lessons just for this once? There's something I need to talk to you about.'

Adela was immediately suspicious. 'Can't it wait?'

'It could,' I acknowledged, 'but I'd rather it didn't.' Which was true. I knew what a coward I could be.

'Very well then,' she said slowly.

The children whooped with joy and vanished upstairs before she changed her mind. A few moments later it sounded as if the whole of Caesar's Gallic wars was being re-enacted above our heads.

'Let's go into the parlour,' I suggested.

Some little time later, I finished the stumbling account of my visit to Juliette Gerrish and, leaning forward uncomfortably in my chair, waited for the storm to break.

There was a long silence, then, much to my astonishment and confusion, Adela said quietly, 'The poor creature. Why ever didn't she tell me the truth at the time? It would have saved so much . . . misunderstanding between us.'

'You're sorry for her?'

'I'm sorry for any woman placed as she is. But are you certain she's telling the truth? That the father is indeed your half-brother?'

'How else could she have known about him? Very few, if any, people, even in Bristol, knew about John Wedmore's relationship to me. I doubt, after three years, if anyone even remembers him. And she called him an Irishman, even though, like the blessed Saint Patrick himself, he's Somerset born and bred.'

There was another silence before Adela's initial suspicions were suddenly reawakened. 'You're not suggesting that we should take this child in when . . . when . . .?'

'No, of course not,' I disclaimed, a shade too hurriedly. 'In fact . . .'

'Roger, we have three children of our own! And another boy! This house is too full of males as it is.'

'And so I told Mistress Gerrish. But I did promise I would try to speak to this Walter Gurney who's head groom to Sir Lionel Despenser.'

'A fool's errand,' Adela told me bluntly. 'You'd do better to save your shoe leather.'

'I know it,' I agreed. 'But a promise is a promise. It will mean a walk to Keynsham, but I can sell some of my goods on the way. I'll pay a visit to Goldsmith Foliot's shop tomorrow and ask him for Sir Lionel's exact direction. I know they're friends. Which reminds me,' I added, relieved that my confession was over, 'I haven't yet told you about the rest of my adventures. What happened at Tintern Abbey. A most remarkable series of coincidences, if indeed it was that.'

And I proceeded to tell the tale.

Adela was intrigued by the story, as I had known she would be, but she had no solution to offer to the mystery. 'But,' she said, 'it does account for some gossip that I overheard in the market the day before yesterday to the effect that Anthony Roper's nephew is dead. There didn't seem to be much information as to how the boy had died, more speculation as to how Master Roper had received the news. The general opinion was that he would have shed no tears over a scapegrace and a ne'er-do-well for whom he had never had much affection in the first place.' Adela broke off for a moment, thinking, then nodded briskly to herself. 'It accounts, too, for the fact that when I passed Ursula Foliot in St Mary le Port Street a day or so back, her eyes were all red and swollen as if she had been crying. You say Master Foliot claims the lad had been hanging around his daughter and wanted to marry her. I must admit that both Goody Watkins and Bess Simnel had hinted as much a while ago, but you know how full of talk they are and at the time I didn't take much notice. But what could he possibly have been after at Tintern Abbey?'

'I've told you, we found nothing on his body, so perhaps there was nothing to find. But he was certainly looking for something even if he failed to discover it. And I could have sworn that he was holding something in his left hand when he rushed past us and out into the night.'

I had hoped that Adela might be in the mood to discuss the subject further, but I knew her well enough to see that her attention had wandered and that she was now struggling with some confession of her own.

'Roger –' she began, then stopped.

I raised my eyebrows and gave her an encouraging smile.

She took a deep breath and began again. 'Roger, I've invited Richard to supper this evening.' Richard Manifold, sheriff's officer and one-time aspirant to Adela's hand in the long-ago days before she had married Owen Juett and gone to live in Hereford, was a constant, if infrequent, presence in our lives and a perpetual thorn in my side. Adela liked him, not only for old times' sake, but also for himself, and while I had no doubt that her heart was entirely mine, I was uneasy when he was around. I felt certain, not without past reason, that he would do me a mischief if he could. And be happy to do it. But he was always smooth and pleasant on the surface so, unless I were to appear unnecessarily churlish, what could I do except treat him with complaisance? Nevertheless, Adela knew that I disliked him and was always tentative when mentioning his name.

'I wasn't to know that you'd be home today.'

'Of course not.' I smiled, but couldn't prevent myself from asking, 'Has he kept you company often while I've been away?'

'No! No!' Her answer was a little too emphatic for comfort. 'Only once or twice. It gets lonely when you're not here.'

'The children?'

'Oh, Roger!' She gave me an exasperated smile. 'Only a man could think that small children are adequate company. Have you ever tried talking in words of one syllable all day?'

'I'm sorry,' I said and, rising from my seat, went over and gently drew her to her feet. I kissed her, but couldn't help adding, 'It was you who sent me away this time, you know. And all for nothing as it turned out.'

She smiled wryly. 'I suppose I shall never hear the last of that.'

I hotly refuted the allegation, kissed her once again and spent the rest of the morning cleaning my boots and washing myself from head to foot in order to wipe away the grime of the past few weeks. Then I donned a fresh shirt and hose preparatory to visiting my favourite inn, the Green Lattis, to discover how the world had been turning in my absence.

It was just my luck that the first person I saw, and who saw me, was Richard Manifold, attended by his two henchmen, Jack Gload and Peter Littleman.

'Ah! Roger!' he exclaimed. 'You're back at last, safe and sound. Not taken prisoner by the rebels, then?' Jack and Pete gave a dutiful snigger at this pleasantry. 'Master Foliot told me that he'd met you and how you'd all taken refuge at Tintern Abbey. I think he was expecting your arrival a day or two ago.'

'I had business in Gloucester that detained me,' I answered shortly. And, with no intention of satisfying his obvious curiosity, I went on, 'Have you seen anything of, or did Master Foliot happen to mention, a pedlar by the name of Oliver Tockney, a Yorkshireman? He left Gloucester ahead of me, bound for Bristol. I'd be glad to know that he was safe. He'd never travelled this far south before.'

The sheriff's officer bit his lip.

'Ye-es,' he answered slowly. 'Master Foliot did say how you and this Tockney – is that his name? – had struck up a friendship. Said you left Tintern for Gloucester together. But then this other fellow arrived in Bristol without you, oh, all of three days ago. Told Lawyer Heathersett, when he met him in the street, that you'd gone to call on a woman.' My companion's eyes gleamed hopefully.

Could one never keep any of one's business private in this city?

'That's right,' I said casually, adding with malicious pleasure, 'Adela knows all about it. Get her to tell you the story at supper tonight. I understand we are to have the honour of your company.'

I watched the light of hope die out of his face. 'I shouldn't dream of being so inquisitive,' he replied stiffly. Again, there came a snigger, muffled this time, from Pete Littleman. Richard Manifold glared at him before turning his attention back to me. 'I'm afraid I have some bad news for you, Roger, concerning this Yorkshire friend of yours.'

'Bad news? What . . . What sort of bad news?'

'The worst, I regret to say. He's dead.'

'Dead?'

'Murdered.'

EIGHT

'**M**urdered?' I repeated stupidly.

'Murdered,' Richard Manifold confirmed, while Jack Gload and Peter Littleman nodded lugubriously.

'When?'

Richard fingered his chin. 'Let me see. The day before yesterday, was it?' He turned to his henchmen but, as usual, the pair just looked blank. Mind you, that was their normal expression, so I don't really know how he told if they were agreeing with him or not. But he seemed satisfied. 'Yes, the day before yesterday. That would have been Saturday, and he arrived in the city on Friday. Several people noted his arrival, which they might not otherwise have done if he hadn't wanted directions to Master Foliot's shop in St Mary le Port Street. Or else to Lawyer Heathersett's, although he wasn't sure of his address.'

'Did he get to see either of them?' I interrupted.

Richard Manifold shrugged. 'You'll have to ask them. Certainly Goldsmith Foliot identified the body, but then it seems he'd met the pedlar before.'

'How . . . How was Oliver killed?' My tongue stumbled over the words as my ears still refused to believe what they were hearing.

'Strangled from behind with a piece of knotted rope.' Richard blew his nose in his fingers and wiped them delicately on his sleeve. 'Favourite trick of thieves and pickpockets.'

'The motive was robbery?'

'Of course it was robbery,' Richard said impatiently. 'His pack was missing, and Master Foliot understood the Yorkshireman meant to fill it up at Gloucester.'

'Yes, he did.' My mind was still whirling. 'Where are you keeping the body?'

My companion looked bewildered. 'Keeping the body?' Pete and Jack gave another snigger. 'We're not keeping it anywhere. It was tipped into a pauper's grave on Saturday afternoon. And it would have gone to the common pit if Master Foliot hadn't offered to pay the fee for a pauper's funeral.'

'You mean,' I demanded hotly, 'that there was no inquest?'

'Inquest?' Richard Manifold was scathing. 'Why would the city be put to such a cost when the cause of death was obvious? And what's more, he was a stranger.'

'Stranger,' echoed Jack Gload, in much the same way as five-year-old Adam echoed me. His crony nodded solemnly in agreement.

'How do you know he was robbed?' My brain continued to dispute the inevitable.

Richard Manifold sighed. 'Because,' he enunciated slowly and carefully like someone speaking to a backward child, 'as I've told you once already, his pack was missing and has never been found, and because strangulation with a knotted rope is, again as we have already established, a favourite method of killing by Bristol's criminal population. Wake up, Roger! Any more stupid questions?'

This last remark provoked a full-scale explosion of mirth from his loyal followers and attracted the attention of fellow drinkers, who looked around to find out what they were missing.

'All right! All right!' I said hurriedly, ordering a beaker of ale from the potboy who had finally arrived, hot, flustered and overworked, to know my wishes. 'Whereabouts was the body found?'

I could see that Richard Manifold was dying to tell me to mind my own business, but he was supping with Adela and me that afternoon and was afraid to jeopardize his invitation.

'In one of those alleyways between St Peter's Church and the Mint,' was the reluctant answer. He went on quickly, 'Now, mark my words well, Roger! Just because you knew this fellow and were friendly with him – although not friendly enough, apparently, to accompany him all the way to Bristol – I forbid you to start poking your nose in, snooping about and asking questions. This is a straightforward case of a man, a stranger, being set upon by robbers, probably putting up a fight and consequently being murdered for his pains. A circumstance which, unfortunately, is all too common in this city. Is that clearly understood?'

'Understood,' I muttered, taking my brimming beaker of ale from the potboy and swallowing an almighty gulp.

Richard Manifold regarded me suspiciously for a long moment, but then, obviously deciding there was no more to be said, finished his own drink, jerked his head at his two subordinates and quit the Green Lattis without looking back.

I sat on, staring into what remained of my ale and feeling, without being able to pinpoint exactly why, uneasy. But this was swamped by my distress as I pictured Oliver's wife and family looking for his return up there in distant Yorkshire, waiting week after week, month after month until, finally, when a year and more had passed, reaching the sad conclusion that he was never coming home again, wondering what had happened to him and if his absence were voluntary or not. And, to my annoyance, I also felt guilt, as if I had been responsible for him and somehow let him down. That was nonsense, of course. He was a grown man and in charge of his own destiny. Moreover, it had been his decision to strike as far south as Bristol and, furthermore, he could have waited for me in Gloucester if he hadn't been so impatient to get on. Of course, if I were being truthful, I had done nothing to discourage his independence: I was heartily sick of his company by that time, and he of mine. All the same, a nagging voice whispered at the back of my mind that I should have done more to protect him. I had been on familiar territory, and had we stayed together, no doubt he would have lodged with us at journey's end. Adela would have made up a bed for him somewhere and he would therefore not have been out alone at night.

I finished my ale and got to my feet, giving only a cursory nod in the direction of several friends and acquaintances who were trying to attract my attention. Outside, it was cold and damp as the pale November sun struggled in vain to impart a little warmth. I made my way down High Street before turning left into the gloom of St Mary le Port Street where the houses' overhanging upper storeys made winter of even the warmest summer's day.

Walking from the High Street, Master Foliot's shop was situated on my right, halfway between St Mary le Port Church and St Peter's Church, the latter being flanked on the farther side by the goldsmith's splendid new house which was the envy of all his friends. That he sold quality wares was obvious by the goods displayed on the counter inside, and by the fact that he had no less than four apprentices, the two younger keeping the furnace stoked, working the bellows and sweeping up the shavings and bits of gold from the floor. The elder lads, one of them probably nearing the completion of his time, learned their craft under Master Foliot's expert tutelage and, from what I could see, would no doubt set up in competition with him some time in the future.

As I entered, the goldsmith glanced up from examining the setting for a ring which one of his pupils had just finished making. He wore a look of expectancy, hoping for a sale, and his face fell a little as he saw who it was. But then he recovered himself and advanced smiling, one hand extended. 'Ah! Master Chapman! You've returned at last. I suppose –' he hesitated briefly before resuming with a suitably altered countenance – 'you've heard about your poor friend, Tockney?' I nodded mutely, temporarily bereft of words. Master Foliot went on, 'A terrible thing to have happened! And to the stranger within our gates! A second death coming so soon after that of poor Peter Noakes . . . Well, it has shaken me, I confess.'

I cleared my throat. 'You . . . You don't think by any chance that the two deaths were connected, do you?'

The goldsmith stared at me in much the same way as Richard Manifold had done, as though there was something amiss with my powers of reasoning. 'Connected?' he repeated, puzzled.

'Yes.'

He frowned. 'But . . . Good God, man! Why should there be? No, no! Whoever told you of the pedlar's death couldn't have explained it to you properly. The fellow was set on by robbers, his goods stolen and he himself strangled. If I've said it once, I've said it a hundred times, the Watch should be more vigilant. There should be more torches left burning in the streets at night and a second patrol is needed . . .'

I interrupted him with an assurance that the details of Oliver Tockney's death had indeed been made plain to me. It was just that . . . But, I didn't bother to explain just what it was that had prompted my question because, to tell the truth, I wasn't sure

myself. Instead, I went on, 'Did Oliver come to see you when
he reached Bristol?'

'Friday last, yes! I gathered that I was his first port of call.'
The goldsmith looked a little shamefaced. 'I think it was merely
a friendly visit, a renewal of our former acquaintance. Nothing
more than that. But I'm afraid I was rather short with him. There
were two customers in the shop at the time, and I was in the
middle of a very lucrative transaction with one of them. A fair
sum of money was involved.'

I could picture the scene. In the presence of a rich client whom
Master Foliot wished to impress, he had no desire to be hailed
as the companion of a shabby pedlar who spoke in a strange
dialect. So Oliver Tockney had been given short shrift and had
probably walked off in a huff to look for, and secure, lodgings
for the night.

'Was this late in the day?' I asked.

If Gilbert Foliot felt any resentment at this continued questioning
by one inferior to him in station, he didn't show it. 'It was getting
dark,' he agreed. 'But then, it gets dark early this time of year. Oh
yes, I recollect now. Both the bells of St Peter's and of St Mary
le Port were ringing for Vespers.'

'And you didn't see Oliver again?'

'No. That is not until the next day, Saturday, when Sergeant
Manifold asked me to identify a body which had been found not
far from here, in Pit Hay Lane. You must know it. It's between
St Peter's and the Mint, close to the castle.'

I knew it, and I also knew the origin of the name because
Adela had once, and rather surprisingly, informed me of it. It
came from two Norman French words, *puits* meaning well and
haie meaning hedge. And the well with the hedge around it was
still there, used every day by many people in the vicinity and by
many of the pilgrims who came to St Peter's to worship at the
shrine of St Mary Bellhouse.

'Why did the sergeant ask you to identify the body? Was he
aware of your previous connection with Oliver?'

A shade of annoyance crossed the goldsmith's face and I
wondered if I had strained his patience too far. But although he
compressed his lips for a second or two, he answered pleasantly
enough, 'I believe Lawyer Heathersett, who Sergeant Manifold

had reason to visit a day or so earlier, had mentioned something of our adventures to him.' (Of course, the three men must have arrived back in Bristol almost a week earlier. The atrocious weather had eased, the rebels had dispersed and the horse ferry across the Severn was most probably again in use. I daresay there had been no need for them to ride north to Gloucester, after all.) 'So when the presence of a strange pedlar in the town was reported to him, Richard Manifold put two and two together and made four. And when the poor man's body was discovered on Saturday morning, not so very far from here, he did the same again and came straight to me. A very intelligent fellow, Manifold.'

I could have argued with that, but it was neither the time nor place. Besides, honesty compelled me to admit that I was biased against the man. Instead, I changed the subject. 'How did Master Roper take the news of his nephew's death?' I asked.

'As one would have expected,' was the tart rejoinder, and I could tell that the goldsmith's goodwill was at last running out. One of the senior apprentices had been standing patiently by for some little while, waiting to attract his attention. It was high time that I took my leave. I had only been tolerated this long because Gilbert Foliot was possessed of this mistaken belief that I was somehow hand in glove with the king.

'I hope Mistress Ursula is well,' I said, turning towards the door.

'As well as can be expected.' Another curt response. Then he relented, adding, 'She's taken the news of young Noakes's death badly, I'm sorry to say.' A snort of derision. 'Far worse than the lad's uncle.'

'Who's this you're talking of? Your daughter?' demanded a deep voice as the door behind me opened, admitting a tall, well set-up man with very blue eyes and a shock of thick, wavy brown hair beneath an emerald-green velvet hat. I recognized him as Gilbert Foliot's friend, Sir Lionel Despenser and, as luck would have it, the very man I wanted to see.

'Who else?' the goldsmith shrugged.

'Well, you know I've offered to take her off your hands at any time,' the knight said, smiling. 'As her father, she'd have to obey you. And –' he gave a falsely modest smile – 'although I say it myself, I'm quite a catch. You'd be surprised – or then again perhaps you wouldn't – at the caps that have been set at me.'

The goldsmith laughed. 'I'll say this for you, Lal, you never try to hide your light under a bushel . . . One day, maybe, we'll arrange it. But not just at this present. So what brings you in from Keynsham?'

'Originally, to find out how you got on during your journey into Wales. But as I had some business with Henry Callowhill first – a couple of butts of malmsey he's been keeping for me – you may assume I know all there is to know about it already. What a gossip the fellow is! All the same, I thought I'd like to hear your version of events.' Sir Lionel, suddenly becoming aware of my presence, gave an irritated frown and raised his strongly-marked eyebrows as much as to say, 'Who is this fellow?'

Gilbert Foliot looked a little surprised himself to find me still present, but made the necessary introduction. 'This is Master Chapman. Roger Chapman. I feel certain you must be acquainted with the name.'

Was there a note of caution in his voice, or had I imagined it?

'Oh, that man.' The knight laughed.

I bowed subserviently. 'Sir Lionel.'

'I needn't detain you further, Roger,' the goldsmith said point-edly, turning at long last to his patiently waiting apprentice.

'No,' I agreed, but made no move to leave, instead continuing to look at Sir Lionel.

'I was wondering, sir, if I might ask you a favour.'

'Me?' He stared down his patrician nose. 'And what would that be?'

'I believe you have a groom in your employ. A Gloucester man, Walter Gurney.'

'My head groom. Yes. What of it?'

Gilbert Foliot, ignoring the poor apprentice yet again, was staring at me as though I'd taken leave of my senses.

'I'd like your permission, Sir Lionel, to walk out to Keynsham some day soon and have a word with him.'

'In God's name, why? What's the man to you? What do you know of him?'

'I'm afraid I'm not at liberty to say. It's a private matter, sir.'

The two men glanced at one another. I felt that they were both disturbed by the request, but I could see no reason for their unease. Then I thought that Gilbert Foliot gave a very slight nod, although I couldn't be sure.

'Well, if you must, you must,' the knight finally conceded. I thanked him and was turning once again to go, when he asked casually, 'And when will that be?'

'Not for a day or two. I only reached home this morning. Thursday or Friday perhaps, with your agreement.'

'Of course! Of course!' Sir Lionel waved a dismissive hand. 'I'll see that Walter is apprised of your visit and is ready to receive you.'

'Thank you,' I said and bowed low to each man in turn before stepping out once more into the shadows of St Mary le Port Street.

Outside, I leaned against the nearest wall for a moment or two while a horse and cart rumbled past, its driver loudly cursing the narrowness of the road and giving it as his considered opinion that someone would get stuck there one of these fine days. I think he was fishing for a little sympathy, but I failed him. I was busy with reflections of my own.

I wondered if Walter Gurney had confided in his new master the reason for his flight from Gloucestershire and if that explained Sir Lionel's obvious reluctance to allow me access to his groom. I didn't know that I blamed him if that were the case. (Maybe Walter had never intended to marry Jane Spicer, with or without Juliette's child.) And yet I couldn't help feeling that there had been something more; some undercurrent of suspicion that had communicated itself to, and been understood by, Gilbert Foliot. But what the goldsmith's interest in Walter Gurney could be, I was unable to fathom. His knowledge of the man would be solely what his friend had told him, and somehow I couldn't see the knight concerning himself with his servants' problems. In the end, I gave it up, decided I had been imagining things and walked on in the direction of St Peter's Church and the castle.

There was the usual bustle around the church porch as a steady stream of locals and pilgrims went in and out. The shrine of Our Lady of the Bellhouse, known generally as St Mary

Bellhouse and situated next to the belfry tower, was the chief jewel in St Peter's crown. A church already rich in history when the body of King Edmund, murdered in the King's Wood, rested there while on its journey to Glastonbury for burial, it had inevitably been rebuilt by the Normans, but its Saxon foundations remained.

I went inside to offer up a prayer and pay my respects.

In a setting glowing with colourful wall paintings and tapestries, the shrine nevertheless managed to hold all eyes. The statue of the Virgin Herself, the deep azure blue of her robes glittering with precious and semi-precious gems, the golden canopy over her head, the scented candles on either side, the wealth of offerings, both large and small, laid at her feet, made everything else pale into insignificance. The shrine's fame was widespread, drawing pilgrims from all over the west and from even further afield. Its maintenance was in the hands of the Fraternity of St Mary Bellhouse, a band of local men dedicated to its upkeep and of whom, I guessed, Gilbert Foliot was probably one. He was a man of substance, an important citizen who would naturally be associated with such a project. Moreover, his house was right next door to the church.

As I came out again into the pale November sunshine, I accidentally brushed shoulders with a young woman just entering. I would have recognized her immediately as Ursula Foliot even had my attention not been caught by her red and swollen eyes and her general air of tragedy. This was so pronounced, her mourning so ostentatious, that I was induced to hope that matters had not gone very deep with her; that it was more show than suffering. I waited for her to emerge once more, enjoying as always the traffic of a busy street, then put myself in her way, possessing myself of one of her hands and bowing obsequiously.

'Mistress Foliot, would you be kind enough to vouchsafe me a word? My name is Roger Chapman' – I was growing used by now to not having to explain who I was – 'and, as your father may have told you, I was at Tintern Abbey when Master Noakes's body was discovered.'

'Yes.' She hesitated before continuing in a low, dramatic voice, 'Whatever it is you want to know, I can't speak to you now. I'm too upset.' She pulled forward the black veil wound around her head so that it partially obscured her face. 'Peter,' she continued in trembling accents, 'was the Abelard to my Eloise. We were going to be married, you know, in defiance of everyone. His uncle! My father! Peter had vowed it. I had vowed it. The only thing that was stopping us,' she added in a much more prosaic, whining tone, 'was money. Neither Master Roper – who, I might tell you, is a skinflint of no mean order – nor Father, who isn't any better, would take us seriously and kept us both on the most meagre of allowances.'

I clucked sympathetically and she glanced around her, suddenly changing her mind and longing only to unburden herself of her sense of ill-usage.

'Very well, come to the house now,' she whispered. 'Father's busy in the shop and there are only Mistress Dawes and the servants there at the moment.'

She spoke as one who had little, if no, regard for the lesser orders. She probably, I reflected, looked upon them as so many additions to the furniture.

The goldsmith's house was a recent addition to St Peter's Street, being at that time certainly not more than twenty years old. Gilbert Foliot's acquisition of it when the original owner died ten years before, had been, so my former mother-in-law and her cronies informed me, the talk of Bristol. I had been too much of a newcomer, and too often absent from the city, to have taken notice of the gossip myself, but I could believe it to be true.

It was an imposing edifice, three storeys high and, I was told, with deep cellars that had belonged to a much older Saxon building, once occupying the site. Mistress Ursula led me across a hall with painted beams and carved figureheads at either end, and into which my entire house would possibly have fitted, to a parlour of equally generous proportions. There was little, however, in the way of furniture, and what there was looked most uncomfortable except for a wooden rocking chair laden with cushions. This was set on a raised platform at the far end of the room with a window overlooking a small garden and velvet curtains that pulled across the front of the dais, thus turning it into a cosy retreat, a room within a room.

My hostess offered me neither refreshment nor a seat, merely asking abruptly, once she had closed the door, 'Well? What did you want to ask me?'

There was nothing for it but to abandon the normal courtesies and be equally abrupt. 'Do you know what Master Noakes was doing at Tintern Abbey?'

Ursula unwound her veil and dropped it on the floor for someone else to pick up. My sympathy for her bereaved state was fast evaporating. 'Not exactly.' I maintained a questioning silence and after a short pause, she went on: 'Peter said there might something there which would make us rich.'

'What sort of thing?'

She made an impatient gesture. 'I don't know. He wouldn't tell me. He said it might prove to be a mare's nest and then I'd be disappointed.' She snorted disgustedly. 'He'd have done better to have told me what he knew. At least I could have advised him whether it was a wild goose chase or not.' Recollecting herself, Ursula gave a tragic moan and momentarily closed her eyes. 'Poor sweetheart! Peter wasn't always very practical, I'm afraid.'

'Did he ever mention how he came by his information?' I asked eagerly, praying for a miracle.

But none was forthcoming. 'He wouldn't say.'

'Was it from your father, do you think?'

She considered this idea, wrinkling her nose. 'My father was at Tintern himself, wasn't he?' Her tone was thoughtful. 'A coincidence, do you think?'

I sighed. 'I have to admit it isn't likely. We were all taking refuge from the weather and the rebels. On the other hand . . .'

'Yes?'

'It was at Master Foliot's suggestion that we took shelter in the abbey.'

'There you are, then!' Her face fell. 'No, that's no good. Father would never have confided in Peter about anything.'

I made no comment, but glanced covertly at the alcove at the far end of the chamber. If someone were sitting there with the curtain drawn, his presence unsuspected, it would be quite easy for him to overhear any conversation in the main part of the room. Was that what had happened? For there was no getting away from the fact that Gilbert Foliot had been making enquiries of the abbot concerning the secret hiding place at the very moment that Peter Noakes was breaking into it.

Unfortunately, neither was there any doubt that the would-be thief appeared to have found nothing. For if he had, where was it?

And what was it?

'I haven't been much help, have I?' Ursula's voice recalled me to my surroundings.

She was looking pathetic again, and I saw to my shame that there were genuine tears standing in her eyes. Contrite, I raised her hand briefly to my lips. She seemed shocked, and probably was. Common pedlars didn't make that sort of gesture.

'You've been very helpful,' I assured her. 'I may need to talk to you again. Meantime, mention nothing to Master Foliot about our conversation or my being here.'

'Of course not. I'm not speaking to him, anyway,' was the taut reply.

I trembled inwardly. In ten years or so, I could foresee Elizabeth saying the self same words.

'I must go,' I said. 'I only arrived home this morning and so far I've devoted very little time to my family.'

'I expect you're a lovely father,' she said yearningly, gazing soulfully into my eyes.

I beat a hasty retreat. All the same, I was shaken and more than a little dashed. When young girls started seeing me, not as a lover, but as a surrogate father, it was high time to be thinking of leading a more settled life.

A most depressing thought!

NINE

I went home, but not before first paying a visit to Pit Hay Lane, a noisome little alleyway in the crowded neighbourhood of the castle. It was a fruitless errand of course, there being nothing to see; no patch of dried and discoloured blood to indicate whereabouts the murder of Oliver Tockney had taken place. I walked its length, glancing at the mean houses and shops on either side, then turned and walked back again.

I was about to get myself a drink of water at St Peter's fountain when someone tapped me on the shoulder. I had been aware for several moments of a more than usually pungent smell – more pungent even than the alleyway's normal aroma of stale urine, dead cats and dog turd – and, turning, found myself staring down into the rheumy eyes of a small man whose verminous head reached to just the middle of my breastbone.

'I been a-watching of thee,' he announced. 'Not that anyone could miss such a gert lump. I reckon thee's looking fer where that there pedlar were murdered Friday evening.'

'How do you know it was Friday evening and not early Saturday morning?' I asked, taking a step or two backward in order to distance myself from the stench of the man's clothes. (Clothes? More like a bundle of very old unwashed rags.)

''Cos I saw him set on, that's why. I were looking out the door of me mother's house down there –' he waved a sticklike arm towards the opposite end of the lane – 'and I seed him walking down on t'other side, coming my way. He were being followed, I seed that at once. Two gert big fellows they were and they meant mischief. I seed one of 'em twisting a rope a-'tween his hands. Thee's for it, me old acker, I thought – and sure enough he were. Mind, he put up the devil of a struggle, kicking and clawing and squirming, but it weren't no good. He were dead as mutton in minutes. Quicker than the hangman c'n do it, I said to meself. Then they stripped his pack from his back and were off, like greased lightning.'

'And you made no attempt to go to this poor man's assistance?' I demanded furiously, and without really stopping to think.

My informant soon put me straight. 'Me? Thee's out thy mind! How tall dost 'ee think I am? They were gert big fellows, I tell 'ee! They'd 'ave made mincemeat out of I. I ain't risking me life fer no stranger. I ain't that stupid, Maister.'

I could see his point of view and apologized for being so foolish, whereupon he flashed me a toothless grin and offered to show me the exact spot where the murder had taken place. I declined – there didn't seem any point – but asked him to confirm that the killers were indeed nothing other than two common footpads looking for an easy mark. 'For I can't see why they needed to kill him,' I said. 'Oliver Tockney wasn't a big man. Moreover, there were two of them to his one. They could have overpowered him easily.'

My companion considered this.

'Maybe they didn't mean to kill him,' he volunteered after a while. 'Maybe one jus' meant to hold him with the rope round his neck while t'other robbed him. But, as I told 'ee, he put up such a fight that I reckons they had no choice.'

I nodded and, taking a coin from my purse, put into the man's greasy palm. His fist closed round it tightly and he disappeared almost at once, no doubt heading for the nearest ale-house. The alacrity with which he received the money made me wonder how true his story was. Had he really been a spectator to Oliver's murder or had he simply made it up, loitering around the alley, waiting for some gullible fool to show an interest in the crime?

There was, unhappily, no way of knowing for certain, so there was nothing to be done. I had my drink at the fountain and went back to Small Street.

'You're just in time,' said my wife, 'to make yourself useful and put out the dishes and spoons for supper. I hope you haven't forgotten that we have company.'

'If you mean Dick Manifold, why don't you say so?' I countered bad-temperedly. 'I don't call him "company". And where's Elizabeth? It's high time she took her share of the household chores.'

'She's gone to the market for me and taken Adam and Hercules with her to get them out from under my feet.' Adela considered me thoughtfully. 'Now, what's happened to put you in such a bad mood?'

I told her and she was immediately all concern. 'Roger, I'm so sorry! What a dreadful thing to have happened. And the poor man, not in the city above a day, if that! No wonder you're upset. Sit down and have some ale. We must question Richard more closely about it, at supper.'

But Richard, spruce and shining, gobbling down his hearty

portion of beef stew – beef was a rare treat in our house, and I felt highly incensed to be sharing it with Dick Manifold – was disinclined to pursue the subject. The death of a pedlar, and a stranger at that, was of small importance to him. As a man of the law, he had news of far greater substance to impart. 'If I should happen to be called away during the course of this evening,' he said, 'don't be offended.' (I shouldn't have been offended, not in the least.) 'It will be on official business.' He paused here to give the rest of us – well, Adela, then – sufficient time to look both admiring and interested before continuing, 'All ports in the south-west have been warned to be ready to repel invasion by Henry Tudor and his troops.'

This revelation did, most gratifyingly, catch and hold our attention. Adela cried out and I dropped my spoon on the floor. (Hercules had licked it clean before I could pick it up again.)

'Henry Tudor?' I queried stupidly.

Richard nodded. 'Royal messengers brought the news express this morning. Henry Tudor with a Breton fleet and an army of mercenaries is off the Dorset coast, at Poole, seeking access to the town.'

'An unwalled town,' I put in swiftly.

'As you say, Roger. However, a further messenger arrived late this afternoon to inform His Worship the Mayor that the invasion had been repulsed by the loyal citizens of Poole and that the Tudor was sailing on westwards, probably – or so King Richard guesses – making for Wales. Henry's grandfather, Owen Tudor, was, as I am sure you know, a Welshman. And the Welsh are very loyal to their own. All ports, therefore, along the south coast and, particularly, those on the English side of the Bristol Channel have been instructed to be extremely vigilant.'

He looked so pleased with himself that I couldn't resist pricking his bubble of self-importance. 'Well, if the invaders have only just quit the Dorset coast, they'll hardly reach this far for several days, at least,' I said nastily. 'So you're unlikely to be called away this evening. We may look forward to many hours of your company yet.'

Adela looked daggers at me, but I was rewarded by guffaws from the three children, two of whom knew perfectly well when I was being sarcastic. (Adam simply followed their lead.)

Richard flushed with annoyance, but long practice had taught him to ignore my jibes. He replied with dignity, 'This is a serious situation, Roger.' He smiled up at Adela as she removed his dirty bowl and placed a clean wooden trencher in front of him, preparatory to cutting him the largest slice of her pear and apple pie. He shovelled a good portion of this into his mouth – he was a greedy man – before turning once again to me. 'What,' he asked, 'do you make of these rumours that the king has had his nephews put to death?'

Richard Manifold could have asked no question more likely to send my temperature soaring. 'Arrant nonsense!' I shouted so loudly that poor Adam, who was sitting next to me, nearly fell off his chair and Hercules started barking like a fiend. When order had been restored and I had received a timely rebuke from my wife, I continued on a less aggressive note, 'One can see how and why they arose, of course.'

'Of course,' Richard agreed at once. But then added cautiously, 'What's your theory?'

Not loath to air my opinion, I laid down my spoon and proceeded to give it – it being, of course, the same as I had already tendered to Oliver Tockney and others. 'As far as I can gather from everything I've heard while on my travels, there has been not just one rebellion, but two. The first was in the south and west by disaffected Yorkists on behalf of the late King Edward's sons. They're outraged by Richard's seizure of the crown and their intention was to restore the elder boy as King Edward the fifth. The second rebellion was fomented in Wales by the remnants of the Lancastrian faction who see King Richard's accession – which hasn't, let's face it, been welcomed by everyone – as a heaven-sent opportunity to stir up trouble on behalf of Henry, their one remaining claimant to the throne. The very last thing they want is the restoration of the House of York in the person of young Edward. So they've spread the rumour that the two children have been murdered on the orders of their uncle. At one fell swoop, this tears the heart out of the Yorkist cause and, in many cases no doubt, wins the Yorkist rebels over to the Tudor's side. There's a very subtle brain at work, and I've a shrewd idea whose it is. The Bishop of Ely has always hated King Richard and he was under house arrest at the Duke of Buckingham's home in Brecknock when all this trouble began. He undoubtedly persuaded Buckingham to throw in his lot with Henry just out of a sense of pure mischief. God knows where both of them are now.'

'Oh, I can tell you that.' Richard's chest once more swelled with the importance of the well-informed official. 'The bishop's reported to have fled abroad, to Brittany. The duke's been captured near Salisbury.'

'He'll receive short shrift from the king then,' I said. 'If there's one thing Richard won't forgive it's disloyalty.'

Richard Manifold nodded, but returned to his original subject of concern. 'If your theory is correct, why has His Highness not repudiated the claim? Why has he not produced the two princes in order to prove that they are both alive and well?'

'Because he's been otherwise employed crushing two rebellions,' I answered tartly. 'And I wouldn't in future refer to them as princes, if I were you. The lords Edward and Richard Plantagenet suit their bastard status better.'

I spoke more hotly than I intended and saw my guest raise his eyebrows. 'You're a loyal partisan, Roger, I'll say that for you. Or is it,' he added shrewdly, 'that you're not quite as convinced by our new king's claim to the throne as you would like to be?'

I was about to launch a vigorous denial when Adam saved me the trouble by banging loudly with his spoon on the table and commanding, 'No more talk!'

Richard Manifold stared at him in shocked surprise. This was a side of my son that he had not seen before and it was not the way in which children were supposed to behave. Nor did they in any other house that I had been in. It was, however, Adela, not I, who dismissed Adam from the table with an admonition for being rude, but even she had a quaver in her voice which our astute little son instantly detected, for he bounced off quite cheerfully while the other two clamoured to go with him. So while we three adults spent a quiet hour or two in the parlour, the usual noisy game was played out overhead; a game which neither my wife nor I did anything to curtail as soon as it became apparent that the incessant shouting and thumping of feet were likely to speed Richard Manifold's departure.

And when, finally, he took his leave, without the usual threat of honouring us with another visit, Adela wound her arms about my neck, kissed me soundly and said, 'You're right, sweetheart. Richard is becoming wearisomely pompous.'

I was so taken aback by this admission that I was struck dumb for a full half minute. But at last I found my voice for long enough to make a highly appropriate suggestion.

Adela laughed and kissed me again. 'Well, I suppose you have been away from home for quite some time,' she conceded.

'And in quite a lot of danger, too,' I reminded her pathetically. 'Moreover, I wouldn't have gone in the first place if you hadn't sent me.'

'Oh, very well,' she agreed and led the way upstairs.

But she still managed to make it sound as if she were doing me the favour. (How do women do that?)

The next week passed in the hurly-burly of domestic life, getting out and about with my pack, doing odd jobs around the house, making it secure against the onset of colder weather. The days were getting progressively darker and shorter and there were window catches to be made fast, an adequate supply of fuel to be laid in, the tiler to be summoned to fix a loose tile on the roof. Adela, too, was busy, salting meat and fish for the winter, wrapping and storing apples in the tiny loft above Elizabeth's bedchamber, drying fresh herbs while they could still be got and generally preparing for that time of year when people burrow deep inside the four walls of their houses and listen to the elements doing their worst outside.

Nearly eight days had passed before we heard of the execution of the Duke of Buckingham at Salisbury on Sunday, November the second. This intrusion of great events into our small domestic circle was a reminder, to me at least, of a larger world outside demanding my attention. The rebellions were now well and truly over, retribution (surprisingly little considering the provocation) exacted and the king, so far as I could gather, settled in London and, for the present, resisting all temptation to return to his beloved north. The rumours about his nephews had died down, although Richard still seemed reluctant to make any statement concerning their well-being. I found this somewhat surprising, but had no time to let it worry me, having suddenly realized that I had not yet honoured my promise to Juliette Gerrish and Jane Spicer to visit Walter Gurney at Keynsham.

'You're not going away so soon?' Adela demanded indignantly when I had made my plans known to her.

'Only for a night. Two nights at most. As long as it takes me to walk to Keynsham and back again. I won't carry my pack. I'll be quicker that way.'

'Well, see that you are. And you can take Hercules with you. The walk will do him good. He's getting far too fat and lazy.'

The sagacious animal, sprawled inelegantly beside the fire, opened one eye and gave her a baleful stare.

Nevertheless, he seemed willing enough to accompany me when I set out early the following morning. It was still dark as we passed through the Redcliffe Gate and a sickly sliver of moon rode high in the heavens, appearing and disappearing between the storm-driven clouds. A strong wind, soughing through the scrubland on either side of the track, sounded like the hushing of the sea.

'I'm afraid we're in for a wet walk, old friend,' I said, pulling my cloak more firmly about me and my hat down over my ears.

Hercules, however, was already investigating various promising scents and noises coming from the bushes and tufts of long grass growing by the side of the road, and was not yet in the mood for playing a dog who was being hard done by. That would come later when he decided it was time to be carried. Adela was right about him, I decided. He had put on weight since I went away.

As a reluctant and watery sun rose over the distant hills, painting the landscape a pale and dirty yellow, the track began to get busier. Hercules and I met an increasing number of farmers and smallholders driving or walking their goods to Bristol market. A weary friar, his bare feet blue and swollen with sores and cold, gave me a cheerful 'God be with you!' and would have paused for a word with Hercules, but the ungrateful beast only growled and went off in pursuit of an imaginary rabbit.

The rain which had threatened since dawn was, in spite of the scurrying clouds, still holding off by the time we sighted Keynsham somewhere around mid-afternoon. The rest of the journey had been as uneventful as its beginning. And with only one stop in the lee of a hedge to eat the bread and cheese provided by Adela, we had made excellent progress. But with daylight already fading, there was no doubt that we should be forced to find accommodation for the night.

But as I passed along Keynsham High Street, I could see no sign of an inn. I had always thought it a mean place, with little besides the abbey to recommend it. The houses were, for the most part, crudely built, one-storey, daub-and-wattle dwellings with thatched roofs and single windows closed by wooden shutters. No worse than many other places of its size and kind, I supposed, and the Romans hadn't spurned it. At least, I had once been shown bits of pottery and tessellated pavement that had been discovered in the bed of the River Chew, the muddy tributary of the Avon which encircled the village.

Enquiries for Sir Lionel Despenser's holding led me up the steep hill at the eastern end of the main street and in the direction of Bath for perhaps some half a mile or so. I was just beginning to fear that I had lost my way when an arched gateway rose in front of me, suddenly appearing out of the gathering gloom and with the light from a wall torch illuminating the massive bell-pull.

An overzealous tug on the rope caused the bell itself to clash loud enough to waken the dead in the abbey graveyard and to provoke a furious response from the guard dog on the other side of the gate. This affront to his dignity sent Hercules into a positive frenzy so that by the time the gatekeeper arrived, Sir Lionel himself had emerged from the house to demand what, in God's name, was going on.

'Who's there, Fulk? Why is the dog making all this racket?'

'Dunno, master. There seems to be someone outside the gate.'

'Of course there's someone outside the gate, you dolt! He rang the bloody bell!' Sir Lionel had by now hushed his own dog and I had picked up Hercules, holding him firmly under one arm. 'Ask who it is.'

I saved the man the trouble. 'It's Roger Chapman, sir. You promised me I might have a word with your groom, Walter Gurney.'

There was a sudden silence, all the more profound after the

recent cacophony. A moment or two later, the knight said slowly, 'So I did. You'd better come in.'

The man he had addressed as Fulk drew back the bolts and eased the gates open just enough for me to pass through.

I found myself in an impressively large courtyard surrounded on three sides by the house itself and its outbuildings. The guard dog was now under the control of a third man who, at a nod from Sir Lionel, led him away towards what I presumed were the kennels. But I was taking no chances: I still held fast to Hercules.

The knight and I sized one another up, then he smiled. 'Have you walked here?'

I nodded.

'You'd better come inside, then. You must be tired. It's all right, Fulk. I know this man. He won't harm me.'

The retainer grunted, closed and bolted the gates again before slouching off into the darkness. Sir Lionel led me indoors, into a great hall with elaborately carved and painted beams, the reds and blues and greens embellished here and there with gold leaf which shimmered in the firelight. On a dais at one end of the chamber a substantial meal had been set out on a long trestle table, and an armchair with a brocaded seat had been pushed back at right angles to it. The knight had obviously been disturbed in the middle of his supper. A tall, lean man who was presumably his steward (his wand of office was propped against the back of his chair) and one or two other household officials were seated at either end of the board, but there was no sign of any female company. I recollected that Sir Lionel was a bachelor.

He slapped me on the shoulder. 'Come and eat with me,' he invited. Taking my acceptance for granted, he addressed a server who had just appeared from behind the kitchen screen, carrying a covered dish. 'Robin, set another place beside mine.' He indicated Hercules, now struggling to be put down. 'And take the dog to the sculleries and find him some water and scraps.'

I wasn't sure that Hercules would go with him – he was wary of strangers – but to my surprise, he trotted off at the fellow's heels quite happily. He had evidently decided that there was nothing to be afraid of.

I took my place on the dais next to Sir Lionel and was soon tucking into baked carp in a galentyne sauce – if this was an ordinary midweek supper, then my host lived in a very high style – followed by a syllabub of pears. I couldn't help wondering why I was being treated with such unprecedented courtesy (for a common pedlar, that is) and came to the conclusion that Gilbert Foliot had imparted his quite erroneous belief that I was an agent for King Richard to his friend.

When I had finished eating, but not before, I once again broached the possibility of a private word with Walter Gurney.

'Ah!' Sir Lionel gave a wry smile. 'Unfortunately, that's impossible.' I said nothing, waiting for the explanation which I felt sure would be forthcoming. 'Walter has, unhappily, left my employ.'

'Left?'

'I'm afraid so. The day after I gave him your message, he packed his things and went, taking one of my best horses with him. As payment of wages I suppose.'

'Do you have any idea why he departed so abruptly?'

My host snorted with laughter, but he was plainly not amused.

'My dear fellow, I should have thought that was obvious, wouldn't you? Your message frightened him away.' He produced a wintry smile. 'I don't know what your business is with him. Nor do I wish to know. It seems to be a matter better kept between the two of you. But whatever it is, he was scared of meeting you.'

'He doesn't even know me,' I protested. I thought I saw an expression of surprise – or was it disbelief? – in my companion's eyes and continued irritably, 'Whatever you may have surmised, sir, that couldn't possibly have been his reason. Have you tried to find him?'

Sir Lionel looked pardonably annoyed. 'Of course I've tried to find him! I told you! He's stolen one of my best stallions, Caesar, a big, handsome black with white stockings. Part Arab. Worth far more than anything Walter Gurney was owed in wages, wizard though he was with the animals. I sent four of my men out in all directions as soon as his and the horse's disappearance was reported to me. But to no avail.'

'And you blame me for this loss.'

He laughed awkwardly. 'No, of course not. I presume you were only acting under orders and weren't to know that the man would take fright.' The blue eyes narrowed suddenly. 'Or did you suspect that this might happen?'

'No. Or I shouldn't have alerted him to my coming. I'd have arrived unannounced. Furthermore,' I went on, 'the message I had to give him was merely one of remembrance from a lady in Gloucester to whom he had once been betrothed.' I considered it more prudent to give this simpler version of events. There was no point, in the circumstances, to complicate matters.

'I see.' Sir Lionel rubbed his chin. 'An explanation which makes Walter's sudden flight seem rather strange.' My host was clearly not convinced by my story, but was too much the gentleman to question it. He smiled and once again pushed back his chair. 'In that case, we'll let the subject rest. You'll do me the honour of spending the night here? I assure you I can offer you better hospitality than you'll find at the abbey.'

'Mine will be the honour, Sir Lionel,' I answered formally, then suddenly grinned. I was beginning to like the man.

'That's settled then.' He gave me an answering smile, but I had the feeling that it was not as spontaneous as it seemed. 'Do you play chess?' he asked.

'Not at all, I'm afraid. I've watched men play, of course, but I've no knowledge of the rules of the game.'

'I believe the Du— I mean, King Richard is an excellent player,' was the seemingly irrelevant response.

'I wouldn't know, sir.'

Once again, my host gave me the leery look that implied he quite understood my discretion. Not for the first time, I silently cursed Margaret Walker and her friends, who had spread the idea throughout Bristol that I was a part of King Richard's inner circle and privy to all its confidential secrets. (In fairness, though, I have to admit that the notion had begun to take hold without the aid of their chattering tongues.)

In the end, Sir Lionel and I whiled away the hours before bedtime with a game or two of Three Men's Morris, and I entertained him with the story of how I had once taken part in a game of Nine Men's Morris played with live 'counters', of which I had been one. This amused him greatly. Halfway through our third game, however, the servant, Robin, a big, burly fellow with a broken nose and a scarred cheek, came in and whispered something in his master's ear, and this seemed to be the sign for our retirement. Sir Lionel's housekeeper was summoned and bidden to show me to the room which she had prepared for me.

'I'd be grateful,' I said, 'if I could have my dog returned. He gets restless in strange surroundings if we're parted for too long.'

'Of course.' The knight was immediately sympathetic and despatched Robin to the kitchens to seek out Hercules. While we were waiting, I told Sir Lionel of the circumstances in which the dog and I had been thrown together, and made him laugh with a description of the animal's less endearing habits. In return, he disclosed that one of his favourite hounds had recently died and that he had been so distressed by his loss that he had had poor Wolf, as he called him, buried within the manor precincts, in a vacant plot of land, close to the chapel.

By this time I had been reunited with Hercules, who greeted me ecstatically and embraced my left leg with embarrassing familiarity. After which, I said a hurried goodnight to my host and followed the housekeeper up to bed.

TEN

The housekeeper had allotted me a small room over the entrance porch of the house which she obviously considered more in keeping with my lowly status than any of the manor's larger bedchambers. In spite of this, the sheets were clean, the mattress comfortable and my 'all-night', consisting of half a loaf and a substantial beaker of ale, placed within easy reach on the ledge of a fine circular window that overlooked the courtyard below. A jug of water and a bowl had been provided for me to wash with, while a lighted candle and tinderbox stood on a handy shelf.

Hercules, as tired by his long walk as I was, leapt on to the bed and had settled down before I had even removed my boots. But as soon as I had stripped and splashed a few token drops of water about my person, I was not long in following his example. Only pausing to blow out the candle, I was asleep in minutes.

I don't know how long I slept before being roused by the dog's restless behaviour. Hercules was standing on his hind legs on the edge of the bed, his front paws placed on the window ledge, his ears pricked forward, every inch of him alert and listening.

'What is it, lad?' I whispered.

I could hear nothing, the window being fast shut, but it was plain that his acute hearing had picked up some noise that he thought it worthwhile to investigate. I slid out of bed and knelt beside him, but the thick, opaque glass prevented any sound from reaching my ears. As my eyes grew accustomed to the darkness, however, I noticed a catch at the base of the window frame, and when this was released, the window tilted on a central crossbar. Cautiously, I eased it open an inch or two, then, removing the 'all-night' to the far side of the bed, wriggled around until I was in a position to squint down into the courtyard. I was in luck. This was faintly illumined by the flickering radiance from a torch placed high on a wall beyond my range of vision, and by its feeble light I was able to make out the figures of two men standing with heads close together, obviously deep in conversation.

After a moment or two, I recognized the man on the left as Lionel Despenser, but his companion was unknown to me. I certainly hadn't met him so far during the course of my visit, but that didn't mean to say that he wasn't attached to the manor in some capacity or other. He was, however, dressed in a travelling cloak with a hood pulled up over his head and I recollected the servant, Robin, bringing a message to his master during supper and wondered if this meeting, which bore all the indications of secrecy, had anything to do with it. Even as the thought crossed my mind, there came the clop of hooves and a moment later Fulk – there was no mistaking him – led up a horse ready for the stranger to mount.

The other two continued their low-voiced, extremely earnest conversation for a short while longer, then clasped each other in a farewell embrace before the second man swung himself into the saddle with expert grace. And at exactly that moment a gust of wind must have torn at the flame of the wall torch making it flare into brightness. For five or six seconds, the courtyard was sufficiently well lit for me to see that the horse the visitor was straddling was black with four white stockings.

I closed the window gently, making no sound, and went slowly back to bed. It was a long time, however, before I fell asleep, my thoughts going round and round like a squirrel in a cage.

There was little doubt in my mind that the horse I had seen was the one Lionel Despenser had accused Walter Gurney of stealing. It was remotely possible, I supposed, that the knight might have two animals with identical markings, but I thought it extremely unlikely. Or did the beast have some additional distinguishing mark that I had missed? Somehow I didn't think so. The horse, fresh from the stables and eager to be off, had shifted, half-turning towards me, but apart from the liquid flash of his eye in the torchlight, I could remember nothing but the 'stockings'.

I awoke the next morning very little refreshed and with unresolved questions still going round in my head. Was the man I had seen Walter Gurney? Was the story of his flight a lie? And if so, why? And would Sir Lionel be on such familiar terms with his groom as to embrace him as I had seen the two men embracing the previous night? Perhaps. I recalled Jane Spicer saying that when a travelling barber had brought word of Sir Lionel Despenser seeking a new head groom, Walter had packed his things and left in a hurry. She had assumed that it was because of her hints about adopting Juliette's baby, but could there have been another motive? Had the two men known one another in the past?

A maid arrived with a ewer of hot shaving water and a message that I would find breakfast waiting for me in the kitchen when I was ready. Sir Lionel, she added in response to my enquiry, had already eaten and left the manor. He would not be returning until late.

So I was to be denied any further conversation with my host. He could have no idea that I had overlooked his meeting with his nocturnal guest – neither man had glanced up and seen me – but he was taking precautions not to be alone with me again. Or, at least, that was how it appeared to me in the suspicious state of mind I was in. But there was nothing I could do about it. Even if I hung around all day waiting for Sir Lionel's return, what could I accuse him of when, finally, we came face-to-face? Of lying to me about the horse? But to do that I should have to admit that I had spied on him the night before, a sad breach of the rules of hospitality. And it was possible, of course, that Walter Gurney had not really run away. Perhaps he had merely asked his master to concoct a plausible enough story to discourage any further visits on my part. In which case, the best thing I could do would be to go home and wait a week or two before making a further, unheralded appearance. Besides which, I had promised Adela to return as soon as possible – probably the most cogent reason of all for not delaying my departure.

It was almost dark when Hercules and I reached the Redcliffe Gate and we passed through with only minutes to spare before the curfew bell began to toll. The streets were still crowded with people shutting up shop for the night or hurrying home for a belated supper. There was a deal of noise and rowdiness along the Backs, where the foreign ships were berthed, and near the marsh in the street known as 'Little Ireland'. It was there that the Irish slavers congregated, carrying on their highly illegal trade with any good Bristolian who wished to rid him- or herself of an embarrassing or unwanted member of the family. I had myself had dealings with a couple of the Irish fraternity in the past, but in general I gave the place a wide berth.

Since Oliver Tockney's murder, I had been more than usually conscious of the evil stalking the streets after dark and so I walked purposefully and with lengthened stride, swinging my cudgel as I did so. As I crossed Bristol Bridge, I stopped to use the public latrine and found it already occupied.

'Who's that?' demanded the gentleman struggling fractiously with the laces of his codpiece. Then, as I began to fiddle with my own, a face was suddenly thrust close to mine and a voice said in relieved accents, 'Ah! Master Chapman, it's you!'

'Master Callowhill,' I acknowledged as I made out the handsome features and bulky physique of the wine merchant.

'Yes. I've been hoping for a word with you. Will you walk as far as Wine Street with me?'

'With the greatest pleasure,' I answered, wondering what on earth he could want. I had a nasty feeling he was going to remain in the latrine with me, but after a second's hesitation, he withdrew to wait for me outside. When I at last emerged from behind the wooden screens, he was standing a few feet off. Hercules, who had taken the opportunity to cock his leg against the wall of a neighbouring house, gave a low growl and tried to bite the merchant's ankles. Cursing, I grabbed the dog and tucked him firmly under my arm.

Henry Callowhill cut short my apologies and, to my astonishment, took hold of my arm as though I were one of his particular cronies, after which we completed our crossing of the bridge in silence.

I was just beginning to wonder if my companion had changed his mind about desiring a word with me when, as we started up the gentle rise of High Street, he said, 'Master Chapman, you may think this an odd question, but since our return home have you noticed any sinister strangers lurking about the streets?'

I was at first inclined to think he was jesting, but peering at his face in the light of two wall cressets above our heads, I saw to my astonishment that he was in deadly earnest. 'But Master Callowhill,' I protested, 'there are always more strangers than one can count in Bristol. For a start, it's a port, which means that there are foreign sailors. French, Bretons, Portuguese, Spanish and from a dozen or more countries you can think of. Not to mention the Irish! Then there are people who come in from the surrounding villages. It stands to reason that not all of them are honest trading folk. And there are plenty of rogues native to the town itself.'

'I know all that,' was the testy answer. 'I'm not talking about those sort of men. I can recognize a foreign sailor when I see one and I've lived in Bristol all my life. I'm able to sort the wheat from the chaff. No, I'm talking about three or four – or maybe in reality it's only one or two – big, strong, ugly-looking fellows who seem, on occasions, to be watching my house. And don't tell me I'm imagining it because Lawyer Heathersett has complained to me of exactly the same thing. So I was wondering if you had noticed them anywhere in Small Street.'

'No,' I said slowly. 'I don't remember seeing anyone of that description. All the same . . .'

'Yes?' he prompted eagerly.

'I was going to say that it might tally with one I was given by someone who witnessed the murder of poor Oliver Tockney.'

Henry Callowhill stopped in his tracks. 'Someone witnessed the murder? Then why hasn't he gone to Sergeant Manifold or one of the other sheriff's officers with this information?'

I laughed. 'Because he isn't the kind of man who would have dealings with anyone in authority. His mother has a house – a hovel – in Pit Hay Lane and he claims he saw the attack on Master Tockney from her doorway. His description of the attackers suggests a couple of ruthless but highly efficient ruffians, although apart from saying they were great big fellows, he wasn't close enough to see any other details. As for himself, he stinks to high heaven and it wouldn't surprise me to know that he's also one of the city's criminal fraternity.'

The wine merchant began walking again, but slowly, obviously lost in thought. After a moment or two, he went on: 'As I said, "great big fellows" would describe the pair I've noticed once or twice hanging around opposite my shop.'

'And you say that Lawyer Heathersett has noticed them as well?'

'Yes. He reckons there have been strangers loitering around Runnymede Court for the past week, if not longer.'

'Are you both sure they're the same men you've noticed every time? After all, there must be a number of big men in the city. I could probably name you half a dozen.'

My companion was silent for a moment or two before reluctantly admitting, 'Well, no! I wouldn't like to say that either of us is absolutely certain. But certain enough to make us both uneasy.'

'Could it be,' I persisted, 'that you and Lawyer Heathersett are imagining things in the wake of Oliver Tockney's death?'

The wine merchant hesitated. 'I suppose it's possible,' he agreed, but in a tone that showed him to be doubtful.

'And do you and Master Heathersett connect these sightings with events at Tintern Abbey?' I asked abruptly.

'You think Geoffrey and I are making them up,' Henry Callowhill accused me. 'You think we're behaving like a couple of hysterical women.'

I did, if I were honest, but I wasn't going to admit it.

We had, by this time, drawn abreast of the opening to St Mary le Port Street. I was struck with a sudden inspiration. 'Why don't you pay Master Foliot a visit and ask if he's noticed any strangers answering to your description anywhere in his vicinity?'

Henry Callowhill paused yet again, mulling over this suggestion. 'Gilbert won't be in his shop now,' he hedged. 'It's after curfew. He'll be at home in St Peter's Street.'

'I feel sure he won't mind a visit from an old friend,' I encouraged him.

Still the wine merchant hesitated. 'Will you come with me?' he asked after further cogitation.

I could see his motive for the invitation. Henry Callowhill was a man who liked to be thought well of by everyone, but particularly by someone such as the goldsmith, whom he plainly revered and whose good opinion he set much store by. Why this should be so I had no idea, for in terms of wealth and social standing there was little to choose between them. Nevertheless, my companion was obviously lacking in the self-confidence his friend enjoyed and was afraid of appearing a fool in the other man's eyes. If I were with him he could, if he were clever enough, make it seem as if I was the one plagued by silly fancies. He could say with perfect truth that I was the one who had proposed the visit.

I thought things over, but for less time than it takes to tell, then nodded. 'Yes, I'll come with you,' I agreed.

The goldsmith's opinion mattered nothing to me. He was welcome to think me a fool if he liked, but somehow I didn't think he would. He struck me as a shrewd man who regarded the world with a sapient eye and was perfectly well aware of his many friends' faults and foibles. Indeed, during the days we had all spent together in Wales I had, on occasions, caught him looking at his companions with something akin to barely concealed intolerance at best, outright contempt at worst. If I were honest, I wasn't sure that I really liked the goldsmith, and yet there was something about him that commanded my admiration: a decisiveness, an ability to make the best of any situation, but with, deep down, a sense of the futility of life. I felt he was all too aware of the stupidity of hopes and dreams in the short span of time allotted to us, but that wasn't going to stop him trying to fulfil his aspirations. Whatever they were.

Henry Callowhill and I turned into St Mary le Port Street much to the annoyance of Hercules who, having sensed that we were on the road home, deeply resented this diversion. He began to snuffle and whine, wriggling and squirming beneath my arm in an effort to regain his freedom.

'Quiet!' I commanded him. He licked my face.

The shops on either side of us were now boarded up, but candle- and lamplight glowed through the chinks of the shutters in the upper storeys. Only one was shrouded in complete darkness and that was the goldsmith's.

'Doesn't it worry Master Foliot to leave his wares unattended at night, in an empty building?' I asked as we drew to a halt and surveyed the house from the opposite side of the street.

'Oh, as to that,' my companion replied, 'I believe he had a special underground strong room built – in addition, that is, to the cellars – before he moved to St Peter's Street. The entrance and how to open it is known only to him.'

'And to the workmen who made it,' I added.

'Yes, yes, of course. But as I understand it, they weren't local men. Not from the town, at least. They were men of that Keynsham friend of Gilbert's, Sir Lionel Despenser.'

'Ah!' I said. 'Him! I slept at his house last night.'

'You know Sir Lionel?' The wine merchant was plainly curious. For a pedlar, I must seem to him to know a great many people who should be far above my reach. On the other hand, if he shared the goldsmith's mistaken belief that I was in the king's employ his curiosity extended only to finding out what my business could be with the knight. I had no intention of disappointing him.

'I know nothing of Sir Lionel himself. I went to Keynsham merely to deliver a message to his head groom, Walter Gurney, from a lady of his acquaintance in Gloucester. Unfortunately, I got there only to discover that Master Gurney had run away, at the same time stealing one of Sir Lionel's most valuable horses.'

'How very odd!' Henry Callowhill made to walk on, then stopped again beneath an overhead torch, wrinkling his brow. 'You say this man's name was Gurney?'

'Walter Gurney, yes. Why?'

The brow wrinkled even more. 'I don't really know. But there's

something about the coupling of the two names . . . Despenser
. . . Gurney . . .' There was a pause while the merchant wrestled
with his thoughts. In the end, however, he shook his head. 'No,
it's no good. Somehow or another I feel there is a connection,
but for the life of me I can't remember what it is. Perhaps it's
just in my imagination.'

'Perhaps,' I agreed.

We moved on at last, and not before time. It had grown very
chilly standing there in the street. I could feel Hercules shivering.
But we had hardly taken three steps when the wine merchant
stopped yet again, grasping my arm. 'Somebody's up there! In
the upper-floor room over the shop. I'm sure I saw a flicker of
light through a chink in the shutters.'

I stared hard at the first-storey window, but could see nothing.
Then I walked across the cobbles, subjecting the whole front of
the house to close scrutiny. Hercules whined suddenly and his
ears went up.

'What's the matter?' I hissed.

He gave a little bark and his whole body tensed, but a moment
later, a cat sauntered out of the narrow alleyway between the
goldsmith's shop and its neighbour. I was caught unawares and,
before I could stop him, Hercules, breathing fire and slaughter,
had wriggled free of my grasp and hurled himself in the direction
of the unsuspecting interloper who dived back into the alleyway
and was soon swallowed up by the shadows.

Cursing fluently, I made a lunge at the dog, just managing to
grab him at the expense of a twisted ankle and a grazed hand.
He protested violently, but I was angry enough to clip him across
the nose, for which indignity he tried first to bite me before
finally settling down again under my arm, but emitting a series
of little growls just to let me know of his displeasure.

'There's no one there,' I said, returning to Henry Callowhill.
'You probably saw a reflection of the torchlight.'

He laughed shortly. 'Even if there was someone there, he isn't
going to show himself now after all that commotion.'

'There was no one there, I tell you. It was your imagination.'
I felt certain that I was right and that it had been nothing more
than a trick of the light.

We proceeded on up the street and into St Peter's Street, where the bells of St Peter's Church were just beginning to toll for Vespers.

There were lights in the ground-floor windows of Gilbert Foliot's imposing house and the wall cressets had been lit. Henry Callowhill raised his hand and knocked on the door, which was answered after a brief delay by the goldsmith's housekeeper, Mistress Margery Dawes, who also acted as a companion to Ursula. As I think I mentioned somewhere earlier, she was a cousin of sorts to Lawyer Heathersett and had his slightly protuberant eyes, although that was the only real likeness. She was a big, full-bosomed creature, not in the first flush of youth, but not old enough, either, to have lost completely the romantic yearnings of her girlhood. It was generally accepted that she had connived at the secret meetings between Ursula and young Peter Noakes, even if she had not actively encouraged them.

'Yes?' she queried, peering at us short-sightedly.

'Who is it, Margery?' asked Gibert Foliot, his face suddenly appearing over her shoulder. It registered surprise. 'My dear Henry! And Master Chapman! This is an honour indeed. Pray come in.'

Mistress Dawes, having been politely but firmly shouldered aside, the goldsmith held the door wide as we stepped into the splendid hall with its painted beams and carved figureheads, while I reminded myself to act as though this were my first visit. I doubted very much that Ursula had mentioned my earlier one to her father.

We followed our host into the same parlour that I had seen before, but this time a fire had been lit on the hearth and the rocking chair removed from the dais to stand beside it. Another armchair had also been introduced into the room, directly facing it, while between them stood a small table bearing a flask of what was undoubtedly wine and two very fine Venetian goblets. The goldsmith had obviously been entertaining.

He must have followed my gaze and said calmly, addressing himself to his friend, 'A good job you didn't come earlier, Henry, or I couldn't have received you.' He waved a casual hand at the chairs and table. 'I'm trying my best to persuade a certain gentleman to buy an extremely expensive gold necklace for his wife's birthday – so far, I must admit, without any luck. This

was a private visit to display the goods without fear of interruption, and I was hoping some of my best malmsey might
have done the trick. But, alas, he's still hesitating . . . Now,
what can I do for you and Master Chapman? If it's about your
wine bill . . .'

'No, no!' Henry Callowhill was dismissive as though money
were of no importance. 'The thing is . . .' He paused, reluctant
to continue, feeling, I could see, a little foolish.

'Yes?' Master Foliot raised his finely marked eyebrows.

The wine merchant glanced imploringly in my direction and,
taking pity on him, I explained the situation.

For a moment our host stared blankly, then he laughed and
indicated that we should both sit down, waving Master Callowhill
to the rocking chair and himself taking the armir opposite. That
left me to pull out a stool from under the table, demonstrating
that however wary of me he might be, and however friendly he
might appear on the surface, there was still a social distinction
between us.

'Now, let me understand this, Henry,' he said, leaning forward
with his elbows on his knees, 'you and Lawyer Heathersett think
you're being watched by two or more bravos whose descriptions,
if you'll pardon my saying so, could be that of at least a hundred
men in this town. Let's face it, Bristol harbours as pretty a set
of rogues as any other city in the kingdom and they are frequently
to be met with in the streets. Why should you and Geoffrey feel
yourself under any particular threat?'

'You haven't seen anyone in particular, then, loitering around
hereabouts?'

'No. Nor do I expect to. Henry, you are allowing your
imagination to get the better of you. Geoffrey also. Why, I'm
not sure. Has it to do with the pedlar's murder?'

His friend looked a little hangdog. 'I daresay,' he admitted.
'But these men . . . their description does tally with that of the
two men who killed Oliver Tockney.'

Up went the eyebrows again. 'I wasn't aware we had a description of Tockney's murderers. Or even that we knew there were two.'

I said quietly, 'I've spoken to a fellow who witnessed the
attack. A beggar – or perhaps worse – whose mother lives in Pit
Hay Lane.'

'Indeed? And have you informed the necessary authorities of this?'

'No one's interested. Oliver Tockney's dead and buried. Moreover, he was a stranger, not one of our own.'

The goldsmith pursed his lips. 'That's true. Very true. You'd doubtless be wasting your time.' He turned once more to Henry Callowhill. 'And having heard Master Chapman's tale, you're now convinced that the same men are the ones you say are watching you. Does Geoffrey agree?'

'He doesn't know. Master Chapman's only just told me the story.'

'And what do you think, Roger?'

The sudden familiarity threw me somewhat. 'I – I don't know,' I stammered.

'Well, I do.' The goldsmith rose and took up a stance with his back to the fire, raising his padded tunic slightly and rubbing his buttocks as they absorbed the welcome heat. 'It's all in your mind, Henry. Yours and Geoffrey's. What with young Noakes's death at Tintern and now poor Tockney's murder, you've allowed things to breed ill fancies until you're jumping at your own shadows and seeing danger where none exists. Although why is a mystery to me. Neither event had anything to do with either of you. So pull yourself together, man! And stop listening to Heathersett. He's an old woman at the best of times.'

'You're right.' Henry Callowhill spoke humbly, like a small boy who'd just been chastened by a schoolmaster. 'I suppose,' he added in extenuation, 'the danger we found ourselves in, in Wales, the rebellion, upset me. I – I assume all's safe now?'

'Of course it is!' The goldsmith spoke scathingly. 'What else did you expect with King Richard at the helm? A soldier of his experience, who's been fighting from his earliest years! And the latest information is that Henry Tudor is sailing back to Brittany with his tail between his legs. It seems he's found it impossible to land anywhere along the south coast of England. So you may rest easy in your bed, Henry. No bogey man is coming to get you.'

The wine merchant flushed scarlet and got to his feet with what dignity he could muster. It was plain that his host had gone a step too far. 'Thank you for your advice, Gilbert,' he said quietly. 'Master Chapman and I will be leaving now.'

'Henry!' The goldsmith gave a rueful grin and stretched out a hand. 'My cursed tongue! I'm sorry.'

His friend inclined his head. 'Your apology is accepted. All the same, it's after curfew and Roger and I must be going. I bid you goodnight.'

And so we left, the two men apparently reconciled. But I had a feeling that the goldsmith's overhasty words, his scornful tone, would not easily be forgotten by his friend.

ELEVEN

Hercules and I accompanied the wine merchant as far as his house in Wine Street and said goodnight to him at his front door. He had been rather quiet during our walk, but roused himself from his abstraction to thank me for my company.

'It's been my privilege, sir,' I bowed.

He raised his hand to knock for admittance, but hung on his heel for a moment. 'Gilbert can be a little brusque at times,' he said, almost apologetically. 'But he's a good friend. He has some peculiar ideas, but there's not a more loyal man in the whole of the West Country than him.'

I made no reply. Indeed, I wasn't at all sure what Henry Callowhill meant by the remark. It seemed to refute some accusation that had not been made, at least not by me. Nor by anybody else as far as I knew. So I let it go and, instead, pressed for an answer to a question which had been bothering me. 'Master Callowhill, you said earlier that you thought there was some connection between the names of Despenser and Gurney. Have you, by any chance, recollected what it is?'

He stared at me for a few seconds, a little bemused by this sudden change of topic, then shook his head. 'No. No, I'm afraid not.'

'But you believe there is one?'

'Well . . . Perhaps "believe" would be too strong a word. It was just a momentary feeling, that's all.'

I hesitated before asking, 'If you should remember, will you let me know?'

He looked faintly surprised, but nodded. 'Certainly if you think it important. Is it?'

'I've no idea,' I replied truthfully. 'Probably not. But it might be.'

'Then I promise.' He extended his right hand, a great conde-scension, and grasped mine. 'Goodnight again, Master Chapman. And, once more, thank you.'

His knock was answered almost immediately by a young servant girl, the candle- and lamplight spilling out into the street and gilding the piles of rubbish overflowing from the central drain and awaiting tomorrow's muckrakers. The wine merchant gave me a final nod before the door was closed behind him.

I glanced down at the patiently waiting Hercules. He was by now too tired even to protest at all these delays. I stooped and picked him up, holding him under my left arm and grasping my cudgel firmly in my right. Both suddenly seemed to weigh a ton and my back was aching. All the same, I wasn't quite ready to give up yet. 'Sorry, lad,' I whispered. 'I just want to go back to St Mary le Port Street. I promise you we won't be long. I'm as anxious to get home as you are.'

He gave a half-hearted growl, but couldn't be bothered to register his displeasure more forcefully.

The streets were far less crowded than they had been, those people who were still abroad being, for the most part, cosily ensconced in their favourite ale-houses, the remainder tucked up safely by their firesides. Of course that meant that those people I did encounter were the more likely to be on some nefarious business of their own, but it was still too early for the real rogues to be up and doing, and I retraced my steps to St Mary le Port Street scornful of any lurking danger.

Once again, I stopped opposite the goldsmith's shop, where I stood looking at it closely for several minutes, then crossed the road and entered the alleyway between it and the bakery next door. It was pitch black here and I had to pause while my eyes grew accustomed to the darkness. Eventually, however, I was able to make out a door which must lead into the back of the ground-floor living-quarters – kitchen, scullery, counting-house

– and beyond that a small yard with a bedraggled-looking tree and a few sad bushes just visible over the top of a wall. There was a gate which gave access to it – an important factor as far as I was concerned for, a moment later, I heard a key rattle in the lock of the door.

The lock, fortunately, seemed to be somewhat rusty, judging by the fact that its wards refused to turn easily. This gave me time to push wide the gate into the yard and conceal myself and Hercules behind one of the bushes before the door finally opened. Someone stepped into the alleyway, cursing softly and the dog gave a little whimper which I hushed, waiting to find out in which direction the unseen interloper would go. He trod quietly, and it was only because his foot disturbed a loose stone that I realized he was heading towards St Mary le Port Street. I emerged from the yard just in time to see him disappear around the corner of the bakery, turning left and making for the junction with High Street.

In a few swift strides I, too, had reached the corner and was staring after the man as he proceeded on his way, every now and then glancing back over one shoulder to ensure that he was being neither followed nor observed. I had drawn back into the shadows cast by the goldsmith's shop, which appeared to afford sufficient protection.

I stared after the retreating figure and suddenly drew a sharp breath. Hercules gave an indignant yelp as he was crushed against my ribs, but I took no notice. Without any justification whatso-ever, I was convinced that I had seen the man before, last night in the courtyard of the Despenser manor, talking to Sir Lionel. Walter Gurney? Maybe. Or then again, maybe not. But whoever the man was, and whatever his name, I felt sure that it was the same person. Why I was so certain I had no idea, but there was something about the shape of his back, his height, the way he moved that was instantly familiar.

Cautiously, I followed him.

I reckoned that at the end of the street he was bound to turn right, into the heart of the town. He must have left the horse tethered somewhere, or else at the livery stable in Bell Lane. Indeed, so certain was I of this, that I had begun to cross the road in anticipation of his move when, to my astonishment, he swung sharply left again, towards Bristol Bridge and the Backs.

'Now where is he going?' I muttered in Hercules's ear, before it occurred to me that the man could just as easily have left his mount at one of the ale-houses in Redcliffe as elsewhere.

But at the bottom of High Street, he made no attempt to cross the bridge, instead walking slowly the length of the quay, looking up at the ships berthed alongside. Suddenly, by one particular ship, he stopped and again looked round, as though something, some noise or movement, had made him suspicious. Hurriedly, I drew back into the shadow of one of the cranes, praying that Hercules would not choose that particular moment to register a further protest at the long delay in getting home. I felt him quiver, but he remained silent, some of my tension obviously communicating itself to him.

After several moments, the stranger seemed satisfied. He turned his head away and gave vent to a piercing whistle. Almost immediately, as though he had been waiting for the signal, a sailor appeared, leaning over the side of the ship and peering down at the wharf. My quarry stepped deliberately into the light of a lamp hanging from the bow, raising a hand, and the sailor nodded. Within a minute or two, he had lowered the gangplank which the stranger mounted before vanishing below deck. The gangplank was then withdrawn.

It had all happened so quickly and so unexpectedly that I was left standing in the shadow of the crane, completely bewildered. Was the man fleeing the country? Or was he simply a foreigner returning to his home? If the latter, then he was not Walter Gurney. If the former, why this precipitate flight? Surely not because of my message that I wished to speak to him. That made no sense. Even if he had guessed I was the emissary of Jane Spicer, all he had to do was make it plain that he had no interest either in her or in returning to Gloucester and that would have been that. I couldn't have forced him.

And there was another, more important question. If this man were indeed the one I had seen last night in the courtyard of the Despenser manor, what had he been doing in Gilbert Foliot's old house? He had had a key, which suggested that the goldsmith knew him, or at least knew of him as a friend of his friend, and had been willing to give him access to the shop . . .

I was suddenly conscious of how quiet and still everything

was. Faintly, in the distance, I could hear singing from one of the dockside taverns, but the wharf itself seemed deserted, eerily silent, striped with shadows of the warehouses and cranes. It was long past curfew now and I was uncomfortably aware of my proximity to 'Little Ireland'.

I decided that it was high time I went home.

'I wasn't expecting you,' Adela said as I walked into the kitchen. 'You said you might be away two nights, and as curfew sounded over an hour ago, I naturally thought . . .' Her voice tailed away and she smiled a little guiltily. 'Not that I'm not pleased to see you.' She came over and kissed me warmly before going on, 'It's just . . . well . . . Richard's here.' She hurriedly placed a finger on my lips. 'Before you say anything hasty and which you might regret later, I didn't invite him. He arrived just as the children and I were sitting down to supper.' Of course he did! That man had a nose for Adela's cooking that would have put a greyhound to shame. 'So naturally I felt I must ask him to join us. He has no one, Roger. He gets very lonely.'

I snorted derisively. 'Then perhaps he should find a good woman to look after him. I resent sharing my wife.' I seized her roughly around the waist and returned her kiss with interest.

She laughed and traced the curve of my cheek with her forefinger. 'You've no reason in the world to be jealous,' she said.

I knew I hadn't. That didn't stop me, however, from indulging in a little childish petulance.

'Where is he?' I asked.

'In the parlour, playing at fivestones with the children.'

My parlour! My children!

Adela smiled at the expression on my face and kissed me again. 'Someone's playing with your toys, is that it? Without your permission.' I flushed, feeling stupid, and she went on, 'Sit down at the table and I'll heat up the pottage for you. Did you manage to speak to this Walter Gurney?'

I sank down thankfully on a stool and began pulling off my boots. Hercules started to bark, nosing his bowls and generally indicating that he, too, was in need of attention. So while my wife bustled about, attending to my wants and his, I gave her a brief history of my visit to Keynsham and of all that happened during the past hour or so since my return home.

'As a matter of fact,' I concluded, 'I'm glad Richard is here. There are some questions I want to ask him.'

Adela stirred the pottage as it began to bubble in its pot over the fire. 'In that case, you'll be pleased to see one another,' she said. 'He came here hoping for a word with you.'

I was immediately suspicious. 'Now what does he want? When that man starts to pry, it usually means there's trouble brewing.'

My wife ignored this and put down a plate of offal scraps for Hercules, who fell on them with all the ravening hunger of a dog who has never had a decent meal in his life. I drew up my stool to the table, stretching and easing my stockinged toes, and waited for my supper.

Adela sat opposite me while the pottage came back to the boil and questioned me about the events of the evening. Who did I think it was in the goldsmith's old house? Why had I not returned and informed Master Foliot of what I had seen? What did I think the stranger could possibly have been up to? Where did I think he was going onboard that ship?

Thankfully, at this point, the stew began to bubble, demanding her attention. And, once a steaming bowlful was placed in front of me, I was able to stuff my mouth too full to give her any coherent answer. Hercules, having wolfed down his portion, came across to see what he might wheedle out of me. He received short shrift.

I had just asked for a second bowlful when Richard walked into the kitchen. 'The children are tired of beating me at five-stones,' he said, 'and have gone upstairs about their own . . .' He broke off, suddenly becoming aware of my presence. 'Roger!' He even managed to sound faintly pleased to see me. 'You're back! Good! I've been wanting to speak to you.'

'So Adela tells me. And I wish to have a word with you, so sit down and we can talk while I eat.'

Adela, to my great annoyance, immediately fetched him a beaker of ale from the barrel in the corner, but as she also brought one for me, I stifled the impulse to utter the acid comment which was hovering on the tip of my tongue and started on my second helping of pottage.

Richard waited until I had swallowed my first mouthful before enquiring, 'Well? What is it you wish to say?'

'There are three ships berthed at the wharf by the bridge. Do you happen to know whereabouts they're from?'

'Doesn't the Quay Master know?'

'I haven't asked him.'

I could see that this answer annoyed my companion – he went red with suppressed irritation – and that he was longing to tell me to consult the proper authority, not bother an important and busy man like himself. But he wanted something from me in return and was afraid that if he angered me, I would refuse my help.

He sipped his ale. 'Let me see,' he said, stroking his chin, a silly, pompous habit he seemed to have acquired lately. 'There was a ship arrived yesterday morning from Bordeaux. Cargo wine, I think. I believe that's anchored along the Backs. But as for the other two – you mentioned three ships? – then I'm sorry, I can't help you. Although . . . Wait! Now I come to think of it, someone did mention that a Breton ship had been berthed there for several days and wondered what it was waiting for because it had been unloaded and reloaded on the day of its arrival.'

'A Breton ship,' I muttered, laying down my spoon and wiping my mouth on the back of my hand.

There was silence for a few moments, except for the children thundering overhead. Then Richard snapped, 'Are you going to tell me what this is all about? Plainly you find this information disturbing. I should like to know why.'

So, between mouthfuls of pottage, I told him briefly of my evening's adventures, but without laying too much stress on the name of Gilbert Foliot.

'And now,' I said, 'I should like to hear what it is you want to say to me.'

Richard hesitated, obviously mulling over what I had told him. Then, after a moment or two's reflection, he nodded. 'Very well! A friend of His Worship the Mayor – what I'm telling you is in the strictest confidence – returned from London this morning. Whilst there, he was told, or heard a rumour, I'm not sure which, that an old friend of yours has secretly been sent here on account of some treason or other which may be brewing in the city. As you can imagine, His Worship is deeply worried by this information.'

'What old friend of mine?'

'That little man who worked for the king when he was Duke of Gloucester. One of his spies, I should imagine. And every time he appears, you seem to vanish with him to London.'

'Timothy Plummer,' I said grimly. 'And he's the King's Spymaster General. Well,' I added with more than usual determination, 'if he thinks he's haling me off anywhere this time, he will have to think again. I'm not going.' Adela was looking unhappy, so I stretched out a hand and squeezed one of hers reassuringly. She managed an unconvincing smile.

Richard shook his head. 'No,' he corrected me, 'I don't think he's here to look for you. Not on this occasion. The understanding of His Worship's friend was that Master . . . Plummer, did you call him?' I nodded. 'That Master Plummer is in the city, but probably in disguise. Now, mind you, Roger, the Mayor has impressed upon me that all this is most secret! His friend has no right to this information and it could mean serious trouble for both him and his informant if it were to be made public. Suspicions must not be aroused. Do you understand me?'

'Perfectly,' I said. 'In that case, why are you telling me? Adela, too?'

My wife grimaced mockingly. 'Me, especially, when it's well known that women are notoriously unable to hold their tongues.'

Richard's face softened as he looked at her. 'I'd trust you, Adela, with my life.' He turned back to me and his features hardened again. 'The mayor and sheriff want your help, Roger. You are the only person who knows this Timothy Plummer well. If it's true he's in disguise, you may be able to penetrate it. If that should happen, then naturally you would be curious as to what he's doing here. Who is he watching? What does he suspect?'

'What if, supposing he tells me, he enjoins me to strict secrecy, as you have done?'

Richard regarded me straitly. 'I feel certain you could find a way round that.'

The implication, of course, was that I was a devious, conniving bastard. It didn't make me feel any more charitable towards my uninvited guest.

'The situation may not arise,' I said. 'I may not recognize Timothy. Or the whole story may be a bag of moonshine. However, if there should be a grain of truth in it, if treason is being hatched in this city, then I would advise you to have that Breton cargo ship searched without delay. Unless, that is, it has already set sail on the evening tide.'

Richard looked startled. 'Why? What has the Breton ship . . .?' He broke off, obviously furious with himself and his own stupidity. 'You think the man you saw boarding her this evening might be a Tudor agent?'

'It's possible. Yet Bristol has always been deeply loyal to the Yorkist cause. I've never heard any Lancastrian sympathies expressed.'

Even as the words left my mouth, I could have given his answer myself.

'But you wouldn't, would you? Not to you of all people.' Richard drained his beaker, frowning. 'Yet what would anyone be plotting here? Very well, we know that Henry Tudor with his Breton mercenaries has been sailing off the south coast for the past week or so, trying to get a foothold on land and that he has now returned to Brittany, disappointed. But he wouldn't have chosen Bristol as a landing place, not with the River Avon to negotiate before he reaches harbour. Any seaman will tell you that the Avon with its hidden rocks is a treacherous beast.'

I finished my ale and Adela fetched us both more.

'All the same,' I pressed, 'I'd have that Breton ship searched immediately. Unless, as I said earlier, she's already sailed on this evening's tide.'

'Her captain won't have risked sailing in the dark,' Richard said positively.

'He might,' I argued. 'It would depend on how desperate he is to get his additional "cargo" away.'

'The man you followed?'

'Yes.'

Richard rose reluctantly to his feet, swallowing his ale in just two gulps. 'I'd better be off,' he said.

Adela fetched his cloak and hat and saw him to the door. Then she came back and sat down again at the kitchen table. 'What is this all about, Roger?' she asked me.

I shrugged. 'I've no more idea than you have, sweetheart.'

'Is that the truth? You haven't . . . You haven't already spoken to Master Plummer?'

I raised one of her hands and kissed it. Adela looked suitably surprised at this wholly uncharacteristic gesture. 'I promise you,' I said, 'that I had no more idea of Timothy being in Bristol than you had. Nor do I know what it is he wants here. Not me, that's for certain; not if he's skulking around in disguise.' I grinned. 'I wonder what he's pretending to be this time.' I thought for a moment, then went on: 'But I should guess that his presence here – if, that is, the rumour is true and he really is in the city – might have something to do with the man I saw.'

'You suspect a conspiracy? On behalf of Henry Tudor?'

I bit my lip. 'I can think of no other explanation. All the same, it doesn't make sense. What Richard says is true. No invasion fleet would have risked sailing up the Avon, and if troops had landed at the river's mouth, the city would have had ample warning to shut and bar the gates against them. No, if the man I followed is working for the Tudor, then he's here for an entirely different reason.'

Adela still looked worried. 'You say Bristol is notoriously Yorkist in sympathy and I know it to be a fact. But that was in the past when Edward was king. Is there the same loyalty, do you think, to King Richard? Especially since the rumours of his nephews' deaths?'

I frowned. She had a point, I had to admit. Adherents of the House of York had just risen in rebellion against Richard's assumption of the crown, and the heart of the revolt had been here, in the south and west. Nevertheless, I still felt sure that if there were indeed a conspiracy in the city it had nothing to do with the landing and invasion of a Tudor force. I had no real reason for this certainty, but I had, over the years, learned to trust my instincts and deliberately closed my mind against the idea that they might be wrong.

Adela changed the subject for one nearer her heart. 'Roger, this Walter Gurney! You say you were unable to speak to him. That he had run away. There's no chance then that he could return to Gloucester and offer to marry the woman you mentioned?'

'Jane Spicer? No.' I shook my head wearily. 'Whether he really has run away or whether he's hiding somewhere on the Despenser manor makes no difference. He's made it plain that he has no intention of going home.'

My wife took a deep breath. 'But in that case what will happen when . . .?'

I knew what she was going to ask. A question to which, as yet, I had no ready answer, and it was with a feeling of enormous relief that I welcomed the children as they suddenly burst into the kitchen with cries of, 'We didn't know you were home!' followed inevitably by, 'What have you brought us?'

Fortunately for my already tarnished reputation, I had had the forethought to purchase some sweetmeats – sugared violets and rose petals – before finally quitting Keynsham. They were, by now, a somewhat sorry, sticky mess, wrapped as they had been in a scrap of rag-paper and thrust into the depths of my pouch, but Elizabeth and the boys seemed not to notice as they devoured them in less time than it takes to tell. They made no comment on Richard's disappearance except to say that they had all beaten him at fivestones, an abstention that pleased me greatly. Nor, I noticed, did they refer to him as 'uncle' any more, another cause for satisfaction. I had a sneaking suspicion that this might be Adela's doing, but I didn't enquire too closely. I preferred to believe that it was the children's own choice.

Adela had not long sent them off to bed – after a Herculean tussle to make Adam wash his face and hands, an act he considered altogether unnecessary – and we had retired to the greater comfort of the parlour, when a knock on the street door heralded the return of Richard Manifold.

'The Breton ship has been searched,' he announced bluntly, dispensing with the courtesy of greetings, 'and there's no one onboard the captain can't account for.' Of course there wasn't, not if he was being handsomely paid for conveying his illicit passenger safely back to Brittany. 'Nor,' Richard continued, 'could we find anyone stowed away in any part of the ship. All right,' he added grimly, noting the expression on my face, 'if the man you saw is still aboard, then he's probably disguised as a member of the crew. But without knowing what he looks like, we can't accuse him. The sheriff wants to know if there is the slightest chance that you might recognize him.'

'No,' I said. 'Not to be certain. When's the ship sailing?'

'Tomorrow morning, on the first tide.'

'Well . . .' I was beginning doubtfully, but Adela cut me short.

'No,' she said, addressing Richard Manifold, a determined set to her mouth. 'Roger is not getting embroiled in this. I scent danger, and he's been in enough of that this past spring and summer.' She turned to me. 'I forbid you to have anything more to do with this affair.'

Our guest snorted with laughter. 'He won't be able to help himself, my dear. When have you ever known your husband to keep that long nose of his out of any trouble that's going? It's against his nature. Roger, if you would only . . .'

I suddenly felt extraordinarily weary. There were a number of queries that needed answering, not least what was the connection – if, indeed, there was one – between the man I had followed and Gilbert Foliot? How did the former come to have a key to the goldsmith's old house over and behind the shop? Why . . .? But here my mind balked at any more questions. I had not completely got over my illness of the summer, and although, in a general way, I had recovered my health and strength, there were still times when the lassitude would reassert itself.

'I'm sorry, Richard,' I smiled, 'but you heard Adela. This seems to me like an affair of state, and therefore none of my business. Tender my apologies to the sheriff, but tell him I would be unable to identify this man. I didn't really see his face.'

Richard looked sceptical, but he knew when he was beaten. Once Adela had ranged herself on my side, there was nothing more to be said. When, finally, he had gone, after one last half-hearted attempt at persuasion, I put my arms about her and kissed her lingeringly.

She was having none of that. 'Bed,' she said firmly, 'but to sleep. You're worn out.'

She was right. I was snoring almost as soon as my head touched the pillow. I don't know how much later it was when I felt her hand shaking my shoulder.

'Wake up, Roger,' Adela hissed in my ear. 'There's someone downstairs. Someone's trying to get into the house.'

TWELVE

I heaved myself into a sitting position, knuckling my eyes like a child.

'I can't hear anything,' I mumbled.

Adela shook my arm. 'Listen!' she urged.

I forced myself awake, resisting the temptation to collapse back on my pillow and be engulfed once more in sleep. After a moment or two, I could hear faint sounds as though someone, somewhere, were rattling a shutter. Sleep went flying. Immediately, I was out of bed, pulling on my shirt and reaching for my cudgel, my trusty 'Plymouth Cloak', which I always kept standing in one corner. As I moved towards the door, it opened and a small figure in a nightshirt stood on the threshold.

'Noises downstairs,' announced Adam.

'I know.' I patted his head. 'Go back to bed.'

He shook his head. 'I'm coming, too.' He produced his right hand from behind his back. 'I've got my knife.'

'Sweetheart, leave this to your father,' Adela ordered, alarm bringing her swiftly to my side as she made a grab for her younger son.

Adam was too quick for her, moving halfway down the stairs before she could reach him. 'I'm a man now,' he insisted. 'I have a knife.'

'I said it was a mistake to let him keep it,' Adela whispered accusingly.

'Well, it's done now,' I hissed in return, guilt making me snappish. 'And this is no time to start an argument.' I followed Adam downstairs, but at the bottom caught him by the tail of his nightshirt, pushing him behind me. 'Stay here,' I ordered, 'and don't move until I call you.' Needless to say, I had no intention of calling him. 'I'm just going to look around.'

He gave me one of those white-eyed looks, as much as to say that he knew that I was lying, but the thick darkness seemed to have subdued him a little and he nodded, sitting down on the bottom step.

I stood still, listening carefully. The noises had stopped for the moment and, except for those small creaks and groans which every house makes at night, as beams settle and doorposts shrink, all was as silent as the grave. Then they began again, and I located them as coming from the kitchen.

Grasping my cudgel even more tightly, I tiptoed forward, pausing in the open doorway to let my eyes become accustomed to the gloom. I could see no one ahead of me, but was there someone lurking behind the door, waiting to attack if I ventured further in? Carefully, with my left hand, I eased the door open as wide as it would go, but it met with no obstruction. The kitchen was empty – except for Hercules who, I realized suddenly, was sitting as still as a statue beneath the window, head raised and teeth bared, waiting for the would-be intruder to finish sawing through a third slat of one of the shutters. Two had already been removed and the gap was now almost wide enough for a hand and arm to reach in and lift the wooden crossbar that held them closed.

I trod silently across and patted his head, marvelling at the intelligence which had prompted him to try to catch the thief instead of raising the alarm and frightening the man away. I ranged myself alongside the dog, hardly daring to breathe . . .

There was a sudden clatter loud enough to wake the dead. Adam, tired of doing as he was told and emboldened by the apparent lack of action, had followed me into the kitchen to find out what was going on. It was only a day or two since Adela, disgusted by the sodden mess that had been Hercules's wooden drinking bowl, had provided the animal with a pottery one, and it was this that my son had accidentally kicked halfway across the floor. Hercules, thinking we were being attacked in the rear, began to bark at the top of his voice, scaring Adam who then began to yell. Furiously, I shouted at them both to be quiet and Adela, frightened half out of her wits by the noise, came running downstairs, calling out to know what was the matter.

The would-be intruder fled. Naturally!

Spitting oaths that even I didn't know I knew, I ran to the street door and flung it open, but Small Street was empty. The rats, busy scavenging among the refuse of the central drain, were the only sign of life. I was just about to step outside to investigate further, when the recollection that I was barefoot and wearing nothing but a shirt sent me hastily back indoors.

Adela had by now managed to quieten both the dog and our son, but Elizabeth and Nicholas, roused by all the commotion, had arrived in the kitchen to find out what was going on. They were interestedly inspecting the damaged shutter and at the same time warding off the pangs of night hunger by devouring two of the meat and dried plum pasties which Adela had made specially for my dinner the following day. (My favourites.) Even as I watched, outraged, Adam, his tears dried, helped himself to the last two from the plate on the table, one of which he gave to Hercules. Speechlessly, I surveyed them all.

Adela began to laugh.

'This could only have happened to us,' I stormed at my wife the following morning. 'There is no discipline in this house!'

I was not feeling my best. I had been forced, for reasons of safety, to spend the rest of the night in the kitchen, and although I had dragged one of the armchairs in from the parlour, even piled with cushions it had not been conducive to sleep. I was tired, cross and out of sorts.

The children, scoffing bowls of porridge at the table, kept giving me cautious, sidelong glances, but seemed undisturbed by my ranting. For this, their mother's faintly amused reaction to my behaviour was largely responsible. They always took their cue from her.

'Sit down and eat your breakfast,' Adela advised, placing a fried bacon collop in front of me. 'You can go round to John Carpenter's as soon as you've finished. He'll put things to rights in no time.' She added, 'You shouldn't really be having meat on a Friday, so keep quiet about it, but I thought you deserved a special treat.'

'Is that all you have to say?' I demanded angrily, but nevertheless wiping my knife on the hem of my tunic before attacking the bacon ravenously. 'Doesn't it worry you that someone tried to break into this house last night?'

'Of course it worries me,' was the indignant reply. 'But you know what the streets of this city are like at night. Full of thieves and villains. If I'm truthful, it surprises me that no one has attempted to rob us until now. With your growing reputation as someone close to the king – thanks largely to Margaret and her precious friends – everyone mistakenly imagines we're a lot richer than we are.'

I grunted, but said nothing. It was the most reasonable explanation of what had happened and yet it didn't satisfy me. I had no idea why not, so judged it better to keep my doubts to myself and changed the subject.

'And what about my meat and dried plum pasties? Between them, these three' – I made a sweeping gesture with my knife – 'and Hercules have eaten the lot. I don't mind about the dog. He displayed more good sense than the rest of you put together. If everything had been left to him and me, we'd have caught the intruder red-handed. Instead of which . . .' I broke off, unable to find the words in which to express my outraged feelings. After a few ineffectual gobbles, I resumed, 'It's what I was saying! There's no discipline in this household. You three do just as you like, especially you, Adam. You disobey my orders, you eat my pasties . . .'

'Oh, for the sweet Virgin's sake!' Adela exclaimed impatiently, finally sitting down to her own breakfast. 'I'll make another batch this morning, I promise. There are still enough dried plums left from the autumn's picking. Just finish your meal, Roger, and get round to see John Carpenter. The sooner that shutter is mended the happier I shall be. The kitchen is freezing with all that cold November air coming in. Perhaps, while you're out, you should report the matter to Richard, as well.'

'He won't be interested,' I snorted. 'It'll be just one of a dozen such incidents to him.' I stuffed the last chunk of bacon into my mouth and laid down my knife. 'I'll go and see John Carpenter right away.' I wagged an admonitory finger at Adam. 'And don't think you've heard the last of this night's escapade, my lad! I shall be speaking to you when I get back.'

I didn't wait for his customary wide-eyed look of suffering innocence, but left the house immediately before I could be seduced by it.

I was lucky enough to find the carpenter still at home in St Leonard's Lane, but only just. As I approached his door, it opened and he came out carrying his bag of tools.

'You as well?' he said when I had explained my errand. 'I'm afraid you'll have to wait a while, Roger. Lawyer Heathersett's house and chambers were also broken into last night, but he wasn't as fortunate as you. The thief managed to get in and, as far as I understand it, ransacked the place.'

'Hell's teeth!' I swore before I could stop myself. (John Carpenter was a very pious man. I always suspected him of having Lollard sympathies.) 'Didn't anyone hear anything? The lawyer himself or one of the servants? Not his mother, of course. Dame Heathersett's too old and deaf.'

The carpenter said excitedly, 'Oh dear me, yes! It appears the lawyer himself went to investigate and got laid out for his pains. Knocked over the head, he was. His man, Godfrey, found him in his consulting room, trussed up like a Christmas chicken, when he got up this morning. One of the ground-floor shutters had been removed.'

'Was much stolen?'

The carpenter shook his head. 'That I can't tell you. The servant who came to fetch me didn't have any details, except that Sergeant Manifold and his assistants were all there and also that the physician had been sent for. The lawyer ain't dead, far from it, but it couldn't have been a pleasant experience for a man of his years.' He added, preparing to move, 'I'll come to your house when I've finished at his. After dinner, most likely.'

'I'll come with you,' I said. 'I'd better report my own affair to the sergeant. There may be some connection.'

My companion nodded. 'Aye, there might be at that. Some gang working the streets. Or maybe just one man. Thwarted at your house, he probably went off to find another, easier mark to rob.'

I wasn't convinced of this. And yet it seemed the obvious explanation.

The lawyer's premises in Runnymede Court were unusually full of people. As well as the physician, who was busy bathing a nasty gash on the top of Geoffrey Heathersett's head with comfrey juice, Richard Manifold, Peter Littleman and Jack Gload were also taking up a great deal of space, while old Dame Heathersett hovered, twittering, in the background. She was a small, bird-like woman with grey hair and washed-out blue eyes, at least seventy years of age by her reckoning (she always maintained that she had been born two years before the battle of Agincourt), widow of a lawyer's clerk and inordinately proud of her only son, who had risen higher than his father to become a fully fledged attorney.

'What are you doing here, Roger?' was Richard's bad-tempered greeting as soon as he clapped eyes on me, but he changed his tune when I had told my tale. 'Bugger!' he exclaimed, scandalizing not just old Clorinda Heathersett, but John Carpenter as well. 'There must be a gang working these streets. I've just this minute received word that Master Foliot's house was also a target for thieves last night. There was an attempt to break into his house in St Peter's Street.'

'St Peter's Street?' I grimaced significantly, slightly raising my eyebrows. 'Are you sure that's what he said? He didn't mention anything about St Mary le Port Street and his shop there?'

'What? Oh! No.' Richard looked more harassed than ever. 'Go away now, Roger, will you? I'll call on you and Adela later, but for the present I wish to question Lawyer Heathersett and his mother, and I shan't be able to concentrate with you hovering over me, listening to every word.'

I grinned. He had never before come so close to admitting that my presence rattled him. I suspected that he was under some pressure from the City Fathers to catch this thief – or thieves – as soon as possible. It was one thing for people like myself to be robbed and inconvenienced without too much effort being expended to apprehend the culprits, but quite another for important personages such as rich merchants and men of law to suffer the same fate and the perpetrators go unpunished.

'I'll leave you then,' I said and turned on my heel. Then I had a thought and turned back. Ignoring Richard and his furious expression, I approached the lawyer who was shifting around on a stool while the doctor tried to bandage his head.

'You're hurting me. You're a damned, clumsy fool,' he was upbraiding the poor man. 'Haven't I had enough to put up with this night without a leech with ten thumbs, who doesn't know his business, pulling me about like a sack of turnips?'

'Then stop wriggling around like an eel on the end of a fishing line,' snapped the target of all this rancour. 'A child would make less fuss. It was quite a nasty blow, I grant you, but not one that was meant to kill. You'll live for several more years yet.'

Before the lawyer could think of a suitable response, I bent down and grasped his arm. 'Master Heathersett, it's Roger Chapman. Did you by any chance see the man who struck you?'

The lawyer nodded. 'He was tall,' he said eagerly. 'Mind you, I didn't see his face. He attacked me from behind. I'd come downstairs to find out what it was had woken me, and as I entered this room, I could see that one shutter was off its hinges. That was when he hit me. But the injury is to the top of my head, which means my assailant was taller than I am. Master Callowhill and I have been complaining for days of our footsteps being dogged by a couple of very tall rogues, but no one would take our complaints seriously.' He ended on a shrill, accusing note as Richard Manifold jostled me angrily out of his way.

'If you say one more word, Roger,' he snarled, 'if you put one more question to this witness, as sure as God's in His heaven, I'll have you clapped up in Bristol gaol.'

'I'm going,' I said hastily, straightening up. There were times when it was safe to oppose Richard and others when it was wise to back down. This was definitely one of the latter.

Matters, moreover, were not improved when the lawyer said fretfully, 'You'd do well to listen to him, Sergeant. Master Chapman has more sense than you and those two dolts' – jerking his head in the direction of Peter Littleman and Jack Gload – 'have put together.'

It was definitely time I left. Richard was swelling with indignation, his face crimson with suppressed emotion, while his two henchmen were doing their best to look affronted. So I took my leave and went to the goldsmith's house in St Peter's Street, where I was told that he was in the church next door, attending a special service for the Wardens of St Mary Bellhouse, but anyone could attend who wished to do so.

The nave was packed as always with pilgrims come to pay their respects at the shrine, and I was forced to stand right at the back, peering over people's heads. I could just make out the figure of Gilbert Foliot at one end of the row of six men in their blue silk robes and holding their white staffs of office. The shrine itself was lit by the glow from a dozen or more candles, all of which guttered in a draught, the source of which I was unable to locate. I glanced over my shoulder but the door was fast shut.

A fat woman standing next to me whispered, 'They always do that. Odd, ain't it? You a stranger here?'

I had to admit that I wasn't. I muttered in extenuation that my wife and I usually worshipped at St Giles's.

When the Mass was finished, I would have moved at once towards the door to lie in wait for my quarry, but the fat woman caught at my arm, wheezing heavily.

'I'm no good in a crowd these days,' she apologized. 'It's me chest.' She patted her ample bosom, suddenly becoming loquacious. 'Got trouble with me breathing. Me daughter's made me a concoction of coltsfoot and honey, but it don't seem to be doing no good. They say breathing up smoke from a fire's another remedy, though I've never tried it meself.'

Once outside in the street, I tried to free my arm from her determined grasp, but she was tenacious and I could see that she was spent. I could hardly leave the poor soul to her own devices.

'Do you have far to go?' I asked, hoping the answer was 'no'. The crowd was beginning to disperse and I could see Gilbert Foliot, who had until then been deep in conversation with his fellow wardens, turning towards his door. I edged a few steps in his direction.

'Me home's in Keynsham,' she panted. 'But I'm stopping a night or two with me sister in St Mary le Port Street. It ain't far. If you'd just be kind enough – and you looks a kind man – to give me your arm to her door, I'd be that grateful.'

I had no option; her growing physical distress was obvious. But in any case the mention of her home village had made me more willing to assist her. 'I was in Keynsham the night before last,' I remarked casually. 'A guest of Sir Lionel Despenser.' She shot me an incredulous, sidelong glance which lingered pointedly over my homespun clothes. 'I was looking for a man recently in his employ, a Gloucester man, Walter Gurney, Sir Lionel's head groom. But he seems to have disappeared.'

As we started down St Mary le Port Street, my companion paused for a moment to catch her breath, palpably excited. 'Ay,' she said. 'Now that were strange. Master Gurney used to drink in the local ale-house now and again. A bit high and mighty my Jacob said – Jacob's my goodman, you understand – but he'd every right to be. It seems he were a wonder with horses. Sir Lionel were overheard to boast he were the best groom he'd ever had. As for Master Gurney himself, he told my Jacob he was settled for life. He'd never leave Sir Lionel. Not ever. And then a day or so later, he's gone. No one knows where.'

I mulled this over, while we continued at our snail's pace down the street. It seemed highly unlikely to me that after such a positive statement as the groom was said to have made, he would have been frightened away by the news that I was about to visit him. He had no reason to think me an emissary of Jane Spicer. And even if he had, he had only to stand his ground and refuse to return to Gloucester, to declare that he was finished with his former life, and what could I have done? Nothing! So why his precipitate flight? It made no sense. And things which made no sense bothered me.

My companion had stopped at a house halfway down the street. 'This is my sister's,' she grunted. 'Thank you, kindly young man. I won't trouble you further.' She was in the act of raising a hand to the knocker when she paused and turned back.

'I'll tell you something else Master Gurney told my Jacob, which my goodman thought odd. He said he hadn't come all the way from Gloucester to offer his services to Sir Lionel just because he'd heard that he was looking for a new head groom. He said he'd come because their two families were . . . now how did he put it? Because their two families were linked together – yes, that was it! – were linked together by the past. Now, what do you think he could have meant by that?'

I said I had no idea, but my pulse was racing. I was remembering Henry Callowhill's words; that he thought there was some connection between the names of Despenser and Gurney.

I was just turning away when I thought to ask my new-found acquaintance's name.

'Elizabeth Shoesmith,' she told me. 'My goodman's the village cobbler.' She gave another wheeze. 'If you're in Keynsham again, come and see me. Anyone'll tell you where our cottage is.'

I thanked her, waited to see her safely inside her sister's house and then walked thoughtfully back the way I had come.

I was fortunate this time in being admitted at once into the goldsmith's presence and although his greeting was not effusive, he nevertheless treated me with civility.

'Master Chapman!' I had ceased for the moment, I noticed, to be Roger. 'This is a pleasant surprise. What can I do for you?'

'You've heard about Lawyer Heathersett's house being broken into last night and himself attacked I suppose?'

'I have indeed. A lamentable business, and I should have visited him 'ere this had it not been for the Wardens' Service at St Peter's.' He indicated his cloak and hat thrown down on a nearby chair. 'I was just about to set out when you were announced, and I . . .'

'I understand from Sergeant Manifold that your house, too, was targeted last night,' I interrupted ruthlessly.

His eyebrows shot up in annoyance, but he answered smoothly enough. 'I should have expected better of Dick Manifold than to spread my business around this town, but since you ask, yes, there was an attempt to force an entrance through one of the windows last night. One of the shutters in the buttery was found to be half off its hinges this morning, but the thief had obviously been disturbed and made off in a hurry. I've very recently had a new consignment of specially fine wine delivered by Master Callowhill. News gets around. No doubt the thief was after a few bottles to sell.'

I shook my head. 'Forgive me for doubting you, Master Foliot, but you and Lawyer Heathersett were not the only people to suffer the attentions of would-be intruders last night. Someone tried to break into my house, as well.'

The goldsmith exclaimed in astonishment. 'Sweet Virgin! You, too? This must be some new gang infesting the Bristol streets. I must have a word with the sheriff immediately. The members of the Watch must be increased. Was anything stolen?'

'No, only a shutter removed from the kitchen window. Luckily, my wife, who, like most women, sleeps with one ear open for the children, heard the noise and roused me. Between us, my dog and I would have caught the man had my younger son not decided to take a hand. I regret to say that he stumbled over a bowl of water on the floor and so alerted our would-be thief, who promptly ran away.'

Gilbert Foliot frowned slightly. 'You have a dog?'

I laughed. 'If you can dignify him with that name. As a matter of fact, he was with me when Master Callowhill and I called here last night, but I left him outside for fear of his dirtying your floors. He was one of the curs that run wild upon the downs above Bristol. Some few years back he attached himself to me, refused to be shaken off and through sheer persistence became one of the family. A scrap of a thing, but with a fierce bark and very sharp teeth. We call him Hercules.'

'Because he isn't? Yes, I see.' There was a fleeting smile, then the frown returned deeper than before. My companion reached for his cloak. 'Now, if you'll excuse me, Roger' – it seemed we were on Christian name terms again – 'I must go at once to see the sheriff. This is a veritable rash of attempted robberies and must be attended to.'

I put out a hand to detain him and was rewarded with another of his haughty stares. 'Master Foliot,' I said, 'there is something else you must know. Yesterday evening, before Master Callowhill and I came to see you, we walked past your shop in St Mary le Port Street and thought we saw a light in the upper floor. At the time, we both imagined we must have been mistaken, so said nothing. But later, after I had parted from Master Callowhill, I went back.' I then proceeded to tell him all that had happened subsequently, but without saying anything about recognizing the man or where I thought I had seen him before.

'And you say this man let himself out with a key?'

'Yes.'

'And he boarded a vessel bound for Brittany?'

'So it would seem.'

'You're absolutely certain of this?'

'Not absolutely, no. Sergeant Manifold could find no trace of the man onboard the Breton ship, which could mean one of three things. Either he had been disguised as a member of the crew, or he was hidden very securely where no one would think to search for him, or he had, by that time, disembarked and returned to the city.' This last possibility had only just occurred to me and I wondered that I had not thought of it before. The man could simply have passed on a message to the captain and left.

'And who do you think this stranger might be?' Gilbert Foliot asked uneasily, chewing on one of his thumbnails.

'A Breton ship,' I said, a little hesitantly, 'suggests a Tudor agent.'

The goldsmith nodded, his face grim. 'It does indeed, a fact worrying enough in itself. But even more worrying for me is how this man came to have a key to my shop and the living quarters above . . . You are certain that he had a key?'

'I'm certain. I heard it turn in the lock of the side door before he let himself out.' But was I certain? Was my memory playing me false? 'The fellow must have got in somehow,' I urged.

Gilbert Foliot was now gnawing at the other thumbnail.

'True,' he murmured. 'All the same, you didn't think to search for any signs of unlawful entry, I suppose?'

'No, because . . .'

'Because you were convinced the man had a key. I understand. Master Chapman.' He drew a deep breath. 'I must go immediately, first to St Mary le Port Street, then, as I said, to see the sheriff.' He donned his hat and grabbed his cloak without pausing to put it on. 'Forgive me! My housekeeper will see you out.'

And I found myself alone, left with a number of questions still unasked and, more importantly, still unanswered.

THIRTEEN

I found myself staring at the fire leaping on the hearth and recalling the scene of the previous evening when Henry Callowhill and I had called on the goldsmith so unexpectedly. Master Foliot had been entertaining and entertaining lavishly. I remembered the second armchair, the flask of wine, the two fine Venetian glass goblets. (I had presumed they were Venetian, so much of the finest glassware came from Italy. But what did I know?) An important customer he had claimed, but suddenly I began to wonder if that were really true. Could it possibly have been the man I later saw leaving the house in St Mary le Port Street, a man who might possibly be a Tudor agent?

No, no! That was ridiculous! Everyone knew that Gilbert Foliot, close friend of the mayor and sheriff, a member of the Fraternity of the Shrine of St Mary Bellhouse and whose late wife had been a Herbert, was a loyal supporter of the House of York, none stauncher. And yet, as I had so recently been reminded, the setting aside of King Edward in favour of King Richard had played havoc with the allegiance of many Yorkists. And the vicious rumours now circulating of the death of young Edward and his brother must have alienated many more waverers who were still uncertain whether the substitution of uncle for nephew had been a good thing or no. Or even legal.

A slight noise behind me broke my reverie and made me spin round to find Margery Dawes, the housekeeper, standing at my shoulder. 'The master said I was to show you out, Master Chapman. He's had to go somewhere in a hurry.'

'Yes, I know,' I answered, smiling. 'He needn't have troubled you. I could have found my own way.'

Her slightly protuberant eyes and full red lips returned the smile as she assured me that it was no trouble, no trouble at all, in her soft, sleepy voice.

'The master's in a bit of a taking. Someone tried to break into the house last night,' she added comfortably, in much the same tones, I imagine, as she would have informed me that the cat had just had kittens.

I was going to say that I knew all about it, when the door opened again and Ursula appeared.

I could see at once that she was in an even more dramatically tearful mood than on our previous meeting. Her black draperies were even more profuse than before, the natural pallor of her face further enhanced with white lead paste and her voice, when she spoke, was low and throbbing. I was more than ever convinced that she was in love with romance and tragedy equally as much as she had been with Peter Noakes.

'I thought I heard you,' she said, coming forward and painfully gripping my wrist. 'Alderman Roper returned last night from Tintern with Peter's body.' A sob escaped her and, freeing my arm, I put it gently around her shoulders. She went on: 'His funeral is tomorrow at St Thomas's Church. I shall attend, even though my father has forbidden it.' The housekeeper made a vaguely protesting sound which Ursula quite rightly ignored. (Even I could tell that it was made from habit rather than conviction.) The girl continued, 'I have been with the alderman this morning and he says he is almost certain that Peter's death wasn't caused by drowning, but that he was hit over the back of his head before he went into the water.'

'What makes Alderman Roper think that?' I asked sharply.

'He claims he can see a bruise and feel a lump under Peter's hair.'

'Has he informed the sheriff of his suspicions?'

Ursula shook her head and gave another sob. 'No, he says he doesn't want to stir up trouble. That Peter's dead and nothing is going to bring him back so there's no point making a fuss and that he's probably mistaken anyway.' She gulped and burst out: 'He and his wife never liked Peter. They always resented having him foisted on them after Master Roper's sister died. Oh, I know Peter wasn't as good a nephew to them as he might have been, but it isn't easy to be good when you're unhappy.' She uttered this last with real feeling and I suddenly found myself genuinely sorry for her. It can't be easy for a girl to lose her mother when she's young.

'I'll go and speak to Alderman Roper,' I said, but she immediately shrieked and clutched my arm again.

'No! I told you, he doesn't want to make any fuss. He only blurted it out in front of me by accident.' She took a shuddering breath. 'If the truth be known, I believe he and Mistress Roper are glad that Peter's dead. They'll bury him tomorrow and that'll be the end of him. Promise me you won't say anything. To anyone.'

Her distress was so evident, and Margery Dawes was looking at me so reproachfully that, much against my will, I gave my word not to approach the alderman, nor to pass on his suspicions to anybody else.

Ursula was plainly relieved and grew calmer. She glanced around the room.

'You asked me once, Master Chapman, if I knew what Peter was doing at Tintern.'

I nodded. 'You said you didn't, but that he had talked of something there that might make you rich.'

'Yes. And then I think you asked how he came by his information and I said I didn't know. That he wouldn't tell me.' I
waited impatiently for her to continue while she once more
glanced about her before turning to the housekeeper. 'Margery,
do you recall an evening last September, an evening when my
father returned unexpectedly while Peter was here?'

Mistress Dawes chuckled. 'And he had Sir Lionel with him.
The master, I mean. Oh yes! Oh, Sweet Lord, yes! Your father
had promised you a whipping if he found you anywhere near
young Master Noakes again.'

Ursula's mouth tightened. 'I remember.' She turned to me.
'Peter and I were in here when Margery rushed in to tell us that
my father had just come home with Sir Lionel and that my father
had ordered wine to be brought to the parlour immediately. We
didn't know what to do until Margery had the idea of pulling
the curtain across the dais and concealing Peter behind it.'

The housekeeper nodded agreement. 'Fortunately, it was a
dark, miserable, wet evening, only fit for huddling around the
fire. Pulling the curtain to make all cosy seemed a natural thing
to do. And it was your forethought,' she added, smiling at
Ursula, 'that made us shift the armchair from the dais and
place it near the hearth. Then we both sat down and pretended
to be toasting our toes at the flames when the master and Sir
Lionel came in.'

'What happened then?' I asked.

Ursula took up the tale. 'Margery and I were both sent out of
the room because, my father said, he had business to discuss.
And it was an age before Sir Lionel left, with poor Peter sat
behind that curtain, on the floor, not daring to make a sound. By
the time Father eventually came up to bed, and I was able to
creep down to let Peter out, he was so cold and chilled and had
such cramp in both his legs that he could barely stand, poor
lamb.'

Margery chuckled again. 'We were nearly caught out that time
and no mistake.'

'Yes, but what I've remembered,' Ursula went on, 'is that it was
not long after that evening that Peter started talking about going
to Tintern, dropping hints that he knew something that would make
our fortune.'

I took a deep breath. The scene she had just described was exactly the one I had imagined to myself when trying to work out how it was that Peter Noakes and Gilbert Foliot had been at Tintern at one and the same time. Whatever the goldsmith and his friend had discussed that September evening must have concerned the abbey and the secret hiding place discovered all those years ago during William Herbert's funeral. And whatever that was had been enough to send both Master Foliot and young Noakes scurrying across the Severn into Wales.

Whatever that was! Could it possibly be anything other than buried treasure? Surely not, if it were to make Peter's and Ursula's fortune. And just as surely, I reasoned, it must have been something, some information, provided by the knight that, after fourteen years, had alerted the goldsmith to the possibility that the hiding place had contained more than the accounts and the pages of diary originally found. But what that information had been and how Lionel Despenser had come by it were riddles to which I had no easy answer. They were problems to be mulled over when I had more time. For the moment, there were other matters needing my attention.

I took my leave of Margery Dawes and Ursula, having once again given my word to mention nothing of Alderman Roper's suspicions to anyone, and went back to the lawyer's chambers in Runnymede Court. I was relieved to discover that Richard Manifold and his two henchmen had gone about their business elsewhere, so I was spared the usual insults about prying ways and long noses and was able to make my own enquiries unmolested. In fact, there was only one question that I really wanted to ask.

The lawyer, I was told, was laid down upon his bed, his mother in attendance, which suited my purpose exactly. I was able to speak instead to his clerk, Edward Pennyfeather, a young, tousle-headed fellow with bright hazel eyes, untidy in his person, but sharp-witted enough for all that.

In reply to my enquiry, he shook his head. 'There was nothing taken, Master Chapman, that's the strange thing about it. A robbery, the whole place ransacked, stuff strewn about everywhere, but nothing, so far as we can discover, absolutely nothing stolen. And old Mistress Heathersett has some fine jewels the master's bought her from time to time, but although they were tipped out of the strong box, they were left scattered about the floor as if they were of no value.'

'So what would be your conclusion?' I asked.

The hazel eyes regarded me shrewdly. 'That the thief was looking for something in particular?'

I nodded. 'My thought exactly.'

The clerk scratched his nose. 'But what?'

'A paper? A deposition against one of your clients? Evidence that could get someone hanged?'

Young Pennyfeather snorted. 'We don't deal with exciting stuff like that, sir. Our cases are about wills and land settlements and other such boring things.' He yawned prodigiously and stretched his arms. 'I don't think I'm cut out for the law as a profession. I'd like to go for a soldier, but my mother has hysterics every time I mention it.' He sighed. 'She's a widow, so I suppose I can't blame her.'

'No.' I was attending to him with only half an ear. 'You're certain, absolutely positive, that nothing was taken?'

'As certain as I can be. Mind you, if the thief took something I knew nothing about, that would be a different matter. But Master Heathersett himself swears that he can find nothing missing.'

I thanked him and took my leave. My next call was at the livery stables in Bell Lane.

The owner greeted me jovially. 'Don't tell me you've come to hire a horse,' he chortled. 'They're not sending you on your travels again, are they? I've got a nice, quiet cob, won't go more than three miles an hour. Just the animal for you.'

My dislike of horses and my uncertain seat in the saddle was a standing joke around the stables. Several of the lads sweeping out the stalls gave way to unseemly mirth. I ignored them. 'Have you recently housed a black stallion with four white socks?' I asked. 'A prime beast, I imagine. Arab blood.'

The owner immediately ceased his joking and became enthusiastic. 'A prime beast, indeed! You never said a truer word. Ay, we stabled him for a night, but the owner came for him first thing this morning, as soon as it was light. Why? What's it to you?'

'Nothing,' I answered briefly and walked away, his curiosity unsatisfied, his eager questions pursuing me along Bell Lane until I reached the turning to Small Street.

So the stranger had not sailed with the ship to Brittany. My belated notion that he might simply have delivered a message to the ship's captain and then returned ashore would seem to be the correct one. I felt certain that this was the man I had witnessed talking to Sir Lionel in the manor courtyard at Keynsham, but whether or not he was Walter Gurney I was still unable to determine.

It was almost dinnertime and my belly was, as usual, rumbling with hunger, but before going home I walked to the Frome Gate. Fortunately, it was quiet at that time of the morning and I was able to engage the gatekeeper in conversation without interruption or distraction.

'Have you been on duty since dawn?'

The man, a new fellow whom I did not remember having seen before, gave me a surly nod, then burst out with: 'And damn cold it was, I can tell you!'

'I'm sure it was,' I murmured sympathetically. 'The City Fathers should provide you gatekeepers with extra clothing during the winter months. With no added cost to your good selves, of course.'

'Now you're talking sense. Haven't I always said the same?' His manner thawed a little as he recognized a well-wisher.

I risked forfeiting his good opinion and asked another question. 'I suppose you didn't happen to notice a man riding a blood horse, black with four white stockings, pass through the gate very early on?'

'Nah! No one on a horse like that has passed this way early or late. And don't,' he went on, anticipating me, 'ask if I'm sure, 'cos I'd 'ave remembered.'

So, the stranger had not passed out of the Frome Gate. The Redcliffe Gate then? Returning to Keynsham? It seemed most probable, but it had been as well to check. I thanked the gatekeeper and was turning back towards Small Street when, reluctant to let me go so easily, the man remarked, 'Heard the news about the robbery?'

'You mean at Lawyer Heathersett's?' I answered.

The gatekeeper looked surprised. 'The lawyer's been robbed

as well? My, my! What is this city coming to? No, I meant the wine merchant's. Master Callowhill's house was broken into last night.'

This time I did say, 'Are you sure?' before he could stop me.

'Of course I'm sure,' he said – or words to that effect. Actually the phrase was a richer and riper one which I committed to memory for future use at the Green Lattis. (It should earn me a few admiring glances.)

I thanked him a second time and made off before he could detain me further.

Adela was in the kitchen where, I must admit, a woman is generally to be found, chopping herbs to sprinkle over the dried fish which was our Friday fare. 'John Carpenter hasn't been yet,' she said accusingly, pointing with her knife to the piece of sacking she had nailed over the gaping hole in the shutters.

'He'll be here,' I promised, 'but he has other folk to attend to first.' And sitting down on a nearby stool I told her of the other robberies and attempted robbery that I had learned about that morning.

At first, my wife was inclined to be indignant that our need seemed to be of less consequence to the carpenter than that of other people, but gradually common sense prevailed. She knew as well as I did that we were indeed of less consequence than men of fortune and civic standing. Besides which, intelligent woman that she was, another thought had begun to form; a thought which had already occurred to me.

'Roger . . .' she said slowly, abandoning her chopping and sitting down on a stool on the opposite side of the table. 'Roger, do you think these robberies and failed robberies aren't just . . . aren't really . . . well, aren't proper robberies at all? If you see what I mean. Has it occurred to you that you and Master Foliot and Lawyer Heathersett and Master Callowhill are all people who were at Tintern Abbey when poor Peter Noakes was drowned?'

I nodded. 'That idea has been nagging at me ever since the gatekeeper told me about Master Callowhill just now. I'm trying to make sense of it. Give me a moment or two while I mull things over.'

I cast my mind back to that stormy night at the abbey and

tried to picture again what had happened. I recalled Peter Noakes rushing past us and my conviction that he was holding something in his left hand as well as the bag of tools in his right. Later, however, when his body was found and nothing was discovered on his person it seemed that I had been mistaken. I closed my eyes in an attempt to recall the exact sequence of events.

Peter Noakes had dashed out into the night, pursued by Brother Mark and his posse of fellow monks, only to elude them in the infirmary by escaping along the latrine drain to the cesspit and climbing over the wall. But why had he risked being trapped inside the infirmary? Our conclusion, apparently accepted by everyone at the time, was that he had gone back to collect the rest of his gear which he had left there. But had that really been the reason? Wasn't there another, far more probable explanation which I, like the double-dyed fool that I undoubtedly was, had carelessly overlooked, but which someone of greater wit and intelligence had instantly thought of? Peter Noakes had indeed found whatever it was that he had been seeking and concealed it in the baggage of one of the rest of us, hoping to retrieve it later. And in that same moment of realization, I understood why Oliver Tockney had been set upon and murdered. And why his pedlar's pack had been stolen.

But last night's events proved that Oliver could not have been carrying the 'treasure'. I leapt to my feet like a madman.

'Where's my pack?' I yelled.

'Where it always is when you're not using it,' my wife answered patiently. 'In the kitchen corner next to the water barrel.' Once more, she pointed with her knife.

I grabbed the pack and tore it open, spilling its contents over the floor.

'What, in the Virgin's name . . .?' Adela began, but I waved her to silence.

Piece by piece I picked up the various items, subjecting each to close scrutiny before restoring it to the pack. But there was nothing out of the ordinary, just the usual collection of needles and thread, bobbins, laces, ribbons, some fancy buttons, a pair of buckles, belt tags, a 'silver' ring and pendant and the two pairs of Spanish gloves that I had purchased in Gloucester. I scrabbled around on the floor, looking for something – anything

– that I might have missed, but in the end was forced to the conclusion that everything was accounted for. Supposing my theory to be the correct one, then Peter Noakes had not chosen me to be his carrier.

I rose stiffly to my feet and heard one of my knees crack.

Adela heard it, too, and grimaced but made no comment. She had, by this time, divined the reasons behind my frenzy and said, 'You think Peter Noakes did find something and hid it in someone's baggage.' It wasn't a question, just a statement of fact. As I have already remarked, she was a very intelligent woman and clever enough, most of the time, to conceal the fact in my presence. I gave her a quick hug and a suggestive kiss. She went on calmly chopping herbs.

'Yes,' I said. 'I feel sure now that that's what happened. I should have thought of it long ago. I must be getting old.'

Adela didn't contradict me. She knew I was thirty-one. Besides, she was busy pursuing her own line of thought.

'But Roger,' she objected after a moment or two, 'if you are right, why would the houses of all of you – Goldsmith Foliot, Lawyer Heathersett, Master Callowhill as well as yourself – be broken into? Apart from yourselves, who else's baggage was there that could have been used as a temporary hiding place by young Noakes?'

'Only Oliver Tockney's. And he's dead.' Adela's great dark eyes were suddenly fixed on me with a look of painful intensity. I gave her another kiss and tried to reassure her. 'Oliver was an easy target; a stranger, a "foreigner" from the north whose death no one would care about. The rest of us are different; men of standing. The murder of anyone of us would provoke immediate investigation.'

This time she returned my kiss and laughed, albeit a little shakily. 'You're a man of standing?' she teased.

'Falsely, yes, because my reputation belies the truth. Thanks to the fact that I was at King Richard's coronation and feast, and thanks to that unholy trio, Margaret, Bess Simnel and Maria Watkins, I'm mistakenly believed to be a royal agent whose murder would bring instant retribution in its wake. However,' I went on, watching as she sprinkled the herbs over the fish and started to fry them in the skillet, 'that doesn't answer your question as to why all remaining four of us have been victims of last night's successful or attempted robberies.'

Adela, leaving the fish to fry gently in the pan, began to put out bowls and knives and beakers. 'So what is the solution?' she asked, although I felt sure she had already worked out the answer for herself.

'If you want to direct attention away from yourself, you arrange with your hired bravos to make it seem that you are also one of the victims.'

Adela sat down on a stool again, thinking deeply. 'What you're saying is that someone knew about the Tintern treasure, knew what it was that Peter Noakes must have found, guessed where he had hidden it and is now trying to recover it. Surely, if that theory is correct, the finger of suspicion can only point in one direction?'

'To Gilbert Foliot? Yes. But if so, what part does Sir Lionel Despenser play in the story?'

'You think he has one?'

'I should say almost certainly. It has to be information traded between him and the goldsmith that sent young Noakes haring off to Wales.' And I told her what Ursula Foliot had said to me only that morning. 'I don't believe, however, that either man knew what it was they were looking for. In that respect, they are as much in the dark as the rest of us.'

'Why do you say that?'

'Because Master Foliot only has a suspicion that there might have been something else in the abbey hiding place apart from the original papers, and that must be on account of something Sir Lionel told him. And . . .'

'Yes?' my wife encouraged me as I faltered.

'We-ell, it seems probable – more than probable – to me that such information came into his possession after he had made the acquaintance of Walter Gurney. Consider the facts for a moment. To begin with, two people have now said that there is some historical link between the names of Despenser and Gurney, one of them, according to Mistress Shoesmith, being none other than Walter Gurney himself. Secondly, Jane Spicer testified to the fact that when Walter heard of Sir Lionel being in want of a groom he was off at once to offer himself for the position. She, of course, attributed it to his anxiety to get away from her and possibly being lumbered eventually with Juliette's child.'

'But you don't believe that was the reason?'

'Oh, it may have been part of the reason, but not all of it. Walter knew there was a tie of some sort between his and the Despenser family.'

'To do with the Tintern treasure?'

'If there is indeed any treasure. Don't let's forget that I am guessing and nothing more. But if there is, then no, I wouldn't think Walter knew of it.'

'Why not?'

'Because in that case, human nature being what it is, I would hazard that someone in the Gurney family would have gone after it long ago. The account books and the pages of the old monk's diary belonged to the early years of the last century. 1326 was the date, if I remember rightly.'

'Does that date mean anything to you?' The fish was now fried and Adela began dishing it out on to thick trenchers of stale bread. She went to the kitchen door and shouted for the children.

I thought back to history lessons with Brother Hilarion, but although I cudgelled my brains, no memory stirred.

Elizabeth, Nicholas and especially Adam were all still full of the previous night's attempted robbery, Adam particularly so as he seemed to think that he had played a major part in scaring off the intruder. Which, of course, he had, although not in quite the heroic way that he regarded it.

'I'm a man now,' he announced with simple pride. 'I have a knife. If that man tries to rob our house again, I shall stick it into him. Straight through his belly button.'

Everyone laughed but me. I was too busy trying to work out why his words bothered me; what chord they had struck in my mind. It seemed to me afterwards that I had very nearly had the answer when a furious knocking on the street door made me jump almost out of my skin and drove all such thoughts from my head. Two minutes later, Elizabeth, who had gone to the door to admit the caller, returned to the kitchen with Richard Manifold in tow.

I groaned. He took no notice.

'Roger,' he said, at his most officious, 'you must accompany me to the bridewell at once.'

'Well, I won't,' I replied mutinously. 'I'm eating my dinner.'

'Now,' was the uncompromising answer. 'Orders of the sheriff.'

I threw down my knife. 'Why?' I demanded pettishly.

'An old beggar has been murdered in Pit Hay Lane. We've arrested a man, another old beggar, who was caught red-handed bending over the body.'

'So?'

'So this second beggar insists on speaking to you. Absolutely insists on it. And you haven't forgotten what I was telling you the other day; the rumour that an agent of the king might be here in disguise?' I gave a start. I had forgotten it. 'The sheriff thinks I'm being overzealous. He says this man couldn't possibly be a royal officer. But I thought it would be as well to be certain.'

FOURTEEN

He was sitting – perched would perhaps be a better word – on a narrow stone ledge beneath a tiny barred window through which the pallid November daylight struggled to make any impression. A rush light provided almost no illumination, and I had to wait for my eyes to grow accustomed to the gloom before viewing the huddled figure with any clarity.

He was a small man dressed in an ancient and very patched tunic, torn hose, rubbed shoes, with several weeks' growth of beard adorning his chin, long greasy hair and a filthy eye-patch over the left eye. The right regarded me malevolently.

I started to shake with laughter.

The prisoner snatched off the eye-patch and threw it to the floor.

'Don't just stand there cackling like a demented peahen!' he yelled. 'Tell this idiot who I am.'

When, finally, I could command my voice, I turned to Richard

Manifold, who was gloomily regarding the pair of us. 'Hard as you may find it to believe,' I gasped, 'this gentleman is the King's Spymaster General, one Timothy Plummer.'

'You're sure of that?'

'Of course he's fucking sure, you dolt!' Timothy bounced to his feet and shook his fist under the other man's nose, something I'd never seen anyone actually do before. 'Fetch the sheriff here immediately so that Master Chapman can identify me in front of His Honour. Go on! Shoo!'

Richard departed, a sullen look of resignation on his face. Timothy resumed his seat and I sat down beside him.

I said, 'I don't think they do, you know.'

'Who? Who don't do what?' my companion snapped.

'Peahens. I don't think they cackle.'

There was a pregnant silence. 'Why are we talking about peahens?' Timothy asked, dangerously quiet.

'You were. You said . . .'

'Shut up! Shut up, you great oaf! I suppose you think that's humorous? Well, it isn't!' Timothy was on his feet again, fairly dancing with temper. 'I just want to get out of here then come home with you and have a good wash while you go and collect my saddle-bags from the Full Moon Inn. I feel certain your goodwife will find me something to eat, even if it's only bread and cheese, and after that we can talk. Perhaps you can tell me what's going on in this benighted town.'

'There's nothing like inviting yourself! And I'm not your errand boy,' I rebuked him. 'And what about this secret mission that you're on?'

'I can't continue with that now, can I? Not now half of Bristol knows my real identity.'

This, of course, was a total exaggeration, but I guessed he was glad of an excuse to rid himself of a disguise which had begun to irk him and which he saw as demeaning to his dignity. I reflected that it must be a very important and delicate matter to have made him undertake it himself in the first place.

'All right,' I conceded, 'provided Adela raises no objection and understands that you're not going to hale me off to London again at any minute.' Timothy made a dismissive gesture. 'In that case, I'll do as you ask.' He was moved to grasp my hand, which left it smelling strongly of decaying fish. I wrinkled my nose. 'I suppose you know you stink to high heaven?'

It must have been well into the afternoon and getting on for suppertime before Timothy and I were at last able to settle down in the parlour for our talk.

It had taken the sheriff a good hour or more to put in an appearance at the bridewell (he was, as he was careful to point out, a very busy man), by which time my companion was at boiling point. It had taken all the tact of which I was capable to prevent him from insulting a civic dignitary and being kept in prison for contempt. However, I finally managed to convince the sheriff that this was indeed the king's Spymaster General and that His Highness would be most displeased if he were mistreated in any way. In the end, the pair were slapping each other on the back and enjoying a laugh at Timothy's unprepossessing appearance, and the latter was promising to pay a visit to both the mayor and the sheriff on the morrow to make them free of anything they desired to know.

'But not of anything I don't desire them to know,' Timothy said later, stretching his feet towards the fire burning on the hearth.

Adela's goodwill had been more difficult to win, and it had only been repeated assurances on my part that I was not to be dragged off to the capital at a moment's notice that had finally persuaded her to let Timothy use the pump and some of her carefully hoarded best white soap while I visited the Full Moon Inn to collect his saddle-bags. She had also fed him a makeshift meal of bread, goat's milk cheese and onions and promised him a share of our supper. But she refused to let him stay for the night.

'Now that he's clean and shaved, he can go back to the inn.'

I didn't blame her. It would have meant Adam sleeping with Nicholas, and that always led to trouble.

'Right,' Timothy said, looking much more like himself in a decent blue tunic and hose and with a chin and upper lip free of hair, 'what do you know of what's going on in this town? And don't tell me "nothing" because I shan't believe you. There's no one else I know who has your talent for getting mixed up in other people's business. If there's any trouble, you're sure to find yourself in the thick of it.'

I was in half a mind to resent his remarks, but decided it would be a waste of effort to do so. I was not, however, going to allow him the ordering of the conversation.

'Tell me what you're doing here first.'

He hesitated briefly, then decided to comply. 'One of our best spies at the Breton court sent back a report that the Tudor is growing short of money. Duke Francis is facing war with France – the French nobles are flexing their muscles now that Louis is no longer alive to restrain them; the new king is too young to hold them in check – and therefore is unable to give the same generous aid to Henry. The latter's attempted invasion during the recent rebellion failed lamentably as you probably know, but even so, mercenaries still need paying, win or lose. But our man wrote that there was a rumour – indeed, more than a rumour – in circles close to the Tudor of the possible windfall of a vast sum of money coming his way. And the source of this money was here, in Bristol. His Grace the king was perturbed by this story as you can well imagine.'

'King Richard took it seriously then?'

'Of course he took it seriously!' Timothy fairly exploded. 'I've told you, this report came from one of our best men; a man probably only second to myself in reputation. A man who, if he works hard and lives long enough, may even one day succeed to my office. That shows you how good he is and how highly his opinion is regarded.'

'You've no need to say more,' I assured him, straight-faced. 'So the king sent you in disguise to Bristol to find out more?'

'Of course. He would trust no one else. It had to be done under a cloak of the greatest secrecy.'

I said meanly, 'Not secret enough, I'm afraid. I was informed of your possible presence in the city yesterday and asked, as someone who knew you well and might be able to penetrate your disguise, to keep a lookout for you.'

Timothy stared at me disbelievingly. 'This is one of your ill-timed jests.'

'No. The absolute truth, I assure you. It would seem that a close friend of His Worship the Mayor had just returned from

London and had been warned of the fact that there might be treasonable activity in the city, and that you were here to investigate.'

Timothy was silent for a long moment, then he burst out: 'Matters are worse than I thought. The king is beset by traitors! Even the people he thinks he can trust betray him! Buckingham was the prime example, but there are others less open in their disaffection and therefore even more dangerous.'

'His taking the crown has incurred a great deal of ill will,' I said soberly. 'Even amongst former friends and well-wishers.'

Timothy nodded grimly and leant forward, clasping his hands between his knees. A flame spurted suddenly between the logs on the hearth and a shower of sparks, like golden thistledown, burned brightly for a moment, then vanished. The shadows of the November afternoon thickened and I realized that my companion was no longer a young man. He was growing old and cares pressed heavily on him. The future, in spite of its bright promise a few months ago, now looked dark. The old familiar bombast, once so laughable, now invited sympathy. It covered a multitude of anxieties.

Timothy,' I said urgently, also leaning forward and lowering my voice almost to a whisper, 'what is the truth in this rumour that the king's nephews have been murdered?'

His head reared up at that. 'False, of course! You, at least, should know better than to believe it.' His tone was accusing.

'I don't believe it.' There was another silence filled only with the crackling of the fire. Then, 'You know for certain it's not true, do you?' I asked.

He flung me a contemptuous glance. 'I know him! I know the king! So do you, and that should give you your answer.'

'It does . . . But he hasn't publicly denied it.'

Timothy turned on me in a fury.

'Why should he? Why should he give himself the trouble, the indignity, of publicly denying what anyone who knows him must be aware is a vicious lie?'

'It would make sense to do so,' I argued gently. 'Produce the boys. Bring them to court. Show people that they're still alive.'

'And remind everyone of their existence? Make them a focus of rebellion yet again? Is that what you want? It's much better, surely, to keep them quietly secluded in the Tower until he decides what to do with them. Given time, and once King Richard has established his rule, people will forget about them. Or they'll appreciate how much better off they are with a man than a boy on the throne. How much better off without the Woodvilles! Then he can establish the boys again in the world without the fear that someone will rise up on their behalf.'

'But you are certain that the lord Edward and his brother are still alive?'

'I've told you, yes!' Timothy almost shouted.

'That's all right, then,' I said.

The trouble was that I didn't believe him. I wanted to. How I wanted to! But I had a feeling that he didn't really know. Like the rest of us who loved King Richard he was saying what he wanted to be the truth, not what he knew to be fact. Why I felt this, I wasn't sure. Maybe it was the way his eyes refused to meet mine, sliding away to focus on the fire or the fleas hopping about amongst the rushes, brought out of hiding by the warmth.

'Now,' Timothy remarked briskly, changing the subject with obvious relief, 'let's get on with the business in hand, shall we? What information do you have for me?' He flung up a warning finger. 'And I've told you, don't pretend you know nothing. If you haven't sniffed out something by this time, then I'm a Chinaman.'

Once more, I risked his fury by countering with another question. 'Who's this beggar you were accused of murdering? And how did you come to be found stooping over his body?'

'For Christ's sweet sake –' he was beginning, but it was my turn to hold up an admonitory finger.

'It might be important. Did someone mention that he lived in Pit Hay Lane?'

'I don't know! Quite possibly. I'm not acquainted with the names of the streets in this town, let alone the alleyways. I just know I tripped over something, crouched down to see what it was and the next moment I was being clapped on the shoulder by that oaf of a sergeant who was putting me under arrest for murder.'

'You're sure the man had been murdered? I know Sergeant Manifold said so, but –'

'Oh, yes! That was plain. He'd been strangled, any fool could see that. His eyes were bulging out of their sockets, his tongue was swollen and protruding from his mouth, his face, what I could see of it beneath the dirt, was suffused with blood.'

'A small man? Stank to high heaven?'

'He didn't appear to be very big and he certainly stank. Like an old fish barrel.'

I nodded. There were a lot of beggars in the city but I had no hesitation in concluding that this was the man who had witnessed the murder of Oliver Tockney. Now he, too, was dead. Strangled. And I was the idiot who had so carelessly made it known that the pedlar's killing had been overlooked. There would have been little difficulty in identifying him. A bribe offered for the person in question to come forward and tell what he had seen, a meeting in a dark corner of the alleyway, a knotted rope slipped swiftly around the neck . . .

'Are these questions relevant?' Timothy's voice broke in on my thoughts and his nails tapped against the arm of his chair impatiently.

I nodded. It was quite dark outside by now and I rose to kindle a taper at the fire and light some candles.

'Timothy,' I said, glancing over my shoulder at him, 'do you have any idea what happened in the year thirteen twenty-six?'

He goggled at me. 'Thirteen twenty-six? Thirteen twenty-six? That's . . . That's more than a hundred and fifty years gone! Sweet Jesu! How would I know what went on over a century and a half ago?' He eyed me wrathfully. 'What's this all about, Roger? Why do you keep putting me off with these ridiculous questions?'

'They're not so ridiculous,' I said, returning to my seat on the other side of the hearth. I sighed. 'I suppose I'd better begin at the beginning and tell you everything I know. But try to refrain from a lot of foolish interruptions. Just wait until I've finished or I'll lose the thread of my tale.'

To do him justice, the only questions he asked were to clarify some point which I had not made clear; other than that, he remained silent throughout the long and sometimes complicated story. I even had to admit to the tangled history of my relationship with Juliette Gerrish in order to introduce the name of Walter Gurney.

When at last I had finished, he said nothing for a while, sitting forward and staring into the flames as though for inspiration. Finally he grunted, 'Then the two conspirators would appear to be this goldsmith, Gilbert Foliot, and Sir Lionel Despenser.'

'I wouldn't even be sure about that. There's no proof against either of them,' I pointed out. 'No solid proof. And both men have a reputation of being loyal to the House of York. Foliot, as I told you, was married to a Herbert and attended William Herbert's funeral after Edgecote.'

Timothy frowned. 'But the man you followed to the Breton ship had, according to you, been prowling around the living quarters above the goldsmith's shop and, again according to you, let himself out with a key. You don't have keys to other people's property unless they've been given to you.'

'Or stolen. Or given to you by some other person than the one concerned. You'll have to tread warily, Timothy. Without positive proof, you can't go accusing a wealthy Bristol citizen, especially not one who is a friend of the mayor and sheriff, of treasonable activities. King Richard won't thank you for alienating a city as rich as this one, whose wealth he may have need of one day. Take it from me, insult a Bristolian and you insult the whole population. You're dealing here with a town that, during the reign of the second Edward, built a wall between itself and the castle and defied authority for three long years until eventually the king had to send an army with siege machines and batter it into submission. The memory of that episode still fills every man, woman and child with pride after more than a hundred and seventy years.'

'Which just goes to show,' Timothy spat, 'what a lot of traitorous dogs the inhabitants of this godforsaken city really are. Oh, all right, all right!' He waved a dismissive hand as I would have protested further. 'I understand what you're saying and I'll walk carefully. But you must admit the circumstances are suspicious. Then there's this odd business of the treasure at Tintern Abbey. Do you have any idea what it might be?'

'How can I?' I was suddenly impatient. 'I told you, it's never been found. If young Peter Noakes did discover anything, he hid it so effectively that no one can find it. But that begs the question, was there anything more than the account books and diary to be found in the first place? For fourteen years no one ever considered that there might be, and then . . .'

'And then?' Timothy prompted.

'And then . . . Oh, I don't know!' I exclaimed, tired and irritated. The smoke from the fire was making my head ache, I wanted my supper and all at once I was sick of the subject, sick of going round in circles, every now and then catching, or so it seemed to me, a little gleam of light, only to lose it again. Who were those men who had arrived at Tintern Abbey all those long years ago whose crime, whatever it was, had so revolted the monks that they had begged the abbot not to give them shelter? And why had the abbot chosen to do so in spite of all their pleadings? Had the criminals brought treasure with them which he had agreed to keep concealed; treasure so valuable that he had had a special hiding place made for it in his own lodgings? And what was the connection between Walter Gurney and Sir Lionel Despenser? Because it seemed to me that this notion of there being more to the Tintern treasure than simply the original documents had arisen only after Walter had become the knight's head groom.

Or was that, too, just my imagination?

'Roger! Are you all right?'

Timothy's concerned voice brought me back abruptly from where I had been floating somewhere near the ceiling, and I realized that in another moment or two I would have lost consciousness. I felt deeply ashamed of such weakness, my only excuse being that it had been a stressful year one way and another, and that I had suffered an illness during the course of the summer which had left me prey to an exhaustion which occasionally threatened to overcome me.

Fortunately, at that moment, Adela called us out to supper.

A further discussion after the meal – more fish as it was Friday – decided nothing but that Timothy would return to London the following day, after visiting the mayor and sheriff, leaving me, as he put it, to 'poke and pry around' in the hope that I might stumble upon some answer to the riddle of what, if anything, was going on in Bristol.

'There's no point in my staying,' he said, 'now that my identity has been revealed. If a plot is being hatched to succour Henry Tudor, then the conspirators won't make a move while they are aware of my presence in the city.'

'What will you tell the king?'

He grinned and slapped me on the back. 'That the investigation is in the capable hands of his loyal subject, Roger Chapman. He will be more than satisfied.'

I groaned. Here I was, mixed up in Richard's affairs yet again, and how it had come about I had no very clear idea. Our lives seemed destined to intertwine. The only bright spot in a day which seemed to have flashed past in a series of not altogether pleasant surprises was that while Timothy and I had been talking John Carpenter had arrived to mend the damaged shutter, so I was spared another uncomfortable night sleeping – or rather not sleeping – in the kitchen.

But if I had expected a well-earned rest, I was destined to disappointment. My sleep was troubled by dreams. In one, Timothy and I were building a wall between ourselves and the goldsmith's house in St Peter's Street when Oliver Tockney arrived to say that the king was coming and asking what I had done with his pack as he daren't go home without it. 'It's in Gloucester Abbey,' I said, and the next minute I was standing looking down at Robert of Normandy's effigy in the choir. A second later, I was tapped on the shoulder by Jane Spicer, holding Juliette's baby in her arms and saying, 'That's the wrong tomb. It's the other one.'

And then I woke up.

It was Adela who was tapping my shoulder. 'Wake up, Roger! You've been tossing and turning all night. I've hardly had a wink of sleep and now it's high time we were stirring.'

She sounded aggrieved, looking as little refreshed as I felt myself. And to make matters worse, I could hear rain pattering at the shutters and a rising wind moaning around the housetops. Moreover, I knew that today I must get out with my pack or money would be in short supply, a circumstance for which I should quite rightly get the blame. As I dragged on my clothes preparatory to staggering downstairs and braving the icy water of the pump, I roundly cursed Timothy Plummer for leaving me with the responsibility of discovering what – if anything at all – was going on in Bristol that was a threat to King Richard's peace.

Breakfast was a quiet meal, even the children appearing somewhat subdued. The next day being Sunday, Adela announced that she would hear the passages of scripture that they should have learned by heart as soon as she had washed the dishes. This was greeted with a general moan which evoked my sympathy. I had endeavoured to teach them a little Latin from my own scanty knowledge, but it was not enough. They learned by rote, reproducing the sounds without any clear idea of what they were saying. Occasionally, in my more heretical moments, I wondered if anyone would ever continue Wycliffe's work and eventually translate Holy Writ into English. It was not, naturally, a thought that I expressed out loud.

I was struggling to make sense of my dream. The building of the wall had undoubtedly been prompted by the episode in Bristol's past that I had told to Timothy the previous afternoon, and that had led on to Edward II and his tomb in Gloucester Abbey. No great mystery there then! And yet I couldn't rid myself of the notion that the dream had been of more significance than that. It had been trying to tell me something, but I was too stupid to see what it was. There was another thing, too, niggling away at the back of my mind; something Adam had said. But what? And I also kept seeing in my mind's eye the contents of my pack strewn across the kitchen floor. Why, I had no idea. I was tired. I was feeling overwhelmed with responsibilities and people. I needed, as was so often the case with me, to be by myself.

What better excuse then than to get out on the open road, away from my nearest and dearest, for the most cogent of all reasons, to make some money? Breakfast over, I rose briskly to my feet and announced my intention.

Adela expressed her approval, but frowned when I said that I might be away for a night, or even two.

'Tomorrow's Sunday. Wherever you are, don't omit to go to church if at all possible.' I gave my promise. 'And take Hercules with you,' she added.

The dog looked up from the bone he was gnawing and gave

me a leery stare. He could hear the rain and wind as well as I could and was obviously not eager for a closer acquaintance with either.

I shook my head. 'Not this time.' I could see that Adela was about to argue the point when I was struck with inspiration. 'With all these robberies going on, you'll need him to guard you.'

'He can sleep on my bed and then I'll feel safe,' Elizabeth announced, a statement at once hotly contested by Nicholas and Adam, who both maintained they had a superior claim to Hercules's protection.

I left them wrangling and went upstairs to put a clean shirt in my satchel, wrap myself in my thickest cloak and hood and then return to the kitchen to pick up my pack and cudgel.

'Where will you go?' my wife asked as she kissed me goodbye.

'I thought I might walk as far as Keynsham again.' It hadn't been my intention, but the words just seemed to form themselves naturally in my head.

'Don't forget to bring us back presents,' my daughter reminded me, breaking off in mid-argument to slide from her stool and put up her mouth for a kiss.

I stroked her soft cheek. 'Be a good girl and help your mother while I'm away.'

A slightly mutinous set to her lips made my heart sink and I said sharply, 'Now, Bess!'

'Let things be, sweetheart,' Adela whispered, drawing me towards the door. 'There's nothing to worry about,' she urged when we were out of earshot. 'She's at a difficult age.'

Gloomily, I agreed. But sometimes it seemed to me that females were always at a difficult age however old they might be. I thought for a moment that it was on the tip of Adela's tongue to demand a definite day for my return, but she refrained. She knew only too well the wanderlust that gripped me every now and again.

I hugged her and stepped out into the storm buffeting its way down Small Street. I had intended to continue straight on to the Redcliffe Gate, but at the junction of Broad Street and High Street I hesitated, then walked a little way along Wine Street to Master Callowhill's house.

FIFTEEN

The servant who answered my knock, a stout body with a gimlet eye, took one look at me and my pack, said sharply, 'Nothing today, my man!' and made to close the door.

I stuck my foot in the narrowing gap and asked to see Master Callowhill.

'Be off with you!' she retorted angrily. 'Neither the master nor the mistress deals with the likes of you.'

'Just tell Master Callowhill that Roger Chapman would like a word with him,' I snapped.

I had no great hope that this information would carry any weight and was preparing myself for battle when, to my astonishment, she immediately stepped back and held the door wide.

'Oh, him!' she grunted, beckoning me in. 'Wait here. I'll fetch the master.'

Nothing could have shown me more plainly that the reputation I was gaining throughout the city was no figment of my imagination. The perception of me as someone who was in Richard's pay, first when he was Duke of Gloucester and now that he was king, was growing. My prolonged absences, both last year and this, the rumours that I had been engaged on secret work for him, had confirmed a steadily increasing belief, no doubt fostered by Margaret Walker and her precious friends, that I was someone to be reckoned with, if not actually feared. It accounted for a certain change in attitude amongst my friends, some of whom had definitely become more reserved in their dealings with me, whilst others, mainly the ones I liked least, were more ingratiating.

I was not kept waiting many moments. Master Callowhill emerged from one of the doors on the right-hand side of the hall, the white cloth tied around his neck indicating that he was still at breakfast.

'Master Chapman!' His tone was effusive. 'Come in! Come in! You're abroad early. We're still eating I'm afraid. But come and share a pot of ale with us.' He laid a broad arm across my shoulders, practically propelling me into the dining parlour where his wife and children were seated around a laden table, and refusing to take no for an answer.

I felt uncomfortable and stupid in my old clothes and looking, I was sure, like a drowned rat. But no one seemed to notice anything amiss, Mistress Callowhill giving me a courteous greeting, the daughter of the house rising from her stool to bob me a curtsey, the elder of the two boys hurrying forward to relieve me of my pack and cudgel and the younger one offering me his seat.

'Now,' Henry Callowhill said as soon as a maid servant had appeared with a clean beaker for me and he had filled it from the pitcher in the middle of the table, 'let me guess why you're here. Rumour has it that this gang of robbers also attacked your house the night before last. You wish to know, as I do – as we all do – what measures the City Fathers are taking.'

Mistress Callowhill gave a visible shudder. 'It's dreadful! Dreadful! So many houses broken into in one night! Ours! Yours! Lawyer Heathersett's! Master Foliot's! And now we hear Alderman Roper suffered a similar fate yesterday evening.'

I gave a startled glance in the wine merchant's direction.

My host nodded. 'Our servant, Molly – the one who opened the door to you – has a sister who works for the alderman and who was round here at first light this morning to tell Molly the news. It seems that not only did these villains search as much of the house as they could without waking the sleeping household, but they went so far as to disturb the body of poor young Peter Noakes which was lying in its coffin. In case, one can only suppose, there was anything of value hidden underneath it to be buried with him. You may not have heard, Master Chapman –'

'Yes,' I interposed. 'Yes, I had been told by Mistress Ursula that the alderman had returned from Tintern with his nephew's body the day before yesterday.' I put down my beaker and, leaning forward for greater emphasis, asked, 'Master Callowhill, what was stolen from this house?'

His wife answered before he had a chance to reply. 'Everything was all over the place,' she shrilled indignantly. 'You never saw such a mess. Cupboards emptied! Drawers emptied! Stuff strewn everywhere. Coffers –'

'But what was actually taken?' I insisted, stemming her flow of words without compunction.

There was a silence, broken finally by Henry Callowhill, who said slowly, 'Well, now that I think about it . . . nothing. At least . . . nothing of any value or one of us would have discovered its absence by now.' He frowned. 'How very odd!'

'Very odd indeed,' his wife corroborated. She turned to the children. 'Are any of you aware of anything missing?'

They shook their heads and suddenly the elder boy saw the funny side of things.

'Whoever heard of robbery where nothing was stolen?' He started to laugh and his siblings joined in.

I waited for their merriment to subside before turning to Master Callowhill once more.

'Lawyer Heathersett – or, rather, his clerk – tells the same tale. The place ransacked but, so far as can be ascertained, nothing taken. It would be interesting to know if Alderman Roper has found anything missing.'

'You think this may be of some importance, Master Chapman?' The wine merchant regarded me enquiringly.

'Master Callowhill,' I said earnestly, 'has it not occurred to you that these break-ins and attempted break-ins have all been at the houses of people who were at Tintern? Yours, the lawyer's, Master Foliot's, mine and now at the home of poor Peter Noakes.'

My host looked startled. 'Sweet Jesu,' he breathed. 'You're right. And that must mean . . .'

I nodded. 'That someone thinks Peter Noakes did discover something and that one of us, knowingly or unknowingly, may well have whatever it is in our possession.'

The elder Callowhill boy, a pleasant, fresh-faced lad whose name I knew to be Martin, objected. 'But would robberies have been attempted at all your houses? I mean, if someone who was at Tintern Abbey is the instigator of the break-ins . . .'

'One could be faked,' I pointed out gently, and he let out a long, low whistle.

His mother frowned disapprovingly and glanced towards her

husband. But the wine merchant issued no reprimand: he was busy wrestling with thoughts of his own.

He addressed me. 'You're thinking that if young Noakes did discover something, he might have planted it on one of us?'

'Yes, in our baggage. You may remember that he ran back into the infirmary before escaping.'

Master Callowhill rose to his feet. 'Let's put this theory of yours to the test. I shall send one of the maids to Redcliffe immediately to enquire of Alderman Roper if anything is actually missing. If the answer is "no", I think that will prove your point.'

'Sir, it's pouring with rain,' I protested. 'Send later in the day if you must.'

'Pooh!' My host rejected this argument with a wave of his hand. 'A drop of rain doesn't hurt anyone.' And he left the room.

When he returned a moment or two later, it was to say that a girl had been despatched and would not be many minutes. Meantime, would I have more ale?

I accepted, although silently cursing this unlooked-for delay. It meant that the morning would be well advanced before I began my walk to Keynsham. But at least there was a chance that the rain might have eased off by then.

The conversation flagged due to the fact that Henry Callowhill seemed temporarily withdrawn, staring unseeingly ahead of him and occupied by his own thoughts. Then, suddenly, he burst out with, 'No, no! I cannot believe that either Lawyer Heathersett or my good friend Gilbert Foliot would go to such lengths as to organize robberies in order to discover if young Noakes had hidden anything in our baggage. And who else is there? It's utterly preposterous. For one thing, they wouldn't know how to set about it. For another, they would only have to ask us. I repeat, the notion is ridiculous. Geoffrey, after all, is a man of the law himself. And Gilbert is one of my most respected friends. He has even offered to admit me to the Fraternity of St Mary Bellhouse. Only last week, he did the boys and me the honour of showing us all over St Peter's Church. Is that not so, lads?'

Both boys nodded and Martin added eagerly, 'Did you know, Master Chapman, that St Peter's is built on the foundations of the old Saxon church? There is still a portion of the original crypt underneath the present bell tower.'

I smiled at his enthusiasm. He was obviously a boy with a thirst for knowledge. 'And did you know,' I asked him, remembering some of Brother Hilarion's more subversive teaching, 'that the Saxon term for a Norman was Orc? A term of abuse, of course. Or that our Saxon forefathers called the great battle near Hastings the Battle for Middle Earth? Middle Earth being where we live, between Heaven and Hell.'

Henry Callowhill gave a loud cough, an indication that he considered the discussion had gone far enough. We were all English nowadays. Memories of the old, divisive times were not to be encouraged.

Luckily, as a rather heavy silence had descended, the young kitchen girl made her appearance, wet and out of breath. She bobbed a curtsey to her master and mistress.

'Please sir, ma'am, the alderman says as how he can't rightly find anything missing, but he's sure there must be summat as'll be discovered later.'

She made another curtsey and withdrew, hopefully to get warm and dry. My host pulled down the corners of his mouth.

'It seems as if your theory could be the correct one, Roger. Well, as I have said, it can't possibly be one of us. So who else could it be?'

I was not prepared to answer this and got to my feet. 'Master Callowhill, I'm afraid I must bid you good-day. I've my living to earn and have determined to walk as far as Keynsham today. Don't refine too much on anything I've said. I could be wrong in my assumptions. It's probably no more than a gang of bravos working the Bristol streets. The Watch will soon have their measure and clap them behind bars.'

He looked unconvinced and when he accompanied me to the front door – a mark of respect he would never have accorded me in the past and yet another indication of my increased standing in the community, however undeserved – he said in a low voice, 'You don't really believe that.'

'I don't know what I believe,' I told him. The rumours of a royal spy having been discovered in the town, or of a treasonable plot being hatched, seemed not to have reached him so I decided to say nothing further. But as he was a man of education and learning I asked him if he had any idea what might have been happening in the year thirteen twenty-six. 'The year mentioned in those account books found in the abbot's secret hiding place.'

But he was unable to help me. Nor, when they were applied to, were either of his sons. There was a limit to their knowledge.

I thanked them and set out once more, heading for the Redcliffe Gate.

The rain had ceased by the time I had walked a mile or so beyond the gate and a thin autumnal sun was trying to penetrate the clouds. The wayside shrines, dedicated to various saints, but mostly to the Virgin, glowed here in all the freshness of a new coat of paint, or showed there the battered, weather-beaten face of neglect. Yet none was truly neglected; even the most dilapidated boasted its posy of flowers or, now that November was almost half done, an offering of leaves and berries. I reflected how much the Virgin was beloved in this country. English names and places – marigold and Lady's smock, Mary's Mead and Ladygrove – all testified to the fact. Her image was everywhere, in gold and silver, alabaster and marble, and every statue studded with a plethora of gems. Poems abounded in her praise and Mary was the most common girl's name in the English language . . .

My ruminations were interrupted by the sound of cart-wheels just behind me, and the next moment, the cart itself had pulled up alongside, a handsome brute of a shire horse harnessed between the shafts. Seated on the box beside the carter was my acquaintance of the previous day, the cobbler's wife from Keynsham, Mistress Shoesmith.

'I thought it were you, young man,' she said. 'There's not many of your height about. I'd like to thank 'ee again for your kindness of yesterday.' She added, lowering her voice confidentially, 'I decided to go home earlier than intended. My sister and I had a few words. We ain't that fond o' one another, but I feel I've got to visit her from time to time. She's my only kith and kin. Apart from my Jacob, that is.' She eyed me speculatively. 'Where're you bound?'

'Keynsham,' I said, 'to sell my wares.'

She at once turned to the carter sitting stolidly beside her and poked him in the ribs. 'Give him a lift, Joseph Sibley,' she ordered.

'I'll pay you. There's room enough if I squeeze up a bit. Or he can sit in the back on one o' them crates.' She turned to me. 'There's only candles in 'em.'

The carter, a man I knew vaguely by sight, having seen him on various occasions in the company of Jack Nym, grunted assent and shifted obligingly to the edge of the box. Mistress Shoesmith followed suit and patted the narrow space thus left. I heaved my pack and cudgel into the cart on top of the crates of candles and climbed aboard. There wasn't much room and, to her obvious delight, I was forced to put an arm around my benefactress's broad waist to prevent myself from toppling off.

'Eh, lad,' she gurgled, 'this takes me back to my girlhood. I haven't had a cuddle with a good-looking man since I married my Jacob.' She grew serious. 'Are you visiting your friend Sir Lionel Despenser again?'

The carter snorted with laughter, evidently taking this for a joke.

I let him think it. And in a way he was right. The knight, I was sure, only treated me with civility because Gilbert Foliot had warned him that it would be circumspect to do so. 'No,' I answered cheerfully. 'Just hoping to make some money for my wife and children. I shall spend tonight at the abbey and return home again tomorrow.'

'You'll do no such thing,' Mistress Shoesmith said robustly. 'You'll spend the night with Jacob and me. What's your name, lad?'

'He's called Roger Chapman,' the carter put in before I could reply. 'And you want to be careful of 'im, Missus. They do say there's more to 'im than meets the eye.'

I sighed, but didn't argue the point. It would have been of no use, anyway, so deeply entrenched now was this belief that I was an agent of some sort – although of what sort exactly no one was prepared to say – of the king.

'Take no notice of the fool,' I told my companion as she turned a somewhat bewildered face towards me. 'He's jesting.'

The carter gave another snort but, thankfully, seemed disinclined to argue the matter. Instead, he asked, 'Not got that dog o' yourn with you, then? Jack Nym reckons 'e's an 'oly terror. Chases anything on two legs or four.'

'You don't want to believe everything Jack says,' I snapped, irked by this criticism of my favourite. I could see by the carter's face that he was getting ready to make a running joke of Jack's numerous anecdotes about his difficulties with Hercules during our journey to London earlier in the year, so I said quickly, 'Sir Lionel told me that he had recently lost a favourite dog. It was an animal he was most attached to, so he had him buried in a vacant plot of land close to the manor chapel.'

Mistress Shoesmith looked puzzled. 'I don't know why he should say that. Not unless you misunderstood what it was he was telling you, my dear. That there grave belongs to one of the manor servants who died sudden-like. One of the kitchen hands my Jacob were told when he took some mended boots and shoes up to the manor. Sir Lionel's chaplain had just finished the burying of him. There weren't nothing said about any dog.'

'Perhaps . . . Perhaps I did misunderstand him,' I said slowly. But I sat staring before me like a man in a dream, a suspicion forming and growing in my mind until it became almost a certainty. 'When was this?' I asked. 'Can you remember, mistress?'

My companion pursed her lips. 'Well . . . Not all that long ago. A week, maybe.'

'About the time that Walter Gurney disappeared?'

She looked at me for a long moment, twisting her head round to stare at me in surprise. Then she burst out laughing. 'Go on with you! It wouldn't be him! He didn't work in the kitchens. He were Sir Lionel's head groom. Sir Lionel would've said if it'd been him. Very upset he were about Master Gurney's disappearance. No, no, lad! Put that notion right out of your head.'

'You still haven't answered my question,' I said.

'What question was that?'

'Was the death of this man, this kitchen hand so-say, about the same time as Walter Gurney's disappearance?'

There was an uneasy silence. 'Well . . . Yes, it was,' she admitted at last. 'The day before. Or maybe the day after.' Mistress Shoesmith thought about this then shook her head decidedly. 'No. It don't make sense. If Groom Gurney had died why would Sir Lionel not say so? And why'd he tell you he'd buried a dog?'

Why indeed? Unless he was afraid I might notice the newly

turned grave and connect it to Walter Gurney's sudden disappearance. But why not simply tell me, if he felt he had to mention it
at all, what he had told everyone else? Because he was afraid of
rousing my suspicions? Because he thought that I knew more
than I did about something? Maybe, if he believed everything that
Gilbert Foliot had hinted about me. But what was it that he thought
I knew?

Perhaps it was true that he and the goldsmith were at the heart
of a conspiracy to raise money for Henry Tudor and perhaps the
latter had been hoping to find something of value at Tintern. But
that begged the question as to why, suddenly, after so many years,
he had thought there might be treasure hidden in the secret hiding
place in the former abbot's lodgings.

Once again it seemed to me that the missing link in the chain
might be Walter Gurney who, on hearing that Sir Lionel Despenser
of Keynsham in Somerset was in need of a groom had not hesitated, but left his home and previous employment and set off to
offer his services to a man whom, as far as anyone knew, he had
never met before. Had it been simply to avoid his obligations to
Jane Spicer? Or had there been another motive? He had, at any
rate, according to Mistress Shoesmith, boasted of a connection
somewhere in the past between the Despensers and the Gurneys.
But what that was, and whether or not it had any significance, I
was unable to decide. Was it the real reason for his disappearance
before I could speak to him?

And had he not really run away, but been murdered? The more
I considered the question, the more likely a possibility it became. I
knew for a fact that the horse Sir Lionel had accused him of
stealing had not been stolen at all, but was being ridden by the
man whom I had seen in St Mary le Port Street and, later, board
the Breton ship. At the time I had thought the stranger might be
Walter Gurney himself, but now I felt certain I was wrong. It
seemed probable that the man was a Tudor agent who had been
visiting Gilbert Foliot. I remembered the supper things set out
before the fire the evening that Henry Callowhill and I had called
on the goldsmith unexpectedly; the best glass and napery
produced for someone of consequence. A valued customer the
goldsmith had said, which had appeared to be a valid explanation
at the time. But now, I wondered . . .

'You've gone all quiet, lad.' Mistress Shoesmith reproached me. 'The cat got your tongue?'

'I'm sorry,' I apologized. 'I was thinking about that grave and . . . and what you said about it being one of Sir Lionel's kitchen hands. You're sure of that? You're certain it wasn't one of his dogs?'

She gave her infectious gurgle of laughter. 'Of course I'm certain. He told my Jacob so, and my Jacob wouldn't have made it up. He's not got your brains, but he ain't stupid either. It's you who must've got hold of the wrong end of the stick, lad. Which wouldn't surprise me – not if you'd been in a trance like the one you were in just now. I'd to speak to you three or four times before I was able to get your attention.'

'I'm sorry,' I said again. 'I was thinking.'

'Well, that's what I mean. My Jacob, he don't do much thinking, but he understands what's said to him in simple, straightforward English.'

It was, and is, my firmly held contention that English is neither simple nor straightforward – there are too many different languages all mixed up together and vying for supremacy – but this was neither the time nor the place to argue the point. In any case, we were now within sight of Keynsham Abbey and the carter was enquiring whereabouts Mistress Shoesmith wished to be set down.

'The cobbler's shop at the far end of the High Street,' she said. 'You can put Master Chapman down with me.' She produced her purse and some coins changed hands which the carter quickly pocketed.

'Are you returning to Bristol on Monday?' I asked him, but he shook his head.

'Goin' on to Glastonbury. Two cases of these here candles are for the abbey.'

I was struck by a sudden inspiration. Brother Hilarion, my old Novice Master, was one of the most learned men I knew.

'Will you take me with you?' I asked. 'And then back to Bristol after that?' I, too, produced my purse and gave it a shake. There was the satisfactory sound of money chinking.

'Done,' he said. 'But I'll be starting early, as soon as it's light. I'll be staying at that ale-house, down in the dip there between them two slopes. Don' be late, 'cos I shan't wait. Understood?'

I assured him it was, grabbed my pack and cudgel from the back of the cart and, with Mistress Shoesmith, watched him drive away back along the street to make his first call.

It was by now well past the dinner hour, the carter having taken the five-mile journey at a leisurely pace, certainly below the capabilities of his horse, and I was ravenous. Fortunately, Mistress Shoesmith, as her comfortable shape implied, was also a hearty eater and her first action, once she had shepherded me through the cobbler's shop to the living quarters behind, was to berate the little maid we found dozing there for taking the pot of stew off the fire. Being a just woman, however, she relented almost at once, admitting she had not been expected for at least another day.

'There, there! Don't grizzle, Betsy. I didn't mean it. Just get the pot back over the heat. This is a friend o' mine, Roger, who's going to stay a night or two. And when you've done that, you can take my bag upstairs. Where's the master?'

'Gone out, deliverin' the mended shoes. 'E'll be back soon.'

Her mistress nodded briskly. 'Very well. Now stop gawping at Roger like you've never seen a good-looking man before and bustle about.' The dame turned to me. 'The accommodation ain't much, lad, as you can see, but what there is you'm more than welcome to share for however long you want to stay. There're two rooms upstairs, one that I share with my Jacob and a little one that Betsy sleeps in. But it won't hurt her to sleep in the kitchen for a night or two.'

I immediately protested, at the same time trying to press my share of the carter's fee on my hostess, who promptly rejected it with every appearance of being mortally insulted. In fact, she began to wheeze in such a distressed manner that I was forced to desist and assure her that I was only jesting. Also, when Betsy reappeared, she expressed perfect willingness to give up her room to me for as many nights as I wished, at the same time giving me such a broad wink, accompanied by an alluring swing of her hips, that I at once scented danger. If I didn't find her in my bed, either that night or the one after, I should be very surprised. Disappointed, too. She was a cosy little armful.

Mistress Shoesmith and I had just finished our bowlfuls of rabbit stew, and I was about to start on my second, when we heard voices raised in the shop and, a moment later, the cobbler entered the kitchen, to be brought up short by the sight of his wife and a perfect stranger sitting at the table. Mistress Shoesmith greeted him rapturously.

'I've come home early, my dear,' she said, rising and casting herself into his arms. 'Mary and I don't rub along too well at the best of times, as you well know, and this visit she just ruffled me up the wrong way right from the start. So here I am, two days early. And this is a young friend of mine, Roger Chapman, who's stopping with us tonight and tomorrow. He's a pedlar and hoping to do a bit of trade today and make some money for his wife and kinder. Roger, this is my Jacob, what you've heard me speak about.'

Jacob Shoesmith was as skinny as his wife was plump, the classic pairing that I had noted so often in my life; the attraction of opposites. But in nature they seemed well matched, he accepting my presence without demur and indeed smiling a welcome without demanding any further explanation. He returned his wife's embrace with a fervour equal to her own.

'I've allus said your Mary's a sharp-tongued shrew,' was his sole comment before turning to the maid. ''Ere, Betsy, you seen a pair o' black Spanish leather boots anywhere? I should've taken 'em with me to Sir Lionel's, but somehow I mislaid 'em . . . Ah! There they be!' He pointed to a corner of the kitchen. 'Now, how did they get in here? Must've walked by theirselves.' He and the two women laughed heartily at his joke. Then he called out, 'Found 'em, sir! They're in here. I'll bring 'em out.'

But before he could do so, another man entered the living quarters without so much as a by-your-leave and stood, looking contemptuously around him.

I knew at once who he was. He was the man I had seen in the courtyard of the Despenser manor house and, later, in Bristol, boarding the Breton ship.

SIXTEEN

Why did I feel so sure of that? At no time had I seen his features clearly enough to warrant such certainty. But there was something about his stance, the way he held himself, the arrogant set of his head on the broad shoulders, that left me in no doubt. I was also convinced that he was not Walter Gurney. His presence dominated the little room and he looked about him with a confidence that no servant, whatever his status, could command. He was a man used to consorting on equal terms with the very highest company. If he had indeed been Gilbert Foliot's recent guest, I could understand the effort made to impress him; the silver, the glass, the leaping fire, the best armchair. The boots, too, which he almost snatched from the cobbler's grasp, were fashioned from the very best Cordoban leather.

'You're a damn careless fellow, mislaying them like that,' he said, and I noticed that his English was slightly accented, not so much in the manner of a foreigner speaking a strange tongue, but more after the fashion of a native who had spent many years abroad. Brittany, perhaps? With Henry Tudor?

'I'm sorry, I'm sure, sir,' the cobbler apologized. 'I dunno 'ow they got in 'ere from the workshop. I 'ope it ain't delayed Your Honour's journey too much.'

The man vouchsafed no reply to this observation, merely repeating over his shoulder, 'You're a damn careless fellow. I don't know why Sir Lionel puts up with you.' The next moment he was gone, the curtain between the inner room and the shop rattling noisily on its rings.

'The impudence of it!' my hostess exclaimed wrathfully. 'What did he mean by that? I think I'll go after him and give him a piece of my mind.'

'Now, now my girl,' her husband said, laying a hand on her arm. 'Not so hasty. The gen'leman's got right on 'is side. I shouldn't've forgotten 'is boots. Nor Sir Lionel's red Moroccan slippers neither. I don' know what's got into me this morning. I'll 'ave t' go to the manor with them this afternoon.'

Mistress Shoesmith was not to be pacified. 'That ugly brute,' she declared hotly, 'could've taken Sir Lionel's slippers with him and saved you a journey. He must be staying at the manor. 'E wouldn't be likely t' be staying anywhere else.'

'Now 'old yer 'orses, dearie. 'Old yer 'orses! First, it's my fault entirely fer bein' so bloody forgetful. Must be gettin' old or something. Second, the gen'leman ain't goin' back t' the manor. 'E 'ad 'is 'orse waitin' fer 'im outside and 'e's off down Cornwall way. Won't be comin' back. Leastways, so 'e says. And there ain't no reason not t' believe 'im. So I'll just 'ave t' trudge to the manor again. Serve me right an' all. Maybe I won't be so careless in the future.' He turned towards me. 'Now tell me again oo this is. Didn't catch it proper the first time.'

So the introductions and explanations were gone through for a second time and Jacob Shoesmith welcomed me as warmly as his wife, generously bidding me to consider their home as mine for as long as was necessary.

'And now, my dear,' his wife exhorted me, 'if you want t' do some selling, you'd best get out right away. Fer it's Sunday tomorrow and I heard you make arrangements with Joseph Sibley to go on to Glastonbury with him on Monday. Besides, it gets dark early these days. You'll be back fer supper, o' course.'

I took the hint and shouldered my pack somewhat reluctantly, the goodwife's rabbit stew lying heavily on my stomach. But it also gave me the opportunity I had been looking for.

'Let me take Sir Lionel's slippers to the manor for you, Master Shoesmith,' I offered, holding out my hand for them. 'It will save you another journey.'

There was the inevitable argument of course, husband and wife both protesting that I didn't need to go beyond the village, and certainly not as far as the manor, while I insisted that it made no difference to me whatsoever. In the end, of course, I won. I made certain of that. I had been wondering how I could get inside the manor again if I was refused entry on the grounds of peddling my goods, and this gave me the perfect opportunity.

So, with the slippers wrapped in a piece of old sacking and tucked safely under my arm, my pack on my back and my cudgel in my hand I set out, promising to return in due course for supper.

To my great relief, the gatekeeper on this occasion was a stranger to me, for my fear had been that the man called Fulk, or the other servant, Robin, would have denied me access, a fear fully justified when I encountered the former as I crossed the courtyard.

'What in the Devil's name are you doing here?' he growled, planting himself directly in my path and showing an ugly, unwelcoming face.

I explained my errand, but almost without knowing what I was saying as I stared, fascinated, at his right cheek where four long abrasions were just beginning to show signs of healing. I noticed, too, as I had not done previously, how tall and muscular he was. I remembered the old beggar telling me how poor Oliver Tockney had clawed at his murderer's face as he was strangled, and also Henry Callowhill's and Lawyer Heathersett's description of two big, burly men who, they were convinced, were watching them and their houses. And almost immediately, right on his cue, the other servant, the one called Robin, appeared around a corner of the chapel and strolled across to join his fellow servant.

'What's the trouble, Fulk?'

Robin, too, was a heavily built man of an equal height with the other, a fact which made me catch my breath and then glance away quickly, in case I should be accused of staring. Could these be the two men who had committed the robberies, who had killed Oliver Tockney in order to steal and search his pack? If I were right, and I felt almost certain that I was, it meant that their master must have put them up to it.

Before Fulk could reply to Robin's question, another voice, that of Sir Lionel himself, posed the selfsame query. The man turned and indicated me. The knight's well-marked eyebrows flew up.

'Master Chapman, what a surprise! I'm afraid that if you are still hoping to see Walter Gurney, you will be disappointed. He has not returned.'

'Nor your horse, either, I suppose?'

He looked a little nonplussed for a moment before he recollected.

'No, nor my horse.'

'Well, that's not why I'm here,' I said. 'I've given up all hope of speaking to Master Gurney. I've come to deliver these.' And I held out the slippers, freed from their sacking wrapping.

He looked startled. 'What . . . I mean why . . .?'

I explained as briefly as I could. 'And Cobbler Shoesmith sends his most abject apologies for his forgetfulness. It seems he also mislaid your friend's boots, but that mistake has also been rectified.'

'My friend? Ah, yes! He's . . . He's left here now.'

'He has business in Cornwall, I understand.' I hadn't seen the stranger ride away, but I drew a bow at a venture. 'A very fine horse he was riding. Rather like the one you described Walter Gurney as having stolen.'

I saw his eyelids flicker for a second, no doubt silently cursing himself for having described the animal in such detail. He said curtly, 'Something like,' and rapidly changed the subject. 'So you're here to sell your wares, eh? I fear you won't find much of a market in Keynsham. A stingy lot, the inhabitants – tight with their money.' He indicated that I should hand the slippers to Fulk and went on, 'I see you have your pack with you. Come inside. You may have something my housekeeper is in crying need of.'

'In that case, I'll go round to the kitchens.'

'No, no! Come into the hall and display your goods in comfort. Robin, tell Dame Joliphant I need her and then take those slippers to my bedchamber.'

He nodded dismissal to both men and turned towards the door, but I hung on my heel. The chapel was to our right and the graveyard, behind its white paling, alongside it.

'This is where your dog – Caesar, did you say he was called? – is buried, I think you told me.' I pointed to a mound where the grass and tangle of bindweed, with its white, trumpet-like flowers, had not yet taken hold. 'Is that it?'

Once again, Sir Lionel appeared to be slightly taken aback before making a recovery.

'Er . . . Yes.'

'A big dog by the size of his grave.'

'A mastiff,' he answered shortly. 'Now, shall we go in?'

Indoors, he led me to the dais at the far end of the hall and bade me set out the contents of my pack on the table. The housekeeper arrived, somewhat flustered by this peremptory summons, and was told to see if there was anything she needed. But I was more interested in the actions of my host who stayed glued to my side, closely scrutinizing every article I produced and laid out for inspection. And, finally, when the pack was emptied and he judged that my attention had been firmly claimed by Dame Joliphant, I saw him, out of the corner of one eye, lift the pack and shake it in order to satisfy himself that nothing remained inside.

Nothing did, and as soon as I had finished supplying the housekeeper's modest requirements, I found myself being shown the door with a most impolite speed. Whatever Sir Lionel had hoped he might find in my pack, he had been disappointed and now had no further use for my company. Indeed, I had probably become an embarrassment to him with my unfortunate recollections of things he had said to me on the previous occasion; lies which he had concocted on the spur of the moment and by now half-forgotten.

I spent the rest of the short autumnal day hawking my wares around the Keynsham cottages, and little reward I had for my efforts. This, however, was not altogether due to the parsimony of the good folk of the village. To say that my heart was not in my work would be no more than the truth. I felt sure that those goodwives who did inspect my wares found me absent-minded and my conversation less than scintillating. After all, much of the pleasure of inviting a chapman, or indeed any itinerant member of society, into their homes was to hear the latest gossip and news of the outside world, and my vague, terse and occasionally downright impatient answers to their questions must have been a great disincentive to part with their money. But my mind was elsewhere.

I was trying to come to terms first and foremost with the idea that Walter Gurney was the occupant of that new grave in Sir Lionel's chapel graveyard. It was obvious that the story of the dog had been a lie told me at the time in order to put me off the scent in case I noticed the freshly turned earth and grew suspicious. (In the event, the untruth had proved unnecessary and had only served to arouse my suspicions at a later date. The knight must again be rueing his too-ready tongue.) But that begged the question as to why he had thought I might suspect him of doing away with his groom.

I recollected his sceptical expression when I had revealed my reason for wishing to speak to Walter. He had plainly not believed me, which could only mean that he thought my business to be of a secret nature. That I was working under instructions from the crown? Yes, probably. If he and Gilbert Foliot were truly hand in glove with one of Henry Tudor's agents, they would be wary of everyone who had known associations with King Richard. But what information had Walter Gurney possessed that might be of value to me as a spy?

The second thing that exercised my mind was the nagging conviction that Fulk and Robin were the two men responsible not just for Oliver Tockney's murder, but also for that of the old beggar who lived in Pit Hay Lane and for the break-ins. But in that case, they had to be acting at the instigation of their master and possibly of the goldsmith, too, which, if true, bolstered my belief that the robbers were after only one thing. And that surely had to be whatever it was Peter Noakes had found – or they thought he had found – at Tintern Abbey.

Timothy had told me that Henry Tudor's coffers were reported as being almost empty, and that money to pay the mercenary troops necessary to help him invade England was his most pressing need. So the obvious conclusion to draw was that the treasure was either cash or something that could be converted into cash. And whatever it was had been left at the abbey a century and more ago by men fleeing from the law; men for whom the monks themselves had felt the utmost revulsion but whom the abbot was willing to assist. Reluctantly, perhaps, and denying them more than two nights' shelter from their pursuers, but nevertheless afraid to withhold his aid.

But if these surmises were correct, where was the treasure? It was not still in the secret hiding place of the abbot's old lodgings because I had myself reached in as far as my arm would go, until my nails had scrabbled against cold earth. And yet if, as seemed most likely, Peter Noakes had hidden whatever he had found in the baggage of one or other of the rest of us, then where was it? It had plainly not been in Oliver Tockney's pack or the search would have ended with his murder. Again, nothing could have been discovered either at the lawyer's house or in Henry Callowhill's. The attempted robbery at my house had been thwarted, but I knew only too well that my pack was innocent of anything unusual or valuable; and if the testimony of my own eyes was not enough, then I had just seen Sir Lionel prove it for himself. That left the goldsmith, but I discounted him. I guessed that the attempt to break into the house in St Peter's Street had been nothing but a blind.

With all this churning around inside my head, it was small wonder that my efforts at selling my goods were met with poor success, and by the time I eventually returned to the cobbler's shop I was bone-weary and dispirited.

'Eh, lad, you've worn yourself out,' Mistress Shoesmith upbraided me, pushing me, unresisting, into the room's one armchair and bustling about to fetch me a beaker of ale and some of her honey cakes, baked, so she assure me, only that afternoon. 'Now, sit still and Betsy'll pull off your boots.'

I made a feeble remonstrance, but was too tired to resist and extended my feet to the obliging Betsy without more ado. She glanced up and gave a broad wink which I returned, but half-heartedly. I was glad when the cobbler himself entered the room and supper was served.

'He's worn himself out,' my hostess informed her husband, who grunted.

'It's hard work getting money out of them skinflints,' he grumbled. 'Don't I know it?'

'You can have a rest tomorrow,' Mistress Shoesmith said. 'It's Sunday.'

Fortunately, my hosts were not ones for sitting up late, nor was their conversation of such a nature as to keep them awake much past mid-evening. The cobbler did ask me if I fancied a visit to the local ale-house, but as the pair of us were already yawning our heads off, I declined – greatly, I thought, to his relief. Mistress Shoesmith, having imparted such gossip as there was concerning her visit to her sister, had fallen asleep at the table, her chin propped between her hands. The only one of us who seemed unaffected by the stuffy atmosphere of the little room behind the shop, its shutters closed and barred against the dark November evening outside, was Betsy. She sat on a three-legged stool in one corner, humming softly to herself, her large eyes fixed on each of us in turn, but mainly, I noticed uneasily, turned in my direction. I could only hope that her expectations of me were not too high. I wasn't sure that I could live up to them.

It was after my hostess had awakened with a snort from her slumbers that she announced it was time to retire.

'For there's no point in us sitting here snoring when we might as well be comfortable in our beds. Betsy, my girl, bustle about and light the candles and lantern while I douse the fire. And then fetch a spare blanket and pillow from the chest in our bedchamber and make yourself a nest in that corner by the hearth. You'll do very well there for a night or two.'

Once more, I was moved to protest, insisting that I should be the one to sleep downstairs, but I was again overruled, most loudly by Betsy herself. So I allowed myself to be persuaded.

'She's a good deal younger than you are,' the cobbler grunted, while his wife nodded agreement. ''Sides, you be a guest.'

The second reason appealed to me far more than the first, and I went to bed somewhat deflated by the thought of my advancing years.

Mistress Shoesmith's reference to lighting a lantern, which I had found a little strange, was soon explained when I discovered that although the main bedchamber was reached by a narrow flight of stairs from the living room, the second could only be entered from outside the cottage by an equally narrow flight of stone steps. As I mounted cautiously, lantern in hand, a few heavy drops of rain fell on my face and I could hear the moan of a rising wind. We were, I guessed, in for one of those storms that so often herald the coldest part of the year.

To call Betsy's room a bedchamber was to give it a dignity it in no way deserved. I doubt if it were much more than six-feet wide by perhaps ten-feet long, while the ceiling was so low that I could barely stand upright. It contained nothing except a bed and, beside it, a small chest which held such spare clothing as she possessed and whose lid acted as a table on which reposed a broken comb, a tinderbox and flints and an earthenware jug full of stale water. There was no window and when the door was shut, no light except from the lantern I was carrying. This I placed carefully alongside the jug while I stripped down to my shirt and eased myself between the sheets.

These, though ripped in several places, I discovered, somewhat to my surprise, to be clean and smelling faintly of lavender. They had obviously been newly put on the bed, probably while I was out earlier in the day, and I was touched by such thoughtfulness. I fished around in my pack for my piece of willow bark and cleaned my teeth, at the same time wishing that Mistress Shoesmith had offered me a basin of water in which to wash away the grime of what had been a long day. But my nose had told me that cleanliness was not of great importance to either the cobbler or his wife.

I sat up in bed and regarded the door. In spite of the lack of a window, there was no dearth of air in the room, the door being extremely badly fitting, with at least two inches of space between the bottom of it and the threshold. It did, however, boast a strong iron bolt near the top, and for a moment or two I debated whether or not to use it. But the memory of Betsy's parting smile as she wished me goodnight made me hesitate. There had been more than a hint of promise in those softly curling lips and although, at the time, I had felt too tired to respond, the fresh air had revived me. There was little chance of her appearing, however, before the Shoesmiths were safely asleep, and as I could still hear them moving about on the other side of the thin wall which separated us, I decided I might as well settle down. I opened the door of the lantern and blew out the candle, then pulled the sheet and the rough woollen blanket up around my ears and closed my eyes.

When I opened them again, how much later I wasn't sure, I could hear that the storm had well and truly broken. The wind had risen to shrieking pitch, gibbering around the cottage as though it were trying to blow it down, and soughing through the branches of some nearby trees, rattling their near leafless branches. The draught beneath the door was lifting the rushes on the floor with such ferocity that several small pieces were floating about the room, one of which had settled on my upper lip, just below my nose, making me sneeze. It was this that had woken me.

I had just brushed it away and was settling myself to sleep again as best I could, when I heard a noise outside. It was a miracle that I could hear anything above the howling of the wind, and precisely what I heard I could not afterwards determine.

'Betsy,' I thought, and marvelled that any girl could be so eager for my company that she was willing to brave the cold, the darkness and the rain to be with me. It was flattering of course, but I wasn't feeling my best and was doubtful of my power to entertain her. Nevertheless, I could hardly turn her away when she showed herself so keen. Besides, honour was at stake. Here was a chance to prove that my advancing years sat lightly on me; that thirty-one was not the end of existence.

I hauled myself up in bed, at the same time groping for the tinderbox and flint and fumbling to open the lantern door in order to light the candle inside. Then I paused. The bedchamber door was opening on a gust of wind and rain, but with a caution that puzzled me. I would not have expected Betsy to be so tentative. I put down the tinderbox and flint as gently as I could and silently swung my legs to the floor. As I stood upright, the wind wrestled the door from the intruder's grasp, flinging it back against the wall with a clatter. The next moment, someone launched himself at me with a grunt, knocking me over and forcing me back against the pillow.

Whoever the man was, he had a knife. I saw the flash of the blade as he raised his right hand, while his left forced up my chin as he sought to expose my throat. But my assassin had not counted on my being awake and therefore alert. I imagine the intention had been to kill me quickly while I slept or, had he had the misfortune to rouse me, before I had time to gather my wits. My vigorous resistance took him by surprise. Moreover, the rain had made his hands slippery, and the blade, thrusting downwards, missed the base of my neck and skidded across my right collarbone, leaving a nasty scratch but nothing worse.

I heard him curse. His breath was foul in my face, but no lasting damage had been incurred. With a great heave, I managed to throw him off and wriggle free from beneath his weight. But big man though he was, he was agile and came at me again almost at once, certainly before I had time to find my feet. This time he forced me, half on, half off the bed, back against the wall at its head. His anger at being thwarted was palpable, and I could see the whites of his eyes glinting in the darkness. He was at me again, stabbing wildly now at any part of my body within reach, and I was having to fend him off with every ounce of strength that I could muster. My heart was hammering so hard it was beginning to make me feel sick. Surely I wasn't meant to die here in this fetid little room! I had been in worse situations than this, I told myself, and survived. I felt the knife nick my left cheek . . .

Suddenly I remembered the jug of water on top of the chest. With an enormous effort I pushed my assailant off me just long enough to reach out with my left hand and grab the jug's handle. Then I poured the contents over him and broke the empty vessel over his head. Temporarily blinded and slightly dazed, he dropped the knife and staggered to his feet, lurching towards the door. In an instant I was after him and had propelled him through the opening. Another shove and he crashed down the short flight of steps, landing with a sickening thud on the rain-sodden ground below. I didn't wait to see if he were seriously hurt or not, but went back inside the room, closing and bolting the door.

It was a long time before I fell asleep. There were too many questions that needed answering.

I had had a lucky escape. Apart from the scratch on my collar-bone, which throbbed a little, there was practically nothing to show for my recent murderous encounter. I was winded, frightened but otherwise unharmed. But who had my attacker been? I thought I knew. He had been either Fulk or Robin, but it had been too dark to be sure, but that it was one or the other of them I would have staked my life on. Which meant, of course, that Sir Lionel Despenser was behind the outrage. He still regarded me as a threat to whatever plot he was mixed up in, and on discovering that I was to spend the night in the village had seized this opportunity to get rid of me. Had he succeeded, I wondered who would have taken the blame for my death. My guess was that Jacob Shoesmith and his wife would have found the finger of suspicion pointing at them.

But how had my assailant known that I was sleeping in the room normally occupied by Betsy? This was something I had

not mentioned that afternoon when talking to the knight. The
fact that I had left the door unbolted might simply have been
fortuitous. On the other hand, it might not. It could be that
someone from the manor had paid a visit to the cobbler's shop
that afternoon while I was plying my trade elsewhere in the
village, and who knew what Jacob Shoesmith might have let
slip? He could well have noticed how the girl had looked at me
and guessed her intention. A salacious jest, a nudge, a wink and
Fulk – or Robin – would have returned home with the information that the coming night presented an opportunity worth the
taking. If it turned out that I had, after all, bolted the door against
Betsy's advances, there was still all day Sunday and the following
night to make a second attempt.

I jerked into a sitting position, sweat prickling across my
skin and my heart pounding against my ribs. I knew suddenly
that I had to get away from Keynsham as soon as I could and
not wait for a lift in Joseph Sibley's cart on Monday morning.
Danger threatened me in this isolated village; the same fate as
had most probably overtaken Walter Gurney. I slid out of bed,
unbolted the door and peered cautiously outside. No black shape
still lay at the foot of the steps: whoever had attacked me had
gone, nursing his injuries. But I felt certain that, sometime
during the next twenty-four hours or so, he would be back. Him
or another.

The moon, a pale sickle of apricot, rode high amid the rushing
clouds, then vanished, but the rain had stopped. I dressed quickly,
wrapped myself in my cloak with the hood pulled well forward
over my head, took my pack and cudgel and let myself out into
the all-enveloping darkness. What the Shoesmiths would make
of my abrupt and ungracious departure I did not give myself time
to consider. My instinct for danger warned me to get away while
the going was good. Apologies and explanations could wait for
some future date, if and when I saw them again. For now, my
safety was all that mattered.

SEVENTEEN

As the crow flies, my home city of Wells lies seventeen or so miles to the south of Keynsham and Glastonbury some five miles beyond that. There was no hope, therefore, of my reaching the abbey for several days, but if I kept to the main tracks, there was a slight possibility that Joseph Sibley and his cart-load of candles might overtake me before my journey's end. It was not much of a chance – most cart-horses went only a little faster than walking pace – but it was a chance nevertheless, and would save my aching legs when they needed it the most. And I kept to the main tracks for another reason: it was easier to see if I was being followed.

I slept for what remained of the first night in an empty barn standing adjacent to the road, wrapped in my cloak on the damp, beaten-earth floor, my cudgel by my hand. I didn't sleep well, but this was not entirely due to general discomfort. I couldn't help wondering if my response to the attack on me had not been somewhat too precipitous, too cowardly and too unfair to the Shoesmiths. But the sense of danger had been strong, begging to be heeded.

The next day being Sunday, the tracks were sparse of traffic, especially when I started off in the chill mist of a November dawn. A broad stream ran alongside the path for a mile or two, the rising sun reflected like a drowned golden orb in the stillness of its water, the mirrored images of trees quivering stealthily across its glassy surface. I forced myself to stop and wash my hands and face, but it was like bathing in snow-broth, and when I drank some of the water from my cupped hands my very innards seemed to freeze.

It being the Sabbath, I was unable to peddle my wares, but in the various cottages where, throughout the day, I found food and shelter, the goodwives were more than willing to accept payment in kind rather than money. The one, who gave me breakfast – hot oatcakes and honey and several cups of mulled ale – chose a pretty leather girdle with pewter tags. (They weren't fools, these women. They knew a good bargain when they saw one.) I took my dinner at a farmhouse where I was given a share of a dish of pig's trotters stewed in butter followed by a baked apple dumpling and home-brewed cider. As a reward for this splendid repast, the goodwife chose the set of carved bone buttons that I had purchased at Gloucester, some needles and thread that she was in crying need of and two lengths of white silk ribbon, while her goodman claimed my company over another cup of cider in order to hear news of the wider world.

'What's with all these here rumours,' he demanded, 'that this new king of ours – and whether or no he ought t' be king is a matter o' debate, I gather – has killed off his little nevvies? If that be the case, he should never –'

I cut him short with more haste than good manners and propounded my theory on the subject with such vehemence that my poor host was left floundering and almost apologizing to me for having raised the matter in the first place. After which, it was hardly surprising that he steered the topic of conversation into less controversial channels and described to me the pleasures and difficulties of farming what he called 'hruther' or 'rudder' beasts; the old Anglo-Saxon term, which I as a country boy was well acquainted with, for horned cattle.

Supper was a much more modest affair – bread and cheese and onions – taken at a small, wayside ale-house where I was also able to pay for a bed for the night and avail myself of the use of a pump in the backyard; a great relief to me as I had not washed properly for the past two days. I was also relieved to notice that the door of my room, a tiny attic under the eaves, sported a bolt, and I was able to strip and tumble into bed with a quiet mind.

But not quiet enough, it seemed. My dreams were troubled and appeared to centre on the farmhouse where I had eaten my dinner, although without any clarity to them. They were also mixed up with a jumble of nonsense where I kept on telling Adam to speak up and repeat what he had just said, while Adela lectured me about throwing the contents of my pack all over the kitchen floor. Something was bothering me, that was obvious enough, but when I awoke in the morning

and tried to assemble the dreams into some sort of order, I
was unable to do so.

'Lord,' I prayed, hastily going down on my knees beside the
bed, 'I know I'm being stupid and dense, but please, please show
me the way more clearly. I realize you are trying to tell me
something, but you know that sometimes I don't have the sense
of a louse. Less, probably. So if you could just see your way to
putting things more plainly . . .'

I stood upright again and listened. The silence was
deafening.

Monday was much like Sunday except that there were more
people on the roads and I was able to sell my goods wherever
possible without straying too far from the main Glastonbury
track. In fact, I was more interested in making progress than in
making money, and I knew that it would take another steady day
and a half's walking before I was within sight of my destination.
The November weather was worsening again, the ground soggy,
patches of mist hanging in the air like damp rags and the trees
rapidly shedding their autumnal glory of yellow and purple,
crimson and yellow, the remaining leaves turning a dull, burnt-
out brown.

I was right in my calculations and it was nearing noon on
Tuesday – judging by the height of a watery sun appearing and
disappearing between lowering grey clouds – when I found
myself walking down the long slope of the Mendips into Wells,
nestling at their foot. The town hadn't changed much since my
boyhood, the cathedral, that mighty church dedicated to St
Andrew, still dominating the huddle of insignificant dwellings
crowding around it as if for warmth and protection. I didn't
linger. I knew no one there nowadays and even if I had, by
chance, encountered some long lost acquaintance of my youth,
I shouldn't have known what to say to him. So I pressed on
along the raised causeway across the flat Somerset levels with
the Tor, crowned by its church, rising out of the plain and
beckoning me on like a beacon.

Legend says that this is Avalon, and indeed the tomb of Arthur
and Guinevere is to be seen in the abbey choir, attracting hundreds
of pilgrims every year who come to worship where the Christ

child is reputed to have founded the earliest church in Britain; a boy accompanying his uncle, Joseph of Arimathea, who had come to buy tin and lead from the Romans. But there were very few pilgrims at this time of the year and I had met practically no one on my walk. Nor were there many inhabitants abroad on this dank late afternoon as I approached the abbey gates and rang for the porter.

Brother Hilarion, my old Novice Master, was taking exercise in the cloisters, getting a little fresh air between Vespers and the evening service of Compline. As I watched him coming towards me, my first thought was that he had aged considerably since I had last seen him seven years ago, when the disappearance of two brothers from the town had kept me here against my will and strained my deductive powers to the uttermost. My second thought was that he was probably thinking the same about me. A second marriage and the responsibility of three children had without doubt added years to my boyish good looks. I certainly felt as though they had. I felt old and careworn. It would have been no surprise if Brother Hilarion had failed to recognize me.

'My child! My child!' He beamed upon me, stretching up to kiss my cheek. 'You look exactly the same. You haven't changed one iota.' He patted my shoulder and regarded my pack and cudgel. 'Now what brings you here at this unseasonable time of year when you should be tucked up safe within four walls? Don't tell me that peddling is such a hard task-master that you have to be out in all weathers. No, no! You look too prosperous, too well fed. Besides,' he took my arm, leaning heavily on it, and began to walk back with me along the cloister, 'we hear things, you know, even in here.'

'What sort of things?' I asked resignedly.

'Oh, this and that.' He smiled up at me proudly. 'I always deplored your decision to follow the calling of a pedlar. You were one of my brighter scholars. You learned to read and write faster than anyone else I'd ever taught and could add up numbers in your head. I knew you to be capable of greater things than just hawking a pedlar's pack around the countryside.'

'But that's what I do.'

My old preceptor chuckled. 'Yes, yes! Have it your own way.
I understand. Your lips are sealed. Your loyalty is to the duke. I
mean, the king.' A frown appeared, creasing his brow. 'That was
a strange business. And His Grace the Bishop of Bath and Wells
mixed up in it, too. One doesn't know what to think. And now
these rumours about the two young boys.' Once again, he glanced
up at me, this time curiously. 'I suppose . . . But, no! I mustn't
ask. You're sworn to secrecy, no doubt. So tell me, what brings
you here?'

I sighed. I felt extremely uneasy. My reputation of having the
king's confidence, of being some kind of secret agent for him,
was growing and expanding well beyond the walls of Bristol. I
could deny it as I had done in the past, but common sense told
me that the more I refuted the suggestion, the more people
believed the opposite. Denial on my part only strengthened their
conviction that I was lying.

'I know nothing about the fate of the lords Edward and Richard
Plantagenet,' I answered quietly. 'But I do know something about
the character of the king.' I did indeed. I might as well admit it.
'And knowing that, I can assure you that these vicious rumours
are untrue.'

Brother Hilarion pressed my arm. 'You relieve my mind, Roger.
I have always considered him a good man, and I should be loath
to think him capable of such a heinous sin. But if you assure me
that all is well . . .'

He let the sentence hang and I realized despairingly that with
every word I spoke I only confirmed his opinion of my standing
at the court. I would do better to hold my tongue. I was just
about to turn the conversation into safer channels when my
companion did it for me.

'So, I repeat, what brings you here?'

'Do I have to have a reason? I might just have walked as far
as this on my travels and decided to renew our acquaintance.'

'Friendship,' he amended and then chuckled. 'No, no! That's
not your way, Roger. There was always a purpose to everything
you did. I'm not deceived.'

'True,' I admitted. 'You never were. I need to pick your
brains.'

He smiled delightedly. 'And so you shall. If I can be of any

help to you, I will be. But first, come and pay your respects to
Father Abbot. He'll wish to see you, but we won't stay too long.
His time is much taken up at present with this latest dispute with
Canterbury. You can guess what about.'

I threw back my head and gave a shout of laughter, much to
the disapproval of other brothers exercising in the cloister, two
of whom turned their heads to frown at me and mutter angrily
under their breath.

'You're not still arguing as to who has the real set of St
Dunstan's bones? Is the matter still not resolved after all these
years?'

Brother Hilarion looked offended and withdrew his hand from
my arm. 'No, and never will be, Roger, so long as Canterbury
disputes our claim.'

'But he was Archbishop of Canterbury and died there,' I
argued.

My companion sniffed contemptuously. 'And he was Abbot
of Glastonbury here in his own home county long before that.
He naturally requested that his body should be brought home for
burial as any good Somerset man would. It's obvious.'

'But not to Canterbury,' I murmured. Brother Hilarion,
however, fortunately did not hear me.

'There is no doubt whatsoever that ours are the true set of
bones,' he stated flatly and in a tone that brooked no further
argument.

I took the hint and allowed him to conduct me to the abbot
without further ado.

John Selwood had been Abbot of Glastonbury since I was
four years old, and would remain so for another decade. Before
that he had been Receiver to two previous abbots, and in this
autumn of 1483 was beginning to display some of that unrea-
soning impatience and irascibility that comes with old age. But
he had always been very kind to me and had shown under-
standing and tolerance when, twelve years previously, I had cut
short my novitiate to take to a life on the open road. He greeted
me now with every courtesy in spite of his being in the middle
of dictating a letter to his secretary, enquired after my health,
my circumstances and my family, and invited me to find a bed
for the night in his own lodging house. But he was plainly

preoccupied and I did not linger, happy to let Brother Hilarion shepherd me out once again into the late afternoon chill of the November day.

It was with a sinking heart that I recollected the monks' main meal had passed some hours earlier (my chief and most abiding memory of my years at the abbey was of desperate, gnawing hunger), but Brother Hilarion took me to the abbot's own kitchen and there begged and cajoled the lay brother in charge to feed me. After making a fuss just for the sheer principle of the thing, this toplofty individual unbent to such a degree that he warmed up a large bowl of pottage over the fire, served me with half a chicken carcass, still with plenty of meat on its bones, and rounded off this princely repast with a dish of figs and honey and goat's milk cheese, all washed down with several cups of the abbey's delicious sweet cider.

Thus fortified, I returned with Brother Hilarion to his cell where he should have spent the time in prayer and preparation for the coming service of Compline, but instead invited me to tell him the reason for my visit. So I put my pack and cudgel in a corner and sat down beside him on the edge of the hard, narrow stone ledge that, with a single blanket and straw-filled pillow, served as his bed. (Another reminder of the discomfort and self-deprivation that had convinced me that a monk's life was not for me.) I then started at the beginning and went on until I had come to the end of the story so far.

'An interesting tale,' he said slowly when I had finished. 'But what is it exactly that you want from me?'

'Your scholarship and learning. When the carter, Joseph Sibley, mentioned that he was coming here, I suddenly thought of you. I was hoping that you might be able to unravel the mystery of the men who sought shelter at Tintern Abbey all those long years ago. The year mentioned was 1326. Do you have any notion of what was happening then? Who those men might possibly have been?'

Brother Hilarion chewed his upper lip while he marshalled his thoughts.

'The year of Our Lord one thousand, three hundred and twenty-six,' he murmured over to himself. 'Yes.' He fell silent while I contained my impatience as best I could. After perhaps another half minute he said slowly, 'This fragment of diary that was discovered under the floor in the former abbot's lodging mentioned four men, you say?'

I searched my memory, desperately trying to recall the exact wording.

I said, at last, 'I remember it said that "they came last night" and two others with them, one of whom was called Reading and the other . . . Baldock, Yes, that was it. Baldock! For some reason my assumption was that the second pair – the ones named – were not so important. It was just the impression I got.'

My companion nodded to himself. Then he asked, 'And you say that this knight is called Despenser?'

'Sir Lionel Despenser, yes.'

'And the groom you mentioned, the one you think may have been murdered, was named Gurney?'

'Yes, yes!'

'And he boasted that his family was linked to this Sir Lionel's in some way or another?'

'So I've been told. But not in recent years, you understand. Sometime in the past.' I curbed my desire to take my former mentor by the shoulders and shake the information out of him. Not that it would have done any good. Brother Hilarion had always proceeded at his own pace, making sure that he had the facts right in his own head before imparting any knowledge to others.

Now he nodded yet again, finally demanding in his best domi-nie's voice, 'What do you know about the second Edward?'

Immediately, in my mind's eye, I was back in Gloucester Abbey standing by the ornate marble sarcophagus built, as so much of the surrounding edifice had been, on the proceeds of the offerings of pilgrims who had come to pay their respects at Edward's tomb.

'I know he practiced the vice of the Greeks. That he preferred men to women, in spite of being the father of four children.'

A faint flush mantled Brother Hilarion's cheeks, but he admitted bravely, 'Yes, that was his great sin. Some blame may be laid at his father's door, I think. The first Edward – Longshaks, the Hammer of the Scots, whatever one chooses to call him – was a great warrior. (As, of course, was his grandson, the third

Edward.) To have a son like the second Edward must have been a bitter pill for him to swallow. There is written evidence to show that the latter, as a young man, was treated with great harshness and contempt by his father. And God knows, he paid for his sins. His murder in Berkeley Castle was hideous.' My companion shuddered. 'I find it impossible to imagine how his gaolers could have devised such a death.'

I said nothing, but found it entirely plausible. A red-hot poker thrust up their victim's anus to burn out his bowels would have appealed strongly to their sense of humour: surely an appropriate death for one whose chief lovers had been men.

'One of those gaolers,' Brother Hilarion went on quietly, 'was a Sir Thomas Gurney.'

'Gurney?'

'Yes. The others were Sir John Maltravers and Thomas of Berkeley himself.'

'Gurney?' I repeated again.

'This groom you mentioned, this Walter Gurney, may well be a descendant.'

'And his connection with Sir Lionel Despenser?'

Brother Hilarion eased his shoulders and wriggled his thin flanks against the hard stone. 'Edward,' he said, 'had two lovers to whom he was devoted. One was the Gascon, Piers Gaveston. He was the first and most beloved. "Brother Perrot," Edward called him, and would have given him the moon if he could have got it for him. As it was, Piers had to be content with most of the great cofferfuls of jewels the Princess Isabella brought with her from France when she became Queen of England after her marriage to the king at Boulogne.'

'What happened to the Gascon?'

'Eventually, he was murdered by the barons who resented his influence over Edward. They hoped that with Gaveston's death, the king would amend his ways.'

'But he didn't?'

'Of course not. The barons were fools to think that he would. He found another lover on whom to lavish his affection. Hugh le Despenser.'

'Despenser?' I demanded excitedly. 'You think Sir Lionel might be a descendant of this Hugh?'

'It's possible.' Brother Hilarion was cautious. 'He might not be a direct descendant, of course, although I seem to recall that the younger Hugh was married and had children.'

'The younger Hugh?'

'He had a father of the same name who became Edward's chief adviser. Both men were greatly resented by the barons, as I suppose I don't need to tell you.'

'What happened to them?'

'Not so fast, my child. Queen Isabella, as you may well imagine, deeply resented her treatment at the hands of her husband. She was an extraordinarily beautiful woman, having inherited the good looks of her father, Philippe le Bel of France, and in the beginning, she was known as Isabella the Fair.'

'And later?' Something stirred in my memory. 'Was she the queen known as the She-Wolf of France?'

Brother Hilarion gave a long drawn out sigh, obviously sorrowing for the weaknesses of mankind. 'Yes,' he agreed sadly. 'Her beauty was not the only thing she inherited from her father. Philippe IV had a cruel, ruthless streak in him, as his vicious suppression of the Templars demonstrates. Isabella inherited that streak. But again, we are getting ahead of ourselves in the story.

'Edward was due to go to France to do homage to his brother-in-law, King Charles, for the fiefs of Gascony and Ponthieu. But he was afraid to go; afraid of leaving the two Despensers without his protection. And so he did a very foolish thing. He sent Isabella as his deputy along with their elder son, the thirteen-year-old Edward of Windsor.'

'Ah!' I exclaimed, memory stirring once more. 'If I remember rightly, she met a man and fell passionately in love.'

The little monk pursed his lips and stared down his nose. 'She was a married woman,' he said repressively, 'and a mother four times over. She should have had more control. But you're right. The great Marcher lord, Roger Mortimer of Wigmore, had been at the French court ever since Edward had sent him into exile for some misdemeanour – fancied or otherwise – and he was as eager for revenge on Edward as Isabella herself. Their love affair became so open, so unbridled, so scandalous, that they were ordered to leave France. So they went to

Hainault, betrothed young Edward to the count's daughter, Phillipa, and set out to invade England with an army of Hainaulters and mercenaries.

'The English, sick and tired of the king and his minions, welcomed them with open arms. Edward's supporters were murdered, including Bishop Stapledon of Exeter, his head hacked off with a butcher's knife on the Cheapside cobbles. Edward and the Despensers fled westward to Bristol, along with Edward's Chancellor, Baldock and a clerk of the court, Simon Reading.'

'Baldock and Reading,' I said excitedly. 'The names in the diary.'

Brother Hilarion nodded. 'The citizens of Bristol declared for the queen and Mortimer, managed to seize the elder Despenser and hanged him from the castle walls. Afterwards, they cut his body into collops and fed him to the wild dogs which scavenge for food on the heights above the city.'

I choked. Perhaps one of Hercules's ancestors had been fed on these remnants of human flesh.

'Go on,' I muttered thickly to my companion, who was regarding me with concern, although by now I could work out for myself the end of the story.

'Are you sure you wish me to?' Brother Hilarion asked. 'It's a most unpleasant tale and you look a little queasy.'

'No, no! I'm quite all right. Please continue,' I urged him.

'Well, there's not much more to tell. Edward, the younger Despenser, Reading and Baldock escaped by the city's Water Gate and reached the coast of Wales on the other side of the Severn. From there they went first to Tintern Abbey where, according to tradition, they stayed two nights, and then on to Neath Abbey where they lingered too long and were finally captured by Isabella's and Mortimer's troops. The favourite was hanged, drawn and quartered at Hereford, while the king was imprisoned firstly at Kenilworth and then at Berkeley Castle where, in spite of the most appalling ill-treatment, he refused to die, so was finally murdered in the barbarous way we mentioned just now.' He regarded me anxiously. 'My child, you look quite pale.'

If I did indeed look pale, it was with excitement.

'And all this happened in the year 1326?' I asked.

'To the best of my recollection. But I will check for you in the annals of the abbey library after Compline or certainly before you leave us tomorrow.'

I didn't discourage him in this self-imposed task – it was always good to have confirmation – but I had no doubt that his memory was good. Everything fitted together: the diarist's and his fellow monks' horror at the sin of sodomy which tainted their unexpected and unwanted guests and the abbot's reluctance to offend the man who, when all was said and done, was still his sovereign. And how could he tell at that point who would finally prove victorious?

That left the mystery of the treasure, if it existed outside our imaginations. But it was more than possible that the king had left something of value in the abbot's care; something which he did not wish to fall into his queen's and her lover's hands, but which he could go back for later if his cause took a turn for the better. Either money or something he could convert into money if the need arose.

What had alerted Master Foliot to its possible existence I was not quite sure, but I suspected that it must have something to do with the arrival of Walter Gurney in the life of Sir Lionel Despenser and the latter's friendship with the goldsmith. The link was undeniably there, two men whose ancestors' lives had both touched that of the second Edward.

But none of this answered the question of where, presuming that Peter Noakes had actually found something in the hiding place, the treasure was now concealed? What had he done with it? Who had it now?

EIGHTEEN

Once again, I slept badly; a sleep crowded with dreams which verged at times on the point of nightmares. Nor was it entirely the fault of the bed I occupied in the abbey guest-house, although to compare the thin mattress to a bed of nails is not such an exaggeration as it might at first seem. I could not help contrasting it with the luxury of the accommodation in the Tintern infirmary, but I reflected that the Benedictines had always paid more than lip service to the rigid rules of their Order, whereas the Cistercians had a more relaxed attitude to the needs of the flesh. At least, that's my opinion. But perhaps others might think me wrong.

But it was not only bad dreams that disturbed my rest. Ideas and theories jostled around in my head until it positively ached with thinking. I lay on my back staring up at the low-pitched, black-shadowed ceiling trying to work out a course of events which fitted the facts and made some sort of sense.

Had members of the Gurney family ever had any inkling that there might be treasure hidden somewhere in Tintern Abbey? Treasure connected to Edward II? Somehow I doubted it, or someone at sometime in the past would have tried to locate it. So, how could I be sure they hadn't? I couldn't, but neither the present abbot nor any of his flock had suggested that such an enquiry had ever been made. Not a valid reason you might argue, and you would be right as far as the argument goes. But those sort of incidents – a stranger arriving and nosing around for buried treasure – have a profound impact on the monotony of cloistered lives, fostering endless discussion and repetition and finally growing into a tradition that is passed on from one generation of monks to the next.

I therefore, rightly or wrongly, dismissed this notion. But the Gurneys had known something, that was obvious; something that Walter Gurney had repeated to Sir Lionel Despenser more, perhaps, as a joke than as any serious suggestion. Listening to the faint drumming of the rain on the guest-house roof – a ghostly tattoo beating to awaken Gwyn ap Nud, the Lord of the Wild Hunt, and his followers from their enchanted sleep beneath the Tor – I made a guess that maybe Edward, during his captivity in Berkeley Castle had tried to bribe his gaolers to let him escape. 'I have money (jewels?) hidden in Tintern Abbey,' he might have told them. 'It is yours if you let me go.' But no one had taken him seriously, treating his claim with derision. The story, however, had persisted down the generations of the Gurney family and was always good for a chuckle.

When a travelling barber had brought the news that Sir Lionel Despenser of Keynsham, in Somerset, was looking for a new head groom, Walter Gurney had seen not merely a chance to escape Jane Spicer and her unwelcome expectations of him, but also an opportunity to serve a man with whom his family shared a distant, if disreputable, past. Despensers and Gurneys both had a connection to the unhappy second Edward, and what would have been more natural than that Walter should have shared the joke of there being something of value which the king had left concealed at Tintern with his new master?

And that is what it might well have remained, a joke, if Sir Lionel had not told it to Gilbert Foliot who, by the sheerest chance, had been at Tintern Abbey for the funeral of his late wife's kinsman when the secret hiding place in the former abbot's lodgings had been uncovered. At the time, the hole in the floor had been only cursorily examined and its contents deemed, although of historical interest, valueless. But Sir Lionel's information aroused the goldsmith's interest, making him wonder if the hiding place had, fourteen years earlier, been sufficiently well examined. Perhaps they had all been too easily satisfied that there was nothing else to be found. Maybe, after all, there was some substance in the Gurney family story. Maybe Thomas of Berkeley, Sir William Maltravers and Sir Thomas Gurney should have taken their royal prisoner more seriously.

These thoughts Gilbert Foliot had imparted to his friend in the St Peter's Street house on the evening that Peter Noakes was concealed behind the curtain shutting off the dais from the rest of the parlour, and the young man had immediately determined to make the journey to Tintern Abbey to discover for himself if there was any truth in the speculation. He and Ursula needed money desperately in order to run away together. He must have set off for Tintern the very next day, beating Gilbert's own departure by a narrow margin.

As for the other pair, what did they want the treasure for? Not to line their own pockets, of that I felt certain. And although, I suppose, they might be allotted some credit for their lack of greed, the truth was that they needed it, if Timothy Plummer were to be believed, for a much more treacherous reason: to bolster the depleted coffers of Henry Tudor . . .

And here, I suppose, I must have fallen into the first of the night's uneasy dozes, for at this point I seemed to be back home, standing in the kitchen with the contents of my pack strewn all about the floor. It was a dream I had had before, except that this time, the woman demanding that I pick everything up and put it away tidily was not Adela but the goodwife of the farm where I had taken my Sunday dinner. I could also hear Adam's voice somewhere in the background although I could not see him, and I was trying vainly to hush both the goodwife and Adela, who had now mysteriously joined her, in order to make out the words. Unfortunately, they only increased their importuning until the noise grew so deafening that I was suddenly awake, sitting up in bed and listening to the autumnal storm which was howling around the abbey.

I shivered and lay down again, all my sympathy going out to the Brothers and novices who even at that minute were probably pattering down the night stairs to the cold and darkness of the abbey to celebrate Vigils, the pool of blackness that was the choir studded with the flickering flames of their candles. I supposed Brother Hilarion thought I should have joined them – a polite gesture from a guest who had once been an inmate himself – but I just pulled the rough grey blanket up to my chin and again reassured myself that twelve years previously I had made the right decision.

I expected to drop off almost immediately, but sleep eluded me for quite a while. To begin with, I spent some time trying to interpret my dream. I remembered Adam making some remark which had stirred my memory, but failed completely to recall what it was that he had said. And what significance the emptying of my pack and the farmer's wife held for me I was still unable to fathom. That they did hold significance I had no doubt, nor that God was trying to speak to me, as he had so often done in the past, through my dreams. The fault was mine. I was growing old and stupid.

I let the dream go. I knew from past experience that I could not force understanding. That would come when it would come in a flash of inspiration. Instead, I examined once more my earlier thoughts, my interpretation of events after my meeting with Master Foliot and the other two at Monmouth and later at Tintern.

I was seized suddenly by the conviction that Peter Noakes's death had been no accident, but deliberate murder. I recalled the gold-smith's determination to follow the boy in spite of the teeming rain and tearing wind. But he hadn't lost him in the darkness as he had claimed. He had caught up with him somewhere out in the open, near the river and had dealt him a swingeing blow to the back of the head with . . . With what? A hefty branch most likely, torn from one of the trees by the raging gale. There had been plenty of those strewn around the following morning. (I recollected Ursula telling me that Anthony Roper had noticed a contusion on the back of his nephew's head.) The goldsmith must then have rummaged through his victim's pockets and his baggage, but all to no avail. If Peter Noakes had found something, it was not upon his person. It would then have been the work of moments to push the body into the river and leave it to be found the following morning.

Gilbert Foliot's chagrin and disappointment must have been great and I tried to recollect his demeanour when he had finally returned to the abbot's lodgings, but for the life of me I could remember nothing definite. That was hardly surprising, however: there had been so much general confusion. I wondered how long it had taken him to work out that young Noakes might have hidden his findings in one of our saddle-bags, intending to retrieve his booty at a later date. Less time, certainly, than it had taken me . . .

And it was about then, lulled by the storm chasing its tail around the abbey buildings, that I finally fell asleep.

It was still early when I awoke to a cold, dark, cheerless autumn morning and the bell ringing for Prime. I dragged myself out of bed and scrambled into such clothes as I had taken off the night before and made my way into the abbey church for the service. I remembered guiltily that I had promised Adela that I would go to Mass on Sunday and had failed in that intention. At least, now, I could assure her that I had done a little towards the salvation of my soul. (For she worried about me, I knew, and especially about some of what she stigmatized as my heretical theories.)

I ate breakfast – if you could call it that: stale oatcakes and only water to drink – in the refectory with a few of the lay brothers. (The monks themselves still adhered to the rule of one main meal a day. However had I borne it as long as I did?) I was just finishing this grisly repast when someone swung his leg over the bench and sat down beside me.

'What happened to you then?' demanded the carter, Joseph Sibley.

I turned my head. 'You made good time.'

He grinned. 'Better than you think. I arrived late last night after you were tucked up in bed.'

I snorted. 'You make it sound comfortable.'

He laughed at that, but then repeated his question. 'So what did happen to you? I was told you'd legged it in the middle of the night. The cobbler and his wife were very upset. Couldn't think what they'd done to offend you.'

I hesitated, then told him a version of the truth without saying who I thought was my attacker.

The carter roared at that and slapped me on the knee. 'Reckon that were young Christopher Wiley,' he gasped, adding in explanation, 'Betsy's swain. Crept in to have a bit of a lark with the girl, found you and jumped to the wrong conclusion. Got a hasty temper has young Chris, by all accounts. Don't know him personal like, but from what Goodwife Shoesmith've told me he's not one to cross.' He was shaken by another paroxysm of laughter from which he eventually emerged with streaming eyes. 'I'll tell the dame next time I see her,' he offered. 'Put all right with her and Jacob.' He gave me a salacious grin. ''Course, I can guess why you didn't bolt the door. So could young Master Wiley, I reckon.'

I said nothing. It was as good an explanation as another and one that would serve my purpose. But I didn't believe it, not for an instant, particularly when the carter described Christopher Wiley as a slender youth whose figure as well as his face made him a favourite amongst the womenfolk of Keynsham. There had been nothing willowy about the man who had assaulted me.

'So,' Joseph Sibley continued, 'you're returning to Bristol with me today as we arranged? I could do with the company. Finished your business here, have you?'

I admitted that I had and thankfully accepted his offer. I had

no desire to walk the twenty and more miles to Bristol over
again, so as soon as I had finished eating I sought out Brother
Hilarion and thanked him for his time and patience.

'And was my history lesson of any use to you?' he asked,
reaching up and bringing my head down to his level so that he
could kiss me on the forehead and give me his blessing.

'Of inestimable value,' I assured him.

He nodded. 'And don't let it be so long before I see you again,'
he chided. 'I'm an old man now.'

With a sudden rush of affection, and because I myself was
growing ever more aware of the passing years, I put my arms
around his slight body and gave him a hug.

'I won't,' I promised.

He smiled ironically. 'You're a good man, Roger. I know you
mean what you say.' He patted my shoulder. 'God be with you, my
child.'

We reached Bristol in just over two days, passing through the
Redcliffe Gate early on Friday morning having spent the night
– at my expense, naturally – at an ale-house in the village of
Whitchurch.

The night before, Wednesday (or Woden's Day as many
Somerset people still insist on calling it, in memory of the old
gods who preceded the coming of Christianity) had, by chance,
been passed at the same farmhouse where I had eaten on Sunday.
The good-hearted couple had been genuinely pleased to see me
again, the husband taking the opportunity to pour into Joseph
Sibley's ear the difficulties of raising his 'hruther' or 'rudder'
beasts – I could see the carter nodding off from sheer boredom
as he was told the tale – while the goodwife, in an excess of
pride, showed me a new gown she had but just finished making
and which was adorned down the front with the carved bone
buttons she had purchased from my pack.

As she spoke, recollections of my recent dreams gave me an
unpleasant jolt, but try as I would I could still make no sense of
them. I stared at the buttons. I fingered them. That they held
some significance for me, I was certain, but what that significance
was continued to elude me . . .

Joseph Sibley lived in Redcliffe, so unloaded me along with

my pack and cudgel close to St Thomas's Church. I thanked him, paid him and then set out with a feeling of relief in the direction of Bristol Bridge. My way took me close to Margaret Walker's cottage, but I had no intention of breaking my journey to pay her a visit. Home beckoned. I just wanted to get there as soon as possible.

Fate, however, decreed otherwise. As I started to cross the bridge, I realized that my former mother-in-law was just ahead of me and no doubt bound for Small Street. I had no option but to overtake her with as cordial a greeting as I could manage.

The pleasantry was not returned. 'Oh, it's you, is it?' she said grimly. 'And not before time. It seems to me you're never around when you're most needed.'

'Why?' I asked uneasily. 'What's happened?'

'You mean apart from your house being broken into?'

'Broken into again?' I was aghast. 'When . . . When did this happen?'

'The day before yesterday, in the morning while Adela was at market with the children. She'd foolishly taken that dog of yours along with her because she had a notion in her head that someone had been trying to poison him.'

'Poison Hercules?' I stopped dead in the middle of a crowded High Sreet, staring at Margaret Walker in horror. At the same time, I recalled a conversation with Sir Lionel Despenser in which he had expressed surprise – and, now I came to think of it, concern – that I owned a dog. I remembered telling him how Hercules had been acquired. 'Is . . . Is he all right?'

'Quite unharmed, thanks to Adela, who kept him indoors after he'd been sick on two occasions. Although considering what that animal scavenges from the drains, why she thought –' Here Margaret broke off and seized my arm, urging me forward. 'For the sweet Lord's sake shift yourself, Roger! You're getting in everyone's way standing there like a great booby with your mouth half-open! Besides, you've a bigger worry than that awaiting you.'

'Was anything stolen from the house?' I asked as we began to move, her last words not sinking in for the moment.

'Adela says not, but of course it hasn't stopped Dick Manifold from being round there every five minutes. If you'll take my advice my lad, you want to keep your eye on him.'

'I do, believe me . . . What did you mean, a bigger worry?'

My quondam mother-in-law snorted. 'That child's turned up again. He's bigger now, about ten or eleven months I should say, and he's not with the woman who brought him here first, before you came home in April.'

'What child?' I demanded. But I knew perfectly well what child. I was simply playing for time.

We had by now reached the High Cross and I came to a halt in its shadow. Margaret Walker stood still perforce and turned to face me. 'The child that woman claimed was yours. Only now it seems the story's changed. It appears that after all the boy is not yours, only has some sort of claim on you.' She gave another snort. 'I've never heard such nonsense. I told Adela that if this present woman shows up again to send her away with a flea in her ear. I don't know what your connection is with that creature in Gloucester, and I don't want to know, but it's obvious she's trying to force this child on you by one means or another. She's afraid to come here herself for fear of coming face-to-face with you, so she's persuaded her friend to do the deed for her.'

If that were only the case, I thought with a sinking heart, how much simpler things would be. It was apparent to me that Juliette Gerrish had died and that Jane Spicer, according to her promise, had brought Luke to Bristol in an effort to persuade me to take my half-nephew into my family and raise him as my own. I groaned inwardly. I could foresee storm clouds ahead.

We walked down Small Street, in silence on my part but with Margaret giving me a great deal of advice to which I paid not the slightest attention. Indeed, most of it I didn't even listen to, one half of my mind being preoccupied with the break-in and what it meant, and the other with my responsibility to my half-brother's child and how I was going to persuade Adela that we had no choice but to shelter the poor little mite.

I had been half afraid, after Margaret's warning, of finding myself confronted by Richard Manifold, but my fears proved groundless. In fact, I had rarely known the house so calm and peaceful and we walked through the hall into the kitchen where all three children were seated round the table calmly doing their lessons. Adela glanced up as we entered with a finger to her lips and indicating the old cradle on the floor beside her and which she was gently rocking with her foot.

'Hush,' she said to Margaret, 'he's sleeping.' Then she saw me and was immediately on her feet to give me a kiss of greeting.

'Roger! You're home!'

Immediately all was pandemonium. Elizabeth, Nicholas and Adam left their horn books with shouts of, 'What have you brought us?' Hercules nipped my ankles as a punishment for going away and leaving him behind, while Luke, just as I remembered him, all copper curls and huge brown eyes, sat up and beamed at all and sundry.

Adela stooped, picked Luke up and tucked him under one arm. 'He's so active,' she explained. 'You have to watch him every minute.'

Margaret Walker and I stared at her.

'Where's . . . Where's Jane Spicer?' I asked.

My wife smiled. 'Gone home to Gloucester.' The smile vanished. 'Mistress Gerrish died two weeks ago.'

'Adela!' Margaret exclaimed, outraged. 'You've not agreed . . . You've not been so foolish as to keep that child, have you?'

Her cousin looked surprised. 'What else can I do? And once I'd seen him . . . He's such a sweet-natured child.'

She turned her head to smile at Luke who grinned in return, revealing two teeth. He patted her cheek.

I sank down on the nearest stool, my head in a whirl. I had been prepared for squalls, but unbelievably all seemed set for fine weather. All the same . . .

'Sweetheart,' I said weakly, 'are you sure about this? Another woman's child! And another boy! What . . . What do the children think about it?' I glanced nervously at the three of them as they rummaged eagerly through my pouch and pockets, extracting the small gifts I had had the forethought to buy them in Wells. I recalled a time when Adam was young and the other two had tried to give him away.

Adela shrugged. 'They don't seem to mind. If anything, Adam

is rather pleased, I think, to have a member of the family younger than himself. It means he's no longer the baby . . .'

'I'm a man now,' my son interrupted. 'I have a knife.'

'. . . while Bess and Nick,' my wife resumed, 'as you well know, have always been wrapped up in one another.'

'You're a fool, my girl!' Margaret Walker declared loudly, making me jump. I had forgotten she was there. 'Another mouth to feed! Another child to cook and clean and sew for! And not even yours or Roger's!' She prodded me hard on the shoulder. 'You'd better go and see King Richard – if king he really is – and tell him you need to be paid more.'

I slammed my fist down on the table. 'I tell you, mother-in-law –' she still liked me to call her that – 'I don't work for the king! And what do you mean, if he really is that?'

'You've no cause to take that aggressive tone with me, Roger. There are plenty of people, I can tell you, who think he has no right to the title, who believe that his claim was a trumped-up one concocted with the help of Robert Stillington. And what has happened to those poor boys, the little king and his brother? Tell me that! Rumour has it –'

'I know how rumour has it,' I snapped, 'and rumour lies! I know King Richard! I know he would never harm his nephews.'

I was shouting, Margaret Walker was looking affronted and all four children were regarding me round-eyed, uncertain as to the cause of my displeasure.

'I shall be going,' Margaret announced. She kissed her granddaughter and nodded at her cousin. 'You know where to find me, Adela, should you need me. I still think you're the biggest fool in Christendom.'

And with that parting shot she was gone, the street door banging behind her.

'Oh, Roger!' Adela said reproachfully, but I could see the smile glimmering at the back of her eyes. She handed Luke to me and fetched me a beaker of ale. 'Have you had any breakfast?'

'Of a sort, in an ale-house at Whitchurch.' I shifted Luke's weight to my left arm and took a long swallow of Adela's home-made beer. 'But never mind that. We've things to talk about. First and foremost, are you sure about raising Luke?'

She smiled, a little wryly, I thought. 'Tell me what else we can do? Mistress Spicer was adamant in her refusal to keep him. And if you're satisfied that he is indeed your half-brother's son . . .'

I hesitated, then nodded. 'I feel sure he must be.'

'Then there's no more to be said, is there? Talking is simply a waste of breath. Besides, he's a very lovable child.'

And as if to confirm this, Luke gave me a beaming smile and put up a hand to tweak my nose, an action which caused his foster siblings a great deal of amusement.

This argument having been settled with far less aggravation than I could possibly have imagined, even in my most sanguine dreams, I turned to the second and far more serious matter. 'Margaret says the house has been robbed again.'

Adela gathered up the horn books and put them away. 'Not "robbed",' she demurred, 'and not "again". On the first occasion, if you recall, whoever it was didn't manage to get in, thanks to Hercules, and this time nothing was taken. Oh, everything had been turned upside down, the contents of every drawer and cupboard strewn about the floor, but neither the children nor I could discover a single thing that was missing.'

Elizabeth, Nicholas and Adam vociferously confirmed this statement.

'When did this happen?'

'The day before yesterday, Wednesday, while we were all at market.'

'Margaret said you'd taken Hercules with you. She had some story that you thought he was being poisoned.'

Adela suspended a pot of stew from the hook over the fire, to heat. 'I thought he might have been. He was sick twice, each time after Bess had reported seeing a man giving him meat.'

I turned to my daughter. 'What was he like, this man?'

Elizabeth wrinkled her forehead. 'A big man. Not anyone that I knew.'

'Did he have a scar or scratch marks on his face?'

Again she furrowed her brow, but to no avail. 'I can't remember.'

'Did either Nicholas or Adam see him?'

But my stepson and son denied all knowledge of the stranger.

'If I'd seen him,' Adam declared stoutly, 'I'd have run him through with my knife. Right through the belly button.'

There it was again, that jolt of recognition that told me he had, as once before, said something of importance, something of significance. And if I remembered rightly, he had used almost exactly the same words. But try as I would, the memory refused to resolve itself. I could only sit there, fuming with frustration.

NINETEEN

I spent the rest of the morning until the dinner hour going around the house, satisfying myself that nothing had been taken that Adela and the children had failed to remember was there. This was not as difficult a task as it sounds for, whatever other people imagined, we were not rich and our possessions were few. The rest of the world might think me an agent of King Richard and assume I was paid accordingly, but most of the missions I had undertaken on his behalf had happened either by accident or out of a sense of loyalty to a man I greatly admired. That I had received very little payment was entirely my own fault because I preferred to keep my independence and be beholden to no man. It was all the more ironic, therefore, that people now assumed I was the very thing I had striven so hard to avoid.

Nothing, however, appeared to be missing. This did not surprise me. It merely confirmed my belief that the intruder – or intruders – had not been intent on general robbery but were searching for something in particular – the Tintern treasure. Whoever was behind these break-ins – and everything, to my mind, pointed to Sir Lionel Despenser and Gilbert Foliot – was growing desperate. The trouble was, of course, that like myself they had no proof that the treasure even existed. We might all be chasing our tails.

I had no doubt that the knight, with the assistance of his friend the goldsmith, had reached the same conclusion as I had done: that there was a strong possibility that Edward II, during his flight into Wales, had left something of value in the care of the then abbot of Tintern, hoping to return later to retrieve it. Unfortunately, there was no proof so far that this had actually happened. Nor was there any real proof that Sir Lionel Despenser and Master Foliot had transferred their loyalty to Henry Tudor and were working on his behalf.

My thoughts were interrupted at this point by the sound of Elizabeth shouting at the top of her voice and Adam yelling in return. My temper being at that moment not of the best, I descended wrathfully from what was now the former's little attic room under the eaves, where I had been completing my inspection of the house, to the chamber next door to mine and Adela's which was shared by the two boys.

'Be quiet, both of you!' I commanded. 'What is this all about?'

'He keeps stealing my things,' Elizabeth said, pointing an accusing finger at her brother.

Adam, red-faced and mutinous, had his hands behind his back. His expression left no possible doubt as to his guilt.

'He keeps going into my room,' my daughter complained angrily, 'and poking about. He helps himself to my toys and private treasures.'

'Adam,' I said sternly, 'whatever you are hiding behind your back, return it to your sister immediately! If you do not, you will get a whipping.'

I saw him weighing up the chances of my carrying out this threat, so I took a menacing step in his direction.

'I mean it, Adam.' And, somewhat to my own surprise, I found that I did.

My son obviously reached the same conclusion because, after a brief moment of continued defiance, he sullenly held out to his sister a small leather bag closed by a drawstring of faded and rather ragged blue silk. Elizabeth snatched it and flounced out of the room just as Adela called us downstairs to dinner.

The meal being over, I announced my intention of visiting Henry Callowhill. I felt it was high time I shared my deductions and theories with the wine merchant as someone who had been involved in this affair from the beginning, and also as someone who, I felt, was not quite so sympathetic to Gilbert Foliot as he at first appeared. I recalled the goldsmith once treating his friend in a somewhat high-handed manner which I thought had been resented.

'Well, don't be too long,' my wife instructed me as she cleared the dirty spoons and dishes from the table. 'I want to visit Margaret and Bess must come with me. She is her grandchild, after all, the only true one Margaret has. And if I take Bess, Nicholas is bound to want to come as well, so I need you to keep an eye on Adam and Luke.'

'Why do you have to see Margaret?' I demanded peevishly, not relishing these sorts of domestic ties and beginning already, even after so short a time at home, to feel leg-shackled.

'Because she's my cousin and I'm fond of her, and because we parted from her this morning on bad terms. I don't like that. She can be irritating and annoying, I know, but she's been good to us and I couldn't do without her help when you're away. And I shall need that help even more now that there's another child to look after.'

I grumbled and argued – in my role as head of the household I could hardly do less – but in the end I gave in.

'Oh, very well,' I agreed. 'I'll be as quick as I can. But,' I warned her, 'that may not be as quick as you would like.'

Adela gave me a look: the sort of look wives give their husbands when they know these gentlemen are being deliberately awkward.

I called to Hercules, intending to take him with me, but the fickle animal had suddenly found another object for his devotion. Luke was sitting up in his cradle, where Adela had left it next to the water barrel, gurgling, dribbling and clapping his little hands, while Hercules lay beside him watching his every move with adoring eyes. To my demand for the dog's company he turned a deaf ear, the merest twitch of his tail acknowledging my presence.

Disgusted and more than a little put out, I left him to it.

The morning was overcast and dank as only a November day can be. A few rays of watery sunlight pierced the clouds and a wind-like thin steel flailed its way down Small Street. I shivered and drew my cloak more closely around me. I had not intended to hurry but the cold drove me on and in no time at all I had reached the wine merchant's house in Wine Street.

He was not at home.

Mistress Callowhill was all apologies, insisting I come into the parlour for a beaker of mulled ale to 'keep out the cold of this miserable morning.'

'Henry will be sorry to have missed you, Master Chapman,' she fussed, shooing the two younger children – a pretty girl of about nine years old and a boy a little older – out of the room and instructing the elder son, Martin, to pour the ale. 'He's gone to the warehouse and might be some time. But if you would care to wait . . .'

I shook my head. 'Thank you, but my business is not that important.'

Once again, I felt uncomfortable, as though I were masquerading under false pretences. There had been a time, not so very far distant, when the wife of one of Bristol's wealthiest citizens would barely have acknowledged my existence, let alone invited me into her parlour and plied me with refreshment. And she herself seemed to find the situation odd. She was not at ease.

By contrast, young Martin Callowhill was as friendly as ever, chattering away in his casual, friendly fashion and accompanying me to the door when I left.

'I'm sorry you can't stay, Master Chapman,' he said, giving a quaint little bow. 'I enjoyed the last conversation we had together. About Saxons calling the Normans Orcs and about the Battle for Middle Earth,' he added when he saw that I was at a loss.

I laughed, remembering. 'I had a suspicion that Master Callowhill was none too pleased.'

The boy shrugged, somewhat impatiently I thought, then smiled. 'Oh, Father prides himself on his Norman ancestry. His mother's family name was de Broke and there was a tradition that they were descended from a bastard son of the Conqueror. I don't put any store by that sort of nonsense myself, but I fancy Father is a little disappointed that he hasn't risen any higher in life. He went to London last year and was introduced at court by one of my grandmother's relatives. The late King Edward made much of him and I think . . .'

He broke off suddenly, flushing to the roots of his hair, realizing that he had no business to be talking of his father in such a free and easy way to a comparative stranger. Or, in fact, to anyone.

'You . . . You won't repeat . . .' he stammered.

'You may rely entirely on my discretion,' I assured him.

He smiled gratefully and wished me good-day.

I started the return journey home, considering whether or not I might run the gauntlet of Adela's displeasure by a quick visit to the Green Lattis for a further beaker of ale. But she was almost certain to hear of it. The women of Bristol had their own ways of being kept informed of what their menfolk got up to, so, in the end, I decided against it; but only, I told myself, because of a sudden decision to call on Geoffrey Heathersett. He had as much interest in the affair as Master Callowhill, and as a lawyer might be able to advise me what to do next.

I walked down Broad Street and turned into Runnymede Court, conscious of various people hailing me or shouting a greeting, but preoccupied with my recent conversation with young Martin. The picture he had presented of his father did not quite tally with the easygoing, rather jolly man I had always assumed Henry Callowhill to be. Perhaps that was why he occasionally seemed to resent Gilbert Foliot's somewhat patronizing air.

Edwin Pennyfeather received me in the outer room of the lawyer's chambers with his usual cheerful grin, but pulled down the corners of his mouth when I expressed a wish to see his master.

'I don't know how he'll be willing to spare you the time, Master Chapman. He's very busy just at present. A new will he has to draw up for Alderman Stoner.'

I was just about to deny, for the second time that morning, that my business was of any importance, when the door to the inner sanctum opened and Lawyer Heathersett appeared, ushering the alderman out. He was none too pleased to see me, but when I begged for five minutes of his time, he grudgingly agreed.

He followed me into the musty-smelling inner chamber, where piles of law books were stacked on shelves and even in piles on the floor, and waved me to a chair in front of a large, ink-stained desk before seating himself behind it.

'Well, Master Chapman, and what can I do for you?' he asked impatiently.

So I told him of my trip to Glastonbury, of what I had learned from Brother Hilarion, of my theory concerning Edward II and even touched on my suspicions of both Sir Lionel Despenser and Gilbert Foliot.

Somewhat to my surprise, he didn't fire up in defence of his friends, but gnawed on the end of a quill pen to the detriment of his remaining front teeth, several of which looked rotten enough to snap under such treatment. Finally, when I had finished, he demanded, 'Have you proof of any of this?'

'No,' I admitted. 'Not what you could call proof. But I have this very strong hunch . . .'

The lawyer snorted. 'Hunches are of no use in a court of law.'

'I know that,' I retorted irritably. 'But what would you advise me to do?'

'Nothing. There's not a thing you can do.' He nibbled even harder on the end of his pen. 'All the same, what you've told me doesn't surprise me. I've suspected for quite some time now that Gilbert has Lancastrian sympathies. As long as the late king was alive, they lay dormant. Edward was too popular with all kinds and conditions of men for there to be much opposition to his rule. Indeed, many people, wherever their loyalties secretly lay, were prepared not merely to tolerate him, but actively supported him. The Bishop of Ely is a case in point. But all that changed with Edward's death. When Gloucester took the throne . . .' He broke off, shrugging his narrow shoulders.

'Old loyalties reawakened?' I suggested.

He nodded and leant forward across the desk, peering at me with his short-sighted, protuberant eyes.

'Quite so. But they'll be careful until they see which way the wind's blowing. Until they see if King Richard remains as popular as he seems to be at present. These rumours we've been hearing about the two princes . . .' He smiled cynically. 'Well, my advice to anyone would be to forget those. They're probably untrue anyway. But southerners don't like Richard. He's a stranger to them. And he's known to be priggish. Strait-laced. A good husband, father, friend, but intolerant of debauchery in any shape or form. That won't appeal to a lot of people.'

'So what are you advising me to do?' I asked.

'I'm not advising you to do anything,' he snapped. 'I thought I'd made that clear.' Frowningly, he reconsidered this statement. 'All right! I'm advising you not to pursue this matter until you have positive evidence that Gilbert and that friend of his, Sir Lionel Despenser, are planning to aid Henry Tudor. And it seems to me that you won't have that unless this Tintern treasure, as you call it – if, that is, it exists at all except in your imagination – turns up. Let sleeping dogs lie. Just accept that these break-ins, the murder of that pedlar who was with us in Wales, young Noakes's death are simply what they seem to be – street robbers going about their business, a chance killing for gain, a youth accidentally drowned in a river.'

He was right, of course. Everything that had happened had a reasonable explanation. Even the attack on me in Keynsham had been explained away by Joseph Sibley. I could suspect what I liked about the goldsmith and Lionel Despenser, but unless I could force them to show their hand, it was all speculation.

'Thank you for your time, Master Heathersett,' I said and got to my feet. 'I appreciate your advice.'

He nodded. 'I'm sure,' he added slyly, 'that your royal master will understand your predicament.'

There it was again, that presumption that I was working for the king! In a way I supposed I was. But not on his orders nor in his pay. I was about to protest my innocence yet again when the lawyer interrupted me.

'Gilbert Foliot isn't the only man you need to look at in this town,' he said dryly.

I turned back, raising questioning eyebrows, but he waved his pen at me. 'I'm saying no more. Now, if you'll please go, I have work to do. Edwin will show you out.'

I hesitated, but he drew some documents towards him, bending his head over them until his nose almost touched the parchment. I should get no more out of him, so I left.

Young Master Pennyfeather, who must have had his ear to the door, was waiting to bid me a deferential 'good morning'.

Adela was watching impatiently for my return.

'You said you'd be as quick as you could,' she reproached me. 'Did you see Master Callowhill?'

'No, he was out, so I went to visit Lawyer Heathersett instead.' I judged it best to be frank.

'Oh, well! In that case your journey wasn't entirely wasted,' my wife commented dryly. She went on, 'I've decided to take Luke with me,' and indicated the box on wheels that I had made five years previously for Adam. 'Margaret must get used to the idea that we're fostering him, so the more she sees of him the better. But that, unfortunately, means that Hercules insists on coming, too.' The treacherous animal, his leading rope around his neck, was already positioned alongside the box, gazing adoringly at the baby who was waving his little fists at him and gurgling something that Adela assured me was the word 'dog'. (How women know these things is beyond me.) 'So you just have Adam to look after,' she concluded somewhat bitterly.

I looked at my son who was regarding me with wide-eyed innocence, a sure sign that he was plotting mischief.

'He'll be more than enough,' I protested feelingly and accompanied my wife and family to the street door, waving them off as they made their way up Small Street. By the time I had returned indoors, Adam had disappeared. Whatever he was up to it was something quiet, so, thankfully, I let him get on with it, substituted my boots for a pair of shoes and went into the parlour for an hour or more of peace and quiet. I intended to think things through and marshal my thoughts into some sort of order, but within minutes of sitting down in my armchair – comfortably adorned with two of Adela's hand-embroidered cushions – I was sound asleep.

I don't know how long I'd slept – probably no more than ten minutes or so, when I was roused by knocking on the street door. Cursing, I forced myself to my feet and went to answer it. To my surprise, Henry Callowhill was standing outside, in company with Gilbert Foliot.

'Master Chapman!' he exclaimed, extending his hand. 'I met your wife by the High Cross and she told me that you are wishful of speaking to me, that you had in fact called at my house a little earlier, so I thought I might as well come to visit you and find out what it is that you want. And as I had just fallen in with Master Foliot here, he's done me the favour of accompanying me.'

I swore inwardly. As what I wanted to say to Henry Callowhill concerned my suspicions of the goldsmith, I was in something of a quandary. Wondering desperately what explanation I could offer, I invited them both inside – I could do no less – and ushered them into the parlour. I felt unjustly irritated with my wife for having interfered in my affairs. The fact that she had obviously thought she was being helpful in no way assuaged my annoyance.

I saw both men glance curiously around the parlour, but whether they were thinking it poor and ill-furnished compared with their own, or whether they were considering it as too well appointed for a mere pedlar, I was unable to decide. If the latter, then it would merely confirm their belief that I was in the pay of the king. But as to how I came by the house itself, they must know the circumstances. Everyone in Bristol knew them.

I begged the two men to sit down, waving them to the armchairs, one on either side of the hearth, and offered them refreshment.

'I don't keep wine,' I said, refusing to make it sound like an apology, but then ruining the effect by assuring them that Adela's home-brewed pear and apple cider was, if not nectar of the gods, not far short of it.

'By all means let's try it,' Gilbert Foliot said. 'I'm sure, Master Chapman, it's every bit as good as you say.'

I detected a patronizing note, but ignored it and went off to the kitchen to find clean beakers and broach an unopened keg. When I returned to the parlour, I found Adam there. He must have wandered downstairs and entered, unaware that I was entertaining visitors.

'Your younger son, Master Chapman?' the wine merchant queried and I nodded, deciding it was high time I accepted Nicholas as also my own. Henry Callowhill smiled. 'A smart little fellow. Now, Roger, what is it you wish to speak to me about?'

The awkward moment had arrived. Whilst in the kitchen, I had been cudgelling my brains to think of a subject of sufficient moment to warrant my having sought him out. But my mind was still a blank. I handed each man his beaker of cider and desperately sought some distraction.

And, miraculously, found it.

In one of Adam's hands he was clutching the worn leather

bag with the drawstring of faded and ragged blue silk that belonged to Elizabeth. Sternly, I held out my hand.

'Give that to me, Adam! You know very well it's not yours. You've been in your sister's chamber again, stealing her things. I told you earlier this morning that you are not to do it. This time it means a whipping.' He looked defiant. 'What's in the bag, anyway, that it holds such fascination for you?'

For a long moment I thought he was going to refuse and make me look a fool in front of our visitors. I could see him turning it over in his mind, whether or not it was worth a beating just for the sheer pleasure of defying me, or whether it was more dignified to capitulate gracefully. Thankfully, he decided on the latter course.

In answer to my question, he said, 'Buttons.'

'Buttons?'

'Yes.'

'What buttons?'

He looked faintly surprised. 'The ones Bess took, o' course.'

'Took?'

My son heaved a sigh, plainly exasperated by my lack of intelligence.

'When you forgot,' he explained laboriously, 'to bring us home any presents, you said we could take anything we liked from your pack. I took my knife. Forget what Nich'las took. Bess took the buttons.'

Vaguely, my memory stirred, then sharpened. Of course! I recollected now. Two weeks ago, on my return from Hereford, I had omitted to bring the children anything. (My mind had been too much occupied with other matters.) Moreover, I had forgotten Elizabeth's birthday. All three had all been upset and I had lost my temper, storming out of the kitchen and shouting at them to take what they pleased from my pack. Neither Adela nor I had seen what they had chosen, but Nicholas claimed to have taken some tags for his belt, Adam the ivory-handled knife – which he had been brandishing under our noses ever since – and my daughter the buttons . . .

But what buttons? The set of carved bone buttons I had bought in Gloucester, of course!

And yet she couldn't have done! Twice my pack had been

emptied, once by myself all over the kitchen floor and the second time by Sir Lionel Despenser when he had invited me in to display my goods to his housekeeper. And on both occasions, if I shut my eyes and concentrated, I could clearly recall seeing the buttons amongst my other wares: six prettily carved buttons threaded together on a length of ribbon. The very set of buttons I had given to the farmer's wife the preceding Sunday in return for a dish of pig's trotters stewed in butter, an apple dumpling and a beaker of homemade cider . . .

I realized suddenly that this was what all my dreams had been trying to tell me. And Adam's remarks about belly buttons – they too had been jolts to my memory, but I had been too dull, too stupid, to see their significance.

I held out my hand.

'Give me that bag at once, Adam,' I said sternly.

He hesitated, but recognizing the note of authority in my voice, the tone which meant I was deadly serious and not to be trifled with, surrendered his prize. For a moment I stood weighing the bag in my right hand, then, loosening the drawstring, upended its contents into my left.

There was a flash of white light, a rainbow of colour, and I stood staring at what I was holding like a man in a dream.

I heard the sharp intake of breath from both Henry Callowhill and the goldsmith. Then the latter murmured in an awestruck whisper, 'Dear Mother of God, the Capet diamonds!'

There were eight of them, the largest and most perfect stones I had ever seen, and each one had been set in a cup of gold, exquisitely shaped like flower petals, with a tiny, pierced shaft so that they could sewn on to a garment and used as buttons.

I looked at the goldsmith. 'What . . . What did you say they are?'

He took one from my hand and stood twisting it reverently between his fingers.

'The Capet diamonds,' he breathed. 'They belonged to Philip IV of France.' He laughed shortly. 'Probably looted from the Templars. When Isabella Capet married Edward II, the goldsmiths of Paris turned them into buttons which she brought with her to England to adorn her coronation robes. Alas, they suffered the

same fate as most of her other jewels. Edward seized them and
gave them to his Gascon favourite, Piers Gaveston.

'After Gaveston was murdered by the barons, the diamonds
disappeared. No one knew what had happened to them. Gaveston
was related in some degree or other to the great banking family
of the Calhaus, and it has been generally assumed that the buttons
were deposited with them and never reclaimed.' Gilbert Foliot
paused, turning the gem this way and that, watching the light
flash and sparkle before going on, 'But it would seem that this
assumption was wrong. Edward must have taken back the
diamonds after all. And when he and Hugh le Despenser fled
into Wales, escaping from Mortimer and Isabella's invading army,
he took them with him, leaving them eventually with the abbot
of Tintern for safe-keeping and until he should need them. Of
course, he never did, and there they remained in the secret hiding
place in the abbot's old lodgings, no one suspecting their
existence.'

'Not,' I said, 'until Walter Gurney went to work for Sir Lionel
when, in view of their families' shared history, he told him about
the tradition amongst the Gurneys of Edward having tried to
bribe his gaolers to let him escape.'

'How did you know about that?' the goldsmith asked
sharply.

'I didn't. It was something I worked out for myself. Sir Lionel
told you. You remembered the secret hiding place and began to
wonder if it had contained more than the original documents
discovered fourteen years ago. Peter Noakes overheard the
conversation between you, and . . . Well, the rest we know.' I
dropped the buttons back in the bag, taking the final one from
Gilbert Foliot's hand and putting it in with the others. 'And
now,' I continued, 'we'd better take these to the Lord High
Sheriff without delay. They're far too precious to remain in my
keeping.'

The two men glanced at one another, then Henry Callowhill
smiled.

'Oh, I don't think so,' he said. 'We'll take the diamonds,
Master Chapman. They'll make a valuable contribution to Henry
Tudor's war chest.'

TWENTY

I laughed. I thought he was joking. Then I saw that he wasn't. He was perfectly serious and there was a hard look in his eyes that I had never seen before. The genial wine merchant had vanished. This was a man with a purpose.

There was another change, also. The two men seemed to have switched roles. Gilbert Foliot was suddenly the subordinate, looking to his friend for instructions, and I realized that their previous relationship had been a blind for the true state of affairs. I remembered, too, Lawyer Heathersett's warning that the goldsmith was not 'the only man you need to look at in this town'. And there had been young Martin Callowhill's description of his father – a man of ambition and pride in his ancestry – that had not tallied with the man I thought I knew.

The meeting in Wales had not been accidental, either. I now felt sure of that. No doubt as soon as Sir Lionel had passed on Walter Gurney's information to his friend, Gilbert Foliot had, in his turn, relayed it to Henry Callowhill. The two men had gone there together to test the soundness or otherwise of the knight's theory . . .

I put the leather bag into the pouch at my belt and backed away until I could feel the far parlour wall behind me. They were two to one and there was bound to be a fight. Not only did I have what they wanted, but I now knew them for Henry Tudor's men, traitors to King Richard, whose agent and spy they thought I was. If it came to taking my word against theirs, they must feel certain that I should be believed.

Neither man, however, made an immediate move to wrest my pouch from me. Instead, Gilbert Foliot turned to his friend. 'There's no Breton ship at present in harbour, nor will be for a week or two. The winter weather's closing in and sailings will be less.'

Henry Callowhill shrugged. 'We must follow Bray to Cornwall. He's making for Rame Head where he told me a ship will lie offshore, somewhere between there and Penlee Point, as soon as it arrives from Brittany. We must go now. Today. As soon as you return home, send a message to Sir Lionel informing him of our intentions and tell him to join us as soon as he can.'

'Today?' the goldsmith queried, horrified.

'As things have turned out, we've no choice.' His friend sounded impatient. 'You must see that! If we'd found the jewels ourselves, it would have been a different matter. As it is . . .' He let the sentence hang.

'But if, when we get to Cornwall, we find that Reynold has already sailed?'

Reynold Bray! Of course! I had in the past heard Timothy speak of this most loyal and capable of Henry Tudor's agents.

The wine merchant shrugged again. 'We must wait until we can find a ship willing to carry us to Less Britain.' I was interested, in spite of myself, to note that he used the old, archaic name for Brittany.

'And our families?'

'My dear Gilbert!' The impatience was fast turning to anger. 'What do our families matter? What indeed do we matter in comparison with the Cause?' He spoke the last word with all the reverence of one referring to a holy crusade.

'But what about him?' The goldsmith nodded towards me. 'First of all we have to take the diamonds from him, and then . . . And then . . . Well, we can't leave him alive, can we?' He looked a little sick. 'But if we kill him, everyone will know who did it. We were seen talking to Mistress Chapman at the High Cross. We must have been seen walking down the street. And it wouldn't be Bristol if someone hadn't observed us being let into the house. The hue and cry will be raised before we're fairly clear of the city and the *posse comitatus* will be after us in the blink of an eye.' A hysterical note sounded in his voice. 'We're trapped!'

'Trapped?' Henry Callowhill smiled. 'I don't think so!' And, before I could make the slightest guess as to his intentions, he spun round and caught Adam such a stunning blow to the side of his head that the child dropped unconscious to the floor. Then he stooped and picked him up, slinging him across his left shoulder like a sack of flour.

I had completely forgotten my son – he had been so quiet, standing at one side of the room watching, I supposed, the unfolding of events and trying to work out what exactly was going on. He would not have been frightened by the two men; he knew them too well by sight.

I started forward, but Gilbert Foliot was too quick for me. He had drawn his dagger and was barring my path. The wine merchant, too, had his dagger in his hand, but was pointing it not at me, but at Adam's back.

'I shan't hesitate to use it, Roger,' he said quietly. And I believed him. He was a desperate man. He went on, 'Give the bag containing the diamonds to Master Foliot, then move back again and I'll tell you what's going to happen.'

I did as I was told. I had no choice. My son's life was at stake.

'Go on,' I said harshly.

Henry Callowhill had put away his dagger – although the goldsmith still had his drawn and was standing at the ready – and with his free right hand pulled the left-hand side of his cloak across the child's inert form.

'Master Foliot and I will now leave you, Roger,' he said. 'If you tell anyone in authority – your friend Sergeant Manifold, for instance – what has happened, you will never see your son again.'

'What are you going to do with him?' I asked, suddenly finding it difficult to breathe properly.

The wine merchant smiled. I was beginning to hate that smile.

'I shall put him somewhere safe,' he said. 'Somewhere where he can't easily be discovered.' I made an inarticulate sound and the smile deepened. 'Don't try looking for him because you won't find him. Now, if Master Foliot and I – and, I trust, Sir Lionel – reach Cornwall in safety and find a ship waiting for us, just before we embark, I'll send someone back to Bristol with a message for you to tell you where your son is.'

'But that could take weeks!' I shouted, pushing myself away from the wall. But before I could make a grab for Adam, Gilbert Foliot had his dagger at my throat.

'Stand still,' he warned.

But I was barely aware of him. 'You can't do that!' I pleaded with Henry Callowhill. 'Alone, in the dark, without food and water for heaven knows how long, the boy could die. You must know he could!'

'He'll have air,' the wine merchant promised. 'And with good horses under us, Master Foliot and I should reach Cornwall – and it is the north of Cornwall, after all, not far to the west of Plymouth – in a couple of days. Three at most. He looks a strong lad. He should survive that.'

'He'll be terrified,' I said. 'And supposing, as Master Foliot suggested just now, the ship being sent for Master Bray has already arrived and sailed?' I had been doing frantic calculations in my head, and worked out that it was almost a week since the man I now knew to be Reynold Bray had set out from Keynsham for Cornwall.

The wine merchant pulled down the corners of his mouth. 'In that case, Master Foliot and I will be forced to return to Plymouth to try to find a ship bound for Less Britain from there. So let us hope that our worst fears aren't realized. But whenever we sail, provided that no one has come to arrest us, I shall keep my promise to try to send you word where your son is hidden.'

'You can't subject a child of five years old to this ordeal,' I croaked. My mouth was dry, my throat constricted. 'Just kill me instead. Let the child go and just kill me. I won't put up any resistance.'

Once more Henry Callowhill gave that hateful smile.

'Very noble, Roger,' he said. 'And a gesture which, as a father myself, I can appreciate. But Gilbert here has already explained why we couldn't do that. No, I'm afraid this is the only way to ensure your silence and our chance of freedom. Our welcome at Henry Tudor's court will be assured when we present him with the Capet diamonds.' He laughed suddenly, a full-bodied chuckle of genuine amusement. 'And to think that your daughter had them all along! She must have hidden them well for Sir Lionel's men not to have found them. I see,' he added, 'that my revelation doesn't come as a surprise to you. You knew who was responsible for the break-ins?'

'I worked it out.'

Where, oh where was Adela? Why didn't she return home? Her entry into the house, with a dog and three children, might

at least prove sufficient distraction to allow me time to do
something. What, I had no idea, but any chance was better
than none. Yet I knew it wasn't going to happen. When Adela
and Margaret Walker got together they could talk for hours.
What they found to say to one another was a mystery to me,
and my wife, when questioned on the subject, always replied,
'Oh, nothing much.'

Henry Callowhill hoisted the still unconscious Adam further
up his shoulder and arranged the cloak so that it covered my
son's head. He could have been carrying anything, and in the
wind and the rain that was now falling – I could hear it pattering
against the windows – no one was going to pay much attention
to a couple of men in an obvious hurry to get home.

'We must be going,' he said to the goldsmith. 'We've a great
deal to do and we must be away before nightfall.'

I made one last, desperate appeal.

'Leave Adam here,' I pleaded hoarsely, 'and I give you my
word that I will say nothing to anyone about any of this. Take
the diamonds; take them to Henry Tudor with my blessing.'

Henry Callowhill shook his head.

'You wouldn't be able to do it, Roger,' he said. 'Your loyalty
to Richard is too great. You wouldn't be able to keep a still
tongue in your head. Besides, the boy would talk. He heard
enough of what was being said before I laid him out. He'd be
bound to ask you questions and say things to other people. He's
a sharp little fellow. No. I'm sorry, but this is the only way. I've
no wish to die a traitor's death, and neither has Gilbert. So . . .'
He turned to his friend. 'Cover my back until we're in the street.
If Roger makes a move, kill the child.'

And then they were gone. I heard the outer door bang to and
the sudden, terrible all-pervading silence of the house while I stood
as though rooted to the spot, unable either to move or even to
think for what seemed like an eternity, but in reality was probably
only a few minutes. Then, on legs that would scarcely hold me
upright, I staggered to the street door and wrenched it open, staring
out into the wind and the rain, but there was no one in sight.

'You mean you didn't go after them?' screeched Adela. 'You
made no attempt to get Adam back?' Her face was chalk white

and tear-stained. Elizabeth and Nicholas huddled together, staring at me accusingly with round, fearful eyes. Hercules began to bark, suddenly aware of the tension in the atmosphere. Even Luke was whimpering fretfully. 'Why, in God's name, didn't you go straight to Richard Manifold? He would have arrested them before they had a chance to get clear of the town.'

'Don't you understand? I couldn't risk it!' I shouted back. 'One or the other of them would have killed Adam out of sheer vindictiveness. If, that is, they hadn't by that time disposed of him in this secret place Henry Callowhill was talking of. And then we'd never have seen him alive again.'

'We . . . We shan't see him alive again anyway,' she gasped, sitting down on one of the kitchen stools and rocking herself to and fro. 'He'll be dead before those two can send word back from Cornwall. If they ever do!' My wife was seized with another spasm of sobbing so severe that she could hardly breathe. When at last she was able to speak, she demanded, 'Didn't it once occur to you that they didn't mean what they said? That it was a trick to ensure your silence? That they're going to kill Adam anyway?'

I nodded dismally, for the thought had come to me but not, although I wouldn't admit it, until too late. 'Where are you going?' I demanded as Adela got abruptly to her feet.

'To see Richard and tell him the whole. He's a friend. He'll not endanger Adam's life. He'll do as I ask and say nothing, but he might be able to help.'

'No!' I grasped her firmly by the shoulders. 'You can't involve him, and he wouldn't do it in any case. Don't you understand? We're committing a felony. Misprision of treason! Concealing knowledge of a treasonable act. We can't ask Richard's silence. And I doubt he would give it. He's an officer of the law and knows the penalty. At least, if the worst comes to the worst, I can throw myself on the king's mercy and appeal to him as one father to another.'

Adela began to tremble violently. I forced her to sit down again and fetched her a beaker of water. 'So what can we do?' she whispered.

'I must try to find Adam before those two villains – three,

I suppose, with Lionel Despenser – have time to get too far on the road to Cornwall. Before it's too late for a posse to be sent after them.' I spoke with more confidence than I felt. 'I think it's just possible that I know where they might have hidden him.'

'Where? Where, Roger? Tell me!' I saw the hope leap in her eyes and felt guilty to have raised her expectations too high.

'Sweetheart, don't . . . don't . . . It's just that Henry Callowhill himself once told me that Master Foliot had a special underground strongroom built under the cellars at the St Mary le Port Street shop after he ceased to live there and moved to the house in St Peter's Street. It's possible that that's where they've put Adam and that either Ursula or Mistress Dawes knows where the key to it is.'

'Then what are you waiting for?' my wife demanded, pushing me in the direction of the door. 'Go now! Go at once, this minute! Just go!'

I found the two women in a state of shock and near hysterics. When I could finally get any sense out of them at all, I gathered that Gilbert Foliot had returned home long enough to saddle his horse, pack a few garments and other necessaries in a couple of saddle-bags and then ride for the Redcliffe Gate. He had told them briefly that he and Henry Callowhill were joining Henry Tudor in Brittany and that they were henceforth on their own until such time as the latter returned in triumph to claim the crown. As neither woman believed that this would ever happen, they saw themselves as abandoned and penniless, and Ursula as the daughter of an attainted traitor. Margery Dawes could at least find other employment and, meantime, cast herself on the generosity of her kinsman, Lawyer Heathersett.

Brutally, I interrupted their lamentations. 'Did Master Foliot have my son with him?' I yelled at them. 'Will you both be quiet for a moment and attend to me!'

I seized Ursula and shook her hard. She was so surprised that she stopped crying and goggled at me. The housekeeper, too, was shocked into silence. Taking advantage of the sudden hush, I explained what had happened as well as I was able given my state of mind. I doubt if they understood anything very clearly, but at last they grasped the essential fact that Adam had been taken hostage and hidden somewhere as the price for my holding my tongue. When I suggested that the underground strongroom in St Mary le Port Street could be the place, Margery Dawes said at once that she knew where the keys to both it and the shop were kept. My heart began to slam against my ribs, and by the time she returned to the parlour with a bunch of keys dangling from her fingers, I had to fight to get my breath.

Barely pausing to utter my thanks, I left the house, the precious bunch clutched in my hand. Even now, after all these years, I can remember nothing of how I reached the shop nor of unlocking any doors or of searching the house and cellars. However, I do recall my agony of mind as I tried to locate the door to the strongroom and the way I yelled Adam's name over and over again in the hope that, if he were imprisoned there, he would shout in return.

But there was no answering cry.

I had discovered candles and tinderbox in the kitchen of the old living quarters and, eventually, by the light of the flickering candle flame managed to find, in the farthest, darkest corner of the cellar, another door. My hands trembled so much that I had the greatest difficulty in fitting one key after another into the lock and cursing myself every time I failed, unsure if it was my clumsiness or the fact that I had not yet tried the right key that was responsible for my failure. Finally, however, the wards grated and turned and the door swung reluctantly inwards.

'Adam!' I called.

Silence.

All around me the glitter of gold was caught by the candle flame. Here, the goldsmith's wares were stacked on shelves, waiting to be transferred, when necessary, to the shop – something that would never happen now. My hand shook and a drop of hot grease fell on my wrist, making me jump.

'Adam!' I cried again.

But the place was empty. He wasn't there.

*   *   *

It is impossible to describe my feelings at that moment. I remember that I felt sick, so much so that I actually heaved and felt the bile rise in my throat. It seemed as though a black cloud had enveloped my mind, and I had, almost literally, to fight my way free of it, using all my willpower to prevent myself from just sinking down by the cellar wall and giving way to grief. I had been so certain that I had the answer to the problem that the disappointment was even more intense than it would otherwise have been. Indeed, I went so far as to search every corner of the strongroom in the ridiculous hope that I had somehow overlooked my son hiding in the shadows.

Finally, however, I came to my senses and forced myself to consider what I must do next. The thought of returning to Adela without Adam was unbearable, as was the realization that if I failed to discover where he was hidden I should have no option, if I were not to involve the rest of my family in treason, but to go to the sheriff with my story.

It was then that I thought of Mistress Callowhill.

I walked – or half-ran – back to Wine Street and hammered at the door of the wine merchant's house. One of the men servants answered it and abruptly refused me admission. The master was from home and the mistress could see no one.

I wedged my foot in the door before he could close it.

'I know your master's not here,' I said grimly. 'I want to speak to Mistress Callowhill and I intend to do so.'

The man did his best to prevent me, but was no match for my height and weight. I pushed him aside easily enough, prepared to search the whole house until I ran my quarry to earth. But this, thankfully, proved to be unnecessary: the wine merchant's wife and children were seated around the table in the parlour, the elder son, Martin, and his mother obviously discussing the situation and what was to be done. The younger boy and girl looked scared and had been weeping, judging by their tear-stained cheeks. All four were ashen-faced and when I threw open the door, jumped up with startled cries and then stood as though turned to stone.

Martin was the first to recover the use of his voice. 'My father isn't here, Master Chapman. I – I'm afraid I must ask you to leave. Something has happened which –'

'I know what's happened,' I snarled, making him flinch. 'I know exactly what's happened! What I want to know is what that traitor has done with my son? Where's Adam?'

Mistress Callowhill whirled back to face her own son. 'Don't tell him!' she shrieked.

My heart gave a great leap. She knew! This woman knew where Adam was imprisoned. Without stopping to think, she had given herself away.

I didn't hesitate. As she sank down again in her chair, my knife was at her throat.

'Tell me!' I demanded. The tip of the blade pricked her skin. The blood welled and trickled down her neck, a thin ribbon of crimson.

The younger children started to scream and two of the servants burst in, only to be brought up short by the sight of my knife. I've often wondered since if I would have had the courage to use it and how different my life would have been if I had. Or indeed, if I would have had a life at all. Looking back on the scene, I firmly believe I was insane enough with fear and grief to have done something desperate.

But I was spared the decision.

'Mother,' Martin said quietly, although his voice shook, 'we can't be responsible for a child's death. I must tell Master Chapman where the boy is hidden.'

'No!' Mistress Callowhill's voice rose hysterically. 'If he finds him, he'll inform Sergeant Manifold immediately and your father will have lost any chance of getting away. And you know what will happen to him! You know how traitors die!' The lad shuddered as his mother went on more quietly, 'There's every chance your father and the other two will reach Cornwall in a day or so. If he sends back word at once to Master Chapman there's a possibility that the boy might still be alive.'

I saw Martin hesitate and indecision flicker in his eyes.

'Martin, if you know where Adam's hidden, I beg you to tell me,' I said hoarsely. 'He's five years old and must be terrified, waking up alone in the dark, not knowing where he is or what's happened to him.'

'If you tell him, Martin,' Mistress Callowhill said slowly, 'I shall never forgive you. From henceforward, you will be no son of mine.'

Another moment stretched into eternity and the boy's hand crept up to his mouth, his gaze flickering between the two of us. Then he said, 'I'm sorry, Mother.' My legs almost gave way with relief and it was a second or two before I realized that Martin was addressing me. 'We'll have to go to Master Foliot's house to get his keys.'

I could have wept with joy.

'I already have them,' I gasped, pulling them out of my pouch. 'I thought Adam might be in the goldsmith's strongroom, but he wasn't there.'

Martin gave a quick nod as though that somehow settled matters. 'Follow me then,' he said.

'Martin!' Mistress Callowhill's voice was now as cold as ice. I felt as if melt water were trickling down my spine. 'If you do this thing, don't come back.'

He looked at her pityingly, speaking with a composure far beyond his years. 'I shall come back, Mother. You and the children will need looking after.' He turned and left the room.

I followed him out into the street. It was still raining, but the wind, though strong, had eased a little. 'Where are we going?' I asked.

'To St Peter's Church.' When I exclaimed in surprise, he went on, 'Do you know the story of how the citizens of Bristol built a wall between the town and the castle during the reign of Edward II?' I nodded, at the same time forcing him to quicken his pace. 'Well,' he continued, 'according to Master Foliot, the constable of the castle ordered that a tunnel should be dug underneath the wall so that his soldiers could take the people by surprise. Unfortunately for the tunnellers, they broke through in the crypt of St Peter's Church where members of the patrol who manned the wall every night were warming themselves before going outside again. They immediately drove the intruders back, killing a couple for good measure, then one of them ran to ring the common bell, alerting the whole city to the danger. Lord Berkeley never tried anything of the sort again, and in commemoration of their victory the tunnel was preserved. Master Foliot showed it

to me the day he took us around the church. In later years, a
door was put at the crypt end and always kept locked for safety's
sake.'

'And you think Adam's there?'

'I know he is. My father told me so before he left.'

And he was, terrified, sobbing, crouched against the wall halfway
along the tunnel which I saw to my horror might well have
collapsed, suffocating him. After well over a century and a half,
the timbers with which it had been shored up were beginning to
rot and the roof was in danger of caving in. I think Martin saw
it, too, and it was some comfort to him to know that he had
prevented a child's death, even if he had risked his father's life
to do so.

For the four men – Henry Callowhill, Gilbert Foliot, Sir Lionel
and Henry Tudor's loyal adherent, Reynold Bray – all escaped
to Brittany. The talk of Cornwall had been a blind. Wales had
been their true destination where a ship had been waiting to take
Bray on board at Milford Haven. And the Capet diamonds
undoubtedly helped to pay the mercenaries who were responsible
for Henry's triumph two years later . . .

But that's to look forward to an event which, in that late
autumn of 1483, seemed inconceivable to any of us. King Richard
III ruled the country with justice and mercy and all was well
with our world.

Adam recovered from his ordeal faster than either Adela
or I would have thought possible, as children do. There were
nightmares at first, but they gradually ceased, as did his
tendency hang around Adela's skirts all the time. He was very
quiet for about two weeks, which worried us, but then his
voice came back and our peace was shattered. Luke loved
him and screamed with laughter at his antics, a devotion
which annoyed Hercules so much that he returned to his old
loyalties and became my dog once again. (I tried not to feel
too pleased, but human nature being what it is I didn't quite
succeed.)

Mistress Callowhill and her children left the house in Wine
Street and went no one knew where. The house in St Peter's
Street also stood empty. Ursula went to live with a distant

relative in Malmesbury and Margery Dawes with Lawyer Heathersett and his mother.

One night towards the end of November, as I climbed into bed with Adela, I said, 'I'm really looking forward to Christmas.'

As she slid into my embrace, she laughed. 'That's a bad sign. When you look forward to something, it invariably goes awry.'